CENTRAL PARK RENDEZVOUS

FOUR-IN-ONE COLLECTION

RONIE KENDIG, DINEEN MILLER,
KIM VOGEL SAWYER &
MARYLU TYNDALL

BARBOUR
PUBLISHING

Print ISBN 978-1-61626-593-9

eBook Editions:
Adobe Digital Edition (.epub) 978-1-60742-013-2
Kindle and MobiPocket Edition (.prc) 978-1-60742-047-7

This book is a work of fiction. Names, characters, places, and incidents are either products of the author's imagination or used fictitiously. Any similarity to actual people, organizations, and/or events is purely coincidental.

Cover image: Kirk DouPonce, DogEared Design

Published by Barbour Publishing, Inc., P.O. Box 719, Uhrichsville, Ohio 44683, www.barbourbooks.com

Our mission is to publish and distribute inspirational products offering exceptional value and biblical encouragement to the masses.

Member of the
Evangelical Christian
Publishers Association

Printed in the United States of America.

INTRODUCTION

Dream a Little Dream by Ronie Kendig
Afghanistan War, present day
Jamie Russo and Sean Wolfe are hiding behind the mistakes of others and avoiding their dreams. When a Civil War–era coin changes the course of Sean's life, Jamie tries to see through Sean's anger and pain to love him the way God does. But in doing so, she is forced to face her own fears. Will they both surrender fear and dare to dream a little dream?

A Love Meant to Be by Dineen Miller
Vietnam War, 1973
After a whirlwind romance, Alan James and Gail Gibson plan to reunite at Central Park after Alan returns from the Vietnam War, but the lies and deceit of Gail's sister foil their reunion. Thirty-eight years later, Alan's niece, Jamie, makes her own plans to bring the couple back together. But will a surprise reunion prove that their love was meant to be?

To Sing Another Day by Kim Vogel Sawyer
World War II, 1941
When Helen Wolfe's fiancé abandons her, she is forced to relinquish her dreams of becoming a singer and seeks employment to provide for her family. Desperately in need of money, she pawns a family heirloom—an inscribed gold piece dating back to the Civil War. But her act of desperation ignites sympathy in pawnshop owner Bernie O'Day's heart. Will Helen allow him to become her champion, giving her a reason to sing another day?

Beauty from Ashes by MaryLu Tyndall
Civil War, 1865
As the war ends, William Wolfe is excited to see his fiancée, Annie. But he is devastated at the sight of the war-torn country he returns to and the repulsion he receives from Annie at his war-scarred face. When he finds a gold coin he had given to Annie as a token of his love among her sister's possessions, William begins to suspect the truth. Can he overcome his pain to find beauty from ashes?

CENTRAL PARK RENDEZVOUS

DREAM A LITTLE DREAM
PART 1

by Ronie Kendig

Dedication

To All the Wounded Soldiers and Veterans—
Thank you for your sacrifices!

Chapter 1

You can't be serious." Jamie Russo tossed her dance bag onto the hardwood floor and rushed around the counter to her uncle. "Closing? But this is your dream!"

Sunlight twinkled off the glass shadow box that held commendation medals dating all the way back to the Civil War. This small corner of history just a few blocks from Central Park West had been his dream, to collect war memorabilia, research the pieces, find out who they belonged to—if possible—and return them to the rightful heirs. It'd allowed Uncle Alan James to find himself, find peace within, after a brutal tour of duty in Vietnam—an experience that left him haunted and alone. When he'd returned, the woman he'd promised to marry was gone.

Jamie believed with all her heart that he kept the shop running because of his yearning to find Gail Gibson, his true love. All these years, he'd never given up on her.

Until now.

"Uncle Alan, please." She touched his arm as she looked up at the man who'd been like a father to her since her own had died fifteen years ago and her mother before him. "This isn't right. You can't give up on Gail. I know she's out there." Who wouldn't wait for a man like her uncle? Handsome and in his midsixties, he was intelligent and had a quiet strength.

"This isn't about her." He thunked a wad of twine-bound

9

letters on a box. "It's about me moving on. I've pined for what will never be. Wasted forty years doing that. I'm through."

She glanced at the crate he'd set the letters on—and gasped at the wolf's head burned into the wood. "That's from the Wolfe Estate." She jerked back to him. "You're getting rid of *that*?" The situation was worse than she realized.

"Jamie, listen, I don't expect you to understand, but I'm ready to get on with my life." Decades of a broken heart had gouged lines into his gentle face. "Please. . .just let it rest."

"But. . .but that crate. It's from Mr. Wolfe's estate." It didn't make any sense. "You said you'd never part with it, that he was like a father to you."

His shoulders sagged. "I already said it; I'm moving on."

Her heart crashed into her stomach. Whatever had set him off, collapsed his hopes, she couldn't just stand here. She looked again at the burnt lettering. "Let me keep the Wolfe crate."

His gaze came to hers, thoughtful. Then stern. "No, I don't think that's wise." Holding her shoulders, he smiled. "Jamie-girl, you've given up your whole life, all your dreams, to help me here." Light glinted off the counter and reflected in his eyes, giving them an unusual shimmer. "I can't let you do that anymore." Pressing his lips to her forehead, he gave her arms a quick squeeze. He jerked around, before disappearing into the stockroom. Was that a tear rolling down his cheek?

What happened? What made him give up, after all these years?

"Daron Nelson will be here any minute for those boxes," Uncle Alan called from the back office. "Let me know if I don't hear him come in."

Trying to sort through the shock, Jamie slumped against the counter. The crate poked into her shoulder as if nudging her attention. She eyed the bundle of letters. The rhythmic scrawl on the envelope addressed to PFC Sean Wolfe, and subsequently stamped RETURN TO SENDER.

Who was Sean Wolfe? Mr. Wolfe's son? She tiptoed and noted the postmark. Only ten years ago. So it couldn't be his son, because his son was—

Duh. Of course. Patrick Wolfe, Uncle Alan's best friend. . . "Who is dead."

So, was Sean Wolfe a younger brother to Patrick? Her mind raced through what little—*very* little—her uncle had shared about the Wolfes. In fact, it'd been next to nothing except to mention Patrick and the heartache he'd brought his father, Mr. Wolfe. But. . .hadn't Uncle Alan said something about Gail being connected to Patrick Wolfe?

Light glinted and slid along the wall, pulling her attention to the opening door where the sun reflected off the glass and burst into the dingy shop. Daron Nelson stepped in with a grin. "Hey, Jamie." He pointed above the doorframe. "Guess the bell's not working."

"Yeah," she said absently, her mind still on the Wolfes.

If. . .what if she could find this Sean Wolfe—assuming he was still alive—maybe he would know what happened to Gail. Why she never showed up on Bow Bridge New Year's Eve, forty-one years ago.

Her heart did a pirouette at the thought. Jamie hiked her dance bag over her shoulder, lifted the Wolfe crate along with the letters from the counter, and motioned to Daron. "He's in the back."

Scurrying out the door, she whispered a prayer: "God, I know hurt is driving Uncle Alan's decision. Please. . .help me help him."

Adrenaline sped her down Seventy-Fourth Street and back to her apartment. After dance, she'd track down this man, find Gail Gibson, and make her uncle's dream come true.

∞

I just can't live like this, knowing you'll be gone, that you could die any minute. So I'm returning your ring. Let's just move on with our lives, okay? You'll always be dear to me.

Sean Wolfe sat on the edge of the mattress staring across the half-empty loft he'd occupied for the last six weeks since his medical discharge, re-reading the letter from his onetime fiancée. Her words, cruel and unfeeling, haunted him and drew his gaze down to the crumpled letter in his hands. The infamous Dear John letter had messed up his focus, messed with his head—and nearly gotten him killed.

"Dear." He'd given her his mother's antique ring. Devoted his heart and mind to staying alive to come home and marry her. And all she could say was that he was "dear"? She'd ditched him. While he was locked in combat in a hot, stinking desert.

Grief twisted and churned through his chest, dropping into his gut with a weight that left him nauseated.

He was through with dating. Through with women.

The soft thump of feet on the stairs to his loft snapped him out of his stupor. He shoved the letter beneath the pillow and stuffed his hands into a cobalt blue T-shirt.

"Why do you keep reading that letter?" Aunt Mitzi's voice rang out in the open-concept area. With only gym equipment, a small desk, and a bed, noise carried easily and loudly. Except when certain aunts glided across floors barefooted. How long had she watched him? "Why?" she repeated.

"To remind me not to get stupid again." He moved to his all-in-one gym, where he sat on the bench and put on his socks and shoes. Standing, he tucked his wallet in his jeans.

"Stupid?" She folded her arms, the burgundy pantsuit

highlighting the hints of red in her graying hair. "Sean, that girl wanted something you couldn't give her."

"My time?" he challenged.

"No, happiness." She drew the letter out from under the pillow and folded it neatly. "She didn't know what she wanted—still doesn't."

"She wanted someone who could be around."

"No, she wanted a hunk on her arm to make her look good." Aunt Mitzi shrugged. "She's a Colhagen, what do you expect?"

The words should've made him feel better. But they only reminded him that he wasn't good enough. Wouldn't ever be, especially now that his neck looked like a failed art project.

She peered up at him and grinned.

Oh no. He knew that look. "What?"

"Merrie Fitzpatrick is on her way over." She seemed to be enjoying something. "She's bringing her daughter."

Sean plucked the letter from her manicured hands, lifted his watch and phone, and said, "I've got to meet someone."

Aunt Mitzi arched an eyebrow. "Oh, do you? A girl?"

"A *guy*," he corrected. "Says he has some letters from my grandfather."

A shadow flickered over her face. "Oh."

Lifting his hoodie from the lateral tower, he hesitated at her expression. "What's wrong?"

Ever graceful, she lifted her chin and flashed a debutante smile. "Why would anything be wrong?"

Sean shrugged as he snagged his shades from the bed stand. "After this meeting, I'm heading over to Harry's, so don't plan on me for dinner."

"Glad to see you're getting out. It's about time." She nodded at him ruefully. "But you'll miss Merrie and her daughter, I'm afraid."

"That's the point." Sean hustled down the stairs to the

foyer of his aunt's immaculate home and stepped onto the front stoop. He slipped on his polarized sunglasses just as a Cadillac slid to the curb. Sean strode down the street, ignoring the shrill call of Mrs. Fitzpatrick.

He didn't want to be rude, but he knew once the social elite females saw his marred neck, they'd suddenly be *dis*interested. That he could do without. As he jogged, he laid out his game plan for the day—heading over to Harry's to see if he could finagle a job out of him. At least he could report back to Aunt Mitzi with a good conscience that he'd looked for one. She'd been patient—mostly. Even he had to admit a month was more than enough time. But when a guy nearly has his head blown off, it wrecks him.

Wreck. Yeah. *That's me.* Pain rolled through his shoulders and crawled into his neck, but he ignored it and kept moving. He'd have to beat the symptoms. Overcome the traumatic brain injury.

He rounded the corner and slowed at the sight of the sidewalk café. Packed! He groaned as he felt the telltale thump of a headache. Stretching to look at the faces of the patrons, he hoped to find this Jamie guy and get the letters. Then bail on the crowd scene ASAP.

He walked toward the fenced-off outdoor eating area, searching for the contact. Backing up, he toyed with just bailing. E-mail the guy, rearrange a quieter setting. Sean swung around—and collided with someone.

A woman yelped.

Sean braced her shoulders. "Sorry! Are you okay?"

Pure honey eyes looked into his, yanked the good sense right out of him. Color shaded her cheeks as she ducked her chin. "Yes, I'm fine. Thanks." She picked up a bag from the ground, cast a sidelong look at him, then entered the café.

Sean trailed her into the teeming area, admiring her

graceful stride. In the pink pea coat, white scarf, and gray jeans and boots, she had elegance written all over her. *Too much like Aunt Mitzi's kind.* Which pushed him to the right when she went left.

Guess his contact wasn't here. Sean grimaced at the crowded café and searched for somewhere to sit. Finally, he spied an empty table to his left and headed that way, all the while watching for the man. Hand on a chair, he jerked it back.

Another groan of the iron against the cement drew his gaze to the right.

Pea Coat Girl had drawn out a chair—at the same table. "Oh." Her gaze skipped around the area. "I. . .I'm sorry." She apparently realized the same thing he had—only one empty table left. This one.

"Go ahead," Sean said, stepping away. "I'm not staying."

"No, no, it's okay." The wind whipped at her tied-back hair, freeing a few strands. She tucked them behind her ear. "I didn't plan to stay either. I'm meeting someone."

Lucky guy. The thought struck him center mass. Where had that thought come from? He had a new rule in this new life— no girls.

Time for an exit strategy. He motioned to the chair. "Go ahead." He skirted around the other tables and aimed for the exit.

"You're not Sean Wolfe, are you?"

Chapter 2

Incredible Mediterranean-blue eyes spun her stomach in crazy circles. Near-black hair, cut military short, framed a strong jaw. . .a jaw marred by a horrendous scar. With one hand in a pocket, he ran the other over the back of his neck as he came back to the table. His jacket was partially unzipped, revealing a bright blue shirt that made his eyes intense.

He cocked his head. "Yeah. . .do I know you?"

"No, not formally." Heart thrumming, Jamie reached into her satchel and drew out the bundle. "We've e-mailed."

Confusion twisted his handsome features. "We have?"

Didn't he remember? Why else would he be here? She held up the bundle. "The letters from your grandfather. . ."

His eyes widened, shock brightening them. "*You're* Jamie Russo?"

The laugh trickled down her throat and evaporated at the dark shadow that fell over his expression. "According to my passport."

He snorted and looked around the café, shaking his head. "I thought I was meeting a guy."

Why did he look mad? Jamie held the letters, wrapping the twine binding around her finger. "Um, sorry?" She wrinkled her nose. Why was she apologizing for being a girl? She passed him the bundle. "These are the letters I told you about."

He rifled through the stack without disturbing the twine. "Well, thanks."

The abrupt end to their meeting stunned her. She watched, shocked, as he navigated out of the café.

Gail! She hadn't gotten to ask him about her. Jamie hurried after him. "Sean, wait!"

He lowered his head and kept walking.

Surely he'd heard her. Everyone else in New York had. "Sean, wait."

He drew to the side, waiting.

Jamie closed the distance, hands in the pockets of her coat. "Sorry to keep you, but you're Mr. Wolfe's grandson, right?"

"Imagine the name would've given that away."

Snarly. "My uncle was close to Mr. Wolfe."

"The only thing a Wolfe is close to is his ghosts."

What was with this guy? "That's really sad. Good thing I don't believe in ghosts." Okay, it was a stupid thing to say, but his attitude rankled her. Especially the way he dismissed what she'd said about her uncle.

He frowned. Again. "I meant ghosts of our past, demons. You know, metaphors."

"I know."

Again, he looked down, slumping against the wall. "Did you need something? Or did you just want to stop and hassle me about my family?"

She widened her eyes. "Wow. That was rude."

Something flickered over his face and he swallowed, turning those magnetic eyes in a different direction.

If she didn't love her uncle so much, she'd leave this guy to his snark. "Look, I just wanted to ask if you know a woman named Gail. Apparently connected to the Wolfes. A friend or what, I don't know. My uncle won't talk about it."

Sean shrugged. "Never heard of her."

"Oh." Hope deflated, Jamie tucked the stray strands of hair from her face. "Well. . .I'm sorry to have wasted your time. Have a good day." She hiked her satchel up on her shoulder and started away but then paused. Something about that conversation sat as heavy as gluten in her stomach.

Stop trying to rescue people, James. Her uncle's warning drifted on the cool October wind. Though he'd used the endearment—James, a leftover from her mother's maiden name, which is how she'd come to be named Jamie—it did nothing to soften his words. Chewing her lower lip, she looked back at the young man who'd thrown her enough attitude to lead a gang.

His tall, athletic frame slumped against the brick wall of a pastry shop. He pinched the bridge of his nose, bent forward, then his hand dropped. Head back against the wall, he slid down. What on. . .earth? Then it hit her—he'd passed out!

Breath backed into her throat, she plunged through the crowds to him and knelt at his side. "Sean?" Her boots scratched over the rocks and dirt. She touched his face. "Sean, are you okay? Sean!"

A small groan. He blinked. Unfocused eyes met hers. Confusion strangled his handsome features. "Wha. . .?"

"You passed out."

He shook his head and pulled to his feet.

Though he was taller and, if the muscles stretching the fabric of his shirt and jacket were any indication, much stronger than her, she held a hand to his shoulder to steady him. "You okay?"

Those blue eyes pierced her. Then he scowled. Pushed off the wall. "Yeah, I'm fine."

"That you are not." Jamie pointed to the café. "Let's get a table. You need to sit down."

He straightened and took a step in the opposite direction, his face drained of color. "I'm fine. I have another appointment." He held up the bundle. "Thanks for these."

Concern squeezed her lungs. What if he passed out and got

hit by a car?

He snapped a salute and vanished into the teeming crowds of New York City.

∞

Shouting pervaded the dark night. Sean huddled beneath the kitchen table, hugging his knees and praying his parents didn't realize he was there.

"You're worthless. Ever since you came back, you've done nothing but sit around."

"I can't work. My head—"

"Is messed up. I already know that. But I don't see anything wrong with your head, and excuses don't put food on the table or pay for clothes, or—"

"I get disability. I'm doing the best I can."

"Well, it isn't enough. I've taken care of four kids while you were off playing war. That baby of yours about killed me. He's just like you. If he'd never been born—"

"Don't say that, Marcia."

"I'm only saying what you won't."

"He's a good kid."

"He's trouble. Just like you."

His father's heavy footfalls stomped over the back deck. His mother disappeared down the hall, yelling at Jennifer to get off the phone. Sean crawled out from under the table and peeked around the kitchen. On his feet, he crept to the back door, wanting to find Daddy. A flash of light erupted from the shed.

Bang!

Sean jolted, blinking against the sunlight streaming through the shedding branches overhead. He pulled himself upright, letters tumbling away. He snatched for the pages, disbelieving he'd fallen asleep in Central Park, propped against a tree.

Rolling to the side, he roughed a hand over his face. Then. . . stilled. The dream. His heart kicked up a notch. Was that real? It felt crystal clear.

What noise had awoken him? He glanced around. A woman sat on the nearby bench.

Wait. Not just a woman.

Jamie Russo.

He tried not to groan. "What, are you following me?"

"No." She lowered her gaze. "Yes."

Sean started.

"After. . .when you. . ." She huffed. "I thought it best to make sure you were okay."

She'd seen him lose consciousness, one of the humiliating side effects of the traumatic brain injury. The look in her eyes, the pity. . .he didn't need that. Didn't want it. Especially not from her.

He tucked his chin and stood, dusting off his legs as he stuffed the—

The screen door. The bang that startled him had been from the screen door. Sean went still, his mind aligning the loud bang in his dream with the facts from the past. Dad had gone out into the shed, grabbed his handgun. . .and never came back. Ever.

Nausea swirled in his gut.

Was it real? He hadn't remembered those details. . .not till. . .now. Letters in his fisted hand, Sean tried to push the memories aside. He stared at the yellowed paper, remembering the message his grandfather had written:

Now, you may not want to hear this, Lord knows it's not easy to write because I bear your mother no ill, but I want you to have what I know to be a true accounting of your father's last months. After your birth, your mother fell

into a deep depression. Some said she had a mental illness.
When your father went to Vietnam the second time and
returned, even more traumatized. . .well, I don't believe
anything short of a miracle could've saved their marriage
or your father.

Don't get me wrong. Your father was a very good man,
very athletic—a lot like you.

Which is why he'd died. His father bred trouble—named Sean
Patrick Wolfe. *Me.* Everyone in the family blamed him, said
after he came things changed.

Sean stuffed the letters in a nearby receptacle. He wasn't
going to fill his head with more guilt trips. Though he tried to
avoid looking at Jamie as he stalked past her, his eyes moved of
their own will.

Mouth open, she looked from him to the bin. She came to
her feet. "Y–you're just throwing them away?" Hurrying toward
the green trash can, she glared at him.

Sean hesitated and followed her with his gaze. When she
plucked the letters from the top of the heap, he turned back.
"What're you doing?"

Another heated glare.

"Those are my letters."

Her chin tilted up. "Actually, they aren't. They're trash.
And I happen to be a trash collector." She smoothed the letters
against her hip then folded them into thirds.

If she weren't so pretty with that chestnut hair and brown
eyes, he'd give her a piece of his mind. The thought of her
reading about his father killing himself. . .about his mom's
purported mental illness. . .about how Sean had messed up his
family by being born—

"Look, just give them back." He held his hand out, but
when she didn't return them, he added, "*Please.*"

Jamie pushed the hair from her face. "Why. . .why would you throw them away?"

"Let's just say they don't bring back good memories."

Finally, she returned them. "We all need the bad memories to recognize the good ones."

As he held the penned reports, Sean considered her words. She had a point. Pretty, dressed nice, intelligent. . . She didn't seem to bear the weight of the world the way he did, so he doubted she understood. "You have bad memories?"

Dipping her head, she brought a hand to her throat. "Yeah, you could say that." She pointed to the Bow Bridge. "Mind if we walk because"—she hoisted her bag—"I have dance in twenty."

"Sorry." Why did he think someone like her would want to talk with him? "I'll let you get on with things."

"Actually, I wouldn't mind the company."

He hesitated. Was she *inviting* him to walk with her? Nobody had given him the time of day since he'd returned, especially after seeing the marred mess on his neck and jaw. And she'd noticed that in the café. Besides, he so wasn't going there after that Dear John letter.

Yet he fell into step with her, his gut churning. *This is a bad idea. . . .* Someone like her—the obvious reason for her invitation was pity.

Quiet settled between them, only the sound of crunching leaves kept them company amid the rustling of the American elms lining the path. Wind whipped the leaves in a frantic dance across the footpath.

Hands stuffed in her coat pockets, Jamie hunched her shoulders. "My parents died in a car accident on the way to my senior recital in high school." A cool breeze lifted her brown hair and tossed it over her shoulder. "As the recital was about to start, I peeked out from behind the curtain, looking for them. They weren't there. I kept watching, hoping. . .they'd never been late before. My uncle showed up as I was about to take the stage and told me about the accident, that they had both died."

"Wow," Sean said, feeling the weight of the guilt she must've experienced. "That's heavy. So you didn't do your recital?"

"What?" She looked at him, her delicately arched brows knitted. "Oh. Well, actually, I did."

"Seriously?"

Jamie smiled, squinting as she gazed into the darkening sky. "My father always said he wanted nothing more than to see me fulfill my dreams. My mother wanted to be a ballerina, so the best way I could honor them. . .was to dance."

"You're not like normal people."

Surprise marched across her pert nose and brown eyes. "Excuse me?"

"Sorry." Heat crept into his face. "That came out wrong."

She laughed. "Yeah, it did."

"I just meant. . .you don't seem to let things bother you." Wow, that made him sound like a person who hung on to bad things. "I mean. . ." Well, what did he mean?

With a sidelong glance, she paused in front of a building. "I think I get what you're saying." She continued, nodding toward a door with stenciled letters that marked it a dance company. "I remember the past, but I don't cling to it." She managed a weak smile. "Well, my uncle would argue, since I'd do anything to find his long-lost love."

A woman leaned out the door. "Jamie, you're late! Martin is getting mad."

Cheeks pinked, Jamie rolled her eyes. "I'd better go."

"Well, thanks for the letters." He held them up. "And the talk."

"Jamie," the woman called.

"I'll be there, Monet," she said over her shoulder then placed a hand on Sean's arm. "Promise me one thing?"

Anything. Whoa. Easy, chief. Where had that come from? "I don't even know you."

"Yes, you do. We met—I'm Jamie Russo, remember?" She had an infectious giggle. "Just promise you'll read those letters. And if you don't want to keep them, return them to my uncle—his shop is on Seventy-Third." She raised her eyebrows. "Deal?"

"Yeah, sure."

"Uh-uh."

"Huh?"

She wrinkled her nose. "You seem like a guy who keeps his promises, so I want your promise."

Tapping the letters against his hand, Sean studied her. How did she know that about him? Could he commit to digging into the past. . .for her? In that instant, Sean knew he was doomed. He'd do anything for this girl. No, he wouldn't. He'd vowed to never again get messed up with girls.

"Okay. I promise." So much for his vow.

A bright smile spread over her tawny features. "Great!" She backed away. "I. . .I hope we meet again, Sean Wolfe." With that, she whirled and rushed into the studio.

He clamped down the smile her words pulled out. This girl twisted up his mind. He'd had enough of that in one lifetime. Meet again? Not if he could help it.

Chapter 3

Tonight's rehearsal had been the longest four hours of her life. Jamie forced her mind from the exotic blue eyes of Sean Wolfe and back to the music, to the moves, her form. Thankfully, when he'd escorted her to practice last week, Martin had left in a hurry, telling them to practice alone. But tonight. . .she still couldn't shake Sean from her mind.

Oh no. Was that a narrowed gaze from Martin? She mentally traced her lines, determined to give one hundred percent to this session.

Wounded. That was the only word that hung with her even now. Seven days had only agitated her thoughts over him. His comment about Wolfes only being close to ghosts worried her. What ghosts did Sean have?

The music faded.

Martin aimed the remote at the player. "Jamie—where is your mind? Again."

"On a six-two, blue-eyed, dark-haired hunk," Monet muttered as she passed behind Jamie to her starting position.

Jamie speared her friend with a sharp look as she retrieved a towel, wiped off, then returned to her spot with her partner, Claude. When he smiled at her, she could only wonder what Sean Wolfe's smile looked like. He hadn't broken one the entire time—well, one almost sneaked past his barrier, but he'd smothered it.

Music streamed through the studio.

She hurried into the dance, missing a step.

"Jamie—*à la seconde!*" Martin clapped frantically. "No! No, again!"

Shaking out her arms and legs, Jamie moved back to Claude.

"Jamie!" Martin's voice held the French accent that had thickened his words. "Where is your mind? I need it here, yes? *Allegro!*"

She nodded and looked to the side, her right arm extended and her feet in second. But as she did, she remembered Sean's hand dropping to the ground when he'd passed out. What caused that? It'd been short lived and embarrassed him. But hadn't surprised him. Was it related to whatever happened to his neck? And why didn't it bother her? *Because something about him draws me in.* Was that true?

The music snapped off.

Jamie stopped in the middle of the polonaise with Claude.

Waving his arms, Martin growled. "Go—out of my studio." He brushed her away. "Come back with your mind! You are better than this."

Guilt should make her want to stay, but Jamie left the floor with the others, grateful for the chance to explore the thought that capsized her focus. She'd never been drawn to a guy before. In the locker room, she slid onto the bench and untied her slippers. As she plied them off, she winced at the sting in her toes. Bloodied, they'd need to be soaked at home.

"So, what's his name?" Monet stuffed her gear in her bag as she slipped on her shoes.

"Sean Wolfe." Jamie dressed then donned her boots and coat.

"Exotic," Monet said with a giggle.

"His eyes are—but there's something haunted about him." She packed her dance clothes away. "Want to grab something from Mario's?"

Monet shook her head. "Sorry, Claude and I have a date."

"Again?" Jamie sighed. The two were forever exploring dating. But didn't have a bone of fidelity in their bodies.

"You haven't had a date since high school, Jamie!"

"It hasn't been that long."

"Craig Mueller."

Jamie froze. Had it really been that long?

"Just because you're holding out for Prince Charming doesn't mean I have to." Monet grinned. "Besides, Claude is fun."

"He's a flirt." Burying the hurt and shock at what her friend had said, she started out of the room.

"Exactly!"

Shaking her head, Jamie shuffled out of the studio. She'd never understand Monet's penchant for dating the wrong men. On the other hand, Jamie just. . .didn't date. *Jamie-girl, you've given up your whole life, all your dreams to help me. . . ."*

Had she really?

Sure, she'd given up her scholarship to attend The Juilliard, but that's what family did for each other, right? Alone, Uncle Alan didn't have anyone besides her when he went through a serious health scare. Nearly losing him—the only family she had left—well, it was too close to home. Too familiar a pain, having lost her parents. So the decision had been easy for her.

But it'd been six years. Now at twenty-four, she found herself jobless, thanks to his closing the shop, attending night dance school to keep her skills fresh and performing with a local civic ballet troupe, and. . .alone.

There was nothing wrong with making tough choices for loved ones.

Unless it's a cover for your fears.

Jamie's gaze rose to the sky as she slowed. *Fears?* What fears?

Fear of losing someone you love.

All at once, she saw the double caskets on that May afternoon. Felt Uncle Alan's arm around her. Remembered his words that they would make it together. But if he found Gail...

Blowing out a hard breath that made her lips flap like one of the Central Park horses, Jamie trudged across the tree-littered lawn. *Was* she living in fear? If she helped Uncle Alan find Gail, he'd have his true love, and Jamie would've been part of finding a piece of his broken life. How was that living in fear of losing someone she loved?

It's no risk when you think it's impossible.

Ouch. Admittedly, she'd harbored the idea that if he couldn't find Gail after almost forty years, nobody could. The thought of his being gone, not being there for her, of the fuzzy warmth of his laughter...

"I hear You, God," she whispered, her breath puffing out in front of her face. "But...what do You want me to do?"

Bow Bridge loomed to her right, tucked aside and austere, elegant. Uncle Alan was supposed to meet Gail there....

Sean Wolfe surged to the front of her mind, the eyes that held both pain and gentility, the deep voice that was smooth yet terse.

"Okay, Lord," she said as she detoured toward the bridge, "if You want me to get to know Sean, let him show up here."

Fleece praying wasn't the best route to knowing the will of God, but...

"'It's no risk when you think it's impossible,'" she said, repeating the words she heard in her heart. Yeah. Sean showing up here, at nearly ten o'clock? Impossible. Leaning on the stone rail, Jamie gazed out over the lake, glistening and reflecting the lights of the city hovering nearby. With a sigh, she set out for her apartment, for her Bible. She needed to dig out some answers about not living in fear. And spend some face time in prayer. Fingers trailing the rail, she admired the blanket of stars and the Fingernail-of-God moon.

Peace filled her. She sighed and stepped off the bridge.

"Jamie?"

∞

Sean slowed to a stop, his breath chugging. Hand on his chest, he tried to still his pounding heart. And it wasn't from the rigorous run he'd just taken. She looked amazing, even with shock written all over her face. Bent, he held his knees to catch his breath, peering up at her through his brows.

"Sean?" She wet her lips. Looked around. "What. . .what are you doing here?"

"Out for a run," he said as he straightened. "Wanted to clear my head."

After meeting with his friend and getting a job—sort of, if you called tinkering on junkers a job—he'd made his way back to Aunt Mitzi's condo. Sitting there, nothing to do, no transportation, no purpose, drove him to reading those letters. But that had pushed his irritation through the roof. And he found himself here. Staring at her retreating form. Though he'd told himself not to say anything, his body—again—betrayed him by calling out to her.

"At ten o'clock at night?"

He lifted a shoulder then motioned at the path. "Headed home?"

She glanced down the sidewalk for several seconds. *Long* seconds. Then looked at him. Why did she look frightened? Had something scared her? Something primal rose up in him. "Want me to walk you home?"

"I. . ."

So he'd been wrong. What he'd taken for interest, for understanding, *was* pity. "Know what? Never mind." Sean ducked his head. "I'll catch you later." What an idiot. Thinking she'd like him. One would think a piece of shrapnel had hit his brain, not his neck. His sneakers grated on the dirt as he shifted back the way he'd come.

"Did you read more letters?"

He slowed at her words. Turned.

She stood, a hand on the balustrade, eyes wide. Her long, graceful throat processed a swallow. Was she scared? Of *him*?

"You know—the letters I gave you, from your grandfather. Did you read more?"

How did she know the letters had pushed him out of the condo and into the cold night? "Yeah, as a matter of fact, I did." Using his arm, he swiped the sweat from his face.

Jamie took a few rigid steps toward the path then glanced back at him.

A silent invitation.

Sean acknowledged her cue, jamming his hands into the pockets of his jacket as he joined her. Man, this felt good—right. Too right. His insides squeezed and left his courage in the fetal position.

"Earlier you'd said the letters brought up bad memories. I'm surprised you read more."

"Well, like someone told me, we need the bad to see the good." In fact, the conviction he felt from those words nudged him to delve into the past. He didn't want to open up this can of worms, but then again, he needed someone to talk to about all this. And he sure wasn't going to do that with his aunt. She went cold every time his parents' names came up.

"I assume 'clearing your head' is related to the letters."

Smart girl. "He. . ." Wow. Didn't think it'd be this hard to talk about it. "My, uh, my dad died when I was four—killed himself."

Jamie's head lifted, her beautiful brown eyes lit with pain. "Oh, I'm so sorry."

"Thanks." Her compassion felt good, like a balm on a decades-old wound. "My grandfather told me some things about my dad that I didn't know."

"Like?"

He hesitated—but realized he didn't feel defensive with her. "Like he wasn't a loser, that he loved me and my siblings. That he went to war and came back changed." Sean watched a leaf tumble from a branch and flutter to the ground. He felt a lot like that leaf right now, tumbling and fluttering through life. "That I can relate to."

"Is that what happened to your jaw and neck?"

"IED hit our Humvee. Killed three of my men." The memories of the day that shattered his career threatened, so Sean quickly redirected the train wreck waiting to happen back to the letters. "My grandfather then said my mom was mentally unstable."

"Do you believe him?"

"Makes sense, I guess. When I think back to her erratic, irrational behavior. . ." He shrugged. "Mom could be real mean without ever raising her voice. She made it clear I was the reason my dad died." Why on earth was he telling her about all this?

"How awful! I can't imagine a mom ever saying that to her own child."

He'd lived with that burden since. . .forever. "Everyone said it was true." Another shrug. "But my grandfather claimed my father was a hero, that he'd just been broken by my mom's ranting and accusations."

"Seems a father would know his own son. Do you think he was right?"

"I don't know. Maybe." Probably. That made more sense than the stories his mom fed him. "I hated my dad for a long time for taking his life, so it's hard to know what to believe."

Jamie adjusted her bag as they turned toward Seventy-Third. "My uncle talked nothing but stars and sunshine about

Patrick Wolfe." Vehemence laced her words as she stopped him, touched his arm, and stared into his eyes. "Mr. Wolfe was my uncle's mentor, and my uncle doesn't trust lightly. So if your grandfather said those things, you *can* believe him."

More than anything, Sean wanted to accept that as truth. To know his father was a good man, that he didn't hate Sean and want to be free from the responsibility of taking care of a family. And even more—to know that Sean hadn't been the reason his family fell apart. But was it only a desperate hope?

He pulled away and started walking again. It felt like progress: a comfortable, steady rhythm—with her by his side. A mental image of something mentioned in the letter popped into his mind. "Oh, hey. Did your uncle have a Civil War–era coin in that stuff you found?"

Jamie shook her head. "No, I gave you the bundle. There are other trinkets—I can bring them to you if you want—but nothing like a coin."

Sean frowned, a curious ache inside him.

"Is it special?"

"My grandfather said it had been passed down through the Wolfes since one of my ancestors, William Wolfe, who served in the Civil War. Said it was a very important piece, and that should I ever marry and have a son, I needed to be sure he carried on the legacy." They'd reached the edge of the park. Across the street and down a half-dozen blocks, their conversation would be over. Inwardly he winced at the thought.

"You don't have the coin?"

He dislodged the feelings. "No. Never even heard of it."

"Did he tell you where it was in the letters?"

"No. I haven't gotten through all of them though." He squinted ahead. "You'd think if it was so important, I'd know about it." He scratched his jaw and cringed at the mangled flesh. "My brother might have it, I guess."

"You have a brother?"

"And two sisters. They took off when Mom died. I think they were in as much a hurry as I was to get away from the memories."

"Is that when you went into the Army?"

"Signed up at seventeen, my aunt signed a release."

"Your aunt?" Her eyes widened as she slowed in front of an apartment building. "Aunt Gail?"

Hadn't he already told her he didn't know a Gail? "Aunt Mitzi. And she's my godmother. Not blood related."

"Oh." She climbed a step, her nose wrinkled.

One foot on the step, Sean cocked his head, noting that she was now the same height as him. "Why do you keep asking about this Gail person?"

She gave a sheepish grin. "She's my uncle's long-lost love. They were to marry when he returned from Vietnam. She was supposed to meet him on Bow Bridge but never showed."

"Is that why you like that bridge?"

Sparkling eyes met his. "Mostly."

Chapter 4

A soft gong resounded inside the condo. Jamie lowered her hand from the doorbell, her heart pounding, and reminded herself she had good reason to be on the doorstep of the condo. She looked at the hand-painted chocolate tin she'd found last night. It was in the Wolfe crate, but she never dreamed it held more of Sean's past. And she'd seen as plain as the scars he bore that God was working on Sean through these letters.

Okay, so she found a morsel of guilty pleasure knowing that God also used her to help bring about this change. When he'd shown up two nights ago in the park, right after her fleece prayer, she'd been knocked senseless, yet at the same time, a deep knowing locked into place within her soul: she was to be there for Sean on this journey. Just like she'd been there for Uncle Alan.

The door swung open and snatched her breath.

Dressed in black slacks and a silk top, the attractive woman, who was fluid and all motion a second ago, stilled.

Whoa. *She's Sean's aunt?* Despite a few silver strands in her red hair and the delicate laugh lines in her eyes, the woman held a corner on Beauty Avenue and Elegant Lane.

A soft, gentle smile brightened her face. "Can I help you?"

"Hi, I'm Jamie Russo. I believe Sean lives here, is that right?"

The woman's smile flickered. "Yes. Sean lives here. Do I know you?"

"I met Sean through a bundle of letters."

Her mouth formed a perfect circle. "Oh. You're *that* Jamie. The guy who wasn't a guy." She extended a manicured hand. "Mitzi Pendergast."

"Nice to meet you," Jamie said. "Yeah, I think both Sean and I were expecting someone else."

A spark lit soft hazel-green eyes. "Isn't that the way God works?"

Jamie's pulse skipped a beat. Ms. Pendergast couldn't know about the prayer that convinced Jamie that God had crossed her path with Sean's for a purpose. "Um, is Sean home?" Jamie held out the tin. "I found more letters last night."

"I bet you did." She motioned Jamie into the house. "He's upstairs working. Come on up. I'll show you."

Stomach in her throat, Jamie wondered what Ms. Pendergast meant. She honestly had found the tin last night. Why would she think she hadn't? Across the marble floor, past the antique chest with mirror in the hall, and up carpet-lined wood steps, Jamie held the box—tight. *Please. . .please be glad to see me.*

"Be prepared. Sean's never really been a neat freak, much to my consternation." Ms. Pendergast's steps were silent and graceful, a striking similarity to the way Jamie's mother had walked and carried herself. The thought sent a pang into Jamie's chest. "But he's a great guy." She turned to Jamie as they walked along a rail that overlooked the grand foyer to the right and a hall to the left. "I'm hoping the girl he marries won't mind a mess."

Heat spread through Jamie's cheeks—just as she looked across the open space. A large room consumed the upper half of the condo. Open concept, the loft sported a futon, a desk, gym equipment, and a bed shoved against a far corner with a nightstand, warmed by the lamplight that spilled over a chair.

Clank. Clank.

A grunt reverberated though the loft, pulling Jamie's gaze toward a pile of...parts.

"See what I mean?" Ms. Pendergast sighed as they rounded the last corner and stepped into Sean's sanctum. "Sean, you have company."

"Me?" His head popped up over a large box. His eyes widened. He punched to his feet. "Jamie."

The way he said that and the smile shadowing his stubbled jaw drew out her own smile. "Hi."

Ms. Pendergast's smile was even larger. She stroked a necklace that looked like a medallion of some kind. "I'll bring some finger sandwiches and tea."

Before Jamie could tell her not to bother, his aunt had floated away.

Wiping his greasy hands on what looked like a torn T-shirt, Sean came toward her. "Sorry about that." He wagged his eyebrows toward his aunt. "She doesn't know how *not* to entertain."

"She's great." *Makes me miss my mom.*

"I wasn't expecting you."

"I know it was presumptuous, but I thought you'd want this." Jamie lifted the black box with hand-painted flowers.

Sean tossed aside the rag, ran his hands down his jeans then through his hair, and nodded to the tin. "What is it?"

"I was going to use the Wolfe crate for some old books, and when I took this out—I realized there was something inside it."

He stood close now. In fact, so close she could smell the grease and oil amid his cologne, that old-world spicy smell. Accepting the box, he glanced at her. "More letters?"

"Yeah."

"Cool, but I'm glad you came by for another reason." Sean looked around then rushed to the futon, removed a small tool box, a canister, and a T-shirt. "Have a seat. I want to show you something."

Jamie eased onto the futon. Hands on her knees, she trailed him with her eyes as he plucked something from the nightstand. *The letters?* He was going to share them? He'd said they brought back bad memories, yet he was going to share them with her? The significance kept her quiet.

Four large strides carried him back to her. He eased down, the wood frame creaking under his weight. "Remember that coin I told you about? My grandfather mentions it in nearly every letter." Sean flipped through the yellowed pages. "In one of them. . .he says"—he turned another page—"he gave it to your uncle."

"*My* uncle?"

Sean pointed to the line. "Here."

Angling in, Jamie read: " 'After your father's death—' " Her gaze leaped to his.

"Go on."

She returned to the immaculately scrawled words. " 'After your father's death, Alan James became like the son I'd lost. So, in keeping with the Wolfe tradition, I gave the coin to him.' " Jamie froze. "My uncle has it?" She heard the squeak in her voice but couldn't stop it. "I've never seen it. And he's never mentioned it."

"Can you ask him about it?"

"Sure, I'll do it right now." She fished her phone from her purse and pressed the autodial. The line connected and rang.

"Hello?"

"Uncle Alan, sorry to interrupt, but I wanted to ask you a question."

"Anytime, Jamie-girl."

"I'm with Sean Wolfe right now, and we were wondering. . . did Mr. Wolfe ever give you a coin?"

Silence pervaded the line.

Maybe he didn't understand. "We're reading letters from his grandfather. Mr. Wolfe says he passed a family heirloom to you." She looked at Sean, noticing the scars weren't visible from this side. His jaw was strong and his gaze piercing.

"Look, James, if I had a coin, don't you think you would've found it in that crate you took—without asking me, I might add."

"I know, I'm sorry." She sighed. "But do you think you might've set it down, or maybe put it in one of the shadow boxes?" Why did his answer sound like avoidance?

∞

Sean's stomach clenched when her jaw went slack. Concerned, he eased into her periphery.

The phone squawked a reply Sean couldn't make out, but it sounded angry.

Jamie flinched. "I know. . .I'm sorry. . .but do you—" She stared at the display. "He hung up." She dropped the phone into her purse then shoved her hands through her thick brown hair. "He was so angry. He's never like that with me." She shuddered.

Guilt swam a mean circle around Sean's mind. "I'm sorry I asked you to check into it."

"It's not your fault." She tucked her chin. "I think he's mad because I tracked you down."

"Why would he be mad?"

"When I saw the Wolfe estate crate, I seized the chance to find you in the hopes of finding her." Her light brown eyes glossed with unshed tears—and he noticed for the first time the gold flecks that brightened her irises. "When he announced closing the war memorabilia shop, I felt like he was giving up not only on love, but on life. Then he told me I had to stop sacrificing my life for him." She worried a string on the black futon cushion. "I wasn't doing that, not really. I just wanted him happy."

"What about you?" The words were out before Sean realized it. He felt bad, but when her lips parted and she looked at him, he knew he'd hit a nerve. "Are you happy?"

"Me?" That lone word plucked at his heartstrings. "Of course I'm happy."

Nice try. The too-defensive answer was more a retort than an honest reply. "Your uncle said you had to stop sacrificing for him—what did he mean? What did you sacrifice?"

Again she dropped her gaze.

"Jamie?"

"Dance." She swallowed, and a smile pushed into her face. "I gave up my dance scholarship."

"But you're going to school."

The smile lost its luster. "No, I'm taking dance to stay on my toes—ha, ha."

He smirked at the pun. "What scholarship did you give up?"

Jamie looked around the room then rose to her feet. "I'd better get going or I'll be late."

"Jamie. . ." Sean stood and hooked her elbow gently. "I think he only cares about you. He wants you—"

"I know. . .it's just"—she sighed as her gaze met his—"I'd do anything for him. Setting aside my dreams for a while to help him, there's nothing wrong in that."

"Only if you forget to pick the dreams back up."

"What about you?" She bobbed her head toward the room. "Is this your dream?"

The question pushed him back. His dreams? What dreams? His only dream had been to be a soldier, but God slammed that door in his face—literally, and left him the scars as a mean reminder.

Sean shifted and glanced at the parts for the old Harley.

He'd have it put together in a week or so, it'd give him some cash, but what then?

I don't have any dreams. . . .

Maybe his mom had been right. There was no purpose for him. No reason for him to be alive except to cause pain—which he'd just done to the one ray of light in his dark world.

"Guess we're not the best and brightest dreamers." Jamie's wide eyes riveted his feet to the floor as she lifted a shoulder in a halfhearted shrug.

"You have a dream," Sean said. "You should follow it."

Jamie shook her head. "I don't think so."

"Why?"

"Sean. . ." Her voice cracked. It sounded like she was on the verge of crying.

The air had thickened, and even he found it tough to breathe. "Tell you what—your class isn't till six, right?"

Her hesitant nod did strange things to his stomach. The innocence wreathing her face wrapped his heart like a vise.

"Wanna grab a burger? Then I can walk you to class?"

"I. . ." She snapped her mouth closed. Then said, "Okay."

A warm thrill raced through his veins as she agreed. "Great. C'mon." He snatched his keys and a couple of the letters from the tin. "You can help me sort through these."

"Well, here we are." Aunt Mitzi topped the stairs, a white rectangular plate in hand.

"Oh," Sean said, "sorry, we've got to head out."

His aunt gave them an appraising look then popped a finger sandwich in her mouth. "Have fun."

There was entirely too much amusement in his aunt's voice and face as he guided Jamie into the brisk November afternoon.

"I thought she'd be upset after making us those sandwiches," Jamie said as they strolled down the bustling street.

"She's cool. Pretty laid-back most times."

"I love that necklace she had on. What is it?"

"What necklace?" Okay, so he might be able to name every make and model of motorcycles, but he couldn't remember what his aunt wore. Was it a crime?

"The one she had on. It was some medallion."

Pressing the crosswalk button, Sean remembered the piece. "She's had that since I can remember. Wears it all the time."

"It looks like some type of coin."

Sean slowed as he walked. Coin? The piece burst into his mind. The engraving. "Wait a minute. . . ." He whipped out the letters from his back pocket and rifled through them, flipping pages. His head pounded, the beginnings of a migraine. He blinked to ward off the haze taking over. The coin. . .was the coin on her pendant the same coin his grandfather had spoken of in the letters? But. . .how? She wasn't even a blood relation. How would she have gotten the coin?

"Sean?"

Jamie's voice sounded distant.

"No. . ." He felt hands leading him to the side. Tensed—then reminded himself to relax. He didn't want to pass out, not in front of this girl who had it all together.

"Sit on the step."

He eased down, feeling as if his pulse would explode in his head. Gray. . .haze. . .clouding. . .

"Sean?" Soft hands touched his arm, the voice growing stronger.

He blinked, slowly coming out of the fog. Only then did he realize he wasn't leaning against a rail or wall, but against Jamie Russo. Swallowing and straightening, he tired to shake off the haze. "Sorry."

The warmth of her hand on his back made him not want to move. "You okay?"

"Yeah."

"Is this connected to the scars?"

He nodded, hating the TBI, the way it crippled him. "A kid threw a soda can at our Humvee. It was actually an IED. Three of my men died, two others went home without arms and legs. I came back with TBI."

"Traumatic Brain Injury."

He looked at her, surprised she knew what he meant.

"My dad got it in Vietnam. It took him years, but he over-came most of the symptoms. It's why dancing was so important to him."

Braving a glance to her pretty face didn't give him what he expected—pity. Instead he saw understanding and genuine concern in her brown eyes. Something inside him twisted and kinked, knotting his stomach.

Sean pulled himself upright. "We should get going, grab that burger." Before he did something stupid. Like break his no-more-women rule.

Chapter 5

After their burgers, Jamie walked with Sean toward the dance studio, her mind still snagged on the necklace his aunt wore. "Do you think. . .do you think your aunt's necklace could be the coin mentioned in the letters?"

"It could be anything, but it doesn't make any sense. Why would she have it? Especially if my grandfather gave it to your uncle?"

"Well, your aunt—godmother—would have been close to your mother, right?"

He gave a curt nod.

"I thought Uncle Alan said Gail was your mom's sister—"

"But—"

"I know. She didn't have a sister. But maybe they were *like* sisters. So, what if Gail. . ." Jamie groaned. "Oh, I don't know. It's driving me crazy. Do you think you could ask her about it?"

"You just want to play Cupid."

"I can't help it. My uncle is an amazing man." She grinned. "Sean, think about it—what if that's the coin? If her name were Gail, I'd lay my life down she was my uncle's long-lost love."

Warm and inviting, Sean's laughter spiraled around the chilled air and drew her in. "You're incurable."

A horse-drawn carriage clopped around the bend, drawing their attention.

"Will you just ask her about it?"

"You aren't going to leave it alone until I do, are you?"

"What if she knows who or where Gail is? What if because you don't ask, Gail is never found, and my poor uncle dies a sad, lonely bachelor?"

"Ouch." He raised his hands. "Okay, okay. Enough with the guilt session."

"So, you'll ask?"

Another laugh. "Yeah, sure."

Jamie threw her arms around his neck and hugged him. "Thank you!"

Sean stood in the kitchen where his aunt chopped vegetables on the marble countertop. What got him here, what pushed him to ask her about the necklace that even now peeked out from her blouse, he didn't know.

Oh yes, he did. It was that hug. Jamie's spontaneous expression of glee. That reaction had a deadly and dangerous effect on Sean because he knew he'd do anything for her after that hug.

"So, what's up, handsome?" Aunt Mitzi popped a piece of bell pepper in her mouth as she lifted the cutting board over the large cooking pot then scraped the knife along the surface and dumped in the veggies. "You look like you have something on your mind." She slid a sly smile his way. "How're things with Jamie?"

Sean ducked his head, hating the way the heat filled his face. He was crazy about the ballerina, but he wasn't sure about stepping into the explosive waters of dating with her—or anyone. "She's. . .good."

"Oh, come on, you clod! She likes you, and if I'm reading this correctly, you're a bit over the moon about her, too." Her hand moved to the necklace, and Sean realized how often she did that. He'd never noticed before. Were those markings the same as the ones in the letter? If they were, how did she get it? Was it possible there was more than one coin like that?

As he studied the piece, he realized she'd frozen with her eyes wide.

Sean reached for the pendent and lifted it. "You wear this all the time." He turned it over, and his stomach clamped at the inscription—just like in the letter. "It must be special to you."

Her mouth opened then closed. "It is." She quickly moved to the fridge and bent over.

"Where did you get it?"

Armed with meat in a white paper wrapper and more veggies, she straightened and nudged the door closed with her foot. She dumped the contents on the counter, her back to him.

Sean switched to the other side, leaning back against the high-end counters. He touched her shoulder. "Aunt Mitzi?"

"Could you grab the oregano and paprika for me, Sean?" She wouldn't face him.

Something was going on. He wasn't sure what, but he'd never been one to back down. In the letters he'd read "The Wolfe honor was as solid as the ships they built. And just as unsinkable." He'd like to think the same was true of tenacity. Tugging the letters from his back pocket, he knew he had to find the answers.

Carefully he unfolded the letter and placed it on the counter, over the food, and noticed his godmother slow her pace once her gaze struck the papers. "Where did you get the medallion, Aunt Mitzi?"

Her shoulders slumped, both hands resting on the edge of the counter as she looked down. She drew in a long, hard breath. "Please, Sean. . ." Her voice hitched. Chin trembling, she shook her head. "Please, don't ask."

A tear streaked down her perfectly made-up face. Slowly, she wiped it, backed up a step, then walked out of the kitchen.

Chapter 6

After a quick shower and change of clothes, Jamie stuffed her gear in her satchel, donned her coat and scarf, then rushed from the dressing room. Since the day they'd gone for a burger before class, Sean had "just happened" to be in Central Park, at Bow Bridge, as she made her way home. As she barreled out the door armed with hope that he'd be there again, she collided with someone.

"What *is* your hurry?" Monet asked, the light from the studio sign reflecting off the hurt in her face.

"Just. . .gotta get home."

"Why? You don't have a job now, you aren't going to school—what are you hurrying for?"

The words touched a raw spot. The job thing. . .well, she needed a job, but she wasn't overly qualified, having spent all her adult years working at an antique store. And she certainly couldn't tell Monet about Sean without her automatically assuming they were dating. They weren't. But Sean had waited for her in the park just about every night after practice for the last two weeks. Monet wouldn't get that they hadn't been on a date, that they hadn't done. . .things. Her friend had other ideas about dating. But this wasn't dating. Not really.

"You're seeing him, aren't you?" The grin Monet sported soured Jamie's stomach.

"No, I mean—we're not dating."

"But that's where you've rushed off to instead of joining us at the Yankee Grill, right?" Monet looked at something behind Jamie. "With a hunk like that, I can understand."

Over her shoulder, Jamie saw Sean talking with Martin. A strange fluttering erupted in her belly. But she wasn't sure if it was the sight of Sean or the fact he was talking to Martin. "Catch you later, girl."

"Yeah," Jamie said absently as she turned toward Sean, who now strode in her direction. "What are you doing here?"

Hands stuffed in his jeans pockets, Sean shrugged. "How was practice?"

"Painful as always. I think I'll need to soak my feet extra long tonight." Her gaze tripped over Martin, who had a curious expression that Jamie couldn't quite make out. "What. . .what were you doing talking to Martin?"

"He wanted to know what I was doing messing with his prize pupil."

She groaned.

Sean chuckled. "Seems I'm distracting you."

Martin told him that? Jamie wanted to crawl into the manhole she'd just walked over. Her gaze hit his, and she was swept into the squall of those Mediterranean-blue eyes.

They strolled down the street, the November air chilling as Thanksgiving neared. Their troupe would perform a few times right before Christmas, which was the reason for Martin's rude behavior. Of course, Martin was all about dance and not much else.

Two more cross streets and stoplights and they'd enter Central Park, which had somehow become "their place." Or at least, it had to her. Sean proved impossible to read, so she wasn't sure what he thought of her, but she hoped their friendship would grow into something. . .more.

"Do you plan to go to the Macy's Thanksgiving Day Parade?"

He poked the button for the final crosswalk. "Nah. Crowds, noise—not a good combination."

"Me, too." She didn't like the crowds, but she knew they had a worse impact on Sean. What was it like for him to live in fear of another shutdown from the TBI? Handsome, strong, with a killer smile, the guy had more wit and intelligence than most men she knew. But he rarely let anyone see it. She adored his quiet strength, his stoic mannerisms. A complete opposite from her tendency to be outspoken and opinionated. Which is why she found herself biting her tongue right now. He looked conflicted about something.

The light flicked green with the twenty-second countdown. Jamie stepped off the curb into the flow of foot traffic. A man on a bike whizzed toward them. Sean reached toward her, guiding her by the elbow, then his touch trailed down her arm and entwined with her fingers as they entered the park.

Jamie's heart rapid-fired. She had to force herself not to gasp or tense. The questions that had plagued her over the last ten days were answered. Warm and large, his hold was tight. As if he was afraid to let her go. Or maybe he was afraid she would let go.

She eased into their walk, determined to relish the moment, the crisp wind, the stars blinking overhead—mostly blotted by the lights of the city—and savor that she was with Sean Wolfe. Touching her ballet slipper necklace reminded her of their dialogue.

"Have you talked with your aunt yet about the pendant?"

"Well, yes and no."

She wrinkled her nose and waited for him to explain.

"It *is* the same one, and I asked how she got it, but she wouldn't talk to me—in fact, she walked out, leaving the meal she was making, which is huge because she considers herself an amateur Paula Deen." He scratched the side of his jaw. "She has avoided me ever since."

"What does that mean?"

"Whatever it is, she doesn't want to talk about it."

"What are you going to do?"

He frowned. "What do you mean?"

"If that's the coin, then she has to know Gail or what happened to her. You've got to ask her."

"No," he said, "I don't. She asked me to leave it alone, and I'm going to."

"Are you—but, you can't!"

"A Wolfe never goes back on his word." Sean's intensity told her he wouldn't back down, but she couldn't accept that. "Besides, if you knew my godmother, if you knew how strong and resilient she was—to see her fall apart like that"—he shook his head—"I'm not touching that with a ten-foot pole."

"Sean, what if she knows Gail? What if—"

"Jamie, if and when she's ready to talk, I'll listen. But I won't push or force it." He came around and faced her. "Listen, I get how much you want to find Gail, but I have to give her room. She gave me the space I needed after I returned and wanted nothing more than to die."

Grief and anxiety over Gail faded as Sean's words sank into her psyche. Jamie locked onto his gorgeous eyes, her heart aching for him. "You wanted to die? Why?"

"I grew up being told I was worthless, the cause of everything bad. Then after my team gets hit, and they die but I don't. . .I wanted nothing more than to *not* be here. It all felt like a cruel joke—God kept me here just to remind me I was pointless."

Though he snorted, she heard the pain behind those words.

"Sean." Her throat felt raw. "You are not pointless. In fact, you're very important."

Sean's brow knotted. His expression changed. Nosedived from pained to intense. The look told her something in him had shifted, his thoughts bounding from his aunt to. . .

Oh, she didn't want to go there, didn't want to get her hopes up. But that prayer. God *had* brought Sean to the bridge, hadn't He?

"Jamie. . ." His gaze bounced over her face. He touched her cheek. "Do I distract you, like Martin said?"

A bubble of nervous laughter trickled past her stunned mind. Her pulse whooshed in her ears. Thank goodness he couldn't see the crimson color filling her cheeks due to the late hour and less-than-adequate light in the park. She wanted to lie, wanted to say she didn't know what he was talking about, but the prayer two weeks ago and his showing up told her she couldn't lie to him. The whole beginning to their relationship had been different, hard.

"I need to know, Jamie." His shoes scratched on the sidewalk as he inched closer. "I can't go through it again."

"Go through what?"

He let go of her hand and started walking. "Right before the IED, I got a Dear John letter from my fiancée. She didn't want to wait for me, didn't want to be a military wife." He huffed. "It was just excuses. She had already hooked up with one of my friends. I realized what she didn't want was me."

"Her loss."

He stopped, staring at the path. Then at her. "I like you. A lot. But I can't. . ." He swallowed and looked away. "I can't do that again."

"I honestly don't know what to say. I can't see the future, Sean. What I do know, what I can see, is that I like you." Whoa. That was a heady thing to say. "I want to be there for you."

"What, am I your new project?"

She blinked, feeling slapped. "Excuse me?"

"You gave up a scholarship with The Juilliard to save your uncle."

Jamie sucked in a breath. "How do you know that?"

"I don't want to be some pet project, Jamie."

"There is nothing wrong with making sacrifices for those you love." She wanted to snatch back that word. Would he think she meant that she loved him? She didn't. At least. . . she didn't think she did. They'd only known each other a month. It wasn't possible to happen that fast.

"It is when you give up on your own dreams, when you stop living."

The back of her eyes burned.

"I want you to be happy, Jamie. I don't want you stuck with a man who passes out when he gets stressed. And I don't want to get left because you can't take it."

"Good grief, Sean! We barely know each other. How dare you accuse me of not living. How dare you impugn me by saying I'd leave you—that is, if this relationship even goes that far."

"I won't have you giving up dreams for me."

"And what about your dreams, Sean?"

The lamppost light danced across his jaw muscle, which popped angrily.

"You don't even know what your dreams are, do you? What kind of person doesn't have dreams?"

He sliced a glare in her direction.

"I'll tell you what kind of man doesn't have dreams. . ." Jamie swallowed, chiding herself for letting her anger over his oh-too-accurate words vault to the surface. "A man too afraid to dream." *Stop*. Stop pushing him! "What are you afraid of, Sean?"

Steel replaced the rugged look of Sean's face. "A woman who would berate a man for what he is." Sean pivoted and strode into the night.

⬭

It felt like an ambush along the Iraqi border all over again. Except this time, he wasn't peppered with bullets, but words.

Piercing, taunting words. The fight he'd had with Jamie last week haunted him. Reeked of the same arguments his parents had over and over. Eerily similar to the last fight his mom and dad ever had.

No, he wasn't going there. Since she'd entered his life, he'd battled nothing but heartache and bad memories. No more. He wasn't going to live like that, no matter how much good she stirred up in him. No matter how much she made him want to be a better man. Setting himself up for failure wasn't his idea of a good marriage.

Sean froze. *Marriage?* Who was talking marriage?

Life. He meant life.

Hands on the grips of the rebuilt Harley, he aimed it toward Harry's garage. Inside, he flicked the kickstand and cut the engine. Straddling it, he grinned as Harry jogged from the back. "What do you think?"

Removing his Yankee ball cap, Harry smiled. "That's amazing—beautiful! Gary Meade is going to be ecstatic."

"Good, just make sure he pays up the rest." Sean handed over the keys. "I need the money. Ready to find my own place and get back on my feet."

Harry replaced his cap. "Don't worry. Meade's good for it. I'll call you as soon as he comes in, which I can just about guarantee will be first thing—he's heading up some committee with the parade, so I reckon he's down there right now."

Sean nodded. "Sounds good. Catch you later, Harry." He strode out and into the brisk November morning. With the parade in a couple of days, a lot of prep went into it. Armed with more letters, he fought the urge to return to the bridge to read them. No sense risking seeing her. They were over, as far as he was concerned. He didn't need someone pushing him and shoving things in his face.

Okay, so she hadn't been mean. Not the way his mom

had, but it was close. Too close. He couldn't sort out what was different, but he didn't want to go there either.

Sitting at an outdoor coffee shop, armed with a hot latte, Sean tugged the letters from his pocket. Though there were only twenty or so letters, it'd taken time to work through them, especially those from his grandfather that tore into the painful past of his father's suicide. One left, then he'd be on to the older letters, the yellowed ones that bore 1940-era dates and even older.

Sean opened the envelope. Short and sweet, his grandfather had written:

Sean, I found this about a year ago. I think it's time for you to read it. Affectionately, Grandpa.

Unfolding the other pages, Sean stilled at the penmanship. He frowned. This wasn't the handwriting of Henry Wolfe. His gaze skipped to the signature. *Your son, Patrick.*

Heart pounding like a .50 caliber gun, Sean realized his own father had penned this one:

Dear Dad,

Got your letter dated 19 April. Thanks for writing. It's nice to hear something from home. Glad to know Marcia and the kids are doing well. Wish I could have seen little William "Sean" Henry born. That just tears at me to have missed the birth of my own son. Thanks for tending to Marcia's and the kids' needs. I know you and Marcia haven't been on best terms, so I really appreciate you stepping in to help while I'm away.

It's hotter than you-know-what here, so everything and everyone stinks. In fact, this whole war stinks, but we are soldiers. It's what we do. You know that, don't you, having sneaked off to war at 16 with forged papers.

We're heading into a hot spot, so I need to make this quick. I know I've disappointed you in a lot of ways. Back home, high on myself, I couldn't see it. But here, a man starts to realize how valuable life is and how much people really mean.

I'm sorry, Pop. I know I made a mess of things. Anyway, if I don't make it home, that coin you tried to give me at the station...did you give it to Alan like I said you should? You always had a soft spot for him, and I think if anyone could protect the Wolfe legacy, it'd be him. Maybe...maybe someday it could find its way back to one of my sons, but I'd be glad to know it was in the hands of a good friend.

A LOVE
MEANT TO BE

by Dineen Miller

Dedication

For Dad,
for your courage in faith and in life

*[Love] always protects, always trusts,
always hopes, always perseveres.*
1 CORINTHIANS 13:7 NIV

Chapter 1

New York City, 1973

From the street, the Wolfe brownstone stood in its usual imposing regality, the domain of Henry Wolfe. The tall glass doors reflected the regal homes on the opposite side of the street, topped with a glimmer of the distant skyscrapers in downtown Manhattan. At the top of the steps, large ceramic urns poured out a green profusion on both sides of the double doors.

Alan James checked the pocket of his new sports coat again to make sure the ring box still lay snug and secure. Grit on the stairs crunched under his shoes. He paused at the door, brushed the hair off his forehead, then adjusted his shoulders. An invitation to a Wolfe party was definitely a step up the social chain, even if he was only there to deliver a ring.

He pressed the doorbell and took a deep breath, rehearsing in his mind again how he would explain things to Henry. Shadows of inner movement broke the reflective sheen of the windows. The knob turned and one door swung open.

"Well, hello there." The lilt of Marcia Wolfe's voice dragged in drunken flirtation. "What brings you my way?" She stood with one hand on her hip. Her low-slung and too-tight blouse bled wild colors onto snug, dark blue bell-bottom jeans.

"Here to see Patrick and his father, Mrs. Wolfe." Alan touched the ring box through his pocket again.

"Oh yes, Patrick said you were coming." She touched her finger to his chest just above his shirt button. Her nail poked into his skin. "To this day you still won't call me Marcia. Why is that, Alan?" She drawled out his name as if to make a point.

"Just being polite, ma'am."

Her eyes scoured over him much like the animal matching her last name. If Patrick's idea that a glitzy ring would bring his wife back to the "sweet little thing she used to be" worked, then Alan would buy more jewels for his antique store and sell them as magic talismans. He felt a twinge of sympathy for his best friend, who hadn't embraced the "free love" attitude that had sneaked its way into the seventies. Unlike his wife.

She snatched her finger back with a huff. "Right this way."

Alan followed her past the entryway into an expansive living room with wide glass doors leading to the first-floor patio. A minibar the size of his VW Bug nestled in one corner of the room. People milled about, cups and food plates in hand. He squelched his sudden discomfort and weaved his way through the crowd to where Henry stood with his son, Patrick.

He shook Henry's hand. "Sir."

"Welcome to the party, son." Henry's broad grin didn't distract Alan from noticing the wince that flicked across Patrick's face. They'd been friends for years, but the past still stung.

Alan patted his pocket and looked to Patrick. Better to deflect the moment and get to business. "I think you'll like what I found."

Patrick's brows perked up and the corners of his mouth twitched in a slight grin. "Let's take a look." He scanned the room. "Marcia must be in the kitchen. We're cool."

The velvet stubble pressed into Alan's thumbs as he opened the box. A large square diamond set against a frame of white gold and diamond chips sat in red velvet. He handed the box to Patrick.

Small bursts of reflected light glimmered across the icy surface of the diamond. "Marcia will love this. It's exactly her style. Loud and flashy."

Clearing his throat, Henry patted Alan on the shoulder. "Well done, Alan. Patrick's been searching for the right ring to replace the one he gave her when he proposed."

Patrick continued to stare into the box, a blank expression on his face as if he were past feeling anything real except weariness. "Maybe this will keep her happy until I get back."

"When do you ship out?" Alan would soon follow his friend into battle.

"Back to the jungle in two weeks." Eyes dark with nightmares and hidden horrors reflected what Alan feared would be his own demise. Patrick never talked about what happened while he was there, but his troubled stare spoke of images too real to be imagined.

Patrick smiled and snapped the box shut. "Excuse me. I need to find Marcia."

Alan nodded then stepped back to let his friend pass. A moment of silence rested between Alan and Henry Wolfe. "I hope she likes it."

Henry blew out a breathy sigh. "We'll find out one way or another. Marcia can be quite. . .vocal."

To prove his point, a squeal broke through the soft classical music serving as background ambiance. Marcia dashed into the room, hand held out high and proud to a woman standing on the opposite side of the minibar.

Alan's gaze slid from Marcia's outstretched arm to the redhead now holding Marcia's ring-adorned hand. Red shiny bangs streamed out from under a wide white headband and swept across her forehead. The back of her short hairdo puffed delicately out in a classic Jacqueline Kennedy style. Creamy smooth skin surrounded the smokiest eyes he'd ever seen. The girl's beauty put the diamond to shame.

He felt a bump on his shoulder and glanced at Henry, who chuckled then nodded toward the scene. "See what I mean?"

Those smoky eyes stared right at him now. Alan forced a swallow down the brittle dryness of his throat. "Yes, sir. I believe I do."

Marcia had dared her, and Gail Gibson never turned down a dare. Her one obvious flaw and probably why her sister had goaded her to check out Mr. Wolfe's apprentice. But the way he returned her gaze gave her mind pause and her heart a jolt. Maybe she was the first redhead he'd ever seen. Or maybe the guy needed to learn it wasn't polite to stare.

Heat rushed to her cheeks, no doubt making her look like a tomato. The bane of her existence. Here she was chastising the poor fellow for staring and she was doing the very same thing. Gail reverted her gaze back to the safety of her sister's ring. "It is gorgeous, Marcia. I hope you told Patrick you love it."

Her sister shrugged. "I told him it was nice."

"Nice? Don't you think he deserves more than that?"

Marcia's smile turned into a glare. "He's just trying to appease me because he knows I'm still angry about him signing up for another tour. I'm tired, Gail. I'm tired of raising our kids by myself while the man traipses around jungles, getting drunk with his buddies."

Gail inhaled deeply through her nose. Her sister's moods changed as rapidly as the fashions did these days. She couldn't keep up anymore. Thankfully she'd be back home at the end of the summer and back to her beloved classes. Books made better companions.

"You should meet him, you know?"

Gail struggled to follow her sister's sudden shift in conversation. "Who?"

Marcia nodded toward the man she'd dared Gail to look at. "Alan James. He's one of Patrick's friends and now a goony for Henry. You two might just hit it off."

"In case you've forgotten, I have a boyfriend."

"Oh yeah, Mr. Wall Street. Better grab him before he finds some cutie ready to play housewife for him."

She glared at her sister. "Troy Pendergast is a good man. He would never do such a thing."

"I bet he doesn't make your heart race like Alan James."

"Marcia, stop it. I will not let you goad me into a fight. I'm very happy with my life, just the way it is."

Marcia stared at her, almost as if she didn't know what to say. But her sister always knew what to say. Just not always the right thing. "A safe boyfriend and stodgy books. Yeah, that sounds downright chipper to me."

Gail thought about Troy. He *was* kind of safe, but she liked that about him. She knew what to expect from him and knew what he expected from her. They were a good fit. She didn't need to be swept off her feet. She smiled. Now was the right time to tell her sister her news. "Troy asked me to marry him before I left."

Marcia grabbed her left hand. "So where's the ring?"

Gail pulled her hand back. Not quite the elation she'd hoped for. "He said he'll have it by the time I get back. That's why he's working for his dad this summer."

"Then there's still time."

"Time for what?"

Marcia positioned her body behind Gail's and propelled her forward. "To have one more fling before you settle for Mr. Safe. And Alan James is as good as any fling I've seen lately."

∞

"Listen, Alan. . . I wanted to talk to you about something." Henry Wolfe touched his fist to his mouth. He pulled Alan back away from the crowd. "I know you activated your draft."

"Yes, sir. I'd planned to tell you tonight—"

"It's quite all right. I dropped by the shop yesterday, and your sister, Tara, mentioned it. I think she assumed I already knew." Henry slipped his hand into his pocket. "Are you sure you're ready for Vietnam, son?"

He'd asked himself that question almost every day since activating his draft notice. Alan glanced across the room to where Patrick stood off to the side, staring at his wife yet not really seeing her. His vacant expression spoke of a man lost in the world of his tormented thoughts and memories. "Don't really have a choice, sir. I finished my college degree, and my sister is eighteen now. It's time."

Henry pursed his lips and nodded. "Tara said she'll be running the antique shop while you're gone."

Everything he'd planned to say fled under Henry's questioning. "Yes, and I think she'll do a great job. I've been training her the last year, and—"

"Good. I agree."

Alan studied his mentor. Not the reaction he'd expected.

Henry chuckled. "Alan, you and I have worked closely this last year to build your antique business and make it something you'll be able to pass down to your own children. If I'd had any doubts of your ability, trust me, we never would have even started on this venture. Goodness knows I've had enough experience with Patrick. . . . Well, let's just say I know determination when I see it."

Alan glanced across the room, grateful to see Patrick wasn't in hearing distance. "Thank you, sir. I was worried you might not approve."

"I do, and I admire your commitment to your country. Just do me a favor and come back in better shape than. . ." Sadness hung on the man's face making him look ten years older. "I have something I want to show you." He withdrew his hand from his pocket and held out a round gold coin in his open palm.

Judging by the markings, Alan guessed the piece dated back to the Civil War, at least. He took it from Henry's hand and examined the detail. The engraving "Love never fails. W.W. Central Park" circled the back.

"It's been passed down through the family since my great-grandfather, William Wolfe, who fought in the Civil War. It's supposed to bring the bearer good luck in war and love." He smiled and looked at the coin fondly. "It served my sister well. . . . Anyway, I'd like to give it to Patrick. . . ." He shifted his gaze toward his son. Shook his head. "Do me a favor before you ship out and see what you can find out about its manufacturer. I'd like to add that to my records. Could use a little cleaning, too, I believe."

Alan flipped the coin on his palm. "It's a beautiful piece, sir. Haven't seen anything like it. I'm sure Patrick will appreciate it."

"I showed it to Patrick, but he didn't seem that interested in the luck part. Patrick and Marcia. . .well. . ."

Alan glanced up just in time to see Marcia heading their way with the redhead in tow. Patrick slogged along behind the two. But the redhead. . . Alan swallowed again and nearly choked. She kept glancing at him with those smoky eyes, appearing shy and unsettled, which only added to her mystery.

Henry's hand on his shoulder brought Alan back from captivity. "What I mean to say is be careful out there. I've come to think of you like a son, Alan."

Alan nodded then shifted his gaze to search for the redhead. He didn't have to look far though. She stood a mere two feet away, smiling at him.

Patrick stared at the coin in Alan's hand. Pain filled his eyes when he glanced at his father just before he turned and stalked away. Alan closed his hand over the coin. Why hadn't he noticed Patrick standing there sooner? The redhead had distracted him before he could play interference between his friend and his father.

He should go after Patrick, but those eyes had caught him again in living color. "Hazel. . .and green."

Had he said that out loud?

Chapter 2

He'd noticed her eyes. For once she got noticed for something other than her hair. Gail didn't hold back her smile this time, and Alan didn't disappoint her with his. She even liked the way it tweaked back the sides of his goatee.

Marcia pushed herself next to Gail, which effectively made her the center of attention. As usual. Alan's smile slipped into concern at something behind her. Gail looked over her shoulder to see Patrick weaving his way through the mingling guests.

Alan started after him, but Marcia tugged him back. "You're not splitting yet, I hope. Not before I introduce you to my sister. Alan, meet Gail Gibson, a wannabe homemaker who's a junior at Brown."

"Marcia!" Even past their teen years, her sister seemed to take sick pleasure in embarrassing her.

"Well, it's true, isn't it?" She returned her attention to Alan. "She's staying with us for the summer."

Gail tried to ignore the heavy implication in Marcia's voice. Had she not just told her sister she was engaged? "I'm sorry, Alan. My sister doesn't seem to know how to behave today." She held out her hand to shake his. "I'm Gail. Gail Gibson. It's a pleasure to meet you."

"Pleasure to meet you. . .Gail." Alan clasped his hand into hers but didn't shake it. Nor did he seem to want to let go.

Neither did she. How was that possible? He held her hand as if he knew her. . .and the warmth of his made her feel. . .safe. But not safe like Troy. More like protected. . .cherished. Was she losing her ever-loving mind?

Marcia clapped her hands together. "I have a fabulous idea. You two should spend the summer together."

Gail yanked her hand back. "What? Marcia, that's inappropriate."

Her sister rolled her eyes. "I mean, you'll be here the entire summer, and I'm somewhat limited with the kids. Alan could be your chaperone. You know, show you around the city, take you to some shows. He could even take you to his antique shop."

Alan kept looking over her shoulder as if searching for someone. Or an escape route. "I'd be happy to. Could you ladies excuse me a moment?"

"Of course." Gail dropped her eyes. Leave it to her sister to ruin the moment. Not that she wanted a moment. She forced an image of Troy into her mind as she waited until Alan passed out of earshot and Mr. Wolfe found better company in a conversation a few feet away, then glared at Marcia. "Don't ever do that to me again."

"What?" Marcia gave her a coy smile. "I did nothing you wouldn't have done if you weren't so stodgy."

"You know I hate that word."

"Of course I do." Marcia waltzed off like a cat that just devoured its catch.

Gail would have faded into the striped wallpaper if she could and become the true definition of a wallflower, but her petals felt wilted and pathetic. Why hadn't she just stayed in Rhode Island with her parents for the summer? She would have at least had her friends there. But she'd agreed to stay with her sister to help with the kids. Patrick and Marcia's marital problems had far outreached anything Gail could offer, but at least she could be an aunt to her nieces and nephew and help them adjust when Patrick shipped out again.

Her anger at her sister shifted to sympathy. Would she handle things any differently if she were in Marcia's worn-out shoes? Gail would like to think so, but in reality she doubted she could stand up under the constant fear of losing someone she loved in a war.

Again, another reason to marry Troy. His health issues had made him ineligible for the military. And there lay another reason to be his wife. He needed someone to help him stay healthy and strong. He *needed her*.

Timing was never Alan's strong suit, but his friend needed him more than he needed to get to know a pretty girl. He scoped the next room and caught a glimpse of Patrick sitting on a wrought-iron bench by the fountain. . .alone.

Leaving regret behind, Alan walked through the open door and closed the distance to where his friend sat like a lost child.

"Patrick, I'm really sorry."

Eyes squinting against the sun, Patrick smiled up at him. "Man, don't worry about it. I totally get it. You think I don't know how my father feels about his messed-up son."

Alan took a seat on the lounge chair next him. "He just doesn't understand."

"He never has understood me. Just like I don't get him."

"Maybe if you tried talking to him."

"No, it will never change. The man is what he is. I've come to accept that."

But Alan knew better. He saw the pained expressions on his friend's face when he heard his father's comment. Alan had even braved an attempt to talk to Henry about it once. Both men were as stubborn as they came.

"Your father only asked me to research the coin. He wants you to have it but doesn't know how to tell you how he feels."

"I already know how he feels. Especially since I told him..."

"Told him what?"

"I don't want to take over the business."

"Why decide that now? You might change your mind when you get back."

Patrick stared at him, a war blazing behind his eyes that Alan could only stand and watch from a distance. "I don't know if I'm coming back, Alan." He lowered his gaze to the gurgling water. "Don't even know if I want to."

Alan inhaled to recapture the breath his friend's words knocked out of him. "Why? Don't you want to be with Marcia and the kids?"

His friend's short laugh dripped with sarcasm. "I don't think Marcia cares where I am. At least over there I know where I stand. I know what needs to be done, and I do it. And I'm good at it. Here...with Marcia and my father...I'm not..." Patrick cleared his throat and stood. "You better get back in there before you miss a chance with Gail. She's one of the good ones, you know what I mean?"

Alan rose and nodded. Patrick patted him on the back then walked inside. Alan would let his friend be for now. But he'd pray for Patrick's safe return and for a future that included his family's respect. A man could do just about anything if he knew someone stood behind him, believed in him.

He'd only come to understand this truth when Henry Wolfe saw something in Alan worth cultivating and mentoring. Henry was the closest thing to a father in Alan's life. He just wished the man had seen the same potential in Patrick, who had become like a brother to Alan over the years. Even his sister had commented about Patrick being like a brother to both of them. And they needed all the family they could get.

Alan watched how the water glistened and rippled in the fading light of day. The coin beckoned for another glance, and Alan obliged. How many hands that had possessed the coin had seen battle? His hunger for history wanted to know more. Where had the coin been, and who had carried it through the years in hopes of love and luck, as Henry had stated?

"I'd say a penny for your thoughts, but that doesn't look like a penny."

He spun to his left and stopped, but his heart kept going. Gail smiled at him, eyes brimming with promise. . .and something else.

With a nervous laugh, Alan thumbed the coin on his palm. "No, definitely not a penny."

She smiled, started to speak, then hesitated. "Alan, I'd like to apologize for my sister's pushiness."

He measured his words, trying to choose a diplomatic response. Marcia's behavior was her own. "No need. And I understand."

"You do?"

"Yes, I've known Patrick for a long time."

Gail nodded but didn't say anything, though she still seemed to have something on her mind.

Could that something be. . . ? "I'd be happy to, you know."

She frowned slightly, which drew her lips into a small bow. "Happy to what?"

"Show you the city. And my shop."

"Oh, please don't let my sister's suggestion push you into anything."

"I'm not. As I said, I'd be happy to. There's a lot to see in Manhattan. If you're here for the whole summer, you might as well take in some of it in. Ever been to the Statue of Liberty?"

"No, actually. My family had planned to when I was younger, but our plans wound up getting canceled."

"Well see, there's one landmark you absolutely have to see." He tossed the coin in the air, pocketed it, and smiled.

"All right then, I guess that could work." She tucked a lock of hair behind her ear.

"Then I'll pick you up tomorrow morning at ten."

"Thank you, but I should tell you—"

"Gail!" Marcia stood by the glass door, waving Gail inside. "Jennifer's crying again."

"Be there in just a second." Gail glanced from her sister back to Alan. "Sorry. My niece seems to think I'm the only one who knows how to play Barbies correctly."

Alan smiled. "I understand. See you in the morning." He paused a moment then followed Gail's direction. Marcia lingered in the doorway.

When he tried to pass, she blocked him. "Planning something with my sister?"

"Just taking your suggestion to show her around the city."

Again, she scoured him like a wolf sizing up its next meal. "Interesting. . .well, I'm sure you two will have a great time. Maybe you can save her from that dreadful fiancé of hers."

"Fiancé?"

"Yes, didn't she tell you?" She skulked off, glancing over her shoulder at him, giving obvious sway to her hips.

The day suddenly felt like a bust. Alan found Henry and Patrick and said his good-byes. Gail remained absent from view but not from Alan's mind. Better this way. He'd be in another country in a couple months, gone for a good two years. Though disappointed, Alan would be the gentleman, keep his word to Gail, and respect that she was engaged.

They would be friends. Just friends.

Chapter 3

Wind whipped around the bow of the ship. Ahead lay Liberty Island and its most famous female regaled in patina green. The sea air held the rumble of boats and the smell of diesel. Sunlight glinted off the rippling water like floating gems. Gail pulled out the scarf she'd thoughtfully stuffed into her purse and tied it over her hair.

Though cordial, Alan had remained distinctly quiet during the brief ride from the Wolfe estate to the city. Had he really only offered out of her sister's bullying? Gail hadn't missed the exchange yesterday between Marcia and Alan as she went up the stairs to check on her niece. When would she learn to not let her sister goad her into rash decisions? Maybe she should have turned Alan down.

Or better yet, face the question head-on: "Alan, why did you offer to show me around the city?"

He studied her a moment then laughed. "Now that's a question I hadn't expected."

Gail smiled, looked back to the water. "My sister isn't the only outspoken one in our family. I just implement more tact than she does. I do hope I didn't offend you though."

"No, I like directness." His jaw tightened then relaxed. "All right, I'll be direct, too. At first I'd hoped to get to know the pretty redhead with smoky eyes better. A lot better. But then your sister mentioned you had a fiancé."

"Oh, she did, eh?" She snapped her attention back to him.

Alan nodded, but his brown eyes remained steady and focused on her. Almost seemed to challenge her to deny the truth.

"I tried to tell you yesterday before Marcia interrupted. Then when I came back downstairs, you were gone. I guess I could have asked Patrick how to contact you and called. . . ." She'd actually thought about doing that very thing but didn't like telling him over the phone, where she wouldn't be able to gauge his reaction.

"But. . ."

She turned to face him and added some spunk to her tone. "But I could use a friend this summer. My sister isn't exactly friendly material."

"Yes, I noticed. She's one extreme to another."

Gail waited a moment to speak, fighting off the familiar embarrassment over her sister. She'd long bypassed offense when others spoke of her sister's behavior, though that alone saddened her. "I guess you've been around her enough."

"Enough."

She wanted to ask what he held back. Her sister seemed to have driven off many of Patrick's friends. Would Alan be next?

An awkward silence fizzed around them.

"I can be a friend."

His blurted words startled her. He held his head partly turned toward her, brow raised with a funny grin lifting one side of his mouth. Now he was just humoring her.

"Is that a willing offer or a duty to be filled, Mr. James?"

"Oh, definitely a willing offer, Miss Gibson. One I dearly hope you'll accept."

"Then, I do, Mr. James. . .Alan. Most gratefully."

"Good, then that's one question settled. Now it's my turn."

She leaned against the railing. "Shoot away."

"This won't be easy, mind you. I'm not in the habit of asking easy questions."

"I think I'm up to the task."

"Are you sure, because I wouldn't want to wear you out before we even get to see Lady Liberty."

"I promise to give it my best effort." She giggled.

"Okay, here goes. Now be honest."

She nodded.

"Do you like hot dogs?"

∞

The mix of relish with mustard, ketchup, and onions sent his mouth on a happy journey. And judging by Gail's sigh as she chewed, she'd joined the ride. Their explorations up and then back down the Statue of Liberty had liberated both their appetites.

He wiped his mouth. "I told you it would be worth the wait. Casey's dogs are the best."

Gail swept a drip of ketchup from her hot dog bun and popped it into her mouth. "Okay, you win. Definitely better than anything we have in Rhode Island."

"That's because we're in the city. Central Park vendors make fast food an art." He bit into his hot dog again.

"You have some mustard on your mustache." She reached out with her napkin and wiped the corner of his mouth.

Though her eyes were focused on her task, Alan still had a clear view of the dark brown band surrounding the hazel color of her eyes. The green shirt she wore brought out more of the green flecks. A waft of her rosy perfume filled his nose. He wanted to touch her hair and see if it felt as silky as it looked. He'd never been more thankful to have a messy hot dog in his hands.

Not good, not good. He shifted on the park bench to disguise his attempt to put distance between them. "Thanks."

She blinked and drew her hand back. "Happy to help." Gail took a bite of her hot dog.

"You like to help a lot, don't you?"

Still chewing, she nodded then swallowed. "Am I that obvious?"

"Just shows through. It's nice."

Her smile hit full beam, bringing a delightful tilt to her eyes. Those eyes. . .

"Really?"

"Yeah, hasn't anyone ever told you that before?"

She sighed. "You would think that with all the money many of our friends and acquaintances have, that they'd be more interested in helping those less fortunate."

"But they're not." He stated his words as fact but lifted his brow in question.

"No, not really."

He couldn't let the wistful expression on her face pass. "What is it you want to do, Gail?"

She shot a quick glance at him, as if waking from a dream. Her passion was evident as she leaned toward him and spoke with her hands. "I want to teach English in underprivileged areas. Literature has so much to teach and show us about perseverance and serves as a powerful witness to what we, as human beings, can overcome and accomplish in our lives." The pretty girl who was quick to laugh at his jokes had transformed into an animated teacher.

"And even more so with faith." He said the words before he even thought them.

"Faith? I guess so, but that's not what these kids need to overcome their difficult circumstances."

"I disagree. It's what they need most." He knew firsthand. Knew what had brought him and his sister, Tara, through those first dark days after losing their parents.

"Why does it have to come back to religion?"

"I'm not talking about religion here. I'm talking about leaning on a belief in God with the understanding that He loves us and cares what happens to us. That's what faith is to me anyway."

At Gail's silence, he realized he'd spoken with the same fervency she had.

He glanced down at what remained of his hot dog, the angry swirl of red and yellow on the wreckage of his bun. "Seven years ago, my parents were killed in a plane crash. I was eighteen. My parents had left me in charge of my sister. Tara was only eleven at the time. Faith is what got us through it all. And each other."

She reached out and squeezed his wrist, her eyes wide and vulnerable. "I'm so sorry, Alan. I had no idea."

He covered her hand with his own. "We're okay now. At first it was hard to accept. I kept thinking there had to be some mistake and that they'd extended their trip to celebrate their anniversary." He laughed softly. "Tara was the one who finally made me embrace the truth with her prayers."

"I can't even imagine. Who took care of you?"

"I did. We don't have any family. Thankfully I was old enough to take care of Tara, and I landed a job at Mr. Wolfe's firm."

"Is that how you've managed to avoid being drafted?"

"No, I was. Just got a deferment because of Tara. She's eighteen now, and I've finished my business degree. I ship out at the end of the summer."

"Oh." Gail leaned back against the bench, crumpling the remainder of her hot dog into the wrapper.

Why did she suddenly seem upset? "Was it something I said?"

She gave a nervous laugh then smiled—but not the easy one that crinkled the bridge of her nose. "No, not at all. It's just that Marcia didn't mention that. . .that you were going to. . .Vietnam."

Alan took a deep breath, prepared to hear the barrage against the United States' involvement there. "I didn't think it would be an issue for you."

By her expression, Alan guessed she was either offended or angry. Either way, he suspected their time together had come to an end.

A vivid picture of Marcia's husband flashed into her mind. She'd seen the changes in Patrick, heard his screams just the other night—all the way down the hall—though she'd told her sister she hadn't. The idea of Alan going through that pained her. . .though she barely knew him.

She didn't have a clue why Alan rose so abruptly and now stood by the garbage can, head down. He hadn't even finished his own hot dog. Had talking about his parents' deaths and then the war hit too close to home? And what did he mean by "*be an issue for her*"?

Gail gave him a moment then ambled to where he stood. "Alan, are you okay?"

He lifted his chin. "Sure. We should probably get going. I'd imagine you probably have more important things to do."

What in the world had gotten into him? She threw her leftover lunch and soda bottle into the receptacle with a loud thud. "I've no idea what you're talking about, and I'm not sure I want to know." She spun away and headed back toward the direction they'd come.

Alan's steps rushed behind her. "You clearly have an issue with the war, despite the fact that good men are there trying to help. I thought for sure you would understand that."

She couldn't hold back her gasp. "I said no such thing!"

"It's what you didn't say, Gail."

"Didn't say?" She stopped and faced him. "How would you like me to say that I hope the war doesn't change you like it has Patrick? Surely you've seen how he's changed. How he hurts. I wish I could do more to help him, but I can't."

She stormed off again. No way would she let him see her cry. She'd find her own way home if she had to.

"Gail, wait!"

A sudden tug on her elbow brought her to a halt and turned her toward him. She kept her head down. "Just take me home, please."

He lifted her chin. "I'm sorry. I misunderstood. I thought you were opposed to the war."

She reached up and batted away a stray tear. "No, I just hate the idea of you being in such danger. I know how much it affected Marcia. . .not knowing if Patrick was okay or even coming home."

Why was she so upset? And why did she feel so drawn to Alan? Had to be that he'd opened up to her and shared his story. Marcia always did accuse her of having too big a heart for those who had suffered loss.

"That I completely understand. The not knowing if someone you love will come home."

She wanted to melt into his arms. The way he looked at her with total understanding based so clearly in his own loss. The man had a heart to match hers.

No, she couldn't let herself think like that. Feel like that. She had Troy, and he wasn't going to war or someplace dangerous. And he wanted to marry her. She had a secure future with him.

Alan tilted his head, giving her that goofy grin of his. "Forgive me?"

She nodded.

"Still friends, Miss Gibson?"

His words made her laugh. "Yes, Mr. James. Still friends."

Chapter 4

They'd spent nearly every evening together over the last several weeks. Alan had taken Gail to see *The King and I* on Broadway, knowing the story alone would appeal to her tender heart. He hadn't expected her tears at the end, which seemed to embarrass her but only endeared her more to him. And tonight, she was coming by his shop. Alan had already planned which of his favorite pieces he would show her.

He stood in front of the cash register going through the receipts.

"You're whistling, little brother."

He smiled and joined in the game they'd played since childhood. "Not little. . .big. And I'm not whistling, little sister. Just enjoying the day."

She leaned against him. "Do I get to meet her?"

"Who?"

"Your girlfriend."

He kissed the top of her head. With auburn hair like their mother's, Tara looked more like her by the day. "Like I said, she's just a friend."

"Then do I get to meet your *friend*?"

"Of course. I'd like Gail to meet you." He glanced at his watch and closed the register. "She should be here soon."

"I don't know. Wanting her to meet your family. . .sounds serious to me." She winked at him then headed to the back room on whatever errand she'd thought of to keep the last word. Another game left over from their parents. They'd clung to the little things—the games and traditions—to keep their parents' memories alive.

But Tara had hit closer to the truth than he wanted to admit. His feelings for Gail had grown quickly. He would have told anyone three weeks ago that he didn't believe whirlwind romances were based in real love, but now. . .now he could almost believe it was possible to fall in love with someone in mere moments. If it was the right someone. . .

Perhaps it was good that Gail was engaged. She didn't need to be worrying about him when he left. He just hoped she'd be happy with the guy. Hoped the guy appreciated her.

The bell jingled on the door. Gail walked in, wearing the same white headband she'd worn the day he met her. The rest of her outfit wowed him, from the miniskirt to the small square purse, which matched her white leather boots.

"Hi there."

Pure pleasure at seeing her in his shop pushed aside any reticence he still held. "Hello. No problems getting here, I hope."

She reached the counter and set her purse down. "No, Patrick dropped me at the station and the train ride was. . . entertaining."

"Entertaining?"

She lifted her brows. "Quite. One of the passengers played his guitar the whole way in."

"Played well then?"

"That depends on whether you like to hear music played with just fingers, or fingers *and* toes."

"Toes?"

"And that was the good part."

Tara emerged from the back room. "Toes?" She clasped her hands in front of her and stood by Alan. She only did that when she felt nervous.

Alan put his arm around his sister and tucked her to his side. "Gail, this is my sister, Tara."

Gail smiled at her. "Hi, Tara. By your brother's description of you, I was expecting to see a girl, not a beautiful young woman. Shame on you, Alan."

He glanced from Gail to his sister's wide smile. Tara wasn't easy to win over, yet Gail had done so in less than a minute. His admiration for her jumped a few notches. "Only because I'm not in a hurry to see her grow up."

Tara elbowed him in the side. "Spoken like a true big brother."

"And how lucky you are to have such a great big brother." Gail glanced at him shyly.

"Not lucky, blessed."

"Oh, I see." Gail kept her smile in place, but Alan didn't miss the surprise in her eyes.

"Tara, you can head upstairs if you want. I'll finish closing up and show Gail some of our better pieces."

Gail shifted her gaze from Tara to Alan. "Upstairs?"

Tara headed for a door behind the counter. "Yeah, that's where we live, in the apartment above." She leaned in front of her brother. "Don't be too long. The roast will come out of the oven in half an hour."

"Roast? I'm taking Gail out."

His sister laughed at him. "Hot dogs are not what I call dinner out."

"No, not hot dogs. Someplace else." He tossed a wad of paper at her.

Tara paused with her hand on the doorknob. Her eyes pleaded with him. "I made plenty."

"I would love to stay, that is, if you don't mind, Alan. I don't get to eat a roast very often. I'd consider it a treat, especially since I can't even boil an egg." Gail winked at Tara.

He felt his chest expand. Why did the perfect woman have to walk into his life just as he was about to ship out, and with a fiancé to boot? Although he had noticed her finger still remained bare.

"Then roast it is."

His sister bounced with her smile. "I'll let you know when it's ready."

Alan glanced over his shoulder as Tara disappeared through the door. The dwindling sound of her footsteps as she climbed the stairs and the rumble of traffic outside kept the store from total silence.

Gail moved closer to the counter. "I see your sister shares your faith."

He bobbed his head and shrugged. "Yes, she does. She's pretty straightforward about it."

"As are you." Gail smiled. Genuine and warm.

He held his arms out to his sides. "Hope you don't mind." He held his breath. Tara was his world. He could only make room for those who wouldn't upset the balance of their diminished family.

"You really didn't do your sister justice, you know."

And a few more notches added to the admiration scale. He wished he could hold her, tell her how much her words meant to him. "Tara's a dynamo in the kitchen. She says she likes taking care of me."

"I bet she's looking forward to getting married then."

"Just because she likes to cook?"

"And take care of you. I know I would—did at her age. Still do."

He didn't miss her stutter and quick cover-up. "What, take care of me?" He loved the flustered look on her face, bordering on mortification. Along with the blush on her cheeks.

"No! I mean as long as I can remember I've wanted to get married and have a family to take care of. I guess that makes me pretty old-fashioned in this day and age."

"No, just more intriguing."

"Marcia says I'm stodgy." She kept darting her gaze away from him.

"I dearly hope you don't listen to her. Based on her judgment—" He may disapprove of Marcia's behavior, but he was wrong to judge, let alone speak ill of Gail's sister.

"I try not to." Her unspoken "but" hung in the air.

Alan wouldn't ask this time though. "How about I show you around?"

Her usual perkiness returned. "I'd love it."

He gave her the full tour of the store, starting with the fine crystal, which seemed to enchant her the most. Especially the salt dishes, which looked like miniature bowls.

"They look like something my niece would love to use with her Barbie dolls."

Alan laughed, soaking in the delight in her expression. "Now that's one idea I don't think I ever would have thought of."

He finished the tour at an old mirror dating from the turn of the century. "This is the piece responsible for my love of antiques. It belonged to my grandmother, who passed it down to my mother."

Gail ran her fingers over the grooves and curves of the wood. "It's beautiful. Almost reminds me of some of the Art Deco designs of the twenties."

"I'm impressed. You're not too far off."

The door behind the counter swung open.

"Dinner is served." Tara glanced between them, waiting expectantly by the counter.

Gail joined Tara then turned around as if waiting for him. Both women smiled at him, standing side by side.

"Let me take a picture." Alan raised the Polaroid he used to record his inventory, capturing them both in the viewfinder. "Keep smiling."

He pressed the button. The camera whirred and spit out the undeveloped picture. Tara turned around then headed up the stairs.

Gail remained, still smiling but different somehow. "You've done a great job raising her, Alan."

He didn't know what to say to the admiration he saw in her eyes. She left him speechless, so he simply returned her smile. The moment locked them together in a mutual communication without words. Gail seemed reluctant to break their silent conversation, but she turned and headed up the stairs.

Alan waved the picture back and forth to dry the coating. The image of his sister with Gail appeared slowly, faded at first, then more vibrant. He hadn't noticed that Gail had put her arm around Tara's waist and that Tara had leaned her head toward Gail.

Just like she used to do with their mother.

"You're right, Tara's a wonderful cook." Gail gazed into the distance, soaking in the blush of sunset resting on the treetops of Central Park. An older couple passed by with two leashed corgis trotting in front of them. Another couple—younger and oblivious to all but each other—walked slowly ahead. Snippets of their laughter drifted back to where she and Alan meandered their own path in the failing daylight.

Alan smiled but kept his face forward. "She really likes you."

"I really like her. She's so charming."

He shook his head. "No, you don't understand. Tara doesn't warm up to people easily. Took her months to finally admit she liked Patrick. Marcia never stood a chance."

Gail couldn't help it. She giggled at first but then flat-out laughed so hard her stomach hurt. Finally, she had one on her sister. She collapsed on a bench, hands on her stomach. "If only I could share the mental picture that creates."

"I had no idea I was so funny." He clasped her hand in his and tugged her back to the path, but he didn't let go.

Gail dabbed her eyes as a way to sneak a peek at their intertwined hands. She should let go but had no desire to. The warmth of his hand made her feel safe. . .protected. Alan was a good man. She mourned again that he'd soon be exposed to the ravages of war. She hadn't really put much stock in praying since she was a little girl, but maybe, just maybe, God would hear her prayers for Alan.

They reached a bridge with ornate railings. A recent rain had turned the wood to a deep red. "Oh, I love this bridge. My father took me on it when I was a little girl."

"Bow Bridge. Did you come in the fall?"

"No, it was winter. Snow covered most of the ground, and the trees were bare. It was gorgeous."

"You should come back in the fall then. The trees turn yellow and red." They'd reached the center and stopped, overlooking the lake. Alan brushed his fingers over her bangs. "And a burnt orange that matches your hair."

Heat raced up her cheeks, most likely making her look like a tomato again. But she couldn't look away.

His warm brown eyes held her, captured her attention and her heart. "I love it when you blush like that."

"You do?" No one had ever told her that.

His hand cupped her chin. He drew her in gently with his hand and with his gaze, full of love.

Love? Was it possible Alan was falling in love with her? Was she falling in love with him? If she let him kiss her, would she know for sure? What about Troy?

She pulled back.

"Gail, I'm sorry. I shouldn't have done that."

Hand held up, she said what she thought she should but not what she wanted to. "No, it's okay. It's late and the setting is so romantic. We just got carried away." Oh, how she wanted to go back. She wanted his kiss, wanted to know what it would feel like to share that with him.

Marcia would have. Why couldn't she be just a little like her sister right now?

"I should get going. I told my niece I'd be there to tuck her in tonight."

"I'll drive you home."

When they reached the shop, Alan guided her around to the back of the building. He rolled up a green metal door to reveal his car.

"I wondered where you parked your car in the city."

"It's a sweet deal. One of the few places that still has space for a car." Alan opened the door for her then shut it once she got in. But he didn't leave her side. Instead he leaned down, his head in the open window.

Gail couldn't stand to keep looking at him. She wanted to though. Wanted more than anything to answer the question in his eyes.

"I hope he knows how lucky he is, Gail."

She forced a smile. "Don't you mean blessed?"

He nodded his head, as if to say she won. "Indeed I most certainly did." He pushed away from the car, leaving the window empty like a gaping hole.

Much like the one that would stay in her heart once he shipped out.

Chapter 5

Alan paced in front of the bus station, waiting to say good-bye to Patrick. Tara sat on the bench nearby, peaceful as a statue. He envied her ability to be still. Compounding his stress for his friend was the aspect of seeing Gail again. He'd left messages twice, but she hadn't called him back.

He reflected on their last evening together, just as he had every day over the week since. Should he have kept his mouth shut about her fiancé? But that would have gone against his growing feelings for her. And if his parents' deaths taught him anything, it was that you didn't always get a second chance to tell someone you loved them.

Love? He rolled the word around in his brain like a rough stone, smoothing its edges to a soft shine. Did he love Gail? Could he fall in love in such a short time? His mother would have said yes, if it was the right girl. So maybe the question he needed to ask himself was whether or not Gail Gibson was the woman he was meant to love. . .to spend his life with. The one God had in mind for him.

How could he answer that question when she was engaged to another man? Plus he wasn't sure if they stood on common ground faithwise. Another piece of wisdom from his mother. . .

He turned around and directed his gaze down the walkway. Patrick walked confidently in his uniform with his duffel slung over one shoulder and his son in his other arm. Marcia swaggered next to him, her face sour and her arms crossed. Behind them came Gail, holding Jennifer's hand. The little girl clutched a Barbie doll in her other one. Henry secured the flank with their other daughter.

After planting a tender kiss on his son's forehead, he set the child down then strode to where Alan stood. He shook Alan's hand and patted him on the back. Alan did the same, but he didn't know what to say to his friend. Their connection had waned since Patrick's first return—he'd come back a different man than when he'd left.

"Be careful. Maybe our paths will cross when I get over there." Alan searched his friend's face for reassurance that Patrick would be okay, that he'd changed his mind and wanted to come back to his family more than anything.

"You never know." Patrick tilted his head down and gave Alan a pointed stare beneath his brows. "Watch your back, Alan. Remember that, and you'll come back okay."

"You got it." He stepped away, noticing his sister standing next to him. Patrick gave her a hug and whispered something into her ear. Tara nodded then moved to stand by Alan, leaning against him, her head tucked under his chin as she did when she was upset.

With his arm around Tara, Alan watched the rest of Patrick's family say good-bye. Marcia even managed to crack a smile, though her eyes were glittery with tears. The kids clung to their father the longest.

Alan used the moment to approach Henry. "Sir, I thought you might want this right now." He took the coin from his pocket, its surface now clean yet still bearing the tarnish, which enhanced the delicate molding of the gold. He handed him an envelope as well. "Here's the information you asked for."

Henry gave him a grin of thanks.

His motive and timing could be construed as manipulative, but Alan dearly hoped Henry would take his cue and give the coin to Patrick. This could very well be the last chance the man had to tell his son how he felt.

Alan sensed more than saw Gail standing behind him. He turned around. She glanced at him shyly, just as she had at the party, giving his entire nervous system a shock. No matter what the future held, her eyes would always hold him captive.

"I'm sorry I didn't call you back." She took a step closer.

"I'm sorry if I spoke out of line." He braved his own step closer.

"You did what you thought was right."

She understood him better than anyone he'd ever known or met. Including his own sister. The thought of walking away and never seeing her again killed him. He stayed silent. Words would only wreck the moment, and he wanted to stay in this place for as long as possible.

Gail pointed to something behind him. Alan turned around. Henry and Patrick stood off to the side, talking. Henry shook Patrick's hand then pulled him into a hug. Moisture glistened in the man's eyes.

When they separated, Patrick looked down at his hand. He clasped his father's hand, shaking his head.

The group of them stood in their staggered places, watching as Patrick waved then boarded the bus. No one moved as the metal beast released a gasp of air and began to roll its giant rubber wheels.

Henry was the first to walk away. As he passed Alan, he opened his hand. The coin rested in the lines of his aged palm. "I gave him the coin, but he gave it back."

Alan fell into step with him. "Sir, I'm sorry. . .but I'm glad you tried."

Henry stopped. "He did say to hold on to it for him. Maybe

that means we'll get to talk more when he gets back. Alan, you know Patrick better than I do. Is that what he means?"

The man was grasping for hope, and Alan had no desire to cut the thread he clung to. No, he'd rather cling to that same strand and believe Patrick wanted to start fresh with his family when he returned. "Yes, sir, I believe so."

His mentor nodded then continued on toward the parking lot. Marcia and the kids walked past Alan as they followed Henry.

Gail stopped next to Alan. "He seems so broken."

"I think he senses time is running out to connect with Patrick. I wish I could do something more to help."

She slid her hand into his. "Just being around comforts him. I know he's going to miss you, too." Her smoky eyes captured his. "I will, too, you know. Alan, we need to talk, but I have to go with Marcia right now. She needs me. Can I come by your shop in a couple days?"

He squeezed her fingers. "Of course. I'll be there."

"Good." She let go and caught up with her sister, who had been watching them. Gail picked up her niece and continued walking.

But Marcia stared at him a moment longer, her lips a tight straight line. She pointed a finger to one of her eyes then pointed at him.

He got the message, loud and clear.

∽

Alan peeled the packing from the Tiffany lamp. Mr. Winston would be pleased that Alan had managed to find a second lamp to match the one he'd bought in the shop last week. With a gentle cleaning, the colors of the glass would come to life again.

The doorbell jingled. Alan checked his watch. Gail said she would come by at one so they could talk while he managed the store until Tara got back at three. But it was 12:45. She was early. He pocketed the salt dish he'd set aside for Gail's niece.

His heart kicked up a notch. He'd tried not to imagine what she wanted to say to him, but the scene had played in his head many a time throughout the morning with two possible endings. Only one gave him hope. He set the lamp on a small table and left the back room. Somehow he would find a way to convince Gail they were meant to be together.

Alan stopped. Dropped his hands to his sides.

Marcia stood by the counter, alone. "You don't look happy to see me, Alan."

"I wasn't expecting to see you here, Mrs. Wolfe."

She sighed. "I know you're waiting for my sister, but I was in the neighborhood and wanted to thank you for being such a good friend to my Patrick." She held her left hand up, looking at her new engagement ring. "It meant the world to him that you helped find the perfect ring for me."

"I was glad to help."

She shifted her gaze back to him. Tears glittered in her eyes. "I miss him so much." She covered her mouth with her hand. Her tears dropped to her cheeks and rolled tracks down to her fingers.

"Marcia. . .let me get you a tissue." Alan strode into the back room and tugged a couple of tissues from the box on Tara's desk. When he turned around, Marcia waited just inside the doorway.

"Here you go." He held out the tissues.

"Thank you." She dabbed her eyes. Moved closer to him. "You finally called me by my first name." She moved even closer until mere inches separated them. "That means so much to me."

Alan backed up, felt the edge of the small table against his leg. He hadn't even realized he'd used her first name. How could he undo that? Marcia appeared genuinely distressed.

He shifted to go around her, intending to return to the safety of the storefront, but his movement brought him momentarily closer to her. She threw her arms around his neck and pulled his head down, crushing his mouth to hers.

He felt her oily lipstick on his mouth. Her strong perfume burned his nose. Alan grabbed her forearms and pushed away. He lost his balance, stumbled into the table. The sound of the front bell jingling came just before the crash of glass. Shards of colored bits lay strewn on the floor along with the rest of the now-mangled Tiffany lamp.

Gail's gasp drew his gaze back up. She glanced between him and Marcia, eyes as round as her open mouth. Only then did Alan realize that Marcia had her arm around his waist and was straightening her skirt with her other hand. The implications appalled even him.

Alan pushed Marcia's arm away. "Gail, it's not what you think." The words sounded hollow even to him.

Marcia walked past Gail. "I better be on my way. The children will be wondering where I am." She stopped, turned around. "Alan, thank you for listening." She dabbed at one eye with the tissues still clutched in her hand and left.

Alan blew out a long breath. The Tiffany lamp was shattered as well as what chance he had with Gail. He didn't know what to say. Nothing sounded right in his head. He wiped his mouth to get rid of the feel of Marcia's unwanted kiss, and by the red smear on his hand, her lipstick, too.

"Maybe it's best that I go, too." The corners of her mouth turned down, making her lips look fuller and pouty. But it was what lay in her eyes that made Alan want to sink to the floor along with the broken glass.

"Gail, please don't go. You know me well enough by now to believe me when I say I have no interest in your sister. She showed up a few minutes before you came. I thought she was upset so I gave her a tissue. The next thing I know, she's kissing me and the Tiffany. . ." He gestured at the lamp, digesting the amount of money he'd just lost. Money that would help Tara keep the store solvent. He crouched down and started picking up the pieces.

"Marcia's not the one I care about." He kept his head down . . .couldn't bear to see her look at him that way again. "It's you, Gail."

From the corner of his eye he noticed her shift in position; then her hands were moving along the floor near his, collecting glass bits.

"I want to believe you, Alan. I know how my sister is. I also know that's why so many of Patrick's friends don't come around anymore, because she's slept—"

"I would never do that."

"I know you wouldn't."

Alan dropped the shards back to the floor. With his hands on her upper arms, he turned her to face him. "Then give me a chance. I think you care about me, too."

"But I'm engaged. I already told Troy yes. I can't go back on my word."

"Do you love him?"

She pulled away and stood. "I guess you could say I do. Troy needs me."

Alan rose then ran his thumb below her cheek. "What if I need you, too?"

Her eyes pleaded with him. "Please don't say that. I'm already so confused. And seeing you with Marcia. . .and you're leaving soon."

"Nothing happened with your sister. She's made advances before, which I've managed to avoid." He fought the anger welling up inside him. Marcia was just a convenient door that Gail chose to hide behind. "And yes, I'm leaving soon, but then

I'll be back and—"

"Like Patrick came back?"

"Not if I know you're here waiting for me." Why couldn't she see what was right in front of her? People didn't just meet and fit together like they did on a daily basis.

"I'm sorry. It's just. . .I need time to think."

Alan stepped back. "Then take all the time you need. I just may not be here by the time you make up your mind." He returned to his task of cleaning up the broken lamp. He'd let his anger take over, not something he wanted to admit.

He didn't stop when he heard her walking away, but then he remembered the salt dish. "Gail, wait."

She turned around and came back, avoiding eye contact with him.

Alan held out the dish. "I set this aside for your niece. It's one of a kind. Usually they come in sets. Thought she might like it for her dolls."

Gail reached out, her hand slow and tentative. Tears glimmered just on the surface of her eyes. "That's so thoughtful. Thank you. I know she'll love it." She paused for a moment then placed the dish in her purse. When she looked back up at him, her eyes were dry, resolved. "Good-bye, Mr. James."

"Good-bye, Miss Gibson."

Even after the bell jingled, he didn't move. Just stared at the door, remembering the last image of the woman he loved as she walked out of his life.

Chapter 6

"Here we are, ma'am."

The taxi driver's words broke into the chaos and confusion buzzing through Gail's head. She hadn't noticed that the taxi had stopped and now sat in front of the Wolfe brownstone. On her way from the train station, she'd tried repeatedly to stop seeing the image of Alan crouched over that broken lamp, to no avail. The man just wouldn't leave her thoughts or her heart. She nearly sobbed in the back of the taxi when she realized she spent more time thinking of Alan than Troy.

She paid the driver and got out. After the car left, she stood glued to the sidewalk, loathing the idea of seeing her sister. She believed Alan when he said he had no interest in Marcia. His integrity exceeded most men she'd met, matching her own father's high standards. In fact, her father would probably approve more of Alan than Troy.

But she'd made a commitment. She knew she could help Troy become a man of potential. He needed a woman to stand by him and support him through his endeavors, especially with his health issues. And maybe he'd even help her pursue her dream of helping underprivileged teens.

She tried to picture him in that capacity, but every time she did, his face changed to Alan's. Why could she see so much more with him? She straightened her spine and harrumphed.

She had a plan, and she would stick to it.

"You know, you can stand there all day, but it won't change a thing."

Gail shot her attention up the stairs to the front door. Marcia stood with her hand on one hip and the other on the doorknob. Gail tugged the short straps of her purse to sit in the crook of her arm and marched to the door, fully intending to ignore her sister.

Marcia blocked her way. "It's clear he's in love with you."

Gail stared at her sister, and for the first time, didn't bother to school her expression. She hoped every bit of her anger showed. "Why do you even care? You've done everything you could think of to try and catch Alan's attention. Why? So you can use him like you've done all of Patrick's other friends? Well, guess what? It didn't work. He sees right through you."

Her sister shifted to face her, both hands on her hips. Defiance blazed a twisted trail on already-hardened features. Gail was ready for it, ready for the fight to end all fights. She'd had enough and had no qualms about putting an end to her sister's antics in her life.

But then Marcia's facade completely crumbled. That's when Gail noticed her sister's eyes were already red and swollen. Had she gotten bad news about Patrick?

"What's wrong? Is Patrick okay?" All her anger dissolved in the flash of pending grief. Suddenly Gail found herself wanting to pray and ask God to bring her brother-in-law home safely, to pray as she had as a child. Why hadn't she done this sooner?

Marcia shook her head then swallowed her sobs. "Are you kidding me? Your first thought is Patrick? Maybe you should have married him." She let out a bitter laugh. "Patrick is just fine and dandy with his good ole boys in Vietnam. In the meantime, I'm stuck here with his latest brat in my belly and no life whatsoever."

She spun around and slammed the door behind her, leaving Gail on the stoop alone. Pregnant? Another baby? Any hope she had for her sister fizzled with a pathetic pop in her heart. What she would give to have a family like hers. Her sister never saw it as anything but a burden.

Her nieces and nephew would need her even more now. Marcia's moods tended to be long and wicked, and pregnancy only seemed to compound them. She should talk to Troy and discuss this with him. What affected her future would affect his, too.

Tomorrow she'd go into the city again and surprise Troy with a visit, maybe entice him to lunch and some time in Central Park. She could show him Bow Bridge. . . .

Again Alan's face nestled into that place in her mind that had a direct connection to her heart. He'd almost kissed her that day.

Gail ignored the part of her that still longed for that kiss. The sooner she put that behind her, the sooner she could make plans for her next little niece or nephew. She'd do whatever was necessary to make sure that little one came into the world knowing he or she was loved.

Alan shoved the box onto an upper shelf in the back room. The contents shifted, clinking the glass bits of the broken lamp inside. Maybe he'd need parts of it to repair another Tiffany down the road. Didn't matter. He'd find another one for Mr. Winston eventually.

"You know, you could send Marcia Wolfe the bill for that lamp." Tara passed him and plopped into the seat at her desk. "Maybe she'd take responsibility for herself for once."

"What delusional dream world are you residing in now, little sister?" Alan tucked the side of his shirt back into the waistband of his jeans. "I seriously doubt that will ever happen."

She leaned forward and propped her chin in her hand. "I just don't get it. Marcia and Gail are so different. I see the family resemblance, but beyond that, it's like they're from completely different families."

Alan ignored the way his stomach clenched right into his chest with the mention of Gail's name. "Nobody's perfect, Tara. Some just have more awareness of how they impact the lives of others. Some don't."

"I think you should call her."

"Marcia?"

"No, you idiot. Gail. Clearly you both have feelings for each other."

"I'd really rather not talk about it. Gail made her choice. She's engaged. End of story."

"I disagree."

Alan laughed. "Cool it, okay? The subject is closed."

She just sat there and stared at him. Wouldn't stop staring at him. He threw his hands up and blew out the breath he was holding. He wanted more than anything to believe Tara was right, but Gail had made her choice clear. She hadn't just said a simple good-bye yesterday. She'd said *good-bye* as in good-bye forever. The door had closed and rung the bell. . . .

He stomped out of the back room and started unloading the small box of salt dishes that had arrived earlier that morning from an estate sale in the Hamptons. Several more boxes were due to arrive the next day, bearing his latest acquirements along with some additional inventory to keep the shop going for quite awhile. Tara wouldn't need to do any estate sales for the first six months of his absence.

Alan finished arranging the salt dishes and went to toss the box in the back room, but a small clunk stopped him. He weeded through the tissue and found another dish. A loner, almost identical to the one he'd given Gail. Small in size, round and simple in design, yet this simplicity was probably what gave it more beauty than some of its detailed counterparts. He pocketed the antique, chiding himself for still holding on to an impossibility but loathe to let it go.

He returned to the back room and disposed of the box. Tara still sat at her desk and resumed her vigilant stare at him.

"What now?"

"You said cool it, so I'm not saying a thing."

"Yeah, well, with that stare you don't have to."

"Does that mean I can say something then?"

"No!" At her hurt expression, Alan's anger bottomed out to regret. He'd let his emotions take over again. He crouched down in front of Tara and held her hands. "I'm sorry, Sis. Forgive me?"

She nodded then hugged him. Her small form hiccuped slightly with her tears. "It's okay. I really liked her, too."

How'd he let this happen? In the past, he'd always protected their family—what was left of it—and didn't easily let outsiders in. Patrick had been the only one to get close to both of them. He should have been more cautious. Tara didn't need more emotional strain added to what she already faced with his leaving for Vietnam. He only had a few weeks left.

"That day at the station. . .Patrick said something to you that seemed to upset you. Do you mind me asking what it was?"

She shrugged. "Yes, but I'll tell you anyway. He said that I shouldn't bother praying for him. That you need those prayers more."

His friend's words struck him to the core. He kissed the top of Tara's head. "Let's split early and see a movie. Sound good?"

She braved a smile and nodded. "How about a romance?"

Alan glared halfheartedly at her. "You're kidding, right?"

Chapter 7

Gail left the station and walked the few blocks to the offices where Pendergast Investments resided. She checked her watch. Thirty minutes early. The cleverly decorated windows called to her. . .she could afford a few minutes for window-shopping.

She stood in front of a bridal store with one finger on her cheek. No matter how hard she tried to concentrate on the beaded wedding dress with matching shoes in the display, she still kept thinking about what to say to Troy. Would he be willing to support her decision to delay finishing school if Marcia needed more help with the kids? They'd talked of their future together only briefly, and any time she'd mentioned children, Troy had been indefinite.

Still. . .what if she did take time off—

"Beautiful, isn't it?"

The woman's question pulled Gail from the oblivion of her thoughts. "Hmm, yes, it is."

"Would you like to come in and try it on? You'd look divine in it." Her red lips matched the thick frames of her cat-eye glasses.

Gail smiled. "Sorry, not today. Maybe soon though." She left the dress behind and dragged her worries with her. Why did everything seem so unsettled and. . .and. . .hazy? She had her life all planned out. Then Alan walked into the picture, and

Marcia was pregnant and miserable. She'd never imagined any of this happening.

She should be excited about wedding things, but staring at that dress had done nothing for her. Maybe once Troy gave her a ring, it would seem more. . .real. . .more certain.

Troy would know how to make sense of it all. One of the things she loved about him was his logical approach to life and the future. She didn't want to wait another thirty minutes agonizing over it all. He'd sounded happy that she was coming to see him anyway. This would give them more time together.

She reached the office building and went through the door. People milled about the first floor, moving in and out of the elevators. She stood with a group waiting to board the next free elevator. A bell dinged, doors whooshed open, and several people poured out. Gail filed in, pressing her purse against her abdomen to make more room.

Finally at the third stop, she reached the floor dominated by Pendergast Investments. Gail squeezed her way out and approached the secretary's desk, but no one was there. She headed toward the back. Doors to individual offices lined the wide and carpeted walkway. Her boots sank into the plush carpeting.

When she reached the T in the walkway, she turned right, remembering the last time Troy had brought her up to see his father and take her around the office. He'd shown her then the office where he would be working for the summer.

She reached the door and paused. Adjusting her short jacket, she lifted her hand to knock. No, she'd surprise him more if she just opened the door. She turned the knob and pushed the door wide open.

"Surprise!" The word fell flat in the air charged with the sight of Troy lip-locked with the petite blond sitting on his lap with her shirt unbuttoned.

Troy jumped to his feet, toppling the woman to the floor. Gail gasped at the sight of the woman's bra then spun around and rushed back down the hall.

"Gail, wait!"

His footsteps thumped behind her, but she didn't stop. She wanted to leave the building before anyone else discovered the source of her humiliation.

"Gail, please." He managed to grab her arm and pull her to a stop.

She braved a look into the eyes of the man she thought she would soon marry. The man she thought she could trust with her future. His loosened tie and tousled hair made her stomach lurch.

"Gail, say something."

A sarcastic laugh bubbled in her throat. "Me? I'm not the one who's cheating on her fiancé." A ping of guilt hit her square in the heart. Could she really and truly profess innocence? Hadn't she continued to see Alan even when she knew she was falling for him?

He swiped his hair back into some semblance of neatness. "I'm sorry. I. . .I didn't plan for that to happen. It just did."

And so had her attraction to Alan. . .

Her life just went from hazy to near darkness, with no flashlight in sight. She'd have to figure this one out on her own.

"Then consider this just happening to you, too, Troy Pendergast. We're through. Enjoy your new life." She strode down to the main hall, turned left, and didn't stop until she reached the elevator, which somehow opened just as she got there. Divine intervention, perhaps?

She dearly hoped so. She needed a good dousing of the divine at the moment. Once she reached the bottom floor, she kept her steps quick until she blasted out the main doors to the building and hit the sidewalk. No one seemed to notice her as she leaned against the building and let the full impact of what had just happened settle on her.

Tears stung her eyes as she rifled through her purse for a tissue. She found one at the same time her fingers grazed the salt dish Alan had given her yesterday. For her niece. She'd forgotten all about it.

She dabbed her eyes then lifted the small dish and set it on her palm. Sunlight glinted off the cut glass, giving it a diamondesque appearance.

Troy had never even given her a ring.

Yet Alan had given her his heart.

Gail gently placed the dish back in her bag and wadded the tissue in her hand. Was she really all that heartbroken about Troy? If she was to be honest, what really stung was being dumped for another woman. Her pride was more damaged than her heart.

Time for a new plan, and she had an idea of where to start. She followed Alan's lead and prayed for a blessing:

Please, God, let it be Alan James.

Just as Alan flipped the sign on the shop door to CLOSED, a figure appeared in front of the door. Alan leaned to the right to get a clear view without the lettering on the glass door to hinder him. He hadn't expected a visit from Henry Wolfe.

Alan yanked the door open, giving the bell a violent jiggle. "Mr. Wolfe, come in."

"Thank you, Alan."

"What can I do for you?"

Henry's smile looked more sad and melancholy these days. This time was no different. "Actually, I want to do something for you, Alan." He reached into his suit pocket. When he opened his hand, the gold coin sat centered in his palm. "I know you're leaving in just a couple weeks. I'd like you to take this with you."

"But what about Patrick? He'll be home eventually. He might want it then."

"No, he sent me a letter. He wants you to have it. Guess he thinks you need the luck more than he does." His attempt to laugh fell short of the heaviness in his eyes. "Do you believe in luck, Alan?"

Alan took a deep breath. "No, sir. I believe in a God who desires to bless the children who love Him."

Henry nodded. "I thought you might say that, but I'd like you to have the coin nonetheless." He took Alan's hand and placed the coin in it. "You've become like a son to me. You've even helped me to understand my own son better in some ways." He pulled a handkerchief from his pocket and wiped his nose.

Alan closed his hand over the coin. "Thank you, Mr. Wolfe."

"Henry, please. I think we're way past formalities here, son."

A knot formed in his throat. Alan had come to see Henry as a father figure over the last several months. Earning the man's respect meant the world to him. He felt compelled to hug Henry as he remembered hugging his own father before he died.

Before he could change his mind, Alan did exactly that. And in that moment, he sensed Henry needed it as much as he did.

After they parted, Henry nodded and sniffed. "Tell Tara that if she needs anything at all—and I mean anything—she's to call me right away."

"Yes, sir, I will."

"And I'll make sure to stop in from time to time, just to make sure she's doing okay. I know you're going to worry about her, Alan, but you've done a good job raising her and showing her the business. I know she'll be just fine."

"Thank you, Henry. I appreciate you looking out for her.

She's still pretty young."

"But wiser than most young ladies her age, I daresay."

Alan didn't miss the implication in Henry's words. Marcia had wreaked havoc in more lives than her own. He could testify to that.

Footsteps came from the stairs, growing louder. "Alan, do you know where—" Tara stopped at the counter. "Mr. Wolfe. How nice to see you. I hope I didn't interrupt anything."

"No, no. I was just reassuring your brother I'd stop by every once in a while to see how you're doing. Gives me an excuse to come downtown." He smiled at her then looked back at Alan. "I better go. Still have a few errands to run before heading home. I'll see you in a few days, Alan. I'd like to have you out at the house before you ship out. You and Tara both."

His sister took a step forward. "We'd love to."

Alan didn't miss the excitement in her eyes. She'd only been to the Wolfe home a few times. "I guess I'll second that."

Henry patted his shoulder then headed out the door.

Tara kept her eyes on the closed door. "He seems so sad."

"I know. The Wolfe men tend to live with their ghosts."

"What an odd saying."

"I know. I heard Henry say it himself." Alan stared at the door. Would he find himself living with his own ghosts when he returned? He didn't want to live a life of regret, but regret had surely found him this summer. And it looked a lot like one Gail Gibson.

"I'm making dinner. Do you want chicken or leftover meat loaf?"

Why did he regret not stopping her from leaving, even though he knew letting her go was the right thing to do?

"Alan?"

"What? No, thanks. I think I'll take a walk. I'll make a sandwich when I get back."

"No, you won't. You're going to get one of those awful hot dogs, aren't you?"

"Maybe I will. Maybe I won't."

"You will. I know you."

He kissed Tara on the forehead. "You think so?"

"Yes. And I think you ought to call her before you leave."

He sighed. "Not that again. I said I didn't want to talk about it."

"I know, but you should."

"Why? It won't make a difference."

"What won't? Talking about it or calling her?"

"Both. End of subject. I'll be back later." He headed to the door and didn't look back. He didn't want to see Tara's disappointed expression again. The girl just didn't understand that Gail Gibson wasn't going to be a part of their future.

Of his future. The sooner they both accepted that, the better off they'd be.

Chapter 8

Gail thrust the money at the cabdriver and ran the last few steps to Alan's shop. The CLOSED sign put a ding in her hopes, but she couldn't stop now. She knocked on the glass but didn't see any movement in the shop or from the direction of the back room.

Again, she tried knocking. No response. She glanced to the side panel where the mail slot was. She could leave a note then try calling when she got home. But that deflated her hopes to nothing.

A small panel beneath the mail slot caught her attention. Barely noticeable. She lifted the right edge and swung the small door to the side. A doorbell. She pressed the button twice, doing everything she could not to bounce up and down in front of the door.

Hours may have passed, let alone minutes, and just forget seconds. Finally, Gail recognized Tara's form come through the door to their apartment above and rush to the front. When her eyes met Gail's, a broad smile broke her concerned expression.

Tara opened the door. "Gail, what a surprise."

She didn't know whether to hug the girl or cry. "Is Alan here?"

"No, he went for a walk. Is something wrong?"

"No, I'm hoping everything's right."

Tara threw her arms around her in a quick hug. "He's in the

park. Go get him."

Gail returned her hug. "Thank you." She rushed away, not even looking back.

People dodged her as she did her best to navigate through the pedestrians like an obstacle course. She had a hunch where Alan would be and even prayed he'd be there. She found herself praying more and more these days.

The arc of the Bow Bridge came into view. Gail slowed to a fast walk. Bodies moved back and forth but none looked like Alan. She kept walking and searching with each step. Her heart pounded so hard in her chest that she heard each thump in her head.

And then he was there, standing in the middle of the bridge, looking over the water. Sunlight glinted off his hair and backlit his profile. A man of strength and integrity.

Fear stopped her. Would he even want her in his life? That day in his shop. . .she'd made her choice clear. Would he give her a second chance?

The greater fear of not knowing propelled her forward. She had to know, but more importantly, Alan needed to know that she loved him.

Just a few feet away. Alan must have heard her steps. He glanced over his shoulder then turned to face her. His face remained placid, though she didn't miss the twitch on the left side of his mouth—where his smile always started.

She stopped within arm's reach. "Mr. James, I had some time to think."

Alan leaned against the stone railing. "And what did you decide, Miss Gibson?"

"That I've been very foolish."

He frowned. "How so?"

"I thought I could plan everything out in my life, and it would turn out perfectly."

"And now?"

"My life's a mess."

"I take it that wasn't your plan." He pushed away from the bridge and moved a step toward her.

Questions filled his gaze, ones she hoped she had the right answer to. Tears pricked her eyes. "Not at all but I'm glad."

"May I ask why?"

Her turn to brave a step closer. "Because I almost walked away from a very special blessing in my life." She dared to rest her hand on his cheek. She pleaded in her heart for Alan and God to give her another chance, to help her not be so afraid.

His hand reached out to cup her neck as he leaned toward her. All thoughts fled once his lips touched hers. She leaned against him, not trusting her legs to hold her. A deep sense that she was right where she was meant to be flooded her entire being.

She didn't know how long the embrace lasted, but she didn't want it to end. Grudgingly, she let go of her perfect kiss but refused to open her eyes. What if she did and discovered she'd dreamed it all?

"Miss Gibson?"

She fluttered her eyes open. "Yes, Mr. James?"

His gaze tender and loving, he continued to hold her. "Did I just hear you use the word *blessing*?"

She smiled and gave him a quick kiss. "Yes, I believe you did."

The Bow Bridge didn't look any different in reality, but to Alan the stone held a darker, grayer appearance to match the overcast sky. Even the water below appeared dull without the sun's reflection. Duty had a way of holding the mind but not always the heart. His body and soul would be in Vietnam, but his heart would be safely tucked away here with Gail.

Just a few weeks before, he stood on the bridge wishing his life could be his own. And for those weeks, it had. They'd spent every minute they could together. Today would be their last for a while.

He saw her before she saw him. Alan smoothed the front of his uniform jacket and then touched his hat and smooth-shaven chin. Even from a distance he could see the heaviness in her steps, the sadness in her face. Would he be asking too much of her? He had no doubts of their future together, but he still saw the occasional doubt in Gail's eyes.

Time would either be his enemy or his friend.

She quickened her steps when she saw him.

He greeted her with a kiss he hoped relayed just a part of what threatened to explode in his chest. He could survive anything knowing she was waiting for him.

When he pulled away, tears glistened in her hazel eyes. "This is harder than I thought it would be."

Alan kissed the tip of her nose. "That's why I wanted to do this here instead of the bus station."

She nodded and dropped her chin.

"I have something for you."

Gail lifted her head and braved a tearful smile.

"I want you to hold on to this for me." He held her hand in his and pressed the gold coin into her palm.

"Alan, I thought Henry wanted you to have this."

"He does, but I think you need it more than I do." He flipped the coin over on her palm. "Whenever you start to doubt, read the engraving."

She looked at the coin. "Love never fails."

"Do you believe it?"

"I want to, Alan. More than you will ever know."

"Promise me you'll hold on to it and remember that our love is meant to be."

"I promise."

"When I get back, I want you to meet me right here, because I'll have a very important question to ask you. Will you wait for me?"

A full smile lit her face, warmer and brighter than the missing sun. "I will, and I promise you'll like my answer."

Chapter 9

New York City, thirty-eight years later

F elicity, start from the beginning. You've almost got it down. Just a little more, okay?" The girl rolled her eyes but still smiled.

Mitzi tweaked her cheek. In two weeks her little troop of teenage actors would give a short rendition of *Our Town* as their final exam to pass ESL. A great way to finish before their Christmas vacation. She couldn't be prouder of how far the group had come in mastering the English language, both written and spoken.

Felicity finished her lines. "How was that, Mrs. Pendergast?"

"Perfect! Now, let's jump to the next scene where—"

A knock came from the classroom door. Mitzi recognized Sean's face peeking through the small window. "Everyone, let's take a ten-minute break. Go get something to drink from the cafeteria."

The students filed out the door, giving Sean curious glances. Mitzi studied his face as he waited. Something was troubling him, that much she could see.

Once the last student left, she waved Sean into the classroom. "Now what brings you my way? Are you okay?"

"Yeah, fine. I'm sorry to interrupt. I thought you usually finished up by three."

"Normally, yes, but the kids wanted to stay later and practice their play."

"Impressive. They must have the best teacher." He flashed her a smile.

Mitzi gave him a quick hug. "You flatterer, you. I'll take that compliment though." She walked over to her desk and sat down with a sigh. "They do keep me running, that's for sure."

Sean grabbed a chair and spun it around then straddled it, resting his arms on the back. "Aunt Mitzi, I need to talk to you about something."

"Shoot, kiddo. I'm all yours."

He pointed at her neck. "I know it upset you the other night when I asked about your pendant, but I need your help." He pulled out a weathered piece of paper and handed it to her.

She fingered her pendant as she read the letter. She knew Henry Wolfe had given the coin to Alan after Sean's father had left for Vietnam, but she never knew about Patrick's letter asking Henry to give Alan the coin. The ache over Patrick's suicide flooded back. Sean had been so young. . .had she made the right choices?

That question had dogged her for the last thirty-seven years.

"Sean. . ." She handed back the letter. "There's so much you don't know."

"Then just tell me." His knuckles turned white where he gripped the back of the chair.

Tears pricked her eyes. "I don't know if that's a good idea. Some things are better left buried with the dead." With her sister. . . If she told Sean about how she got the coin, then he'd know she'd lied to him. But she'd made a choice to honor Troy's wishes and held to them even after his death.

He rubbed his hand over the scars running down the side of his head. "I almost was one of the dead, Aunt Mitzi. That makes a person look at the truth in a whole new way. You don't need to protect me from it."

"I know, but I just can't help it. You've been through so much." Again, the question plagued her. . .had she made the right choices? Would choosing to tell him the truth be the right one, too?

He gestured to his head. "After this, I think I can handle just about anything."

She stood, smiled, then kissed the scar that angled down the side of his head. He may still see himself as less than the man he wanted to be, but she knew he was more and would become even greater than he could see himself at the moment. His scars would make him stronger if he just believed there could be a blessing in it all.

That word still brought back such memories. . . .

She didn't sit back down, just stood clasping and unclasping her hands. "Sean, first you need to understand that I had to make choices I thought were best at the time. I made sacrifices that I thought would help my marriage and my family. But it meant living a partial truth. . .a lie. Sometimes I wonder if I did more harm than good to my sister."

He frowned. "Sister? You never mentioned a sister."

She sat on the edge of the desk for support and laid her hand over his. No turning back now. Hopefully he wouldn't hate her. "Your mother was my older sister. When she got really wild, Troy asked me to disassociate myself from her because of his political associations. So I started using my nickname, Mitzi. My first name is actually Gail."

The tape made a ripping sound as he dragged the dispenser across yet another box destined for storage. Each sealed carton felt like another place in his heart being stored and put away until he knew what to do with his life. New York wasn't the same city it was when he'd opened the shop. He'd managed to keep the doors open and the property owner had been good to him over the years, but the man couldn't pass up an offer to sell the building that would make him a millionaire.

Alan didn't blame him one bit. The store had run its course in the city. And in his life. No point holding on to something for no reason. And Jamie had given up enough for him—for the store and for his recovery. She needed to move on and live her own life, too.

His cell phone buzzed in his pocket. Jamie's name and picture lit up the screen. "Hey there, Jamie-girl."

"How's my favorite uncle?"

A soft chuckle rumbled from his chest to the phone. Whenever she said it, she sounded just like her mother, Tara.

"How's my little brother?"

"Not little. . ." He never finished the line anymore. He hadn't felt like a brother since her death.

"Uncle Alan?"

He cleared his throat. "I'm your only uncle so that's an easy win."

She giggled. "So how about dinner and some last-minute Christmas shopping?"

"Love to. What time?"

"How about now? You look like you're about done with that box."

Alan jerked his attention to the front door. Jamie stood in front of the main window. She smiled and waved her fingers. Snowflakes fell gently around her, and for a split second, he thought he was looking at Tara.

He pocketed his cell and rushed to the door. "Why didn't you tell me you were coming by?"

She glanced up at the door bells, a questioning look on her face. "I wanted to surprise you."

"Yeah, they're still not working for some reason."

"Weird."

"Telling."

"Huh?"

He waved his hand. "Never mind. Where do you want to grab a bite? And I'll treat. I know you're still looking for a job."

She gave him a sly look. "I have reserves."

So like her mother. "Okay, you're buying. Let's grab a burger."

"And onion rings. You still need to gain some weight."

Alan kissed her forehead. "I'm fine, James. Never better. Doc said so himself last week."

She bounced on her toes. "He did?"

"Yep."

"Why didn't you tell me you had an appointment? I would have gone with you."

"It was just a checkup. Routine. No reason for you to sit with me in a boring doctor's office."

"Still."

"Jamie, it's fine. Trust me, okay? The doctor's pleased with my scans and said I don't even have to come back for another six months."

Her mouth became a circle, as did her eyes. She threw her arms around him in a tight hug. "That's wonderful! I'm so glad."

He hugged her back then gently pushed her away so he could look at her. "I know you sacrificed a lot for me—"

"I didn't mind—"

"Let me finish."

She snapped her lips shut, but the corners upturned in the smile that had melted his heart since she was ten years old.

"You let go of The Juilliard to take care of me and the shop while I underwent chemo. That's a lot. . .your dream. Now we need to figure out how to make your dream come true."

She pulled one side of her mouth between her teeth. "Uncle

Alan, do you think I've given up on my dream?"

He frowned. "Why do you ask?"

"No reason really. Just something a friend said to me." She looked distracted as if remembering a lost conversation.

"No, I don't think you've given up on your dream, but I do think you're scared."

"What do you mean by that?" She pulled away from him, arms crossed. "That's not true."

"Okay, you're not afraid. But I think you're hiding from something. Figure that out, and you'll know what to do next."

She stared at him through the corner of her eyes. "Speaking of hiding something. . ." She unfolded her arms. "Remember that coin I asked you about. I think a certain uncle who is near and dear to my heart has a secret."

He'd tried to avoid telling as much about the wound that still held his mind and heart captive. Maybe it was time to tell Jamie the truth.

He sighed. "Yes, I used to have it, but that was years ago. I gave it to Gail."

"Why didn't you just tell me?"

"Because it's not easy to talk about. I'd hoped I'd find it again."

Jamie looked around the shop. "Is that why you were always so interested in war memorabilia?"

"Partly. . ." He rubbed a hand down his face. How could he put in words what he didn't quite understand himself? "I was so sure, Jamie. So sure Gail would be there and that I'd get the coin back. I'd planned to give it back to Patrick. But then he killed himself, and I didn't have the heart to find out what happened to her. There didn't seem to be a reason to get it back anymore, you know?"

Tears sat in her eyes as she nodded.

He put on his coat. A chill ran through him at the memory

of waiting for Gail at their favorite spot on New Year's Eve. Bow Bridge had never looked so glamorous covered in a fine dusting of snow as it had that night. He'd sent her the letter, telling her he'd be there waiting, but she never came. . . .

"Part of the inscription on the coin was 'Love never fails,' but I guess in my case, it did."

Chapter 10

The yoga stretch pulled at the residual tension in her shoulders. Gail could blame it on the extra work she and the students did on their makeshift stage that afternoon, but in reality, she still hadn't bounced back from her discussion with Sean the day before.

He'd said he understood—that she didn't doubt, but the truth meant some of the old wounds had to be reopened and exposed to the air of forgiveness. As much as Sean didn't want to deal with it, he needed to if he ever wanted to move on with his life and live it free of the ghosts of his parents.

The doorbell chimed. Gail left the spongy yoga mat in the middle of the living room and padded to the front door. She caught only a glimpse of the person dressed in a heavy jacket and knit cap standing with her back to the door.

As she swung the door open, she remembered the young woman's name. "Jamie, right?"

The girl was quick to smile. "Yes."

"I'm sorry but Sean's not here."

"Actually, I was hoping to talk to you."

A moment's hesitation kept her rooted in silence. Fear told her to shut the door, but hadn't she lived enough of her life trapped by it? "Come in."

"Thanks." Jamie took off her hat and coat and hung them on the hooks by the door.

Gail headed toward the kitchen. "I was just about to have some tea. Care to join me?" She smiled over her shoulder.

Jamie nodded, looking around the house as she followed Mitzi into the kitchen. "Your home is so lovely. I love all the Christmas decorations."

"Me, too. Love this time of year." She opened the glass-fronted cabinet and pulled out the two teacups and saucers. "Would you like sweetener?"

"No, thanks. Better if I don't."

Mitzi kept her gaze on the golden liquid flowing from the teapot into the cups. "Sean mentioned you were a dancer."

"I am. I'm part of a dance troupe at the moment."

"Sounds exciting." Gail looked up as she handed Jamie her tea. The girl's eyes remained locked on the pendant on Gail's neck. "I'm guessing you talked to Sean."

She set the cup on the tiled counter, shaking her head. "He's not really talking to me at the moment."

"Give him some time, my dear. He'll come around."

Jamie stared into her tea.

"Is that what you wanted to talk about?"

"No. . .I. . .I need to ask you about your necklace."

Gail nodded. "I thought so."

"You did?"

"Yes, so I'll tell you what I told Sean yesterday. Maybe that will help you understand some of what he's grappling with." She sighed and slid into one of the padded stools at the counter.

Jamie followed her lead and sat on a stool, leaving an empty one between them.

"Sean showed me the letter you brought him. He also told me you suspected that I was your uncle's lost love, Gail Gibson."

She blinked and nodded, lips parted.

Gail believed the girl was holding her breath. Time to finish this quest for the truth. "You were right."

Jamie gasped. "I knew it! You have to come see my uncle. He's searched for you for a long time. I just know—"

She held up her hand. "Jamie, things are not as simple as we sometimes think they are." Here came the hardest part. "I made your uncle a promise a long time ago, one I wound up breaking. As I told Sean. . .I fully intended to wait for Alan. I wanted more than anything to believe what he said. . . ." She fingered the pendant. "I wanted to believe our love wouldn't fail, but so much happened after he left."

"I know he'd understand."

Gail smiled. "You remind me of him. He was so sure of himself. Of life. Of his faith. I thought I would marry him one day."

"You still could. I mean, why not?" She lifted one shoulder and held her hand out.

Gail leaned toward Jamie. "Because I betrayed him. I can't imagine he could forgive me. You see, I was engaged when I met your uncle. To my late husband, Troy. Your uncle showed me what real love was, and it terrified me." Her voice dropped to a whisper with her words. "I told him I would wait for him, but I didn't. My sister, Sean's mother, led me to believe that Alan had no intentions of marrying me. She even showed me a letter that he'd written her, telling her he was only going to marry me so that he could be close to her."

Jamie shook her head and frowned. "But he'd never do such a thing."

Gail smiled. "I know, but you didn't know my sister and how convincing she could be." She stood and paced the kitchen. "Then my ex-fiancé—Troy—was diagnosed with MS. They didn't have the medications then like they have now. He begged me to give him just a few years, to help make the rest of his life worth something. He needed me, and in a way, I guess I needed him. He was my safety net."

Jamie fisted her hands on the counter and frowned. "I don't understand. My uncle loved you so much."

She went back to the stools and sat by Jamie, resting one hand on the girl's fist. "That's what scared me so much, Jamie. I knew that if I loved Alan like that and he didn't come back from the war, I'd never survive that kind of loss. I'd watched Sean's father deteriorate so badly. . .I couldn't go through that either."

"You ran away." Jamie swiped a tear from her cheek.

The truth stung, but having it out there was somehow cathartic. "Yes, I did. And I'm not telling you all this to justify my choices. At the time I did what I thought was best to honor my husband and to protect Sean."

"How was this about protecting Sean?"

"When Patrick killed himself, Troy asked me to distance myself from my family, namely, my sister." She diverted her eyes. "I did as he asked, but I kept in touch with Sean, as his godmother. That part Troy didn't know. I'd already started using my nickname, Mitzi, so it wasn't that hard."

"Sean said you raised him."

She nodded. "His mother died when he was ten. The rest of the kids had already moved out. Sean needed me as much as I needed him. . .my husband had died just a few months before. I don't know what I would have done without Sean. He was the one bright spot in my life."

"You never thought about looking for my uncle?"

"I did a few years ago. I even went to his shop. I watched him through the window. . .with you. At first I thought you were his sister, Tara."

"My mom. . ." Jamie's gaze bounced down then back up. "She and my father were killed in a car accident."

Tears burst from Gail's eyes. "Oh no, I didn't know." Alan had lost so much. His parents then his sister. Her heart ached for him. "I'm so sorry."

"Uncle Alan was my rock. He kept me going. . .kept me dancing. Then he got sick and—"

Gail leaned forward, her heart in shambles. "Is he okay?"

"He is now. Just got a clean bill of health from the doctor. The cancer's gone."

The weight of it all began to crush in on Gail. Prayers started forming in her heart and formulated in her mind. So much loss. "Your uncle always believed in the blessings that came in life, even in the midst of loss and pain. He taught me that, showed me what it meant to truly believe."

"That sounds like him—*before* my mother died. Since then, I think he's struggled. He won't talk to me much about it." Jamie clutched Gail's hand. "But if he saw you, knew you still cared for him, I think his hope would be restored." She touched the pendant. "He never married, you know. All through the years he kept searching for this. For you. Now he's closing the shop and says it's time to move on, but I know his heart is broken."

Despite the pleading in Jamie's eyes, Gail shook her head. She remembered the day in Alan's shop when she said good-bye, thinking Troy was her future. Alan hadn't come after her. He'd let her go. He'd given her a second chance though. . .but she couldn't imagine, after all he'd lost, that Alan would give her a third. He'd allowed her to make her own choice. She owed him the same respect.

"I'm sorry, Jamie. I think it's better to let the past be and let your uncle move on. He deserves that much."

Snow crunched under Gail's feet on the sidewalk. Christmas tree lights glowing in storefront windows cast a wash of colors onto the snow-blanketed sidewalk like paint on a canvas.

Some of the people she passed were already dressed in

formal attire on their way to various New Year's Eve parties. She could only imagine how crowded Times Square was already.

Gail stopped just short of Alan's shop then braved a few steps closer. The sign on the door said CLOSED. She shivered against the cold and pulled the lapels of her coat up around her neck. A peek in the window revealed only empty shelves and tables, but a light glowed from the back room.

She went to the door, all the while watching for him to come out of the back room. What was she doing here? Hadn't she told Jamie that she should let Alan move on? But she had to know. . .had to make sure he was okay. Finding out about his close call with cancer had rocked her world more than she imagined. If she could have been there for him through all that. . .

Before she realized what she was doing, her hand was on the doorknob. It turned freely. She hedged the door open just a few inches then stopped. Her heart pounded in her chest so loud she thought surely he would hear it. Once she stepped in that door there was no turning back.

She took a deep breath and pushed the door open. The overhead bells tinkled just like she remembered. She caught a slight whiff of the cologne she remembered Alan wearing. A slew of memories flooded in and pricked her eyes with threatening tears.

Shuffling came from the back. A voice hollered out, "Sorry, we're closed."

His voice. Gail closed her eyes. Why had she come? She turned around and ran out the door.

Chapter 11

Alan stacked another box, adding to the pile waiting by the back door. He'd rented a small truck to haul the rest to the storage room he'd leased. Most of his inventory had been sold to other dealers, but what remained, what he couldn't part with, would stay in storage until he decided what to do with it.

The front door bells jangled. Didn't the person realize there was nothing to buy? He left the back room but only caught the back of a figure in a mint-green mid-length jacket as she rushed past the main window.

He returned to the back room. Empty shelves stared back at him. Even his desk was empty, except for one thing. The small salt dish he'd kept on his desk through the years as a reminder of Gail. He picked it up. Jiggled it in his palm then set it in the last open box next to the faded Polaroid of Gail and Tara. Time to let go.

The bells rang again. The bells hadn't worked for weeks, then suddenly they work today? He headed to the front part of the store.

"Uncle Alan?"

"Right here, Jamie-girl."

She pointed to the door. "You fixed the bells?"

"No, they just started working today."

Her cheeks were bright pink from the cold, and she seemed

distracted. Jamie went to the window and looked out the direction he'd seen the unknown figure just pass. When she turned around, a frown puckered her lips. "Did someone just come in the store?"

"Yeah, I think so. I was in the back and hollered out that we're closed." Alan laughed and gestured toward the empty shelves. "I think it's pretty obvious—"

"Let's go for a walk. Right now."

He dropped his hand to his side. Why was she so anxious? "Okay, just let me get my jacket."

"Hurry."

"Okay, okay. He grabbed his coat draped over the counter and shrugged into it. Jamie stood in the open doorway waving him along.

"Good grief. What are you so worked up about?"

"I need to show you something."

He locked the door and quickened his steps to catch up with her. The girl went back and forth between a fast-paced walk to a light jog. Her long hair swung back and forth with her hurried steps.

"Jamie, wait up. I thought you wanted to walk *together*." For a moment he lost sight of her in the pedestrian traffic. More people than usual for any night but tonight. New Year's Eve. He'd totally forgotten what day it was. Poor Jamie. . .she should be out celebrating with friends. Not babysitting her uncle.

He recognized Bow Bridge ahead. Jamie stopped at the bottom then turned around. She made eye contact with him and waved frantically again.

Alan closed the distance between them. "Jamie, what's going on?"

She pointed to a figure standing by the bench at the mid-point of the bridge. Alan followed her directions. Even from a side view, he'd recognize that profile anywhere. The upturned nose. Her hair was shorter, and the red had toned down more to an auburn, but it was her.

Gail.

∽

She sensed him before she saw him. Gail glanced to her side. First she recognized Jamie then the man rushing up to her. He'd hardly changed through the years. The same tall figure, strong and brimming with integrity. Gray dusted the sides of his hair heavily, with a small amount throughout the rest. But she'd know him anywhere. She wanted to run to him, pretend the last thirty-eight years hadn't happened. But they had. She'd made choices out of fear and lived with them since. If he didn't want anything to do with her, she'd completely understand.

She wanted desperately to hope though. She did the only thing she knew to do at this point.

Pray.

∽

"I don't believe it." Alan's breath came out in rapid white puffs. His heartbeat remained accelerated, kept in rhythm by a sight he never thought he'd see again.

"Go to her. I think she's waiting. . .hoping her true love will arrive."

Alan glanced at Jamie. The hope brimming in her eyes cinched it for him. How could he disappoint her? She'd lived with his heartache for years. Imagined his happy ending for him when he could no longer dream it.

He made himself move forward. Step after step. Just a few feet separated them now. "Gail."

She faced him. Her lips parted with unspoken words, and her eyes sparkled with tears. "I tried to come into your shop to see you."

"I heard the bells."

She shook her head. "Not just today. But before. . .a few years ago. But I couldn't bring myself to go in. I didn't think you could ever forgive me."

He took another step closer. "Why didn't you come that night?"

"I couldn't." She dropped her head. "I was married."

"Troy." His heart shattered into bits again, just like the Tiffany lamp that day in his shop.

She nodded. "Marcia made me believe you'd written her this letter. . .and Troy begged me to marry him. He was sick, Alan. He needed me."

"I needed you, too."

"But I needed you more, and that terrified me." A sob escaped her lips along with the tears running from her eyes.

He couldn't stand the distance between them any longer. Alan wrapped his arms around her. Time raced back thirty-eight years. She was his girl, and he was a soldier about to go to war. Only this time he didn't have to leave her. Was it too late to build a life together?

She sniffed against his chest then pulled back, searching his face with those amazing eyes that even time hadn't touched. "Alan, I'm so sorry. I let fear run my life—"

He silenced her with his own lips, savoring what he'd dreamed about for years. Of holding her again. Of kissing her. Time may have moved on, but what sparked between them hadn't changed one bit.

And the way she clung to him and kissed him back told him she believed it, too. Maybe this time they had a chance to turn a love they'd allocated to dreams into a reality they could live out for the rest of their lives. Together.

Alan broke the kiss gently. Kissed her eyes and ran his thumbs over the delicate line of her jaw. He didn't want to stop taking her in, all of her, because if he looked away, she might disappear.

She pressed her forehead against his mouth. "Alan, I love you. I've never stopped loving you. I wish I could go back and make different choices out of love instead of fear." She looked up at him again. "I'm so sorry. You believed our love wouldn't fail. . . ."

Inwardly he wanted to shout. Years of loving her threatened to burst out in a ruckus louder than anything Times Square would offer. He touched the pendant at her neck. "Don't you see? Our love didn't fail. It just got delayed."

She trailed a finger over his lips. "Didn't you have a question you wanted to ask me?"

He laughed. "Yes, I do. Miss Gibson, will you marry me?"

"Yes, Mr. James. I do believe I will."

Chapter 12

Alan stood on the platform admiring the antique wedding ring. This time the ring hunt had been for the love of his life—the soon-to-be Mrs. James. The dream had kept him alive in Vietnam and kept the spark of his love going through many years. He chuckled to himself. How like God to move in and do a miracle when he'd given up hope.

The minister nudged his arm just as the pianist and violinist started to play. Alan snapped his attention down to the end of the aisle separating a moderate number of attendees, who were now rising to their feet.

Then he saw her. Her champagne gown, elegant and simple, flowed down and swished around her ankles. Sean guided her down the aisle, looking handsome in his tuxedo. Alan looked to where Jamie sat in the front row, glanced pointedly at Sean and winked at her. She smiled and rolled her eyes upward. He wasn't blind to the chemistry forming between her and Sean.

He didn't know what God had in mind for his niece, but if that plan included Sean, Alan would consider himself doubly blessed. Sean was a good man. He just didn't know it yet. If their love was meant to be like his and Gail's, nothing would keep them apart.

Gail stepped onto the platform next to him. The pendant rested on her neck. She never took it off. The next thirty minutes were a joyful blur. He couldn't keep his eyes off Gail.

She radiated beauty both inside and out.

The minister led them in prayer and finally reached the part Alan wanted most.

Alan answered at his prompting. "I do."

Gail smiled at him.

He'd waited to hear her answer for thirty-eight years.

Her turn. "I most certainly do!"

The attendees laughed along with Alan. He squeezed her hand and relished sliding the ring on her finger and hearing her gasp.

She lowered her voice to whisper. "It's gorgeous, Mr. James."

He kissed her hand then lost himself in her incredible eyes. "She most certainly is, Mrs. James."

Music filled the reception room with soft rhythm. Gail continued to search for Jamie among the tables. She had a mission to complete and hoped Alan would understand.

Sean came up beside her and stopped her path toward the stage where the band played. "Aunt Mitzi. Or should I start calling you Aunt Gail?"

"Whichever one you prefer, kiddo." She kissed his cheek and spoke into his ear. "Thank you for understanding and forgiving your old aunt."

"I could never stay mad at you. Even as a kid. . ." Sean took her hands in his. "You look so beautiful. And so happy."

"I am, sweetheart. Very happy. And I want that for you, too."

"Don't worry about me." He braved a smile and walked away.

She whispered to herself. "But I do, my sweet boy. I do so very much." She would step her prayers up and trust God to bring him through. But watching him struggle made her ache so deeply at times.

"Did you say something?"

Gail jumped. Jamie had somehow come up next to her without being heard. "Nothing, my dear. But I was looking for you. I have something I want to give you." She unclasped the coin pendant from her neck and secured it around Jamie's neck.

The girl's face was a picture of shock as she touched the coin. "Oh Gail, I can't accept this. It means everything to you and Uncle Alan. It's what brought you two back together."

"No, our love is what brought us back together, Jamie. And I know Alan would want you to have it. It was always meant to be passed on." How did she explain what she sensed in her gut, that Jamie and Sean were meant to be together? Time would have to show the two of them.

"Thank you." Tears brimmed in Jamie's eyes.

Gail hugged her. "You're the keeper of the coin now, and I daresay you'll soon be the keeper of my Sean's heart."

"I don't think—"

"I know Sean, and I've gotten to know you. Be patient with him. He's on a tough journey right now. Having you there to help him...well...I'll keep the rest to myself for now. Just trust God, Jamie."

A slow song started.

Alan crossed the room to her. Dressed in a black fitted tuxedo, Gail had a flashback to the day he met her on the Bow Bridge dressed in his uniform. He took her breath away now just as he had then.

He kissed the top of Jamie's head. "May I steal my beautiful wife away for a dance?"

She giggled.

Gail beamed at him. "I'd be delighted."

Alan held her hand as he led her to the dance floor then waited as she made an arc into his arms. They moved across the floor, comfortable in their silence. She fit perfectly against him, in the nook of his neck, in the crook of his hand. Joy surged through her so strongly that she felt breathless. "So blessed."

Alan lifted her chin. "Did I hear you say *blessed*?"

"Yes, you did."

"Even after a month of spending every moment with you, your faith still surprises me."

"Why should it? You were the one who planted the seeds." She gave him a light kiss.

"So, tell me why my niece is now wearing the coin I gave to you, Mrs. James."

"I don't need it anymore. You made your point. Love never fails. I believe it completely now. Besides, I have this." She held up her hand. The ring sparkled softly in the dim lighting.

"I love that, and I love you. I just thought. . ."

"What?"

"Patrick was my best friend and Sean is his son. He should have the coin."

"What makes you think he won't get it?"

He gave her a sideways glance. "What are you up to?"

"Not a thing. I just know what my gut says."

"Which is?"

"Sean and Jamie will wind up together. Their love is meant to be, just like ours was." She nodded toward the direction he'd just come from. "Speaking of which. . ."

Sean and Jamie made a stunning couple, dancing together just a few yards away. But then Sean stopped and walked away. By the look on Jamie's face, the girl was crushed.

Alan frowned. "What just happened?"

"Like I told Jamie, Sean just needs time."

"I hope you're right." He stared at his niece, the ache in his heart written all over his face.

Gail cupped his cheek, turning his head to look at her. "Have you already forgotten that love never fails?"

His smile returned, washing away his worry. "Well, maybe just for a moment."

"But you know it's true." She kept her tone playful.

His expression turned serious. He searched her face as if he had the most important news to tell her. "I do, and I promise I'll never doubt again."

DREAM A LITTLE DREAM

PART 2

by Ronie Kendig

Chapter 7

Jamie let herself into her apartment and dumped her satchel on the floor. She flipped the locks then went to the fridge for some orange juice. Raking her fingers through her hair, she groaned at the light blinking on her machine.

She pressed the PLAY button.

"Hey, Girl." Monet's voice sailed into the air from the answering machine. "Did you see tryouts for The Juilliard are coming up? Be sure to turn in your app. No time like the present, know what I'm saying? I mean—since your uncle is married and all, you have nothing to lose, right? Claude and I think you totally oughta go for it. Okay, well. . .see ya. Ciao!"

Jamie deflated against the counter. "Nothing to lose?" She twisted around and slumped back against the Formica. She had everything to lose—her courage, her pride if she didn't make it, then her grief when she did. There was no way she could come up with the money for that school anyway. And a scholarship had to be applied for *waayy* in advance. The only possible means of getting into that school was a miracle.

Irritated, she abandoned the OJ idea and trudged to the bedroom, where she quickly showered and changed. Curled up on the sofa with her newspaper, she dragged a red pen over the employment ads. With Uncle Alan married, the storefront sold, and life just a total bust, it was time to enter the insanity of a part-time job.

But twenty minutes of the black-and-white print declared her inadequately skilled. Jamie flung the paper onto the small coffee table.

Pounding on her door pulled Jamie off the couch. "Who is it?"

"Me, who else?"

Monet.

Jamie unlatched the locks and let her friend in. "What are you doing here so late?"

Producing a brown paper bag, Monet grinned big. "Rocky Road for you, and Monster Berry for me."

"Are you kidding? That will blow my diet, which will blow the recital. Martin will kill me." Jamie locked the door and followed Monet into the kitchen.

Completely at home, Monet grabbed spoons, peeled the lids off the pint-sized containers. "I'm sick of you pouting over that guy, so we're going to eat, cry, and laugh like best friends should."

Groaning, Jamie plodded toward her bedroom. "Let me get some socks. It's freezing—can't believe you brought ice cream when it's twenty degrees outside."

"Forty. And it's never too cold for ice cream."

Jamie tugged open her top dresser drawer and pulled out a thick wad of wool socks. Bending to put them on, Jamie stilled as a glint of gold caught her eye. The Civil War coin pendant. She'd been so hurt by Sean after the wedding reception that she'd tossed it in the drawer with the intention of never touching it again.

Sean's gorgeous blue eyes moved into her line of determination, breaking it. The metal felt cool against her fingers. She lifted it, an ache worming through her chest. *Oh Sean. . .* Her eyes fluttered closed as she remembered Sean in his suit, walking Mitzi down the aisle. Several young ladies—daughters of the bride's friends—vied for his attention. But he'd not given any of them a second glance. Or dance. But he'd asked Jamie.

Then he'd noticed she was wearing the necklace. A storm erupted in his gaze. He left without another word.

"A love meant to be. . ." Mitzi clearly had misunderstood Sean's interest in Jamie.

"What's that?"

Jamie jumped at Monet's voice.

Her friend tugged the piece from her hand. "Whoa, this is pretty cool. Wait—wasn't your uncle's new wife wearing this at the wedding?"

Jamie retrieved the necklace and returned it to the drawer. "I'm ready for that ice cream." She sidestepped her friend and moved into the living room. Tucking her feet under her, she settled on the sofa with the ice cream.

"Okay, don't think you're going to get away with the silent treatment about this." Monet folded herself into the opposite corner of the couch. "You've been moping for the last few months over that man."

"What man?"

"Oh, don't even try that." Monet spooned the chilled dessert and gave a soft moan as she raised the pint. "To die for." She smiled then nodded. "Go on. What happened? You two danced at the wedding. . . ."

"That necklace—he saw me wearing it. His aunt put it on me, said I should wear it because Sean liked me, because we had a love meant to be." Two spoonfuls sated the burn in the back of her throat. Almost. "I mean, seriously—we only knew each other a little over a month before everything fell apart. How she thinks we were meant for each other, I don't know."

The bridge. . .the fleece prayer. . . *What did that mean, Lord?* Besides trying to teach her not to fleece pray again.

"But you hoped she was right?" Monet asked, her voice soft.

Jamie lowered the pint to the table, drew her knees up onto the cushion, and hugged them. Her vision blurred. "Yeah." Holding the cuffs of her sweatshirt, she pressed her knuckles against her lips. "He's. . ." *Smart. Strong. Encouraging. Stoic. Quiet. Wounded. Sweet.* "So. . ." They got along, it seemed so natural. Talking, walking through Central Park to their bridge.

When did she start thinking of Bow Bridge as *their* bridge? Would they ever meet there again? She thought of the pendant, of her uncle and Mitzi waiting nearly forty years. That was as long as the Israelites had wandered in the desert.

Oh, Lord, please don't make me wait that long. The thing was—would she wait? If it took forever? How on earth had her uncle ever managed? No wonder he'd given up!

"Sean is. . ." What could she say?

"Perfect?"

Jamie met her friend's eyes with an expression she knew bordered on desperation but couldn't stop it. "Am I pathetic?"

"No." Monet set aside her frozen delight. "But if he's not talking to you, Jamie, then you need to move on. I can't stand seeing you moping around."

"But. . .I believe. . ." Why did it sound so foolish? "I believe I'm supposed to be there for him. First Corinthians thirteen— love always perseveres."

"There's persevering, and there's not living."

"I don't want you giving up your life for me." Sean's words echoed through her head.

"Jamie, God wants us to persevere, but He doesn't want us losing ourselves the way you are."

Was she doing it again? Losing her own life trying to fix someone else's? Finding meaning through what she did for others, rather than just being who she was?

When Monet leaned forward, her blond crop swept along her jaw. "Listen, I don't know what Sean feels, but my guess is that you hit a nerve. I mean, I saw the way he looked at you during the wedding. He kept stealing glances, but then when y'all were dancing...it was like he was terrified."

"He is." Jamie batted loose strands from her face. "His father killed himself. His mother drove him to it and convinced Sean he was worthless. We were in the park one night, things were going great—he held my hand." She licked her lips and rested her chin on her knees. "Things got a little tense, we argued. I asked what he was afraid of—he said a woman who couldn't accept him and walked off." She shook her head. "I just wanted him to reach for his dreams."

"Stop trying to fix him."

Oh man. She *was* doing it again. "You're right." She hung her head. "But it's too late. He won't even talk to me now."

Monet chewed her lower lip for a minute, lifted her ice cream, and ate several indulging bites before her eyes enlivened. "Here's the plan...."

Skirting the boxes that still lined the one-room space, Sean navigated his way to the door. Harry had agreed to lease the apartment above his shop to him, on the condition that Sean would work at the shop, repairing bikes. It'd been a no-brainer.

But who on earth knocked on a door this early on a Saturday morning?

"Coming!" Sean threaded his arms through a long-sleeved shirt. He tugged open the door, letting in a blast of icy air. He froze. Not because of the blast of icy air, but because of the man standing on the cement landing that led down to the garage. "Simon."

"Hey, Sean."

What was his older brother doing here? And how? Running a hand through his hair, Sean scrambled for a brain cell. "Wha...

how. . . ?" He shook his head.

Simon snorted. "I saw the wedding announcement for Alan James. Hard to forget the only person who tried to save Dad." Emotion clogged his brother's words. He cleared his throat. "Anyway, he told me where to find you." His brother looked down at the parking lot. "I brought you something. Wanna come check it out?"

Mind reeling from the sudden reintroduction of his brother into his life, Sean glanced over the flimsy iron railing and saw a red Dodge Ram with a tarp-covered trailer. "Yeah, sure. Let me grab some shoes." When he emerged a few minutes later with running shoes on, he spotted his brother unhooking the tarp. Sean hustled down the steps. "So, what is this?" Man, his brother looked like their dad. Spitting image. Creepy.

"Had it sitting in a shed at the back of our property. Lynette wants it gone." His brother lifted a shoulder. "When Alan said you lived here, I thought. . ."

He whipped back the grungy covering—

Sean sucked in a breath at the motorcycle anchored to the flatbed trailer. "Where did you get this?" He ran his hand along the seat, eyeing the body. Adrenaline surged as he realized what this might be. Bending, he eyed the stamps. "Good night! This is a 1962 Panhead FLH Duo Glide." His gaze shot to his brother. "*Where* did you find this?"

With a smile that faltered, his brother broke away. Tucked his head.

Sean hesitated, wondering what he'd said wrong. How did he manage to mess up—

"It was Dad's." Drawing up his shoulders, Simon turned, his eyes wet. "You're so much like him."

Sean gritted his teeth. He'd heard that all his life, along with a string of curses from their mother. "Yeah, Mom made sure I didn't forget that."

"No." Vehemence coated his brother's words as he clamped a hand on Sean's shoulder. "Dad. . .Dad came back from 'Nam different. But he was a *good* man. You were too young to see what was happening, but being like him—it's a good thing." He squeezed the shoulder muscle. "A really good thing, little brother." His brother's eyes glossed. "I'm sorry, Sean. Sorry we left you behind. Sorry for all the things I said back then. I was angry at life."

Burning at the back of his throat kept Sean from replying.

"Mom. . ." Simon swallowed. "She was certifiable, literally. I went into the Navy as soon as I could get her to sign the early entrance papers."

"I remember when you left." It was one of a handful of painful memories locked in Sean's mind.

Harry's blue antique Ford rumbled into the parking lot severing the tenuous moment.

"Anyway," Simon said, swiping his eye with the pad of his thumb. "I've kept this in the shed—for you. It was Dad's pride and joy. Mom told me to run it off a cliff when I was fifteen." He grinned. "I ran it all right—straight into hiding."

Sean stared at the beauty. "Why? Why're you giving it to me?"

"I think he would've wanted you to have it—you used to always squat next to him when he'd tinker on it, and he'd talk, explain what he was doing as if you understood." Simon smiled. "I know you don't remember much, but he was really proud of you. Lynne helped me see that Dad probably saw you as a chance to start over."

Sean grunted. "Some start." It ended in suicide. "Do you remember the day he died?"

His brother sobered. "Every day."

Surprise lit through Sean, his gaze snapping to his brother. In that moment, he realized he didn't even know the man before him. "Lynette—she's your wife?"

"Yeah, married twenty years. Met her right after the Naval Academy. Our son, Will, is eighteen, got an appointment to West Point, and our daughter, Lori, is fourteen."

"You must be proud."

"I am. He's a good kid," Simon said. "Listen, Will's graduation is coming up. I'd like you to join us. If you want to. I know. . .what we did, me, Jen, and Catherine, well—"

"I'd like that, get to know my nephew and niece. Maybe I can give Will some advice on avoiding IEDs."

"That how you got those scars?"

"Yeah. Came with traumatic brain injury and a medical discharge."

"Sorry to hear that."

"No worries."

Hands on his belt, Simon cocked his head. "What about you? Got a wife?"

Sean looked down as a pair of brown eyes flashed before his mind's eye. Jamie. Wearing the coin. The very coin that held the Wolfe legacy and promise of love never failing. When it did fail. With regularity in his life. "No." He looked at Simon. "No wife. Or girlfriend."

"That sounded like a painful answer."

"Getting a Dear John letter while at war. . ."

"Yeah, sounds like you haven't found the right girl yet."

Oh, I found her.

Then what's the problem?

I am.

The truth rankled him as he and his brother rolled the 1962 beauty into the back of the shop, to the rear bay Harry had set up for Sean. After exchanging phone numbers with his brother, Sean promised to see them for Will's graduation party.

A new goal, new energy surged through him at the thought

of restoring the bike. First thing, he'd give it a solid looking over, record the stamps to see if the parts were original—wow, the thing would be worth a pretty penny in pristine shape. But the bike held a greater value. Sentimental value. It felt like he'd gotten back a piece of his life—one of the few *good* pieces.

It was the only way to get Sean Wolfe to stop avoiding her.

Armed with the coin pendant and floundering courage, Jamie stalked up the drive to Harry's Garage. The distinct odor of grease and oil assaulted her as she stepped into the bright fluorescent light of the work bays.

A man in coveralls approached, rubbing his hands on a gray rag. "Can I help you?"

"I'm looking for Sean Wolfe. Is he here?"

With a lecherous grin, the man glanced over his shoulder and hollered, "Wolfe!"

"Yeah?" The shout reverberated off the metal ceiling but seemed to originate from the back.

"Visitor." The man bobbed his head to the back. "Go on."

"Thanks." No doubt her pale pink pea coat stood out among the smelly coveralls, oil pits, and dirty mechanics. Two heads popped over the engine of a BMW as she made her way toward the back. What were they staring at?

She rounded the corner—and stopped short, barely avoiding a collision with a wall of muscle. Her gaze rose and slammed into Mediterranean blues.

Sean's eyes widened. "Jamie." He scowled as he looked around then motioned for her to follow. "What do you want?"

"Be brave. Be strong." That's what Monet had said after their prayer and before she set off. "I need to talk to you."

"Sorry, I'm backed up." Sean indicated to the half-dozen waiting bikes.

"Then we can just talk here." She tugged out her cell phone. "I'll order some pizza or Chinese."

Sean tore his gaze away, irritation clawing through his face. His jaw muscle popped and bounced beneath the scarring. "Look, I don't think that's a good idea."

Smile. Just be calm. "I know, but I do."

Whoops and hollers from behind them turned her cheeks—and Sean's—red. He slammed down the wrench. Stuffed his hands on his hips. "Fine. Let's go out."

She told herself not to take his frustration and terse words personally. "Okay, whichever."

He turned away, hunched over a counter, and grabbed something from behind it. When he pivoted toward her, hand extended, Jamie stilled. Looked at him. Then at the motorcycle helmet he held. An accident on a bike could wipe out her entire career and dreams. "No way."

He smirked. "Then no dice."

Heart thumping, Jamie took a cursory glance around his work area. The motorcycles were sport bikes. Which meant they were fast.

"The red one," Sean said.

Her gaze lit on a sport bike in a deep crimson color propped near the rear door. Before she could answer, Sean stepped forward and slid the black dome over her head. He popped up the visor as he snapped the chin strap. He tapped it. "Looks good."

Mouth dry, she silently chided Monet for not predicting this. "What if you pass out?"

He grinned. "Only when I'm stressed. You planning to stress me out?" He took her hand. "C'mon." Helmet on, Sean straddled the bike and glanced back to her.

Jamie swallowed—hard. On a bike there was no room for ladylike distance. "No." Not being able to afford The Juilliard would be a moot point if they wrecked. She shook her head, palms clammy. "One crash—"

Sean took her hand and drew her to the bike. "Trust me."

Oh, Lord. . .why did he ask me to do that?

Tucking her messenger bag around to the back, she licked her lips and climbed on. Arms wrapped around his waist, she tensed as the engine roared to life. Hoops and hollers followed them out of the garage and onto the congested four-lane road. The two-minute ride to Luigi's proved terrifying. . . exhilarating!

Weaving through the lot, Sean aimed the bike toward the front. They parked in a narrow slot by the door, and Sean helped her with the helmet.

"What'd you think?"

Jamie looked into the eyes that could convince her to walk off a cliff, and right now, those beautiful irises sparkled. Alive and vibrant. He was monitoring her, gauging her reaction. In that moment, she realized he'd shared something special with her. She had to admit both the ride and the man before her were thrilling. "It's fantastic!"

His smile could light the night! Slowly, still watching her, he nodded. "Yeah."

Inside, they sat across from each other in a small window table and ordered. Jamie set her messenger bag on an empty chair between them. "Thanks."

Sean paused in wiping the condensation from his glass of water. "For what?"

"Coming."

He hesitated then nodded.

Food delivered, they bypassed awkward conversation and dug into their meals—he a bowl of fettuccini Alfredo, her a Cobb salad. After twenty minutes of avoiding each other's gaze and pretending their food to be gourmet, Jamie couldn't take it any longer.

Quietly, she set down her fork, took a sip of water, then opened her messenger bag. She rummaged through it, searching for the pendant. As her hand dug deeper, the bag slid. . . .

Thunk. It landed next to Sean.

Groaning, Jamie noticed several papers skidded under his chair. "Sorry."

Sean retrieved them. Holding the small bundle, he tapped them into line. He cocked his head, reading. "What's this?"

Jamie reached for them, but Sean plucked one out as she did and let her take the rest. But her focus rested on the one he scanned.

Her heart seized. The Juilliard application. "Can I have that back, please?"

Sean's gaze bounced from the paper to her. "The Juilliard?"

Anger skittered around the edges of her composure as a blush heated her face. "Please, let me have it."

"I thought you gave up on this?" His gaze narrowed. "Are you going to turn that in?"

When he wagged the paper in front of her, she snatched it back. "No." She stuffed it back in her satchel and refocused on finding the pendant.

"Why?"

"Because."

"Because why?"

She bit down on the snide comment she wanted to make. "I can't afford it."

"Get a loan."

Her fingers grazed the metal piece. Ahh, success! "Here. At the wedding, Gail—Mitzi—gave me this." She lifted the coin pendant from the front pouch. "And I know it really upset you that I had it, so I want to return it to you. I know it's important to your family." No, she really didn't, but more than that, she didn't want grief between them. She wanted to get back on that road to beautiful exploration of life with the man before her.

Sean stared at the piece as she gently laid it on the table next to his hand. . .which slowly coiled into a fist and withdrew. He sat back, hands in his lap, and looked toward the front door. As if contemplating leaving the restaurant, leaving her.

Okay, not exactly what she planned. "I'm sorry, Sean. I didn't mean. . .Mitzi. . ." She closed her eyes. *I'm botching this.* "I never meant. . ."

He shoved it back across the table. "Keep it." He tossed down a twenty and pushed to his feet. "I need to get back."

"Wait." She grabbed the pendant and her bag then hurried after him. "Sean, wait." She caught up with him at the bike as he stuffed on his helmet. "Stop doing this, Sean. Stop shutting me out."

Swinging his leg over the back of the bike, he shoved his gaze in her direction. "Trust me, it's better this way."

Jamie stepped to the bike. Placed a hand over his on the gear. "No. No, it's not." She waited till his gaze met hers. "Trust *me.*"

Again, he looked away, tormented. "That coin. . .it means things. Things I don't believe in."

Incredulity gripped her. "What? Like love?"

He held her gaze for a moment then quietly said, "Yeah." He revved the gear, severing any reply. And hope.

Sean watched as Jamie walked out of the garage after their impromptu lunch. Her shoulders sagged, drawing him after her. Sun streamed down, drawing a line of demarcation between the darkness in the shop—*in my life*—and the world, life. *Love.* The thought stopped him cold at the wide-mouthed entrance, watching. Head tucked, she wiped her face.

Tears?

Something inside him knotted. What kind of guy makes a girl cry? But that pendant, knowing his aunt had held on to it for almost forty years, knowing its legacy. . .he didn't want anything to do with it. And yet, when he'd told her to keep it, that he didn't believe in it or the legacy. . .he'd never forget the pain gouged in her beautiful brown eyes. The gold flecks that normally sparked like glitter lost their luster.

You're a heel.

Just like Dad.

Sean rubbed the back of his neck. Riddled with guilt and confusion, he headed to his apartment and locked the door. There, he dropped against the bench to the total workout system and cradled his head. The waters of his life trembled, slowly heating till they worked into a boil.

Over the next hour, he took out his frustration on the lat bar and the leg press. Still thrumming with frustration, he grabbed his hoodie. A run was the only way to clear his mind when he was this addled. He snatched his keys—and when his gaze hit the unopened letters, he froze.

He'd stopped reading them. They'd overloaded him with guilt and feel-good stuff he just didn't know what to do with. He lifted one, thinking about the times he and Jamie sat on the bench facing Bow Bridge and talked about the letters.

One of the only times in his life when things felt right. Quiet. . .peaceful.

Sean stuffed a letter in his pocket and set off. As if one of the magnetic poles of the earth had shifted, his body kept aiming toward Central Park. Sean corrected course. He wouldn't go there. Wouldn't give her false hope. Wouldn't bait himself with seeing her. Beautiful, warmhearted, and sweet, she saw past his scars. Past his grouchiness. What was with her showing up today? Seeking him out. His heart had clawed its way into his throat when he spotted her walking across the grease pit in her soft, pink coat. Him a grease monkey. Her a beauty. Like water and oil.

"What are you afraid of, Sean?" Her words snaked through the budding branches swaying overhead. Only as he noticed the branches did he realize where he was.

He stopped short. How did he get here?

"Why did you come?"

The soft words slapped him in the gut. He turned and saw Jamie on the bridge. Her eyes were puffy and red-rimmed. His wince couldn't be helped—he'd made her cry. Seeing her like this, seeing the strong woman who'd braved his backlash reduced to tears. . .

I'm a coward.

"If you don't believe in love, why come?" Her words cracked.

Breathing deep as his heart rate settled, he made his way toward her. Palmed the rail of the bridge. "There's not much I believe in anymore."

"That's a shame."

Gaze on the blue sky and cotton-ball clouds, he nodded. "Yeah. I know."

Jamie stood beside him, back against the rail. "What *do* you believe in then?"

"You." The word escaped so quick, he wondered if he'd really said it. But the way her gaze snapped to his told him he had.

"What do you mean?" Voice as small and squeaky as a mouse, Jamie shifted toward him.

Yeah, what did he mean? "I don't know." He ground his molars. "I come from bad stock, Jamie." Man, it felt worse than breathing mustard gas. He didn't want her to misunderstand. This wasn't about pity. It was about protecting her. "I don't want to hurt you. Besides, you deserve someone better."

"What if I don't want someone else?"

He cast her a sidelong glance.

"I know you're hurting," she said. "I know you're transferring that hurt, that pain, to me." She slowly shook her head, the long dark strands curling and bouncing. "But Sean, I'm not going anywhere. I know where I belong."

It felt as if someone had detonated a brick of C4 in his chest. *Run.* It was his only thought. His feet burned to pound the pavement again. His heart throbbed, panicked at the thought of giving this a shot.

Jamie grinned.

Disoriented by her smile and unwavering stance, he barely noticed her pluck something from his pocket.

"Another letter? Shall we read it?" She took his hand and led him to the bench.

But Sean had this deep foreboding that she was leading him to a much different place. . .a terrifying place.

Love.

Chapter 8

Songbirds chirped overhead in the freshly budding branches of the trees. Jamie couldn't help but draw a parallel to what was blossoming between her and Sean. It wasn't that he didn't like her. She was certain he did—a lot, which scared him. While she didn't know all of his past, she knew it was painful enough to force Mitzi to hide her identity and relationship to him. Painful enough to divide siblings.

Unfolding the letter, she focused her attention on the words, not on Sean, who had yet to join her on the bench. Maybe it was too much like yielding, something she was certain he rarely did.

Lord, give me wisdom. Show me how to reach past his fears, his pain, to his heart.

She scanned the words. "It's from your grandfather, but. . ." Jamie went to the next page and drew back. "Wow. The date—oh my!"

"What?" Sean eased down next to her, leaning in to see.

"This is a letter from World War Two."

Sean took the letter. Bent forward, elbows on his knees, he started reading. "This is my *great*-grandfather. I was named after him."

"Sean?"

A cockeyed grin. "No, my given name is Henry William, but mom hated the family names, so she called me Sean."

"So, what's it say?"

"He's writing from 'Somewhere in France,'" Sean said. "'Dear Helen'—that's his sister—'Just a quick note while I have a chance. Wanted to let you know I ran across someone who knows Bernie. Amazing thing that—imagine of all the people I run into. But it just reminded me. . .I need to thank you for all you did for me, Carl, and Lois—for taking care of us, for protecting us. The things I'm doing here remind me of your sacrifice. And boy, do I sure know I gave you a run for your money as a lad. . . .'"

TO SING
ANOTHER DAY

by Kim Vogel Sawyer

Dedication

For Mom,
whose faith could move mountains

*[Charity] beareth all things, believeth all things,
hopeth all things, endureth all things.
Charity never faileth.*
1 Corinthians 13:7–8

Chapter 1

New York City, September 1941

"Henry, are you upset with me?" Helen Wolfe held her breath as she waited for her brother's answer. Henry's pose—elbows on knees, head slung low—indicated sadness. Henry was a good boy, helpful beyond his years, but at fifteen his moods were often mercurial. Although in the past she'd reprimanded him for moodiness, she wouldn't blame him if he spouted angrily at her now.

Slowly Henry lifted his head and met Helen's gaze. "I don't like it. Wish it didn't have to be. But. . ." He released a deep sigh. "I understand."

Helen's breath whooshed out in an expulsion of mingled relief and regret. She leaned forward from her perch on the red velvet sofa. Reaching across the expanse of faded cabbage rose carpet, she grasped Henry's hand. They both squeezed hard—a silent communication that spoke more eloquently than words. Tears stung Helen's eyes. Henry'd already lost so much. This wasn't fair, but what else could they do?

"I'll get it back for you somehow." She stated the promise with more confidence than she felt.

Henry nodded then pushed to his feet, releasing Helen's hand. "I'll fetch it." He scuffed from the parlor, his heels dragging over the scarred pine floorboards that led to the bungalow's bedrooms.

Helen covered her face with her hands, fighting tears. She wouldn't cry. She wouldn't! Would tears bring back Mom and Dad? Of course not. Would tears make Richard change his mind and marry her? No. Tears fixed nothing. They served no purpose except to frighten her younger brothers and sister. She drew in fortifying breaths, and when Henry emerged from the hallway, she was sitting upright, her chin high and her eyes dry, although her insides still quaked.

Henry pressed the twenty-dollar gold piece into her palm. The engraving glared up at her, accusing her with its message: "Love never fails." She certainly felt like a failure, taking Henry's inheritance—his only belonging of value—from him.

Closing her fingers over the coin, she rose and wrapped one arm around Henry in a fierce hug. Then she stepped back and assumed a brisk tone to conceal her inner heartache. "Check on Lois if I'm not back in an hour, and give her another dose of tonic." The medicine stifled the child's cough enough to allow her to rest, and rest was important the doctor had said.

"I will. Don't worry."

"I'll put supper on the table when I return, so tell Carl to stay out of the icebox." Their twelve-year-old brother would devour the entire baked chicken in one sitting if Helen let him.

"I'll tie it shut if I have to."

Helen headed for the pegs beside the front door where her knitted cap and scarf hung next to Mom's old wool coat. Outside the oval window, rain fell in a drizzly curtain. Helen grimaced. The heavy coat would do little more than absorb the moisture, but she had no other covering, so she tugged the plaid wool with its round wooden buttons over her simple cotton dress and covered her curly hair with the bold red cap. Her hand on the doorknob, she sent Henry one more sorrowful look.

Henry waved at her, scowling. "Just go already." Then his lips quirked into a grin. "Hope you get a lot for it." His bravado pierced Helen more deeply than pouting or fury would have.

The coin in her pocket, she set out into the dreary late afternoon.

∞

Bernie O'Day swished the feather duster over the shelves climbing the wall behind the tall wooden counter of his family's pawnshop. His pop had dusted twice a day—once before opening and again before closing—and Bernie followed the familiar routine partly out of habit, partly because it felt right to do what Pop had done.

He whistled as he worked, the tune for "There Is Power in the Blood" warbling from his pursed lips. Pop's whistling had been clear and sweet, where Bernie's sometimes hit a sour note or rasped into breathy blasts, but there wasn't anyone in the shop to complain, so he continued onward to the chorus. With each shrill hoot for "power," he gave the stiff feathers a sharp flick. By the time he finished, the rows of the little ceramic figurines and gold-plated statues stood completely devoid of so much as a speck of dust.

Satisfied, Bernie wheezed out the final note and plunked the duster under the counter. He glanced at the pendulum clock tick-tocking on the wall. Three more minutes till closing. His stomach rumbled in readiness. But even though he hadn't seen a customer all afternoon, he wouldn't put out the CLOSED sign one minute early. Pop had instilled a solid work ethic in Bernie—*"Always stand true to your word, son, and you'll never have reason to hang your head in shame."* The painted sign above the plate-glass window of the O'Day Pawn Shop stated HOURS: 9:00 AM TO 6:00 PM MONDAY THROUGH SATURDAY, and he'd honor the hours, just as Pop always had.

At one minute till six, Bernie removed his bleached apron and hung it neatly on a hook on the back wall. Then, sliding

159

his hand over his short-cropped hair to smooth the strands into place, he headed for the door to lock up. Just as he turned the cardboard placard hanging on a string inside the door to CLOSED, a young woman in a rain-soaked plaid coat and bedraggled knit cap trotted to the opposite side of the glass door.

Her gaze fell on the sign, and her blue eyes widened into an expression of panic. Then her shoulders wilted, and she turned away, shoving her hands deep into the pockets of the threadbare coat. Her dejected pose stung Bernie's heart. Without a second thought, he gave the brass lock a twist and flung the door wide, causing the little bell above the door to clang raucously. The girl spun around, her rosy lips forming an O of surprise. Brown curls framed her cheeks, which were pink from the cool breeze.

Bernie smiled. "Did'ja need something?" He suspected she could use a new coat. He had several from which to choose, and he'd make her a good deal.

She pointed to the little sign. "Aren't you closed?"

"Haven't locked up yet. C'mon in."

Uncertainty marred her brow. She hunched into her soggy coat and nibbled her lower lip.

Bernie held the door wider. "At least get out of the drizzle for a minute or two. You look chilled all the way through."

A shiver shook her frame, and it seemed to spur her to action. She darted forward, scooting past him into the store. Bernie let the door close then turned to face her. She stood rooted between aisles, dripping, her hands clasped in front of her. "I'm sorry to be so late," she said, her voice very prim although it quavered slightly. "It took longer to walk than I thought it would."

Bernie offered a smile, hoping to put her at ease. "No need to apologize." From the looks of her, she'd covered a fair distance in the rain. He wondered why she hadn't taken a trolley. Quicker—and drier—than walking. Her drooping curls and waterlogged coat gave her a sad, waiflike appearance that stirred his sympathy. He gestured to the stove in the far corner of the room, where a few coals still glowed in the round belly. "Why don'tcha move closer over there—warm up a little. Then you can tell me what you're shoppin' for. I got pretty much anything a person needs." Pop had prided himself on their wide array of merchandise. Bernie felt certain whatever the girl needed he'd have it.

She hung her head, toying with one limp curl. "Actually, I'm not here to make a purchase. I. . .I'd hoped. . ." Her voice trailed away, and she stared off to the side.

Since she still hadn't moved toward the stove, Bernie headed in that direction. To his relief, she scuffed along behind him and released a little sigh when she reached the warmth radiating from the black iron. She stood stiffly beside the potbellied stove, her arms folded over her ribs. He waited, but she didn't speak.

Leaning his elbow on the counter, Bernie assumed a casual air he hoped might put her at ease. She seemed as skittish as a newborn colt. "What is it you're needing today, miss?"

She jerked as if roused from a sound sleep. Her hand slipped into her pocket, and she withdrew a round gold coin. "I need to sell this."

Bernie pinched the coin between his thumb and finger and held it to the bare bulb hanging overhead. The Liberty twenty-dollar piece had been rubbed nearly smooth on the front side, and someone had carefully engraved the words "Love never fails" in an arch on the upper part of the coin. Below, "W.W." and "Central Park" filled the bottom half. Bernie rubbed his thumb over the engraving, his brow puckered.

"William Wolfe was my grandfather," the girl said. She bobbed her chin toward the coin, her eyes shining. "He gave this coin to my grandmother as a token of his affection after fighting in the Civil War. It's been in our family for almost a hundred years."

Bernie wondered why she would part with it when the coin clearly meant a great deal to her. He turned it over to examine the back side. The tips of the eagle's wings were marred by some sort of grayish blobs. Bernie angled the coin toward the girl. "What happened here?"

"My father soldered a pin back onto it so my mother could wear it as jewelry, but the fixture fell off. Does. . .does that diminish its value?"

Bernie hated to tell her a defaced coin held little monetary value even without the lumps of solder on its back. He rubbed the coin between his thumb and finger, trying to decide what to say. Then, without conscious thought, he blurted, "Why are you selling it?"

The girl ducked her head, her cheeks flooding with color. "To be honest, Mr. O'Day, I'm sorely in need of the funds. My sister has been ill for over a month. I had to quit my job to take care of her, and the doctor bills have eaten up what little reserve I had in my bank account."

He wondered why she was caring for her sister. Where were her parents? But he decided not to be nosy. He'd already made her uncomfortable with his blunt question. He stepped behind the counter and pulled out his cash box and pad of tickets. "I tell you what. . . Since this is a twenty-dollar piece, I can give you a straight trade—twenty dollars for the coin. Does that sound reasonable?"

The stricken look on her face gave the answer. Bernie bit on the inside of his cheek, his business side warring with his sympathetic side. He'd never recover even twenty dollars for the coin. Who would want it besides the Wolfe family? But the girl clearly needed money. A Bible verse flitted through the fringes of his mind: "Inasmuch as ye have done it unto one of the least of these..."

Bernie pulled three ten-dollar bills and two fives from the cash drawer then slammed the lid closed before he could change his mind. He picked up a pencil and quickly scrawled the amount—$40—on the ticket and added a description, reading it aloud as he wrote. "One twenty-dollar gold piece, inscribed with 'Love never fails. W.W. Central Park.' " He looked at the girl, who hovered next to the stove, her fingers woven together. "Your name?"

"H–Helen Wolfe." She skittered forward, her gaze on the short pile of bills. "You're buying it?"

Bernie shot her a quick grin. "Isn't that what you wanted?"

She nodded, her drying curls bouncing around her cheeks. "Yes. Yes, that's what I wanted." Yet sadness lingered in her blue eyes. "Th–thank you very much, Mr. O'Day."

"Bernie," he said. At her puzzled look, he added, "My pop's Mr. O'Day. I'm just Bernie."

A soft laugh trickled from her lips. An enchanting, lighthearted sound that broadened Bernie's grin. It pleased him more than he could understand that he'd brought that laugh out of her.

"Thank you, Bernie."

He liked the way his name sounded in her musical voice. "You're welcome. Now. . ." He turned the ticket pad to face her. "This is how things work. I put the coin away for thirty days, and anytime during those thirty days you can come in and reclaim it with this ticket and the same amount of money I gave you. After thirty days, I put the coin out as merchandise with a price on it, and if you want it back, you'll have to pay the full price. Does that make sense to you?" The only way he'd break even on this deal was if she returned. Bernie didn't hold out much hope of that happening, and it saddened him.

But not for himself.

Her blue eyes dimmed, but she nodded. "Yes, that makes sense."

"All right then. Sign here." He pointed to a line at the bottom of the ticket and watched as she picked up the pencil and wrote her name in neat, slanting script. He tore the ticket from the book and handed it to her. "Don't lose that now."

She folded the yellow sheet and slipped it into her pocket. "I won't." Her gaze seemed to caress the coin, which lay on the counter. "I truly hope to reclaim it. It. . .it means a great deal to my brother since my father left it to him."

Bernie wished he could coax another smile from her lips. He dipped down slightly, catching her eye. "I'll say a prayer that it finds its way back to you. God has a way of workin' things out even when we don't think it's possible."

She didn't smile, and when she spoke, her words chilled him with their finality. "I thank you for the prayer, Bernie, but it's been a good long while since I felt as though I could trust God to answer my prayers." Snatching up the bills, she wadded them in her fist and darted for the door. The bell clanged wildly when she departed, hurting Bernie's ears nearly as much as her pained statement had hurt his heart.

Bernie lifted the coin and tipped it this way and that, watching the play of light on the carved surface. His gaze drifted to the doorway, where Helen Wolfe had disappeared. He didn't know what hardships she'd encountered, but he did know God could bring healing. And he sensed the coin could play a role in her receiving that healing.

Crossing to his rolltop desk—the desk where Pop had sat to do paperwork, pay bills, and study his old leather-bound Bible—he pulled a silver key from his pocket and unlocked a tiny drawer. He placed the coin in the drawer and locked it again. Then, his hand on the drawer's handle, he closed his eyes and offered a solemn prayer. "Lord, I'm trusting You to find a way for Helen to reclaim this coin. Bring it back to her, and when she holds it again, let it serve as a reminder of Your perfect presence in her life."

Peace chased away the feelings of melancholy his brief encounter with Helen Wolfe had brought. With a smile on his heart, Bernie hurriedly closed the shop and headed up the back stairs for his supper, satisfied the Lord would work, as He always did.

Chapter 2

Helen waited until Carl had mopped up the shiny patches of grease from his plate with the last slice of bread before instructing him to get started on his homework.

The boy scowled and slumped in his chair. "But tomorrow's Saturday! Got the whole weekend to do it. Why do I gotta do it now?"

Helen missed her parents the most in these moments when she was forced to be the disciplinarian. "Because that's always been the rule, Carl. Homework before play." She softened her tone. "Besides, if you get it tucked out of the way, you can enjoy your weekend without the task hanging over your head. Wouldn't that be better?"

Carl grumbled under his breath, but he pushed away from the table and clomped to his bedroom. A door slamming let her know he wasn't pleased.

Helen sighed and reached to begin clearing the table. Lois, her pale cheeks and thin hands giving evidence of her lengthy bout with pneumonia, picked up her bowl and spoon and started to rise. She wobbled. Helen rushed to her sister's aid. "Here, honey, let me do that. You go stretch out on the sofa with a book and rest."

Lois sighed and scuffed her way to the parlor where she flopped onto the sofa, the too-short hem of her nightgown exposing her skinny ankles. Helen's heart caught. Lois had lost so much weight over the past month. Somehow she'd have to encourage the child to eat more than broth and crackers now that her fever was finally gone, hopefully for good. With the money she'd received for the coin, she'd buy some of Lois's favorite foods. Perhaps that would entice her to eat.

Pushing aside her worry for Lois, she carried the stack of dishes to the kitchen and placed them in the sink. As she reached for the tarnished brass spigot, Henry moved in front of her. "I'll wash," he said.

Helen shot her brother a startled look. Henry hated housework. She had to battle with him to pick up his dirty socks. She teasingly pressed the back of her hand to his forehead. "Are you sick?"

He offered a sheepish grin. "Need to talk to you. Figure this's as good a place as any." He angled a quick look over his shoulder toward the parlor, where Lois now snoozed on the sofa with a book open, upside down, across her knees. "Didn't want to talk at supper and upset the youngsters."

Helen's chest ached. At fifteen, Henry was a youngster, too, but he was being forced to grow up too quickly. She put her hand on his shoulder, all teasing forgotten. "What is it, Henry?"

Henry snapped off the water and shifted to look at her. His face—still boyish despite the hints of impending manhood—turned serious. "I think I need to look for a job."

Helen's hand fell away, and she shook her head wildly. "No, Henry! You know how important school was to Mom and Dad. They'd roll over in their graves if—"

"But that money you got for the coin won't last forever. Some groceries and a load of coal—that's all it'll cover." Henry spoke in a fervent whisper, his brow pinched tight. "You've used up the money Dad saved for you to go to the Conservatory. And your job cleaning at the hotel. . .it doesn't give us any extra.

How're you gonna go to the Conservatory now?"

Henry's words stabbed as fiercely as a knife. Her dream, and her parents' dream for her, had been to complete the music courses at the Music Conservatory and become part of an opera company. But Mom and Dad's death two years ago had stolen Helen's opportunity. She'd allowed the dream to fizzle and die, too. With her brother's mention of the Conservatory, the dream tried to rekindle itself from the ashes in her heart, but she couldn't allow so much as a flicker to rise. Only a selfish person would continue chasing a dream when she had three younger siblings dependent upon her.

"You know I've given up on the Conservatory." Helen angled her way in front of Henry and began slipping dishes into the sink before the water turned tepid. She scrubbed, the activity a means of dispelling the longing that filled her as she considered singing on a stage.

"But you shouldn't give it up." Henry lifted a coarse towel and dried the plate she handed him. "Even Richard said—"

Helen dropped the plate and dishrag and whirled to face Henry. "Do not speak his name again."

Henry gawked at her, mouth open.

She drew in a breath, gentling her tone. "Richard Mason has no bearing on anything anymore, Henry. He's gone. Talking about him is too. . .painful."

Henry gulped and placed the dry plate on the shelf. "I just know he really wanted you to become a singer—the same way he's doing." Henry flicked a glance at her. "So you don't think if you go to the Conservatory, he'll change his mind and marry you after all?"

Helen frowned. "Is that why you want me to finish the music course? So Richard will marry me?"

Henry shrugged, his head low. "Thought that's what you wanted. To travel together. Sing together, as husband and wife."

At one time, it was what she'd wanted. How many nights had she lain awake considering her future with Richard? But Henry didn't know Richard hadn't broken their engagement because she had no money for the Conservatory. And she'd never tell Henry—or Carl or Lois—the truth. Why burden them?

She sighed. "Sometimes things just don't work out." A man who could callously demand that she place her beloved brothers and sister in an orphanage had no place in her life. "Besides that, singing on an opera stage is a rather childish desire." Her voice caught. Childish or not, letting go of the long-held plan had proved much harder than letting go of Richard. "I'm twenty-one now. It's time for me to let go of youthful daydreams. But as for you—" She sent him a stern look. "You are going to finish school. And that's that!"

Henry drew back his shoulders. His jaw jutted stubbornly. "Helen, you might be the oldest, but I'm the oldest male in our family. That makes me the man. And I've made up my mind. We need more money coming in, so I'm going to find a job." His eyes squinted as he glared at her. "And you can't stop me."

Wednesday afternoon, while Bernie assisted a customer in perusing his selection of gemstone rings, the little bell above the pawnshop door jangled. Bernie glanced past Mrs. Horton's flowery, kettle-shaped hat to smile at a young man who hovered in the doorway, allowing in a rush of cool, damp air. Winter seemed to be sneaking up on them early this year.

"I'll be with you in a minute," Bernie called, gesturing. "Step on over by the stove, if you like, and warm your hands."

The boy, gloveless, blew into his cupped palms for a moment before inching his way toward the potbellied stove. "Thanks, mister."

Bernie nodded then turned his attention back to Mrs. Horton. The older woman already wore a ring on every finger, yet she searched the flat display case for another gem to add to her collection. Bernie appreciated Mrs. Horton's business, but sometimes he wondered if she sought happiness in places that would never satisfy.

While Mrs. Horton fingered each ring by turn, Bernie flicked a surreptitious glance at the youth who hunkered beside the stove. Brown curly hair stuck out from beneath the brim of his newsboy-style cap. A tan jacket with patched elbows looked to be at least one size too small for the boy's lanky frame. Despite the boy's somewhat ragged appearance, his face and hands were clean, his clothes neatly patched. Bernie'd had trouble in the past with teenage boys pilfering stock, but he suspected he could trust this one. He turned his full focus to Mrs. Horton.

"All right, Bernie, I believe I'll take this opal ring." Mrs. Horton's wrinkled face bloomed into a bright smile. "I counted eighteen stones in all, perfectly matched! How much is this one?"

"Thirty-seven fifty."

The woman didn't even flinch. She opened her pocketbook and withdrew crisp bills. Bernie noted the youth watching, his eyes wide. The boy almost seemed to salivate.

"There you are," Mrs. Horton said. "And if you receive earrings that might coordinate with the ring, you send me a message, will you? I prefer drop earrings, with a back that screws into place rather than simply clamps." She slipped the ring onto her right pointer finger, above a sapphire and diamond ring, and held her hand straight out. The opals shimmered with color in the light. "This ring will be lovely with my blue dress."

Bernie gave Mrs. Horton her change and then walked her to the door. When he turned from closing the door behind the woman, he discovered the youth next to the counter, very near the cash box, which Bernie had left on top of the wooden surface. But even though his eyes were on the box, his hands were deep in his pockets, as if controlling an urge to snatch the box and run. Bernie hustled to the counter and put the box underneath before temptation overcame the boy.

"Now then." Bernie brushed his palms together and fixed his attention on the young man. "What can I do for you?"

The boy whipped off his cap, revealing thick, tousled hair in need of a cut. He glanced around. "You run this place on your own?"

Bernie frowned, unease wriggling through his middle. Had he misjudged this boy's intentions? He hoped the kid wasn't scoping out his shop. Bernie chose to answer with a question of his own. "Why do you want to know?"

The boy raised his chin and met Bernie's gaze squarely. "I was hoping maybe you could use some help. I need a job."

Bernie looked the boy up and down. Tall, slender, with an open face holding a hint of defiance. Or desperation. Bernie couldn't be sure. He examined the boy's face more closely. No whiskers dotted the youth's smooth cheeks. He frowned. "Aren't you a little young to be job-seeking?"

His jaw jutted a little farther. "I'm old enough."

"How old?"

For a moment, the boy pursed his lips, his eyes flicking around as if afraid to look directly at Bernie. If the kid lied, Bernie would boot him out in an instant. He couldn't trust a liar.

The boy drew in a breath that straightened his shoulders. "I turned fifteen in August." He rushed on. "But I'm strong for my age, and I'm a fast learner. I'm willing to do anything you need—cleaning, deliveries, anything you say. And I can start tomorrow if you'd like."

Bernie rested his elbow on the counter edge. Pride nearly

pulsed from the boy. Although he'd encountered many young men seeking employment and had turned down every one of them—he just didn't need the extra hands in his small shop—there was something about this boy that tugged at him. He chose his words carefully. "Seems to me a fifteen-year-old ought to be spending his days in school instead of at a job."

The boy hung his head. "I'll finish my schooling. . .someday. But right now. . ." He raised his face, and the desperation Bernie thought he'd glimpsed earlier returned. "My family needs the money I can make." He blew out a frustrated breath. "I've been walking the streets since last Saturday, and nobody'll give me a chance. If you say no, too, I don't know what I'll do."

Bernie ambled from behind the counter and curled his arm across the boy's shoulders. He drew him to the pair of rocking chairs that had sat in the corner for as long as Bernie could remember. He and Pop had sat there on evenings, sometimes talking, sometimes not, but always at ease with each other. Even though Pop was gone now, Bernie still viewed the rockers as a place of comfort. He gave the boy a gentle push toward one, and he sank into the other.

Holding his hand out in invitation, he said, "Why don'tcha tell me why your family needs money so badly. Might be there's a solution that wouldn't involve you dropping out of school."

The boy sat erect in the chair, his feet planted wide. "My folks died a couple years back, and my sister's been taking care of my little brother and sister and me ever since. She has a job, but it doesn't pay as much as the one she had to give up when my little sister came down with bad pneumonia. She was supposed to go to the Conservatory—become a singer—but she had to use her Conservatory money to pay our bills while my little sister was so sick. Now we've got hospital and medicine bills and not enough money to cover it all."

Bernie's scalp tingled. This story sounded familiar.

"Winter's coming on, and the doc says if we don't want Lois to get sick again, we gotta keep the house warm. Takes a heap of coal to keep the furnace going, and I don't see how we'll be able to do it on my sister's measly salary. So. . ." The boy gulped. "I need a job."

Bernie looked into the youth's earnest face, the blue eyes glowing with determination. Suddenly another face flashed in Bernie's mind's eye. He sat upright. "Your sister—is her name Helen?"

The boy's jaw dropped. "How'd you know that?"

Bernie set the rocker into motion, trying to combat his churning emotions. The sympathy that had compelled him to overpay Helen Wolfe now spilled over on her brother. Even so, a hint of suspicion tickled the corners of his mind. "Did she send you here to ask for a job?"

"No, sir." The boy shook his head, making the brown curls—so like his sister's—bounce on his forehead. "She's plumb irate with me for even hunting for work. Wants me in school. We've argued about it every day, but we need the money, so. . ."

Bernie pinched his chin, thinking. The boy's sister was wise to want the youth to finish his schooling. In these changing times, an education was becoming more and more important. But clearly the family needed help, and for reasons Bernie couldn't begin to comprehend, he wanted to help them. "What's your name?"

"Henry, sir. Henry William Wolfe."

"Well, Henry William Wolfe, I could use someone around here to organize the stock room, keep the sidewalk outside cleared of leaves and snow, and do some general cleaning."

The boy's face lit. "Oh?"

"But I don't need somebody full-time."

The elation died. "Oh."

"And I happen to agree with your sister that you should be in school."

Henry crunched his lips in a tight line.

Bernie stifled a chortle. "But if you're willing to work after school and all day on Saturdays, I'm thinking maybe we can find a compromise that'll help your family and also satisfy your sister. What do you think?"

Henry bounded to his feet. He stuck out his hand. "I think we got a deal!"

Chapter 3

Although Bernie had hired Henry out of sympathy, thinking he was doing the boy a favor, it took less than a week for him to change his attitude. Henry became an unexpected blessing, providing not only assistance but a level of companionship Bernie hadn't even realized he needed. After working side by side with Pop from the time he was knee-high, he'd missed his father's presence in the shop. Busyness had held the loneliness at bay, but now that Henry came in every day, Bernie discovered the pleasure of having someone around to talk to, laugh with, and teach the trade.

As Henry'd said, he was a quick learner, and by the end of the boy's third week in the shop, Bernie felt secure enough to leave Henry in charge for brief periods of time so he could go next door and sip a cup of coffee or fetch a newspaper from the stand on the corner. He enjoyed the new sense of freedom having an employee offered, and he wondered how he'd managed so long on his own.

Bernie started out giving Henry a fifty-cent piece at the end of each school day and two silver dollars at closing on Saturday. As a boy, he'd always liked the larger coins, and he figured Henry would, too. So it surprised him when he held out the round half-dollar the third Friday of October and Henry sheepishly asked to receive his pay in dimes and nickels.

Bernie coughed a laugh, dropping the coin back into his

cash box and fishing out four slim dimes and two nickels. "You wantin' some rattlin'-around money in your pocket?"

Henry shrugged into his jacket. "No, sir. I don't carry it long—just hand it over to Helen. But my little brother, Carl, has been doing my chores since I'm here in the afternoons. I figured it might be nice to give him a little something now and then—a dime or nickel—so he could go see a picture show or buy a candy bar as a treat."

Carl nodded in approval. "That's a right good idea." He tipped his head, giving the boy a serious look. "It'll also make it easier to tithe." Henry had indicated he and his brother and sisters attended Faith Chapel each Sunday. "You're givin' a portion of your earnings to the Lord, aren't you?"

Henry hung his head. "To be honest, Mr. O'Day, I haven't been. I know Dad tithed. Saw him drop money in the offering plate after every payday. But since he and Mom died. . ." He scratched his head, making his newly cropped hair stand on end. Those curls, even short, were untamable. "Just never seems as though there's enough to give to the church."

"You know, Henry, it's always been my experience that when we give God a portion of what He's given us, He makes the rest stretch to meet our needs. Not that we give to get, understand—we give because we love Him and want to honor Him. But I think you'd find a real blessing in giving God a portion of your earnings."

Henry examined Bernie's face, his brow puckered thoughtfully. "I'll do some considering on that, Mr. O'Day. And talk to Helen about it, too."

The mention of Helen sent Bernie's pulse racing. Although he hadn't seen her since that day over six weeks ago when she came in to sell her grandfather's gold coin, she'd often crept through his thoughts. Having Henry in the store each day talking about his sister contributed to Bernie's fascination with the young woman. He'd had no more than a few minutes of time with her, yet he felt as though he knew her from Henry's description of her hardworking attitude, her willingness to care for her siblings, and her desire to keep the family together. He found he admired this woman, whose sweet face and beguiling curls haunted his dreams.

"You do that," Bernie said, "and tell her if she has questions about tithing to come see me. I'd be glad to share some scripture with her."

Henry plopped on his hat and turned toward the door. "I'll tell her, but don't count on her asking. Ever since our folks died and Richard ran off, she hasn't been too interested in talking about God. I think she believes God let her down, and even though she takes us to church 'cause Mom and Dad went, she doesn't really want anything to do with Him anymore." The boy waved on his way out the door, unaware that he'd just thrown icy water over Bernie's heart. "See you tomorrow, Mr. O'Day."

∞

Helen awakened early on Saturday, teased from sleep by a recurring dream that pricked her conscience—a dream in which Bernie O'Day, attired in fine clothing including a top hat that glistened as if covered in sequins, offered her his elbow and invited her to attend the opera with him. Why couldn't she set that dream aside?

Bernie had been exceedingly kind to her family. Besides purchasing the coin, his putting Henry to work after school and paying him a fair wage had eased their financial burdens significantly. Henry's pay covered their weekly groceries, allowing her to put extra toward the hospital bill that had seemed insurmountable after Mom and Dad's accident followed by Lois's lengthy illness. In another few months, the bill would be paid in full, and then she'd be able to put money into the bank to save up for—

No! She needed to stop thinking about the Conservatory. That time was past. She had to focus on the children—getting them raised, putting them through school, seeing to their needs. Lois was only nine. Helen would be far too old for the Conservatory by the time Lois grew up enough to be on her own. Helen resolutely pushed aside the sting of regret. The children were more important than some silly aspiration about singing on a stage.

So why did she continually dream about being taken to the opera by Bernie O'Day?

She sat up, careful not to bounce the bed and awaken Lois, who slept on the other half. On tiptoe, she crept out of the room and down the hallway, past the room Henry and Carl shared, and on to the closed doorway behind which Mom and Dad's bedroom remained undisturbed. She rarely entered their room because it brought back too many painful memories, but on this morning she discovered a need to visit it. To visit them and the days before they'd left her.

Almost feeling like a burglar, she creaked the doorknob and stepped into the room. A musty odor tickled her nose. Sheets covered the bed and bureau, protecting the furniture, but she stirred dust with her feet as she crossed the wood floor to the bed and sat on the edge of the mattress. She closed her eyes, allowing memories to surface. The first one to rise from the dark corners of her mind was a Sunday-morning memory—Mom and Dad in their church clothes, Bibles held in the crook of their arms, leading her and the children down a sunshine-splashed sidewalk toward the chapel.

Helen tried to push the memory aside to focus on something else, but it persisted. The memory collided with her dream, and Henry's comments at supper last night rang through her mind:

"Mr. O'Day says God can make what's left over meet all our needs when we bless Him with our tithe." And she finally understood why the dream and memory were so closely intertwined. They both pertained to God.

Longing filled Helen's breast—a longing to return to the carefree days when she truly believed God cared about her, heard her prayers, and met her needs. Mom and Dad had believed it, and they'd taught her to believe it. But first Mom and Dad died from injuries in the awful trolley accident, and Richard said he didn't want to be responsible for three snot-nosed kids and deserted her when she needed him most, and then Lois fell ill and came so close to slipping away. And somehow in the midst of all that heartache, Helen had lost her belief in a caring God.

But Bernie O'Day believed in Him and now encouraged Henry to believe. Would Henry one day suffer the same deep disappointment that plagued Helen by placing his trust in a God who kept His distance? She couldn't allow that to happen. As much as they needed the money Henry made at the O'Day Pawn Shop, she'd have to tell Henry to stay away from there if Bernie was going to fill his head with unrealistic notions.

A scuffling sound in the hallway intruded on her thoughts, and moments later Henry poked his head in the room. He scowled across the shadows at Helen. "What're you doin' in here?" He stayed in the hallway, not even the loose toes of his socks crossed the threshold.

"Thinking." Helen pushed off from the bed, the creak of the springs discordant in the quiet morning hour. She stepped into the hallway, pulling the door shut behind her and sealing away her parents' room the way she wanted to seal away the troubling thoughts that plagued her. "Henry, when you go to work today, I want you to turn in your notice."

Henry gawked at her. "What? But why?"

"We're caught up on bills now." Her conscience pricked. They weren't caught up, but the more time Henry spent with Bernie O'Day, the greater the chances for his heart to be broken. "We don't need the money."

"Oh yes we do." Henry folded his arms over his chest. He'd grown so tall in the past year—he now peered down his nose at his older sister. "And I'm not quitting."

"Henry. . ."

"No, Helen. It's a good job, and I can still go to school, just like you wanted." Henry inched backward toward his bedroom. "Both of us working is better than only one of us, and I'm going to do my part to take care of the family. I'm keeping my job." He stepped into the bedroom and clicked the door closed behind him.

Helen stared at the closed door, her heart pounding. Should she go after him, insist on him quitting? Dad wouldn't have allowed Henry's backtalk, but she wasn't Dad, and she had no real authority over Henry even if she was responsible for him. She buried her face in her hands, the longing rising to have someone else to help her with her brothers and sister. Someone on whom she could depend. She wished she could still rely on God.

Lifting her face, she pressed her fists to her hips and scowled at the ceiling. She had no help anymore—not from her parents, from Richard, or from God—and she'd manage. If Henry wouldn't quit that job, then she'd just have to make sure his boss understood what he could and couldn't say to Henry. On her way home from work today, she'd stop by the O'Day Pawn Shop and have a firm talk with Bernie O'Day.

Chapter 4

Tired, footsore, and frustrated by her nearly empty pockets, Helen trudged down the street toward the O'Day Pawn Shop. Cleaning hotel rooms wasn't beneath her—it was honest work, and she was grateful to have been hired—but her dependence on guests leaving a few coins behind as a thank-you for her service worried her. She never knew from week to week what she might be bringing home to pay bills. Even on a good week, the money barely stretched to cover their needs. And now Henry, thanks to Bernie O'Day's prompting, wanted her to give some of her precious earnings to the church? The man obviously didn't understand how much she needed the money she made!

We also need the money Henry makes. The thought had plagued her all day as she planned exactly what she would say to Bernie O'Day. She wished so much she could say, "Henry doesn't need a job, so please release him from your employment immediately." But wishing didn't change the facts. They did need Henry's money. All of Henry's money. So Mr. Bernie O'Day would simply have to understand he was Henry's boss, not his preacher or father or even his friend. No more advice-giving.

As she approached the shop, she saw the door open and Henry step out. He paused to wave at Bernie, a smile on his face, then he trotted down the street in the opposite direction, heading home. Helen slowed her footsteps to allow Henry to get well ahead of her. When he turned the corner at the end of the block, she hurried to the door, which now sported a CLOSED sign, and rapped on the glass.

Moments later, Bernie O'Day appeared on the other side. A smile broke across his face when he spotted Helen, and he opened the door quickly. "Miss Wolfe! How good to see you. Please come in."

His cheerful greeting stung, considering the purpose of her visit. How she hated to see his bright smile fade. Just as she'd noted from her dreams, Bernie was a handsome man, with neatly combed sandy-colored hair and thick-lashed hazel eyes. If circumstances were different, she'd be drawn to him. But her intention was to push him away. Away from Henry, and consequently away from herself. She swallowed a lump of regret and forced herself to meet his friendly gaze.

"Mr. O'Day, I must talk to you."

His smile faltered, but then he released a light chuckle. "From the sound of your voice, I'd say it's serious. Should we have a seat?" He indicated a pair of cozy-looking rocking chairs nestled in the far corner of the store.

Although her sore feet and tired body yearned for the comfort of one of those chairs, Helen shook her head. This wasn't a social call, and she must remain brisk and impersonal. "I'll only be here a short while. Mr. O'Day—"

"Bernie, remember?"

She pursed her lips. Would he stop being so kind? This task was growing more difficult with each second that ticked by. She cleared her throat. "Bernie, I've come to request that you do not speak about God with Henry. He holds a great deal of respect for you, and he likes you as well. Everything you say, he takes to heart. If you continue to speak of God, Henry could very well begin to accept your words as truth. And I know all too well that God is not the loving Father my parents believed Him to be."

Sadness clouded Bernie's hazel eyes, bringing a rush of sorrow through Helen's frame. He slipped his hands into his trouser pockets and set his head at a thoughtful angle. "Exactly how'd you come to the conclusion that God isn't a loving Father?"

Helen nearly snorted. "A loving father gives good gifts. He doesn't bestow hardship and trials on his children."

"He doesn't?"

Bernie's genuine surprise took Helen by surprise. She blinked at him. "Well, of course he doesn't!"

Setting his feet widespread, hands still tucked in pockets, Bernie gazed at Helen with twinkling eyes and chuckled. A low-in-his-throat chuckle like distant thunder that sent a tremor of pleasure down Helen's spine. "Miss Wolfe, when you were growin' up, did your father ever find it necessary to bestow a little pain on your. . .er, sittin'-down place?"

Heat flooded Helen's cheeks. She looked sharply away. "I suspect most fathers inflict the occasional rod of discipline. Mine was no exception."

The chuckle rumbled again. "And did that make you think he didn't love you?"

She jerked her face around to meet his grin. "Of course not! If he didn't love me, he'd let me grow up without any sense of right and wrong."

Bernie nodded. "That's exactly right. Your father—being the loving man he was—guided you with painful lessons every now and then, knowing there'd be a good result." He shrugged slowly, his eyes never leaving her face. "So why is it so hard to believe God wouldn't do the same? Use painful lessons for a good result?"

Helen couldn't think of an answer. Which irritated her.

She glared at Bernie.

For long seconds they stood in silence, staring into each other's eyes. Finally Bernie sighed. "I don't wanna overstep any boundaries, Miss Wolfe. I like Henry. He's a good boy, and I'd like to keep him employed here. But I can't promise not to talk about God. You see, God and me. . .we're pretty close. I can't shut Him in a drawer and pretend He doesn't exist when Henry's around. So I'll probably keep talking about Him." He shrugged again. "I just can't help myself, Miss Wolfe."

Helen suddenly realized she'd think less of him if he agreed to change. The thought confused her. Her tongue refused to form a retort.

Then Bernie confounded her even more. "Miss Wolfe, do you and your brothers and sister enjoy picnics in Central Park?"

Immediately, memories swept through Helen's mind of the many summer picnics she'd shared with her parents and siblings when she was a girl. She gulped. "Y–yes. Yes, we do."

"Would you care to join me for a picnic after church tomorrow? My treat. Nothin' fancy—just sandwiches and fruit. Maybe a jug of sweet tea. But I'd like to get to know you and Carl and Lois after hearing Henry talk about you all so much."

Helen shook her head. "Tomorrow? But. . .it's late October. Not summertime."

He used his chuckle again to disarm her. "There some rule says you can only have picnics in the summertime? I happen to think October's a fine time for a picnic. No leaves to hide the blue sky from view. Nice crisp breeze drifting from the lake. And no flies."

Helen's lips twitched, fighting a giggle.

"We can spread a blanket on the bridge at the pond and toss bread scraps to the ducks. What do you say?"

Deep regret pierced Helen. She lowered her head so he wouldn't see the desire to join him glimmering in her eyes. "I'm afraid it's out of the question. My sister, Lois, is still recovering from a very serious illness. She shouldn't breathe in the cool air." She flicked a gaze upward and caught a disappointed frown on his face. "I appreciate the invitation, though." She did appreciate it. No wonder Henry liked his boss so much. Bernie O'Day was a very kind man.

Flustered, Helen turned toward the door. "I need to get home. My brothers and sister expect me."

He reached past her and opened the door. "Thanks for stopping by, Miss Wolfe, and thanks for letting Henry work for me. He's a fine boy, and you should be proud of him."

Helen scurried out the door without answering. Not until she was halfway to her bungalow did she realize she'd completely failed in what she'd set out to do. And to her chagrin, she discovered it really didn't matter.

Sunday morning Lois pushed her barely touched bowl of oatmeal toward Helen and wrinkled her freckled nose. "This doesn't taste right."

The milk had started to turn. Helen had hoped, mixed into the oatmeal with a tiny dash of cinnamon for flavoring, no one would notice. But the way Henry and Carl stirred their oatmeal rather than eating it, Helen knew she hadn't managed to mask the slightly spoiled taste. Even so, they couldn't waste food, so she assumed a brisk tone. "You're probably just hungry for something else, so your taste buds are feeling fussy." She sent a nod around the table. "It's all we're having for breakfast, so eat up or you'll be awfully hungry by lunchtime." She scooped a bite and resolutely swallowed, ignoring the little tang on the back of her tongue.

With sighs, her brothers and sister followed her example. Within minutes, the bowls were empty. Helen gathered the spoons and bowls. "Go dress in your Sunday clothes now. And bundle yourselves well. The wind howled all night, so it's likely to be chilly this morning."

"Wonder if it rained, too." Carl screeched his chair from the table and bounded toward the door. He swung it wide and stuck his head out, looking left and right. "Nope. It's not wet, but—hey!"

Helen's hands stilled in their task at her brother's excited exclamation. "What is it?"

Carl darted onto the porch, letting the screen door slam behind him. Moments later, he clomped back inside with a large basket in his arms. "Look what I found on the porch!"

Lois and Henry bustled forward to meet him, and Helen followed, curiosity filling her. She reached past Lois to lift the checked cloth covering several lumps within the basket. When she revealed the contents, she gasped.

"Lookit all this!" Carl's face glowed with wonder. "Sliced ham, deviled eggs, sweet and dill pickles. . ."

Lois reached into the basket and withdrew a fat jar. She squealed. "Spiced peaches! My favorite!" She hugged the jar to her skinny chest, beaming.

Henry pushed items around, continuing the recitation. "A whole loaf of bread, white cheese, two packets of cookies— looks like Snickerdoodles and oatmeal raisin. Mmm."

Helen's heart began to pound. Spiced peaches for Lois, Snickerdoodles for Carl, deviled eggs for Henry, and oatmeal raisin cookies for her. All of their favorites were nestled in the basket, wrapped in wax paper and cushioned with checked napkins. Only one person besides Mom and Dad could have put this basket together with each of their favorite items. The person who'd often joined her family for summer picnics in years past. Richard. . .

Dashing past her clustered siblings, who continued to

gaze into the basket and ooh and aah in delight, she clattered onto the porch and searched the street. Her heart thudded almost painfully against her ribs. When she'd broken off their engagement, Richard had vowed to make her change her mind. An entire year had slipped by without any contact from him, and she'd given up hope of reconciliation. But now, this basket of treats both she and the children loved ignited a flame of emotion that couldn't be quelled.

She hugged herself, seeking any sign of Richard, both hopeful and apprehensive. Was he back? And more importantly, did she want him back?

Chapter 5

Bernie could hardly wait for Henry to arrive after school on Monday. It had taken some doing to gather the food items he recalled Henry mentioning as family favorites, but putting that basket together had brought more pleasure than anything he could remember in quite a while. After Helen had left his shop, he'd prayed for a way to show God's caring to her. Feeding her physical body seemed a good place to start. Would she recognize the gesture as evidence of God wanting to meet her needs?

Henry sent the bell above the door clanging at 3:45 p.m., prompt as always, and darted directly for an apron and the broom. "Lots of leaves out front. I'll get to sweeping, and when that's all done, I'll—"

"Hold up." Bernie caught Henry's jacket sleeve. In the past weeks, Henry'd grown even taller, and at least three inches of his arms stuck out from the bottom of the sleeves. His current jacket wouldn't last him through the winter. Bernie led Henry behind the counter then held up a brown corduroy jacket with a sturdy zipper and pockets that buttoned shut. "Can you make use of this?"

Henry took the jacket and held it up in front of him.

Bernie said, "It isn't new. It's a trade-in, but it looks to be your size. If it fits, you can have it."

Henry removed his old jacket and slipped on the brown

one. He wriggled his shoulders, as if testing the fit, then stuck his arms out. The cuffs reached halfway to his knobby knuckles. Bernie nodded in satisfaction. Plenty of growing room remained, which was good since a boy of Henry's age would probably keep adding to his height for a while yet. The heavy corduroy with its wool lining should keep Henry warm.

"So what do you think? You like it?" Bernie examined Henry's face, seeking signs of approval.

Henry sighed, rubbing his hands up and down the chest of the jacket. "I like it plenty, Mr. O'Day, but I can't keep it." He removed it and offered it to Bernie.

Bernie didn't take it. "Why not?"

"Helen'd have a fit." Henry laid the jacket on the counter and stood gazing at it, longing on his face. "She's got a lot of pride. Wants to take care of us herself. She'd feel like she'd failed if I brought this jacket home."

"Helen won't let you accept a gift?" Bernie wondered what she'd done with that basket of food. He sure hoped she hadn't tossed it out!

"Well..." Henry scratched his head. "Don't really know what she'd think if I called it a gift." He looked at Bernie, his brow puckered. "Are you giving it to me outright, or am I earning it? 'Cause if I did something extra for you—something beyond what I usually do around here—then I could say I earned it."

"And then Helen would let you keep it?"

Henry nodded.

Bernie's thoughts bounced around erratically. He'd wanted the jacket to be a gift—a sign of God meeting her family's needs. But he didn't want to insult Helen. That would distance her even more. Distancing her was the last thing he hoped to do. But only to draw her to God, of course. He nearly laughed. He wasn't fooling himself any more than he could fool God. Sure, he wanted to draw Helen back to God, but he wanted to draw her to himself, too.

But getting her focused on God was most important. Therefore, he couldn't ask anything in return for that coat or it would destroy the message that God cared enough to meet her needs.

Bernie put his hand on Henry's shoulder. "Henry, this coat is a gift, pure and simple. God laid it on my heart that you needed a new coat, and this coat—a coat just the right size for a boy like you—showed up in my shop. It would be wrong of me to take payment for it, because it really came from God, not me. Does that make sense?"

Henry crunched his face into a scowl of indecision. "It kind of makes sense to me, but I don't know how I'm gonna explain it to Helen."

Bernie scooped up the coat and pressed it into Henry's arms. "You just tell Helen your loving heavenly Father wanted you to be warm this winter and leave it at that."

Henry pushed his arms into the sleeves and closed the zipper all the way to his throat. He smoothed his hands over the sleeves, noting how they reached beyond his wrists. He sighed. "Thanks, Mr. O'Day."

"Don't thank me," Bernie said. "Thank God."

Henry gave a solemn nod.

Over the next weeks, as Thanksgiving approached, Bernie spent a significant amount of his prayer time lifting up Helen Wolfe and her siblings. He'd learned from Henry that their parents died in the horrific trolley accident that claimed more than a dozen lives two years ago. It gave him a start to realize he and Pop had prayed together for the accident victims' families, unknowingly praying for the Wolfe siblings even before he met them. It connected him more firmly to Helen, Henry, Carl, and

Lois, and made him all the more determined to reawaken the faith their parents had lived.

Henry seemed to enjoy talking to Bernie, and Bernie filed away everything the boy said about his sisters and brother. He learned Helen loved to sing but now rarely lifted her voice in song, too busy working and caring for a household. He learned Carl was a good baseball player, and that Lois hoped to learn to play piano someday. He also discovered Henry had a head for business and possessed a number sense that exceeded Bernie's. Henry could add in his head faster than most people did on paper. A boy like that should think about college, and Bernie began praying for a way to make sure Henry had the chance to further his education after he graduated twelfth grade.

Learning bits and pieces of the Wolfe siblings' lives offered lots of ways for Bernie to reach out to the family. He began a practice of leaving packages on the porch of the Wolfe home. Never anything elaborate, fearful Helen would reject items of great monetary value, but little things he knew they needed or that would bring one of the family members some pleasure. Baseball cards for Carl, new gloves for Lois, paper tablets for Henry. And song sheets for Helen—vocal arrangements for a mezzo soprano. According to Henry, she had a rare gift, and her parents had encouraged her to use it. Apparently, her song died when she buried her parents. Bernie hoped holding those song sheets would entice her to sing once again. And he prayed raising her voice in song—using her God-given talent—would help her open her heart to God again.

The Wednesday before Thanksgiving, Henry arrived early since school let out at noon. As soon as he donned his apron, he offered an apology. "I hope it's all right, but I can't stay clear till closing today. Helen asked me to stop by the grocer and get everything we'd need for our Thanksgiving dinner." He flapped a sheet of paper, covered on one side with neat lines of script.

"She's been saving up so we could have a good dinner. If I wait too late to choose our sweet potatoes and roasting hen, all the good ones'll be picked over."

Bernie smiled. "That's fine, Henry. In fact, I rarely get much business the day before Thanksgiving—people are too busy cooking. So why don't you just take today off? Tomorrow I'm closed, too, so that'll give you a nice break."

"Are you sure?" Henry fiddled with his apron ties. "I don't wanna shirk my duties."

Bernie clapped the boy on the shoulder. "Henry, if there's one thing I would never suspect you of doing, it would be shirking your duties." He pointed to the hooks. "Hang up that apron and scoot on out of here. Pick your sister the biggest, freshest sweet potatoes you can find. But. . ." He stepped around the corner and grabbed the crate he'd put together that morning. "You won't need to spend money on a roasting hen. There's a fine turkey in here—enough to feed your family and then some." Bernie had also packed in bags of flour and sugar, a dozen eggs, and two loaves of bread—one for slicing and eating, the other to chop into pieces for stuffing. The Wolfe siblings would have a veritable feast.

Henry stared at the crate. "A–are you sure?"

"Yep." Bernie thumped the crate on the counter. He rested his elbow on the corner of the crate, peering at Henry over the slatted side. "Y'know, it's not uncommon for employers to give their workers something at holidays. Your sister won't fuss about this, will she?" Bernie hadn't asked about Helen's reaction to the gifts he'd been leaving. Partly because he feared Henry would say she resented them, and partly because he wanted to remain anonymous.

Henry shrugged, zipping up his brown jacket. "I think she'll appreciate it. Getting harder and harder to satisfy Carl's appetite. He eats more than the rest of us put together."

Bernie snorted out a laugh.

Henry balanced the crate against his belly. "I'll let her know it's from you, though, so she doesn't think Richard gave it to us."

Richard. . . That name had come up before, and every time he heard it, Bernie prickled. He didn't want to feel jealous of the man who'd once asked for Helen's hand in marriage, but despite his best efforts, the emotion welled. His voice tight, Bernie said, "Why would she think it's from Richard?"

Henry waddled toward the door. "He's been leavin' stuff on the porch for us. Helen's sure it's him, 'cause he leaves things somebody who'd have to know us pretty good would leave."

Bernie's mouth went dry. Helen credited Richard for the gifts? But that meant she wasn't seeing them as God-blessings. "She—she's certain it's Richard?"

Henry shot Bernie a puzzled look. "Who else could it be?"

Bernie clamped his mouth shut so he wouldn't blurt out the truth. He swallowed. "Is she. . .happy. . .that Richard's leaving her presents?"

For a long moment, Henry stood silently, rubbing his lips together. Then he shrugged. "I dunno about happy, necessarily. It hurt her pretty bad when he broke off their engagement. But I know she's lonely. I know she'd like to have somebody to help her out with the youngsters. So maybe she's happy Richard's back. I haven't really asked."

Bernie shuffled past Henry and opened the door for him. "Well, I better not keep you. You've got some shopping to do." He shifted out of the way so Henry could push through. It made a tight fit with the bulky crate in his arms. Once the boy was on the sidewalk, he said, "Have a good Thanksgiving, Henry." He heard his sad undertone and forced his lips into a smile. No sense in worrying the boy.

Henry angled his head to peer over his shoulder at Bernie.

"Thanks. You, too." He took one step then cried, "Oh!" Henry whirled around, nearly tipping the crate. "Mr. O'Day, what're you doing for Thanksgiving?"

Slowly, Bernie lifted his shoulders in a shrug. He had no plans. He'd just be here at the shop, probably going through unmarked inventory in the back room. Things tended to stack up back there. "Not much. Why?"

Henry's cheeks streaked with red. "Helen told me to ask you if you'd like to eat Thanksgiving dinner with us. A thank-you, she said, for giving me this job."

All of Bernie's sadness washed away in one swoop. A smile broke across his face. "I'd like that, Henry. I'd like that a lot."

"Good." Henry flashed a quick grin. "See you tomorrow then, around six. Can't eat earlier than that 'cause Helen has to work."

"Six o'clock." Bernie touched his forehead in a mock salute. "I'll be there." He closed the door and danced a quick jig, excitement stirring in his middle. Helen had invited him to dinner! As a thank-you. But not for the gifts he'd sent. She didn't know they'd come from him. Bernie's feet paused mid-step. The joyful feeling faded and a lump of consternation settled in his stomach.

Had Helen invited Richard, too? And if she had, how would he be able to sit at the same table with the man who'd so wronged this woman who'd sneaked her way into the center of his heart?

Chapter 6

Standing on the porch of the Wolfe family's bungalow, Bernie adjusted his bow tie one last time. Nervousness, excitement, and apprehension created a flutter in his belly. He hadn't been to a real family Thanksgiving since he was a boy, when his grandparents were still alive and the aunts, uncles, and cousins all gathered together. With Grandmother's death, the family get-togethers ceased, and not until he'd received the invitation from Henry had he realized how much he missed being part of a family gathering.

But today, thanks to the Wolfes' kindness, he'd once again have the chance to sit at a noisy table. But exactly how noisy, he couldn't help but wonder. Would Helen have invited the man named Richard as a thank-you, too? A thank-you he didn't deserve?

Pressing one palm to the buttons of his best blue suit coat, he raised his other hand and gave the doorjamb several brisk knocks. Within seconds the door creaked open, and a young girl with a thin, pale face and a tumble of shoulder-length sausage curls gazed up at him. Thick black lashes swept up and down with each blink of her bold blue eyes.

Bernie found himself immediately smitten. "Hello there. You must be Lois." He stuck out his hand. "I'm Bernie O'Day."

The child hunched her skinny shoulders and took his hand in a quick, embarrassed shake. "Hello, Mr. O'Day. Will you come in, please?"

Wonderful aromas greeted Bernie's nose as he stepped over the threshold. His stomach turned, but this time from eagerness rather than apprehension.

Lois closed the door behind Bernie then fixed him with a serious look. "May I take your hat?"

Her impeccable manners and formal speech belied her tender years. Bernie swallowed a grin and mimicked her courtly attitude. "Why, of course, miss. And thank you."

A tiny giggle found its way from the little girl's throat. She placed his hat on a chair in the corner then gestured toward a wide doorway at the far side of the simple parlor. "This way, please." She led him through the doorway to a dining room where a long table covered in a crisp white cloth, flowered China plates, and gleaming silverware sat ready for Thanksgiving dinner. Bernie gawked in amazement. Helen had gone all out to make this dinner a festive affair. He quickly counted the chairs—six in all, but the one at the foot of the table had no place setting. Apparently he was the only guest. He nearly collapsed in relief.

Lois gestured toward a chair on the left-hand side of the table. "Helen, Henry, and Carl are dishing up the food right now. We'll be eating in a few minutes. You can sit down, an' we'll be out in a little bit." She dashed through a doorway in the corner of the dining room, her voice trailing after her. "He's here, Helen! We can eat now!"

Bernie stood behind the chair, unwilling to sit until his hostess had taken her seat. Clanks, scuffles, and mumbled voices carried from beyond the doorway, painting a picture of busyness. He wished he could go in and offer his help, but he didn't want to intrude. So he stood, gaze aimed at the doorway, alternately smoothing his hair into place with his palm and checking the buttons on his jacket while he counted down the seconds.

In less than two minutes, his patience was rewarded by a

small parade led by Lois, who carried a basket of sliced bread and a round dish of creamy butter. Henry came next, his hands filled with bowls of steaming mashed sweet potatoes and buttery green beans. A shorter version of Henry—Carl, no doubt—clomped behind Henry with some sort of green wobbly tower balanced on a plate. And finally Helen emerged, holding a platter containing a beautifully browned turkey and a mound of moist stuffing. Bernie barely noticed the bird, however; he couldn't take his eyes off the woman.

She'd done something different with her hair—pulled it up so it formed a smooth sweep from her slender neck to the crown of her head. Soft curls spilled toward her forehead. Her cheeks sported soft pink, and the color also graced her full lips. The deep blue of her two-piece, well-fitted suit brought out the bright blue of her eyes. She was beautiful. Breathtakingly beautiful.

The three younger Wolfe siblings placed their offerings on the table and settled into chairs with a noisy scraping of legs against the wood floor. Lois took the chair next to Bernie, and Henry and Carl sat side by side across the table, leaving the seat at the head for Helen. She wiped the back of her hand daintily across her perspiration-dotted brow and sent Bernie, who stood stupidly behind his chair staring at her, a shy smile. "Welcome to our home, Bernie. Won't you be seated?"

Bernie darted to her chair and pulled it out. "Ladies first."

Henry coughed into his hand, and Carl smirked. Bernie chose to ignore the boys and kept his focus on Helen. Her cheeks deepened—a natural blush much more appealing than the powder she wore—and she slipped into the chair, her head low.

"Thank you, Bernie."

"You're welcome."

She smoothed her skirt over her knees and lifted her face

slightly. "You already met Lois, and of course you know Henry. Please meet our other brother, Carl."

The freckle-faced boy grinned at Bernie. "Hi, Mr. O'Day. Nice to meet'cha."

Bernie stifled a chuckle at the boy's lack of formality. He gave a quick nod in reply then returned to his chair, feeling clumsy compared to Helen's swanlike motions. As soon as he sat, Carl reached for the nearest bowl—green beans—and started to serve himself.

Automatically, Bernie cleared his throat. "Would you like me to say grace?"

Carl's hands froze on the serving spoon.

Bernie wished he could kick himself. He was a guest— he had no business inflicting his belief system on this family. But how could they sit down to such a fine feast and not offer thanks? He flicked a glance at Helen. She wasn't smiling, but neither was she frowning. Her sweet face wore a pensive expression Bernie wished he could translate.

After a few tense seconds of silence, Helen folded her hands. "Please do so."

Everyone folded their hands and bowed their heads, and Bernie delivered a short prayer of gratitude for the food and the hands that had prepared it. He finished, "Thank You, our Father, for Your bountiful blessings. May we be ever mindful of Your presence in our lives. Amen."

Helen swallowed the lump that filled her throat at the sweetness in Bernie's tone as he talked to the God he called Father. Dad had spoken to God with the same ease and familiarity, and as a child she'd experienced such security while listening to her father pray. Bernie's prayer sent a spiral of warmth around her, as comforting as a cozy quilt on a winter day, but at the same time a chill whisked through her heart. The emptiness that had plagued her since her parents' deaths and Richard's departure returned, coupled with an aching realization: the emptiness was due to more than burying her parents and her dreams of a future with Richard; it was due to her decision to refuse God any part of her life.

Her hands shook as she carved the turkey and placed succulent slices on each plate. But no one seemed to notice her turmoil. Her brothers and sister passed the bowls and dove into the hearty meal. While they ate, they chatted with each other. And with Bernie. Carl and Lois seemed as at ease with this newcomer as if he'd visited a dozen times. Bernie, too, appeared completely comfortable after his initial shyness. He teased Lois, talked to Henry like a peer, and drilled Carl on baseball facts. Helen found she needed to contribute nothing to the conversation, which suited her—she couldn't think of a thing to say—yet also left her feeling left out. Her topsy-turvy emotions confused her, and the food that she had so anticipated lost its appeal.

When they'd nearly emptied the bowls and consumed a good quarter of the turkey, the boys clamored for pie. Helen brought out the sweet potato and pecan pie made from Mom's recipe and cut it into six equal portions. Conversation ceased while they ate dessert. Helen wasn't sure if they'd all run out of words or if they were just too full to speak, but in the silence that fell—only the clink of forks on plates and satisfied sighs creating a soft backdrop—she grew more and more unsettled. If only she could make sense of her tumbling emotions!

As soon as the boys were finished eating, they staggered to their bedroom to change out of their church clothes, which Helen had insisted they wear for the dinner. Lois yawned widely and asked to be excused. Looking into the child's dark-rimmed eyes, Helen decided not to insist Lois help with cleanup. Lois scuffed around the corner, and Helen and Bernie were left alone at a messy table with chairs all askew.

Bernie sat back and patted his stomach. "That was delicious, Miss Wolfe. Thank you so much for including me."

"You're very welcome." Helen's voice sounded unnaturally high. She cleared her throat and tried again. "After your kindness toward Henry, it's the least we could do." She hadn't intended to intimate she'd invited him out of obligation, but she realized her statement could offer that meaning. She scrambled for a way of rephrasing, but before she could think of anything, Bernie spoke.

"Henry gives as much as he gets. He's proved himself invaluable."

Relieved that he hadn't seemed to take offense, Helen rose and began stacking dirty plates. "He loves his job, and—truthfully—his income is very helpful."

Bernie gathered silverware, filling both fists with forks, spoons, and knives. "I'd like to keep him on until he's finished with school. But after that. . ."

Helen gestured for Bernie to put the silverware into the empty green bean bowl. When he'd released the handfuls of clattering silverware, she put the bowl on top of the plates and lifted the stack. "After that. . .what?"

Bernie sent her a serious look. "I'd like to see him quit working for me and go on to college. He's a bright boy. He oughta aim higher than being the helper in a pawnshop."

Although he'd paid her brother a compliment, his words stung. Mom and Dad had wanted college for Henry. But how would she provide it? Forcing a laugh to hide the hurt his comment had inflicted, Helen turned toward the kitchen. "Well, if Henry's to attend college, my gift elf will need to leave more than school supplies and woolen socks on the porch. We'll need a bag of gold."

Bernie scurried after her. "Your gift elf?" Humor and interest tinged his tone.

Helen placed the dirty dishes on the counter then faced her guest. "Have you ever heard the story about the elves and the shoemaker?"

Bernie nodded.

"Apparently we have our own version. Someone. . ." It had to be Richard, trying to butter her up. Helen's stomach churned. ". . .has left items on our porch once or twice a week for the past couple months. It reminds me of the little elves seeing to the needs of the shoemaker when he isn't looking."

A smile twitched on Bernie's clean-shaven cheeks. He smelled of bay rum, too. He must've cleaned up and shaved right before coming over to look so fresh. Helen hurried to the dining room before the temptation to run her fingers along his smooth cheek overcame her.

He followed. "That story always reminded me of a Bible story—the one about a pitcher of oil that never ran dry. God made sure the widow and her son's needs were met."

Helen paused in gathering the dessert plates. She shifted slowly to look at Bernie. His open, honest gaze met hers. "Do you really believe God meets our needs?"

Without so much as a moment's hesitation, Bernie nodded emphatically. "I believe that with all my heart. He might not meet them the way we think He ought to do it, but He gives us exactly what we need."

The past months of worry, frustration, and heartache rose up in one mighty tidal wave of emotion and spilled from Helen's mouth before she could stop it. "What I need most is a helpmate, and if God puts him on my front porch, maybe I'll finally believe He really does care about me."

Bernie stared at her, openmouthed and red faced. Embarrassed, Helen spun away from him. She reached for the last dessert plate, but as her fingers closed around it, a loud knocking sounded on the front door. "Excuse me," she muttered and bustled through the parlor.

The knocking came again—harsh and impatient. Helen called, "I'm coming!" She threw open the door then stumbled backward in shock.

Richard Mason swept his hat from his head and gave a dapper bow. "Happy Thanksgiving, Helen!" His gaze roved from her head to her toes and up again. A knowing grin climbed his cheek. "You're just as pretty as you always were." He held out his arms. "How about a hug, honey?"

Chapter 7

B ernie strode around the corner from the dining room in time to see a well-dressed young man with a dark mustache step into the house and wrap his arms around Helen. Helen stood within the circle of his embrace with her arms dangling, as if she'd suddenly turned into a giant rag doll. The clatter of footsteps intruded as Henry, Carl, and Lois thundered into the room. The man released Helen and turned his broad grin on the children.

"Well, lookit here, if it ain't the whole gang! How you doin', Hank? Looks like you've grown a foot since I saw you last." He punched Henry's shoulder then whirled on the younger two. "Carl! Little Lois!" He rubbed his hand over Carl's head, further tousling the boy's unruly hair, then swooped Lois in the air. The moment he released her, she scooted behind Henry. The three stared at the man, unsmiling. But his wide smile never dimmed. "Good to see you all." Finally his gaze found Bernie, and a scowl quickly marred his brow. He pointed. "Who's that?"

Henry answered. "My boss, Bernie O'Day. We invited him for Thanksgiving dinner."

The man's lips formed a smile, but his eyes remained narrowed slits of distrust. "That so? Well, nice to meet you, Mr. O'Day. I'm Richard Mason, Helen's fiancé."

Helen delicately cleared her throat. "My former fiancé."

She folded her arms across her chest. "Children, would you please finish clearing the table for me?" She raised her brows at the trio, and they trooped past Bernie. Still holding her arms in the defensive position, Helen faced Richard Mason. "Richard, I wondered when you'd finally show your face."

From her tone, Bernie couldn't determine whether she was pleased, apprehensive, or controlling herself for his sake. He knew he should leave—he had no place here—but his feet seemed mired in concrete.

Richard tossed his hat onto the sofa and leaned his shoulder on the doorjamb, his easy smile pinned directly on Helen's face. "Aw, you know how busy stage life can be, doll. Hardly a minute to spare. But I couldn't let the holiday go by without at least popping in and saying hello."

Helen inched backward, her fingers holding tight to her elbows. "Well, I suppose I should thank you for the gifts you left on the porch."

Mason smoothed his finger over his mustache. "Gifts?"

Helen's curls bounced with her nod. "I know they're from you. Who else could have known that spiced peaches are Lois's favorite, or that Carl loves baseball cards?"

Bernie nearly bit through the end of his tongue, trying to hold back the truth. Helen needed to hear it from Mason rather than him. He waited for Mason to admit he had no idea about the gifts.

Mason cleared his throat, his head ducked low as if modesty held him captive. "Yes, well, spiced peaches are a delightful treat. And of course what boy doesn't like baseball cards, hmm?"

Bernie found the ability to move. He stormed forward, his elbow brushing against Mason's sleeve as he went. "Thanks again for the invitation to dinner, Miss Wolfe. I enjoyed my time with your family." Aware of Mason's steely glare on him, he paused long enough to give Helen a soft smile. "You and the children enjoy the rest of the holiday. I'm sure we'll talk again soon." Without waiting for a response, he charged out of the house and down the street, his strides wide and arms pumping.

He was halfway home before his chilly ears reminded him he'd left his hat behind. With a disgruntled huff, he slowed his pace. Should he go back and get it? Part of him itched to turn around. To check on Helen and make sure that weasel Mason—because he was certain the man was a weasel—was behaving himself. But in the end he let out a sigh of resignation. His breath formed a cloud of condensation in the evening dusk then dissipated. Watching the puff disappear, Bernie wished he could make his feelings for Miss Helen Wolfe float away so easily. It hurt more than he cared to admit to think of her taking up with Richard Mason again. Especially if what Henry said was true and the man callously tossed her aside when she gave up her dream of singing in lieu of caring for her siblings. A woman who acted so unselfishly deserved a man who would cherish her.

Lord, what's Your will for Helen. . .and me? The prayer whispered from his heart. *I want to show her Your love in action, but would it be all right if I let her see my love in action, too? Can I be the helpmeet she's seeking?*

Bernie didn't receive an answer, but he felt better having asked the question. In time, God would answer. He trusted his Father to lead him when the time was right. He set his feet in motion again, determined to leave Helen and her needs in God's hands, where they belonged.

Sunday morning as Helen dressed for church, her thoughts drifted back to Thanksgiving Day. Bernie's prayer and the emotions it had stirred contrasted with the surprise of the visit from Richard. He'd stayed well past bedtime and had apologized repeatedly for his hasty exit from her life. She still wasn't completely sure she wanted him back—not in the way he wanted to be back—but she couldn't honestly say she was ready to permanently sever her ties with him. They'd known each other since they were youngsters, and they shared a common goal of singing on the stage. Surely they'd be able to build a life together if only she could learn to trust him not to abandon her again.

Carl's and Henry's voices drifted to her ears—fighting over first turn for the washroom. She should go break up the argument before it turned into fisticuffs, but she stood behind Lois at the mirror and shaped her sister's naturally curly hair into fat rolls instead. While brushing, she idly asked, "Lois, would you like it if Richard moved in here with us and became part of our family?"

"Richard?" Lois wrinkled her nose at her reflection. "He's a dandy."

Helen snorted out a laugh. "Where did you learn a word like that?"

"From Henry. He called Richard a dandy, and I think Henry's right. Richard smiles funny—like he doesn't really mean it—and he's afraid to get his hands dirty. He wouldn't even help you with the dishes the other night. He laughs too loud, and sometimes he laughs when you don't mean to be funny, which I think is mean."

Helen supposed she should scold Lois for speaking ill of Richard. But she couldn't make herself condemn her sister for her honesty. The things Lois mentioned were things that bothered Helen, too, yet Richard also had good qualities. He was very talented and already had a good paying job with the opera company as their lead singer. He'd claimed he could easily get her hired into the troupe, as well, allowing her to live out her long-held dreams. When she'd asked about the children, he'd said, somewhat disparagingly, "Well, this isn't a traveling troupe, doll." She took his comment to infer she'd be available to them.

Lois stepped away from the hairbrush and sucked in a big breath. "None of us are very fond of Richard, Helen. He's hardly the cat's meow."

Helen clapped her hand over her mouth to keep from laughing out loud.

Her hand on her hip, Lois tossed her hair. "But if you like him, then. . ." She flounced out of the room in a perfect Mae West imitation.

Helen sank onto the edge of the bed, shaking her head. She'd have to forbid Carl from taking Lois to the picture show if her sister was going to pick up such habits. But she had to admit, Lois's antics were amusing. And her depiction of Richard far too accurate. Helen sighed. She wished her parents were there to advise her concerning making a commitment to Richard. Without warning, her mother's voice echoed through her memory: *You should pray before making any decision, Helen, and ask for God's guidance.*

Helen whispered, "But I don't pray anymore." She waited, her head tipped, expectant and hopeful. But her mother's voice didn't return. With another sigh, she pushed off from the bed and retrieved her black pumps from the closet. She'd be late getting the children to church if she didn't hurry.

As she buttered slices of toast for a simple breakfast, another thought crossed her mind, carried with the remembrance of Bernie's easy prayer at their Thanksgiving table. Helen no longer prayed, but Bernie did. And Bernie obviously cared about Henry's future, which meant he'd want the best for her brother. If she asked Bernie to seek God's guidance about allowing Richard back into their lives, she had no doubt he'd do it.

Helen desperately needed answers. She could send a message

with Henry tomorrow to give to Bernie, and he'd probably send a reply on Tuesday. But she really wanted him to begin praying now. She needed financial help now. She needed an emotional helpmate in her life now. She didn't want to prolong seeking an answer.

Setting aside the butter knife, she dashed to the hallway and called, "Henry?"

Her brother poked his head out of the washroom. "What?"

"Which church does Mr. O'Day attend?"

"The big brick one on the corner of Fourth and Applewood."

Helen nearly groaned. The church was huge! How would they locate Bernie in that massive sanctuary? She tapped her chin, thinking. If they sat in the back, they could scoot out the doors quickly at the end and watch every parishioner leaving. If they were lucky, they'd spot Bernie in the crowd.

"Everyone, hurry now," she ordered, clapping her hands to emphasize her words. "We're going to Mr. O'Day's church this morning, and it's quite a walk." The distance to his church was much greater than to their own little chapel, so she'd need to bundle Lois well and make sure she kept her scarf over her nose and mouth.

For a moment she hesitated, uncertainty holding her captive. Was she doing the right thing, taking her siblings to meet Bernie O'Day and placing such an important issue in his hands? And why did she trust him with her dilemma? She hadn't a clue. She only knew, for the first time in a long time, she believed she'd found someone who wouldn't let her down.

"Please let my trust in this man not be misguided," she mumbled as she hurried back to the kitchen to pour juice. But she told herself the plea wasn't a prayer.

Chapter 8

Bernie rose after the closing benediction and turned toward the aisle. His heart felt burdened by the minister's impassioned plea for the parishioners to pray for the people in Europe caught up in war. Here in his cocoon of security, Bernie admitted to giving little thought to the horror raging overseas. While he moved toward the double doors leading to the street, a man brushed against him, nearly knocking his Bible from his grip.

"Sorry about that," the man said.

Bernie grinned. "No problem." He slipped the Bible into his jacket pocket and glanced around. "Crowded today—hard to walk without bumpin' each other."

The man nodded. "Holiday Sundays always bring in a lot of visitors."

Bernie agreed. He wished those who flooded the pews at Thanksgiving, Christmas, and Easter would make church attendance an every-Sunday event. He couldn't imagine getting through the week without the nourishment his soul received each Lord's day. As he stepped from the warmth of the sanctuary into a blustery Sunday noon, his gaze roved across the small groups of people chatting together. Although he glimpsed many cheerful faces, he also noted somber ones. He passed between groups, overhearing snatches of conversation, and realized many of the sober expressions accompanied comments about the war. Bernie blew out a little breath of relief. Apparently he wouldn't be the only one praying for peace in Europe.

He stepped from the crowds and turned his feet toward home, but then a female voice—a familiar female voice—called his name and stopped him in his tracks. He whirled around to see Helen, with the younger Wolfe siblings on her heels, scurrying toward him. She wore the same blue suit she'd worn on Thanksgiving Day, but a cream-colored hat with blue feathers and red beads sat at a jaunty angle over her curls. Bernie gulped. Had any woman ever been as appealing as Helen Wolfe?

She reached his side, and the fervency in her blue eyes nearly stilled his heart. "Oh Bernie, thank goodness we caught you."

Bernie whisked a glance over each of their faces. Rosy cheeks and bright red noses let him know they'd waited in the cold for quite a while. "Is something wrong?"

"I needed to speak with you." She curled her hand through his elbow and turned to her brothers and sister. "Wait right here. I'll be back in a minute." Then she guided Bernie a few feet away to the curb, where she released his arm and clasped her gloved hands in front of her. "Bernie, you're a praying man, and I need to ask you a favor."

Bernie's heart swelled. She'd just paid him the biggest compliment ever. Whatever favor she needed, he was ready.

"Remember Richard Mason? He came over Thanksgiving evening as you were leaving."

Bernie stifled a growl. He gave a brusque nod.

"Well. . ." Suddenly Helen turned shy, angling her gaze away from him. "He's asked to begin seeing me again—courting me. But I'm very confused about whether or not to allow it. You see, he. . .he. . ." She didn't directly meet his gaze, but her eyes fluttered in his direction. "He broke off our engagement when I refused to send Henry, Carl, and Lois to an orphans' home. He didn't want the responsibility of seeing to their needs."

"Is that so?" Bernie tried to rein in his contempt for a man who'd ask Helen to cast aside her siblings, but when she blanched he knew he'd failed.

"But he must have changed his mind," she hurried on, once again looking off to the side, "because he's back, and he's been very kind to the children. So I was wondering if, maybe..." Very slowly she turned her face to look fully into his eyes. "Would you please pray for me to know what to do? I desperately need someone to help me support the family. If I were to marry Richard, our financial problems would be solved. He's well established with the opera company, and he says if we're married, he'll secure a spot for me, too. The salary would far exceed what I make now as a hotel maid." Her words tumbled out faster and faster, her breath forming little clouds of condensation that drifted beneath Bernie's chin. "The children deserve security, Bernie, but I want to make the right decision. Will you pray for me?"

Bernie lifted his hands to cup her shoulders. Her tight muscles beneath the fabric of the blue suit spoke of her inner turmoil. How he wished to draw her into his embrace, to offer her comfort. But she'd only asked for prayer. A lump formed in his throat, and he swallowed before speaking. "I already pray for you, Helen. Every day I pray for you, and for Henry, Carl, and Lois."

She blinked up at him, her pink-painted lips slightly open. "Y–you do?" Tears flooded her eyes, deepening the blue irises.

"God put you on my heart, and I've been praying for Him to give you peace and strength."

One tear broke free of its perch on her thick lashes and rolled down her cheek. Gratitude glowed from her eyes.

"So now I'll pray for God to make clear to you what you're

to do. But, Helen?" He paused, uncertainty making his pulse pound. "Be careful. Don't be looking for a man to meet your needs. Men'll let you down. They can't help it—they're human, and they fail. But God? He can't forsake you. It's not in His nature. So lean on Him before anything or anyone else. Trust Him to meet your needs. Will you do that?"

She swished away her tears with her fingertips. Her chin trembled. "I–I'll try."

He knew what effort it took for her to make the concession. He squeezed her shoulders and then let his hands fall away. "It's cold out here, and you need to get the youngsters on home. You ridin' the trolley?"

"We never ride the trolley."

Bernie understood. He reached into his pocket and withdrew two quarters. "Then take this—get a taxicab."

She stared at the coins. "Oh, but. . ."

He grasped her wrist and pressed the coins into her palm. "For me, Helen, so I don't hafta worry about Lois catching a cold. Please?"

With a deep sigh, she closed her fingers over the silver disks. "Thank you, Bernie. You're a very kind man." She gestured to the children, and they dashed to her side. Curling her arm around Lois's shoulders, she offered Bernie a quavering smile. "Thank you for your prayers, Bernie. I promise, I'll be listening for God's voice."

Over the next week, Helen honored her promise to Bernie. As she cleaned hotel rooms, she kept her heart tuned to guidance concerning continuing the job or taking up singing in the opera company with Richard. While she saw to the children's needs, she searched her mind's eye for images of someone stepping in beside her to help her parent her siblings. When she lay in bed at night, she petitioned God to give her the peace and strength Bernie had mentioned. And, although her circumstances didn't change, she discovered she slept more soundly and felt less burdened than she had before. Could that mean God was answering her prayers? Her heart fluttered with hope that maybe, just maybe, God was near.

Richard began the habit of visiting each evening. He always brought gifts—frivolous items like lace handkerchiefs for Lois or chocolate bars for the boys. Helen tried to be grateful, but she wondered why he'd ceased leaving items they could really use, the way he'd done before. With each visit, she tried to envision him as a permanent fixture in their lives. He was willing to accept her and the children—he'd said so— but somehow she couldn't get comfortable with the idea. So although he pressured her continually to set a wedding date— "*And make it soon, darling*," he'd whispered into her ear—she hesitated. Only when she knew for certain Richard was the helpmate God wanted for her would she give her answer.

Sunday morning, December seventh, bloomed like many other December days. Cold, crisp, with snowflakes dancing on a stout breeze. Helen held a steaming mug of coffee between her palms and looked out at the gray morning. Both Carl and Lois had the sniffles, so although she hated to skip church services, she chose to let them sleep. Henry was dressing, however, unwilling to miss attending church. He'd stated firmly he could go on his own.

Her heart swelled, thinking of the fine young man her brother was becoming—responsible, caring, mature beyond his years. And much of the change she'd seen in the past months was the result of Bernie O'Day's influence. Henry quoted Bernie, emulated Bernie, and respected him as a mentor. Henry didn't have a father anymore, but he had Bernie, and Bernie filled the hole their father's passing had left in Henry's boyish heart. *What a kind, good man is Bernie O'Day.* A flutter in her chest accompanied the thought.

"Sis?" Henry bustled into the room, interrupting Helen's musing. "Want me to stop at that hamburger stand and pick up some burgers for our dinner? They'll be yesterday's leftovers, so only a nickel apiece."

Both Lois and Carl loved the greasy sandwiches with ground beef and grilled onions. They might be enticed to eat if offered such a treat. Although Helen had little money to spare, she retrieved her purse and gave Henry two dimes to purchase burgers. Then, as if something—or Someone—encouraged her fingers, she plucked out one more dime and dropped it into Henry's waiting palm. "Put that in the offering plate."

Henry beamed in approval. He dashed out the door, his knitted cap tugged low over his ears.

The house quiet, Helen curled on the sofa with her coffee and her Bible. If she couldn't attend service, she could at least read from God's Word. She flipped pages, scanning passages, and finally settled on one of the letters to the Corinthian churches. Nestled in the corner of the sofa, she read, content. When she reached the thirteenth chapter of First Corinthians, her reading slowed, her finger underlining the words describing God's idea for love.

Without conscious thought, she began to read aloud. "'Charity suffereth long, and is kind; charity envieth not; charity vaunteth not itself, is not puffed up, doth not behave itself unseemly, seeketh not her own, is not easily provoked, thinketh no evil; rejoiceth not in iniquity, but rejoiceth in the truth; beareth all things, believeth all things, hopeth all things, endureth all things. Charity never faileth. . . .'" She closed the Bible, the final line replaying in her thoughts. Charity—love—never fails.

An image of the engraved coin she'd sold to Bernie O'Day

flashed before her mind's eye. Slipping to her knees, she clasped her hands and offered a heartfelt prayer: "God, Bernie told me Your love never fails or forsakes. I want so much to believe You'll always be there and You'll meet the needs of my brothers, sister, and me. Bernie is praying for my strength to find You. I'm seeking You. Will You please make Yourself known to me? Make Yourself known to me in a way I cannot misunderstand, because I need You, God. I need You. . . ." Her last sentence choked out on a sob.

She pushed to her feet just as the front door burst open and Henry charged into the room. He dropped a grease-stained brown paper bag as he raced to her and took her hands in his icy grasp. "Helen! The burger man said there's a rumor that Japan attacked the United States!"

Chapter 9

In all of his twenty-eight years, Bernie had never kept a radio going day and night, but the events of December 7th, 1941, changed that. For the next three days he hovered near the Philco, determined to stay abreast of the latest developments concerning the United States' involvement in the war that, up till now, had seemed distant.

When Henry arrived after school, he, too, drifted to the radio frequently, and more than once Bernie overheard the boy mutter, "Soon as I'm old enough, I'm puttin' on a uniform and going to battle. Won't let nobody attack my country and get away with it!" Bernie admired Henry's determination, but at the same time, his heart quaked. He prayed the war would be over long before Henry reached his eighteenth birthday. At the same time, a desire to do as Henry stated—don a uniform and march in defense of America—continually played at the fringes of his mind.

Posters of Uncle Sam with his finger extended and the words *I Want You!* appeared in windows all over town. Banners claiming the Army's need for fighters hung from lampposts. Everywhere Bernie went, the tug followed him, and by mid-December, he'd made a decision: After Christmas he'd close the shop, visit the Army Recruitment Office, and sign up to defend his country.

He had only one concern. What would Helen do without

the income Henry earned? He added another prayer to his list of daily petitions. *Lord, help me find a way to ascertain the Wolfe family won't go hungry. Even if I'm not here, meet their needs, my Father.*

∽

"What are you saying, Richard?" Helen stared at the man, disbelief raising her voice several decibels.

"It isn't difficult to understand," Richard retorted, his eyebrows fixed in a supercilious angle. "With the U.S. focus on that European skirmish, people will lose their interest in attending operatic performances. We have no choice but to move the opera company into Canada."

"But. . .but I can't move to Canada!" Helen held her hands outward, indicating the simple yet homey parlor in which they sat together on her parents' sofa. "This is my home."

Richard huffed out a breath, adjusting the lapels of his suit jacket. "Then stay. Honestly, Helen, you can be so stubborn."

Helen reared back, her pulse thudding so hard she felt as though a bass drum beat in her head. A snippet from her reading in First Corinthians whispered through her heart— "Charity. . .seeketh not her own." Richard claimed to love her, yet he was willing to walk away from her to pursue his own interests. Again.

She jolted upright and marched several feet away. Aware of her brothers and sister studying in their bedrooms, she deliberately kept her voice low although every part of her wished to rail at him in righteous indignation. "Richard, why did you bother to come back? You haven't changed. All you really care about is seeing to your own selfish desires."

He glowered at her. "What about you—insisting on holding on to this little house and wasting your life taking care of a bunch of kids that aren't even yours? You aren't concerned about me and what I want or need. We had plans, you and me, and you threw them all away!"

"If you truly loved me, you'd understand how much Henry, Carl, and Lois mean to me. You'd never ask me to discard them."

Richard rose and advanced at her, his lips curled in contempt. "I thought a year of separation would be enough to bring you to your senses—to make you see what a fool you'd been. But apparently I was wrong." He released a derisive snort. "Well, I'm going on to Canada where I will continue to build my career. And by the time the war ends, my name will be up in lights. But what of you, Helen? What will you have achieved?"

Helen shook her head slowly, silently berating herself. How could she ever have desired this man's presence in her life? He was right when he'd called her a fool, but he'd chosen the wrong reason to accuse her of foolishness. Now that she recognized the truth, she was more certain than ever that she did not want a future with Richard. Not even for the financial security he could provide.

She spoke softly, her voice quavering with conviction. "I love singing—I always have and I always will—but I love my brothers and sister more." Peace swept through her, assuring her she'd made the right choice. "Someday, Richard, God will give me the chance to sing again. But not for myself. When I sing again, it will be for Him."

Another snort blasted from Richard's sneering lips. "That won't bring much fame and fortune, my naive little Helen, but who am I to stand in your way?" He buttoned his jacket and headed for the door.

Helen called after him, "Before you go. . ."

He turned back, his expression impatient.

She drew in a breath, gathering the strength needed to set aside her pride and utter the thank-you so she'd owe him nothing. "I appreciate the boxes of food and the other items you left. They helped us a great deal."

He rolled his eyes. "Helen, I don't have the foggiest notion about any boxes. I didn't leave anything here."

"Y–you didn't?"

"No." He wrenched the doorknob. "Good-bye—this time for good." He stepped out, slamming the door into its frame behind him.

Helen stood in the middle of the room, confusion coiling through her middle. If he hadn't left the boxes, then who had?

"Sis?" Henry's voice sounded from the hallway. Helen turned and spotted her brother half hidden in shadows. He held the brown corduroy jacket he'd been given. "I've got a loose button on the pocket. Can you fix it?"

Helen stared at the jacket. Comprehension tickled the far corners of her mind. Could it be. . .? Hopefulness tried to rise in her chest, but she refused to allow it free rein. She'd made a grave error in assuming Richard was the mysterious gift-giver. She wouldn't jump to another conclusion. She needed solid proof.

She held out her hands. "Give me the jacket, and I'll stitch that button on securely for you." As Henry placed the warm coat in her hands, she smiled. "Come sit beside me while I stitch. I need to talk with you about something important."

Bernie rose from his knees in prayer. His knees and shoulders ached—he'd remained on the wood-planked floor of his bedroom, hunched over the edge of the bed, for nearly an hour— but he smiled in satisfaction. God had answered his prayers in bigger ways than he could have imagined. The plan was perfect. *If only Helen agrees.* He winged up one more petition for God to move in Helen's heart as effectively as He'd moved in his own so they could be in one accord.

He headed down the darkened stairway to the lower level of the building. He tugged the overhead string dangling from the single lightbulb just inside the shop. Light flooded the room. For several minutes Bernie stood in the glow and examined the shop, allowing memories to creep from every corner. He'd lived his entire life in the upstairs of this shop. He'd worked side by side with his father, learning the trade, earning an honest living. He loved this shop—loved serving people. How it had pained him to think of it closing. And now it wouldn't have to.

Thank You, God. Thank You.

Gratitude warming him, he moved to the storeroom and rummaged around for a suitably sized box. He had one more task to complete before marching into war. One final gift for Helen and her siblings. Then he could leave, secure that she— and his shop—would be just fine.

As the calendar inched toward Christmas, Bernie took advantage of every minute to prepare for his time away. In the past, he'd only given Henry cleanup and organization chores. Now he taught the boy every aspect of running the pawnshop. He drilled Henry on the value of items so he could offer a fair exchange without losing money on the transaction. He taught the boy how to keep the meticulous records and to make out tickets as well as how to rotate stock on the shelves so his regular customers wouldn't miss any new arrivals.

Henry soaked up the information, never questioning an instruction. Instead, he listened attentively and applied the lessons, proving his trustworthiness. Yes, Bernie had made the right decision.

During the evening hours, Bernie accumulated items for one last, special delivery to the Wolfe family. Clothing in sizes he hoped were appropriate for Lois, Carl, and Henry. Bolts of fabric so Helen could sew suits and dresses. Canned goods and bags of beans, flour, and sugar. Necessities—those things needed for survival. Satisfied with his choices, he turned his attention to things intended to bring pleasure.

For Henry, he selected a set of Encyclopedias Britannica— the 11th edition, published in 1911—but still very serviceable and containing information perfect for a studious young man like Henry. He chuckled as he wrapped a Little Slugger baseball bat, mitt, catcher's mask, and chest gear for Carl. He wished he could be a fly on the wall when Carl spotted the signature in the mitt's pocket—Jumbo Brown, pitcher for the Giants in 1940. A baseball fan like Carl would take excellent care of the mitt— Bernie just knew it.

The biggest gift—too big to wrap—lurked in the corner beneath a moth-eaten white sheet. Bernie'd had to promise the produce stand owner a silver dollar to borrow his horse and cart to deliver the clavichord, but it would be worth it to please Lois. The old clavichord wasn't a piano, but it was pretty with its elaborate paintings of flowers and vines, and it would take up less space in their parlor. He needed to find someone willing to give the little girl lessons, but he had a few more days to work out that detail.

Helen's gift was the smallest. It fit perfectly in a foil-covered box with a hinged lid. And he knew the item nestled in the velvet interior would deliver a message directly from his heart to hers. His fingers trembled as he tied a bright red bow around the box. Only two more days, and he'd make one more trip in the darkness of night to leave gifts on the Wolfe family's porch. Then, on Christmas evening, he'd visit to share his plans. And after that, he'd leave.

Pain stabbed. It would be hard to leave them, but it was the right thing to do. His country needed him. And he was leaving his shop in good hands. God would carry them through. Bernie had no doubt.

Chapter 10

Lois and Carl awakened Helen early Christmas morning, bouncing on the bed and squealing for her to get up now! Although Helen would have considered it a gift to sleep in a bit on her one day off, she stifled a groan, tugged on her robe, and allowed the rowdy pair to drag her to the parlor where they'd decorated the tree the evening before. Their cries of delight at the sight of the packages she'd tucked beneath the sagging branches of the little tree chased away the vestiges of sleepiness, and she instructed Carl to fetch Henry so they could open their gifts.

Although the presents were simple and mostly practical, the children raved anyway, pleasing Helen. How proud Mom and Dad would be of them—so unspoiled, so unselfish. Despite her misgivings and stumbles, they were growing up just fine. She whisked a prayer heavenward in gratitude to God for working in their hearts, even when she'd wished to refuse His presence.

Henry bestowed Helen with a package marked "To Helen from all of us," and Helen pretended great surprise before removing the ribbon and lifting the lid. Inside she found a neat stack of yellowed music sheets—hymns and ballads and even a couple of haunting spirituals. The desire to burst into song exploded through her chest as she fingered the music. *Someday, God, I know You'll let me use my voice again.* She thanked her siblings enthusiastically, giving each of them a heartfelt hug, and then they trooped to the kitchen for a Christmas breakfast of pancakes with globs of strawberry jam.

When they'd finished, Helen shot an impish grin around the table. "All right, are we ready to deliver our Christmas surprise?"

Carl and Lois cheered, and Henry pushed away from the table. "Let's go!"

"Dress warmly," Helen admonished as the trio raced for their bedrooms. She followed, trying to imagine Bernie O'Day's face when they showed up outside his shop. Over the past two weeks, they'd practiced Christmas carols in three-part harmony, with Henry singing baritone in his newly discovered man's voice, Carl and Lois sharing the alto line, and Helen carrying the melody. Although they had no other gift for Bernie, she was certain he would accept their offering with much appreciation. His kindness knew no bounds.

Carl led the family out the front door, but he came to a stop just over the threshold, causing Lois to slam right into his back. Henry—hunched over Lois's short frame like a gargoyle in his attempt not to run her down—scolded, "What're you doing, Carl?"

"There's stuff out here," Carl bellowed.

Helen peeked past her siblings and gasped. Stuff indeed! Their gift elf—whoever he was—had outdone himself this time. She couldn't believe the bounty! They dragged everything inside and then spent a happy half hour examining it all. Helen watched her siblings with the little box bearing her name on it held between her palms, unopened.

When the clamor died down, Lois pointed at the red-ribboned box and said, "Aren'tcha gonna open yours?"

Curiosity battled with apprehension. The box—the kind of box that held jewelry, specifically a ring—certainly would reveal their unknown benefactor. She knew who she wanted it to be.

Her heart nearly twisted in agony, hoping. What would she do if it turned out to be Richard once more trying to manipulate her into bowing to his will?

"Open it, Helen," Carl prompted, and Henry and Lois added their encouragement.

Painstakingly, Helen removed the bright red ribbon and set it aside. Then, holding her breath, she eased back the lid of the box. Gold glinted at her. With a gasp, she snapped the box closed and shoved it in her pocket.

"Helen!" her siblings protested, but she jumped to her feet and urged them up from their spots on the rug. They had a concert to deliver. When it was over, she'd share the box's contents with them. But not until she'd had a chance to look into Bernie O'Day's face and find the truth in his hazel eyes.

Bernie sat at his little table tucked beneath the front window and sipped his third cup of hot black coffee. He looked at the clock—10:35 a.m. Only ten minutes had passed since he'd last peeked at the round face. He'd told himself he wouldn't intrude on the Wolfes' Christmas until evening, but the day stretched endlessly before him. How could he while away the hours? Before he settled on a suitable pastime, something reached his ears.

Music. Voices. Sweet voices, the highest line delivered so beautifully gooseflesh broke across his arms. Feeling like the man in Clement Moore's " 'Twas the Night before Christmas," he threw the sash open. Cold air blasted him, but he stuck his head out the window and looked down at the street. His heart galloped happily in his chest—Helen, Henry, Carl, and Lois stood in a half circle on the pavement below, their faces lifted toward him and "Joy to the World" pouring from their throats.

He couldn't stop a joyful laugh from escaping as he peered

downward. They finished the carol then launched into "O Little Town of Bethlehem," followed by "Hark! The Herald Angels Sing." By the time they finished with "We Wish You a Merry Christmas," tears stung Bernie's eyes. He'd never received a sweeter present.

When the last note trailed away, he waved his hand and called, "Wait right there!" He nearly skidded down the stairs in his eagerness to get to the door, his slippers treacherous on the slick stair treads, but he made it without mishap and flung the door open, nearly bopping Carl, who stood too close. Laughing, Bernie ushered them inside then stood staring at them with a goofy grin on his face and his hands shoved in the pockets of his sloppiest pants.

"Merry Christmas, Mr. O'Day," Lois chirped, and Carl and Henry echoed the sentiment.

"Merry Christmas," Bernie said, bouncing his smile across each of the younger Wolfe siblings before allowing it to rest on Helen. Her sweet face, bold pink, wore the most tender smile he'd ever seen. Her blue eyes bored into his, shimmering with a myriad of emotions. Looking into her eyes, Bernie found it difficult to draw a breath.

Then, without speaking, she reached into her pocket and withdrew a little foil box. She held it aloft on her mitten-covered palm, giving it a gentle bounce. "All this time, it was you."

Bernie gulped. He didn't know what to say, so he simply nodded, aware of three pairs of eyes looking back and forth between Helen and him in curiosity.

Helen tipped her head, her brown curls brushing the shoulder of her plaid coat. "Why didn't you tell me?"

He shrugged slowly. "Didn't want you to thank me. Wanted you to thank. . ." Would she understand? Would she accept the gifts once she knew?

Understanding bloomed across her face, her rosy cheeks

deepening. "I do thank Him." She swallowed, tears winking in her eyes. "Mostly I thank Him for bringing you into our lives."

Bernie forgot all about Henry, Carl, and Lois. He lurched past them, reaching, and moments later he held Helen in his embrace. Cold air scented her hair, and he buried his nose in her curls, savoring the aroma of Christmas. She laughed against his chest, the little box digging into his back where she clung to him. But he didn't mind. Not at all.

"Merry Christmas, Bernie," she whispered, her breath caressing his cheek.

"Merry Christmas," he replied. How he longed to press his lips to hers, but whispers and soft giggles reminded him they had an audience. With reluctance, he released his hold on her and stepped back. "I was going to come see you all this evening, but since you're here, should we go upstairs? There's something I need to tell you."

The four of them preceded Bernie up the stairs to his apartment, Lois and Helen in the lead with Henry and then Carl trailing. Bernie resisted the urge to hurry Carl—the boy's gaze bounced here and there, taking in every detail of the shop. Now that the time had arrived to share his plans, Bernie experienced a sense of urgency. What would he do if Helen said no? He pushed the anxious thought aside. God had planted this idea in his heart, and he'd prayed about it. If it was meant to be, Helen would see the sense and agree. He needed to trust.

They entered the big room that served as sitting room, dining room, and kitchen. Bernie pointed to a long, low settee, and the four of them lined up on the peach-colored cushions. Bernie took his father's overstuffed chair across from the settee and rested his elbows on his knees. For the next several minutes, he spilled his intentions to enlist in the Army and his hopes that Henry and Helen would assume management of his pawnshop while he was away. They were silent and attentive as they listened, eyes wide.

Sitting up, Bernie heaved a sigh. "That's about it, I guess. I know I'm asking a lot. Don't know how long I'll be gone—I'm praying the war won't drag on, but I don't reckon any of us can know for sure. But while I'm away, whatever the shop brings in, it'll be yours. I won't have need of anything while I'm off fighting. And—if something should happen and I don't come back—I've already drawn up papers to transfer the shop to Henry." Warmth filled Bernie's chest as he gazed at the serious-faced young man seated so straight between Lois and Carl. "I know I couldn't place it in better hands."

Henry swallowed twice, his Adam's apple bobbing in his skinny neck. "I won't be taking it, Mr. O'Day, 'cause you'll be back. I know you will."

Helen added, "We'll all be praying for your safety every day. You can rest assured of that, Bernie."

Both Carl and Lois nodded, adding their agreement.

Helen still clutched the little box in her hand, and she now placed it on her knee. She opened the lid and withdrew the gold coin she'd brought into his shop only four months ago. Such a short time, but such a changing time. Bernie felt as though his life had turned completely around since the afternoon she'd entered his shop, breathless and needy. She held up the coin, and the gold glinted as brightly as the twin tears shimmering in her eyes.

"Bernie, you've showed me that love—God's love—never fails. You've taught me to trust again, and for that I will be forever grateful."

Thank You, Lord. The words sang from Bernie's heart. His life had changed but so had hers. God had answered his prayers.

෨෨

On January 3rd, 1942, Helen and the children accompanied Bernie to Grand Central Station. Snow dusted their caps and froze their noses, but she was determined to keep a happy face for Bernie's sake. They'd spent part of each day since Christmas together, and in those precious hours she'd grown to love him more than she'd thought possible. It hurt to send him away, yet pride filled her as she thought about him serving his country. Everything about Bernie—his kindness, his strength, his steadfastness, and mostly his love for God—pleased her.

As they walked hand in hand along the boarding ramp with Henry, Carl, and Lois trailing behind them, she inwardly prayed for God's protection over him while they were apart, and she knew he prayed the same thing for her and her siblings. Their hearts were in one accord, just the way God designed them to be.

At the end of the ramp, a cluster of men in matching green blouses and baggy trousers with duffel bags lying in piles around their black boots, waited in a noisy throng. Henry pointed. "Guess they're all goin', too, huh?" A thread of longing colored Henry's tone.

"Guess so," Bernie said. He curled his hand over Henry's shoulder. "But don't be thinking their job is the only important one. Taking care of your family—that's your job, Henry. I'm trusting you to work hard in school and keep the shop running." A lopsided grin climbed Bernie's smooth-shaven cheek. "Gotta have something to come back to, y'know."

"Yes, sir." Henry stood straight, his chin high. "You know I'll see to everything."

"I know you will." Bernie turned from Henry to deliver hugs to Carl and Lois. The pair clung hard, their fingers catching handfuls of his shirt fabric. He held them as long as they wanted while Helen battled tears, waiting her turn.

Finally the two stepped back, rubbing their noses. They shuffled over to Henry, and Bernie reached for Helen. She held on to him as tightly as Carl and Lois had. Maybe more tightly.

It didn't seem fair to have to let him go after only just finding him—this man she loved and trusted, with whom she longed to build a lifetime of memories. But she respected his desire to go, and she wouldn't stand in his way.

He cupped her face between his palms and pressed his lips to hers, the kiss sweet and warm and rich with feeling. A whistle blared, and he stepped back. Although his arms hung at his sides, he caressed her with his eyes. "That's my cue," he said, his tone gruff.

She nodded.

Henry darted forward, his hand extended. "Here, Bernie."

Tears distorted Helen's vision when she recognized the object Henry pressed into Bernie's hand.

Henry said, "My grandma held on to this as a promise. Now I want you to hold it as a promise from all of us"—he gestured to Carl, Lois, and Helen by turn—"to you. That we'll be here waiting when you come back."

Helen closed her hand over Bernie's, the coin pressed between their palms. "And on that day, we'll take a picnic to Central Park."

Bernie winked. "What if it's October?"

Helen thought she might cry, but she managed a smile instead. "Is there some rule that says you can't have a picnic in October?"

Bernie laughed—the sound like music. He pocketed the coin and gave a nod. "You got a deal. We'll meet at the bridge."

"And throw bread to the ducks," Helen said. Tears filled her eyes, making his image waver.

The whistle blasted again, and the men at the end of the ramp began boarding. But Bernie didn't move. Then Carl let out a huff. "Mr. O'Day, if you don't leave, you can't come back. So would'ja please hurry up and get goin'?"

Her brother's petulant query was just the splash of humor

Helen needed to cast aside her doldrums. Rising up on tiptoe, she planted a kiss on Bernie's cheek and gave him a little push. "Go, Bernie. God be with you."

"And with you." He offered a quick salute, yanked up his bag, and trotted to the train car. Just before stepping inside, he looked back and lifted his hand in a final wave. And then he was gone.

Helen remained with her arms around Carl and Lois's shoulders until the train rolled out of the station with a screech of wheels on iron and mighty huffs of steam. Lois sniffled and Carl stood with folded arms and distended lower lip. Beside them, Henry held his chin high and proud, his fingers on his brow in a salute until the train disappeared from sight. Then he lowered his arm and turned to Helen.

"Well, guess it's time to get busy. Got a shop to run."

Helen nodded.

Henry's eyes twinkled. "We'll be all right, you know."

Again, Helen nodded, a smile growing on her lips without effort. "We will be. God will carry us through."

Together, they turned toward home.

DREAM A LITTLE DREAM

PART 3

by Ronie Kendig

Chapter 9

Wow, that's some legacy."

Sean peeked to the side, to the brown and gold eyes that dazzled him stupid. "Yeah?" Too bad he wasn't like them. Too bad he was the black sheep of his family. Like his dad.

The thought gave him pause. Not only had Granddad said his dad was a good guy before he broke, but so had Simon. So. . .what happened?

"You're part of that, Sean." Jamie's soft voice warmed him as she bumped shoulders with him. "You come from a great line of warriors."

He folded the letter, thinking back over the story. Everything in him wanted to debate the point, to argue that his family was just messed up, but he was seeing the fruit of the Wolfe legacy. This time, not from a tainted source, not from his mother.

"You're not unlike Helen Wolfe."

He arched an eyebrow at Jamie.

"She had tough circumstances. She fought and won a happy life. In doing so, she paved the way for your grandfather—her brother—to have a good life."

"And how do you figure I'm like that?"

"You're prepared to do whatever it takes to end the painful side of the legacy that your mom started."

He clenched his teeth at the mention of his mother. "Even

if I could overcome that—I'm broken in other ways, Jamie."

"We all are."

"Yeah, how are you broken?"

Jamie ducked her head, cheeks going pink.

"Sorry. Guess that was too personal—or maybe I'm the only one who's so broke he needs fixing."

"No." Jamie touched his arm. "I just. . .well, honestly, it's not easy to talk about. God's been challenging me lately about. . ."

"Dancing?"

Surely he could see the color from the heat seeping into her face. "Yeah."

"What are you afraid of?" Whoa, that was weird hearing his voice asking the very question she'd thrown at him.

Jamie scrunched up her shoulders. "I don't know." She drove her gaze across the green field, to the street where traffic slithered past. "I guess. . .maybe that I'm not good enough. That even if I got in, there's no way I could afford tuition in addition to living expenses. Maybe, when Uncle Alan was still single, he might've let me stay with him, but now that he's married—"

The two lovebirds were almost sickening. "The very reason I moved out of Aunt Mitzi's place." Besides, seeing the two of them. . .it was just hard to watch. Not everyone got lucky in love like that. "That, and I was too afraid to watch the marriage dissolve."

Jamie's eyes widened. "Why on earth would you say that?"

He shrugged. "It happens. To a lot of people."

"And it *doesn't* happen to a lot." Jamie swept her hair back and craned her neck. "Is that why you're so afraid of. . .us?"

It felt like he was manning that .50 caliber gun again, the report rattling through his chest. "Just don't want to hurt you."

Her expression warmed, eyes softening.

Don't look at me like that. Sean shifted his gaze back to the letter, tried to push his thoughts from the beautiful woman sitting beside him. The one who turned his brain to mush, the one who made him want to break his no-women rule. Could they make a go of it? He'd managed his anger, his frustration. What about the TBI? He couldn't imagine Jamie ditching him the way his fiancée had. But. . .what if she did?

He couldn't take another rejection. Not from Jamie. The idea smothered him. He sloughed his hands together, mind racing. Thoughts careening through the possibilities. What if—was she—worth the risk?

A burst of nausea swelled up his throat. Breathing grew hard. His vision blurred.

"Sean?"

Warmth on his back. Rubbing. Soothing.

"Sean, are you okay?"

The panic abated, leaving him drained but also acutely aware of Jamie Russo. Her delicate touch against his spine. Her soft voice. Her floral scent. Heat darted through his gut as he pushed his gaze to hers.

"It's okay," she said softly with a smile. "You're okay."

Beautiful, sweet Jamie. Wavy brown hair, cinnamon-colored eyes. Full, soft lips. What would it be like to kiss her?

"Hi, Jamie."

At the strange voice, Sean blinked. Hard. A lot. He drew a breath and turned toward the path. A gangly man stalked toward them.

"Martin." Jamie punched to her feet, as if she felt guilty. Did she? What did she have to feel guilty about? Or was Sean lighting up her personal radar the way she did his?

Ah, Sean thought he recognized him. The guy from Jamie's studio. The one who'd given a ubiquitous warning about how Jamie needed to be focused, not distracted by a man.

Jealousy coiled around Sean's chest and tightened as Jamie hugged the goon.

"What are you doing here?"

"Heading to the studio. Hey, listen..." He gave Sean a look. "If I'm interrupting..."

"No," Jamie said. "What's up?"

"We could use some help on the last piece. It's not coming together. Do you have time?"

The test. Would Jamie leave Sean for this guy?

Of course she would. Dance was her life. Sean was a distraction.

"Um"—Jamie's brown eyes darted to him then back to the goon—"right now?"

This didn't need to be painful for her. Sean shifted on the bench and reached for her satchel. He glanced down and saw the application, practically begging him to put it to good use. He'd once told her he wouldn't let her sacrifice her dreams for him. And he meant it.

He stuffed the application in his back pocket and handed the bag to Jamie. "See you later."

Chapter 10

Mouth agape, Jamie stared at the e-mail that hit her in-box. Then she stared at her phone, where she'd gotten the notification.

"What's wrong?" Monet slid into the booth seat beside Jamie.

"I got an e-mail."

"Yeah, that's amazing." Sarcasm dripped off Monet's words and her expressive green eyes.

"It's from The Juilliard."

Monet squealed and wrapped her arms around Jamie. "You applied! I am so proud of you. Man, you really had me fooled, saying you weren't going to."

"I didn't!" Jamie frowned at the screen as its brightness faded. "I had the application, filled it out—for what reason, I don't know. There's no way on earth I could afford it. I even told Sean—"Jamie clamped her mouth shut. A swirl of cold washed through her stomach.

"What?"

She wet her lips. "I. . .I showed it to Sean. He told me I should apply." Covering her mouth, she realized she hadn't seen the application since that day in the park. Surely, he hadn't. . .

"You think he turned it in?"

"No. Yes." She slumped. "Why would he? I *told* him I couldn't afford it." She jammed a hand through her hair. "Now

I'm going to have to call the school and tell them it's no use."

Monet clapped her hand over Jamie's. "No."

"No?"

"You have to try out, right?"

Dumbstruck, she nodded.

"Then go, try out—at least this way you'll know if you've got what it takes."

"But it's weeks of practice and rehearsals."

"So? Martin's not doing anything now. He's jetting around the globe, touring other troupes. You haven't gotten a job yet, so you've got the time—"

"Thanks for pointing that out."

"Hey, I'm just saying Sean has given you an opening, so take it!"

"First, I need to talk to Sean, let him know I don't appreciate this."

With a questioning glance, Monet asked, "Do you really want to ruin what you guys have going?"

Again, Jamie fell silent.

"He probably thought he was doing a favor—"

"Favor? I can't afford this!"

"Get a loan."

"No way. Not after all the debt my parents left behind getting their doctorates. I won't put myself or anyone else in that situation." She brushed the loose strands of hair from her face. "Digging myself into debt makes me look and feel irresponsible."

"Or like you're figuring out how to chase your dreams."

"That is a thing of beauty."

The words pulled Sean around, ratchet in hand.

A man in a brown leather jacket and boots strode toward

him. Purpose defined the man's steps. Wealth and power defined his presence. "Is she for sale?"

Sean placed a hand on the Harley. " 'Fraid not." He'd never felt closer to his father than he had in the last several weeks working on this. It was as if he'd gotten a piece of his life back working on the antique bike. To give it away, he'd be giving away his father, his heritage.

The man planted his hands on his belt, his leather jacket winging back. "You sure?"

"Positive."

"Marc Riordan." The man shoved his hand toward Sean.

Arms up revealing his greasy paws, Sean shrugged. "Sorry. Wouldn't want to get you dirty."

Mr. Riordan produced a business card and slid it in Sean's shirt pocket. "You change your mind about that bike, give me a call. I'd pay a pretty penny for her."

"Why?"

Riordan grinned. "Guess you could say I'm a collector. Runs in the family."

Huh. "Well, sorry. She belonged to my dad, and it's got a lot of sentimental value. It'd be like giving away my dad."

Chuckling, Riordan squatted and ran a finger over the parts. "Amazing. It's all original."

"Yes, sir. Just not running quite right yet. Won't be much longer."

A throaty growl emanated through the warehouse, drawing Sean's attention to the main bay doors where a sleek car slid out of the bright sun into the bleak anonymity of the garage. *Whoa.* Was that an. . .Aston Martin? Old. Vintage.

Stunned, Sean watched as Harry climbed out from behind the wheel. He strode toward them. "Hey, Marc. Yep, I heard that rattle you mentioned. We'll get her fixed up and back to you tomorrow."

Riordan straightened and clapped Harry on the shoulder. "Knew I could count on you. Thanks." He turned back to Sean. "Twenty thousand."

Sean's heart stuttered. "What?"

"I'll give you twenty grand for her."

Mouth dry, Sean looked at Harry, uncertain the man was legit. Harry's curious expression told Sean there was no fluff to this man's offer. "All the same. . ." He wiped his mouth. "I just can't."

"If you change your mind, call me. The offer stands as long as she's running."

Harry watched his friend leave then spun toward Sean. "Are you out of your mind? He just offered you twenty large!"

"Yes, and I told him no. The Harley belonged to my dad. I'm not giving her up."

"It could solve your problems."

"Sorry," Sean said with a chuckle. "Money's not that powerful." But God is. And if he were that desperate for money, God would provide a way that didn't involve a transaction that felt like selling off his soul.

Harry shook his head then pointed behind Sean. Over his shoulder, he spotted Jamie walking up the drive to his bay. His heart did a crazy jig at the sight of her stepping in out of the spring morning. Even after their walks in the park every night, she still turned his insides to Jell-O, especially seeing her wearing the coin pendant. Scared but thrilled him. "I'll get cleaned up, and we can head out."

She nodded but said nothing. Weird. But maybe that meant she was just getting comfortable with him.

It wasn't until they were halfway across the park that the quiet grew uncomfortable. Something was wrong. He could feel it. Feel the tension rolling off her with the way she kept her arms folded, barely spoke.

Normally he was the quiet one. She the exuberant. He liked that. Liked experiencing life through her. He'd wanted to ask her if she was okay, but it was a stupid question. Of course she wasn't. Or she'd be talking, laughing, matching the summer day.

The thought that stalled his brain was: *Is she going to break things off?*

What things? They weren't dating.

"You're quiet."

Jamie stopped. Pivoted as if she'd been just waiting for him to break the ice. Her eyebrows dove. "Did you do it, Sean?"

He drew back. "Do what?"

"My application—did you send it in?"

He lowered his head. Rubbing a hand over his neck, he remembered how his gut had churned as he'd put the cashier's check in the envelope and dropped it in the mail.

Jamie flinched away, pain etched in her tawny features. "Why?" Her voice hitched. "Why would you?"

"You deserve to go, Jamie. You're an amazing dancer. You've sacrificed everything for Alan. It's your turn now."

Face crimson, she whirled on him. "No. It's not. I can't!" Her eyes glossed.

"Why? You got accepted—that's how you knew I sent it in, right?"

She dragged her fingers through that light brown hair. "I can't afford it."

"I'm sure—"

"No." Jamie jerked away from him. "No, don't say anything. You had no right to send that in, and now. . ."

Had someone run a knife through his chest it would not have hurt as much as seeing Jamie in pain. "I'm sorry."

"You had no right!"

His vision blurred and the world darkened with one last visage: Jamie running away from him.

Alone in his apartment, Sean sat on the kitchen chair staring at the brown padded envelope sitting on the table. Fingertips pressed to his lips, he eyed her name on the return address. JAMIE RUSSO. A weight in his chest made it hard to breathe.

He knew what was in there. The same thing that had been in there since he received the package a week ago: the pendant. Jamie was giving up on them. On him.

"I'm broken and nobody can deal with it."

"You ruin everything."

"If he just wasn't born, we'd be okay."

Head cradled in his hands, Sean tried to get a grip on reality. On his life spiraling out of control. It'd be okay. He'd lost other girls.

But nobody like Jamie.

Eyes closed, he tried to steady his breathing. The thought of her leaving him, cutting herself out of his life, had brought on episodes just about every day. He'd bailed on Harry and the garage this week. The fact was he couldn't face the bike knowing he'd run Jamie off. It was like facing his father, and seeing all over again how he just wasn't good enough.

Maybe. . .was it the scars, too? Had she figured out a pretty girl like her could have any guy she wanted? She deserved The Juilliard. She deserved a man who was a man—one who could hold it together.

I don't deserve her, God. But. . .I don't want to lose her. Show me. . .what can I do?

The letters.

No, he didn't need any more history lessons that proved he was the weak link in the Wolfe line. He needed a solution.

Read the last letters.

That's right. There was only one bundle left. Penned by his

great-great-great-grandfather, William Wolfe during the war.

Maybe. . .

Sean dragged the tin from the counter and flipped it open. He dug out the last envelope.

Why. . .why should he even care?

Somehow. . .his fingers managed to unfold the oldest letter. The very first letter of the Wolfe legacy.

BEAUTY FROM ASHES

by MaryLu Tyndall

Dedication

To anyone who has been scarred by life,
both on the inside and on the outside

*To console those who mourn in Zion, to give them beauty for ashes,
the oil of joy for mourning, the garment of praise for the spirit
of heaviness; that they may be called trees of righteousness,
the planting of the Lord, that He may be glorified.*

ISAIAH 61:3 NKJV

Chapter 1

*The Shaw Plantation, outside Williamsburg,
Virginia, May 23, 1865*

Permelia Shaw's stomach growled. Wrapping her arms around her waist, she gazed out the front parlor window. Evening shadows fell upon the cedar and birch trees, coating them in a dull, lifeless gray. Gray like the Confederate uniforms that had been conspicuously absent from Williamsburg these past three years.

Except those that were torn and covered in blood.

A moan rumbled from her belly again. Though she'd eaten an hour ago, the meager fare had not been enough to assuage her hunger—a recurring condition during this horrendous war. Four years was a long time, a lifetime for a young girl who had been only nineteen at the beginning. A lifetime in which she had grown from a pampered daughter of a wealthy plantation owner to a mature woman who could fend for herself.

"I'm hungry." Sitting upon the flowered sofa, her sister Annie voiced Permelia's thoughts. "Jackson said he'd come by with some meat today."

Permelia rubbed the blisters on her palms and gazed down at the dirt beneath her fingernails, trying to gather what patience she had left after her long day's work. "It is not right to take food from that man, Annie."

"Oh fiddle. Who cares?" her sister whined.

Spinning around, Permelia made her way to the mantel. Striking a match, she lit the gilt-bronze sconces on either side of the fireplace. Golden light spilled into the parlor, chasing away the gloom and cascading over Annie's lavender taffeta evening gown. No matter the war, no matter their destitute condition, Annie always dressed to perfection.

Just like their mother had done. A quality sorely lacking in Permelia. Sorrow dragged her to sit beside her sister, who drew her lips together in one of her perfectly adorable pouts.

"Without Jackson's help"—Annie thrust out her chin—"we wouldn't have been able to keep our furniture, our gowns, and most of our things. Not to mention the occasional pig and rabbit he brings for supper."

Permelia touched her sister's arm. "But it's wrong to entertain his affections, Annie. Not only is he the enemy, but you're engaged."

"I haven't heard from William in over three years." Annie waved a hand through the air. "For all I know, he is dead."

Permelia's heart collapsed. "You shouldn't say such a thing. You haven't heard from him because you stopped writing to him." She slid her hand into a pocket she'd sewed inside her skirts, where the hard shape of the coin brought her comfort— hope that he was still alive, though his last letter had been dated eight months ago.

Annie's eyes moistened. She lowered her chin. "It was this war. I couldn't bear the thought of him on the battlefield."

"There, there." Permelia flung her arm around her sister's shoulders and drew her close. "It is, indeed, a hard thing to consider." She knew that fear all too well for she had thought of nothing else for three years. What she couldn't understand was how her sister could abandon the man she loved in his darkest hour. When he needed most to read her comforting, loving words. But Annie was different from Permelia. More sensitive to such brutalities.

Drawing a handkerchief from her sleeve, Annie dabbed her eyes. "Why hasn't Jackson come to call in over two days?"

The quick shift of topic from William to Jackson made Permelia wonder who the tears were really for. "Now that the war is over, perhaps he's gone home." At least she hoped so. The Union soldier was all charm and good looks. A man who had taken advantage of Annie in her weakened condition.

"How can you say that?" Shrugging from Permelia's embrace, Annie rose and straightened out the braided ruffles of her gown. "He said he loves me. He said he would never leave me."

Though the words bristled over Permelia, she studied her sister, trying to understand. The war, the Union occupation of their town, both had taken so much from Annie. Including Colonel William Wolfe, a month before their wedding. No wonder Annie had rushed into the arms of the first man who offered her his protection and love. Yet. . .

"Jackson shouldn't say such things when you are betrothed to another." Permelia held out a hand toward her sister. "Besides, never fear, I'm sure William will arrive any day now."

Annie swerved about, her hoop skirt nearly knocking over a porcelain vase on the table—one of the objects Mr. Jackson Steele had returned to them. "Everyone leaves me. Papa left me, then Samuel. Then William."

Rising, Permelia eased beside her sister and took her hand, swallowing down a burst of her own sorrow as she remembered the letter from President Davis announcing the death of her father at Cross Keys. And the one that followed informing them that their brother, Samuel, was listed as missing in action. They'd never heard from him again and could only assume the worst.

"Then Mama last year." Annie faced Permelia, her eyes swimming. "I cannot lose Jackson, too."

Permelia squeezed her sister's hand. "Many have lost much during this war. Some their entire family and homes. We have each other. And God. He has taken good care of us."

"*I* have taken care of us." Annie tugged her hand away. "By accepting Jackson's courtship. Otherwise those Yankees would have stolen everything we had."

Permelia's jaw tensed. "So I suppose my toiling in the fields every day is of no consequence?"

Annie's eyes softened, and she gave a gentle smile. "Don't be cross, Permi." Turning, she traversed the room then settled back on the sofa. Her smile faded beneath a heavy sigh. "Oh, what are we to do?"

"We are doing fine. Thank goodness Papa left the plantation to us in the event we should lose both Samuel and Mama. Besides, we have Martha, Elijah, and Ruth to help."

"Slaves," Annie said with contempt.

"How can you say that?" Permelia took a seat beside her sister. "They are family now. This is their home, too. With Elijah's help, we will plant tobacco like Papa did and start all over again."

"Us?" Annie's face scrunched into a knot. "Women growing tobacco?"

"Why not? Wouldn't it be wonderful to be so independent? To run this plantation by ourselves and answer to no one?"

"I hate this dull, old plantation. All I want is to get married." Annie gazed out the window.

Permelia studied her sister, wondering how they could be so different, wondering why she could so easily throw away a liberty that few women enjoyed. If their brother did not return, whoever Annie married would inherit all the land. Permelia had accepted that fact. But for now, she relished her freedom, relished being in charge of the plantation that had meant so much to her father—and now to her.

"Ah, William," Annie said dreamily. "So successful, so

wealthy, and *so* handsome."

Permelia smiled. "And honorable and kind and good. He is still all those things, Annie. If God permitted him to live, he'll be here soon to marry you."

"Do you really think so?" Annie's eyes regained their sparkle.

"Yes." Though the thought both elated and pained Permelia. Elated her that William lived. Pained her that he would never be hers.

"Then I shall marry him and live in New York, wealthy and happy and strolling the streets on the arm of the most handsome man in the city." Annie sat up straight and spread her skirts around her. "He is handsome, isn't he, Permelia?"

"Yes, very." Permelia's face heated, and she turned away. Handsome indeed, but so much more than that.

While her sister went on about all the cotillions, plays, and concerts she and William would attend, and the attention they would draw as they sauntered down The Boulevard in New York, Permelia returned to her spot at the window. Darkness settled over the Virginia landscape. A slight breeze stirred the hair dangling about her neck, bringing with it the scent of wild violet and moist fern. Pulling the coin from her pocket she caressed it lovingly—the coin William had given Annie in Central Park as a vow of their love the night the war had separated their families. Permelia had carried it on her person ever since Annie had tossed it out her window in a fit of rage. She brushed her fingers over the engraving on the back:

"Love never fails. W.W. Central Park."

She prayed that was true. For if William ever came to claim his bride, Permelia would need all the power of her love for both William and Annie to keep her own heart from crumbling.

∞

William Wolfe nudged his weary horse down the path. Weary like him. Removing his cap, he wiped the sweat from his brow.

His head throbbed, his back ached, and his legs cramped from riding for five days, stopping only long enough to sleep. He must see Annie. He couldn't wait another day. Another minute. Even for a quick bath and shave in Williamsburg to remove the stench from his clothes. Besides, the condition of the town had spurred him onward: the crumbling buildings, whiskey-drinking loafers, and hundreds of graves dotting the churchyards. Not to mention the hate-filled looks of the citizens as he rode past in his Union uniform. He'd heard Williamsburg had been occupied by Union forces since early in the war. But what he hadn't expected was that his fellow soldiers would have caused so much destruction. His only hope was that the pernicious Union arm had not stretched as far as the Shaw plantation, an hour outside of town.

Darkness transformed the landscape into a battlefield of prickly monsters and sinister dwarfs. Or perhaps it was just his war-weary mind. William rubbed the back of his neck. An owl pealed a *hoot, hoot* from his right, sending a chill over his skin. He chuckled. He'd faced the enemy head-on in battle. Was he now afraid of the dark?

Or perhaps exhaustion and excitement had befuddled his mind. Regardless of the late hour, he must see Annie. He must ensure her safety. He must know if she still loved him.

And whether she would still love him after she saw his face.

William swept fingers over the ripples of burned flesh on his right cheek. Though numb to the touch, the pain of molten iron lingered in an agonizing memory.

He was no longer handsome. He was disfigured, a monster. Wounded on the outside and on the inside in a war that he could not wrap a shred of sense around. A war in which he'd seen thousands of his fellow Americans die.

Ducking beneath a low-hanging branch, William released a heavy sigh and patted the bundle stuffed in his coat pocket.

Dozens of letters from his beloved Annie. Letters that made him believe she would love him no matter what he looked like. Letters that had exposed a heart so pure, so loving, it astounded him that he'd not seen it in her before.

Rounding a large oak, his eyes beheld the Shaw plantation house. Still standing! Three Greek-style columns guarded a wide front porch on the first and second levels. Moonlight dripped from the roof like silver rain, making it seem surreal—an ancient palace in another world. Yet the lantern light flickering from the parlor window and in one of the upstairs rooms spoke of an earthly reality. Of living, breathing people inside.

William nudged his horse onward. "We're almost there, fellow."

The beast begrudgingly complied, even heightening its pace as the gravel crunched beneath its hooves, mimicking the pounding of William's heart. He halted before the house, slid from his saddle, straightened his coat, and slowly made his way up the stairs to stand before the door.

He raised his hand to knock when he heard the distinct cock of a gun, a booted footfall, and the words in a female voice. "Stop right there or I'll shoot you dead where you stand."

Chapter 2

The musket shook in Permelia's hand. The intruder turned his head in her direction, but she could not make out his face. What she could make out was that he was tall and muscular. And that he wore a Union uniform. All three things together portended disaster. She had spotted him from the window, sent a trembling Annie upstairs to rouse Elijah from his bed, then grabbed her gun and sneaked around the side of the house.

"I said, don't move. I know how to use this."

"I have no doubt of that, miss." His voice was low and rich, like the soothing sound of a cello. Somewhere deep within her, it nipped a memory. A pleasant one, for her heart took up a rapid beat. He lifted his hands in the air, revealing the gleam of a saber hanging at his side.

"Who are you, and what do you want?" Permelia demanded.

"Miss Shaw?" He addressed her as if he were making a social call. "Is that you?"

Again the voice eased over her like warm butter. She gulped, attempting to steady the musket. "And who, sir, are you?"

Lowering his arms, he took a step toward her. Memories assailed her exhausted mind—memories of Union soldiers rampaging through her home, tossing everything they could find into sacks: jewelry, silverware, expensive vases and figurines, her father's collection of East Indian tobacco. All accompanied by the sound of her mother wailing in the distance.

And one soldier in particular who wasn't satisfied with only objects. Whose eyes burned with lechery as he crept toward Permelia in her chamber.

"It's me, William." *William.* The name echoed through the night air as if traveling through molasses. Permelia shook her head, corralling her terrifying thoughts.

The soldier took another step toward her. *No, not again!* She must defend her family. Her sister, herself.

She fired the musket.

The crack split the dark sky. The man ducked. His horse neighed. Smoke filled the air, burning her nose, her mouth. Grabbing the gun, he ripped it from her hands. But instead of assaulting her, he wrapped his arms around her and held her tight. He smelled of gunpowder and sweat and earth.

"It's all right, Miss Shaw. It's me, William. You're safe now." The comforting words drifted upon that familiar voice, sparking hope within her. *William?* Against all propriety, she melted into him, never wanting the dream to end. For surely it must be a dream. The same one that had made her endless nights bearable these past years.

But then he was gone. A whoosh of chilled air sent a shiver through her.

"What you doin' there!" Elijah shoved William back and leveled a pistol at his chest. Martha, ragged robe tossed over her nightdress, appeared in the doorway, lantern in hand, their twelve-year-old daughter, Ruth, behind her.

William raised his hands again. "Whatever happened to southern hospitality?" He chuckled and a quizzical look came over Elijah's face.

Shaking off her stupor, Permelia charged forward. "It's all right, Elijah." She nudged his pistol aside. "It is Colonel William Wolfe, Annie's fiancé."

"Then why did you shoot 'im, miss?" Elijah studied William but did not release his firm grip on the weapon.

"I was about to ask the same question," William said, his tone playful.

Permelia faced him, his expression still lost to her in the shadows. "I'm so sorry, Colonel Wolfe. I didn't know it was you."

"Quite all right, Miss Shaw." He lowered his hands. "I've grown used to being shot at."

"Well, I'll be." Martha held up her lantern and moved forward. "Annie's fiancé. We thought you was dead." The light crept over the porch and up his blue trousers, blinking off his saber, the three gold buttons on his cuff, and brightening the red sash about his waist.

"I am happy to report otherwise." William dipped his head.

"Elijah, put down that gun," Martha scolded.

Recognition loosened the overseer's features. "Good to see you, Colonel." He lowered the weapon.

Martha took another step forward. Light from the lantern slid over William's steady jaw, regal nose, penetrating eyes, and glimmered off the epaulette on his shoulder.

The breath caught in Permelia's throat. She'd dreamed of him for so many nights, she could hardly believe he stood before her all flesh and man.

But then Martha's smile faded. Ruth turned away and retreated into the house. Elijah's eyes widened.

William raised a hand to his right cheek, hidden from Permelia's view.

"Let's not stand here staring at the poor man. Do come in, Colonel." Permelia swept past him, leading the way into the parlor. "Annie will be beyond herself with delight."

Delight that now spiraled through Permelia, igniting all her senses.

Dragging off his hat, William stepped through the doorway.

Elijah grabbed the musket and took a spot beside his wife, while Ruth clung to the shadows beyond the stairway. All three lowered their eyes to the floor. Something they hadn't done since before Lincoln's proclamation had freed them from their chains.

Whatever was wrong with everyone?

Closing the door, Permelia tried to settle her erratic breathing. *William was alive!* Not only alive but standing in her foyer. She studied him while his back was turned, trying to gain her composure. Light from an overhead chandelier cascaded over him, accentuating the war-honed muscles stretching the fabric of his coat. Hair the color of rich coffee grazed his stiff collar, curling at the tips.

Why would her heart not settle? He came for Annie. Not for her. Taking a deep breath, Permelia moved to face him.

The first thing she noticed was the depth of pain in his eyes. The second, that the right half of his face hung in shivered purple flesh. What was left of Permelia's breath escaped her lungs. She stifled the gasp that tried to force its way to her lips. His jaw stiffened, and he looked down, fumbling with his hat.

Permelia took a step toward him. His eyes met hers. Those brown eyes, deep and rich like the soil within a lush forest. The same eyes she remembered. Yet not the same. The haughtiness, the innocent exuberance, was gone, replaced by wisdom and deep sorrow. Her own eyes burned. For the agony he must have endured. For the pain, the heartache.

"Martha, would you please go get Annie," Permelia said.

"I'll put some tea on." Elijah grabbed Ruth and pulled her from the room as Martha headed upstairs.

William attempted a smile. "You are not repulsed?"

Permelia shook her head. "No. Of course not." Shocked. Grieved. She wanted to tell him that he could never repulse her, but the words faltered on her lips. "I cannot imagine what you must have endured. How did it happen?"

William shifted his boots over the marble floor. "An exploding cannon."

Permelia threw a hand to her mouth. "Oh my. When?"

"Nearly nine months ago."

So that was why his letters had stopped. "When I—Annie didn't hear from you, we feared the worst."

Miss Permelia's eyes flooded with concern as she reached up to touch William's face. He shrank away, uncomfortable. Yet she kept her eyes upon him. She did not run away in horror as so many others had done. That alone gave him hope. A hope that had stirred at the mention of Annie's name. A hope that kept him rooted in place, willing to risk allowing her to see him in full light.

And perhaps, dare he hope, to look at him in the same way her sister was doing right now. Not in pity but with concern, and something else that gave him pause. He shrugged it off when he heard light footfalls on the stairs. The swoosh of satin and the lacy bottom of a gown materialized. The steps increased. The gown bounced, and the angel appeared.

His Annie.

Hair like gold silk was pinned back from a face that rivaled perfection: alabaster skin, pink lips, luminous blue eyes. Curls danced over the nape of her neck with each graceful movement down the stairs. She raised her gaze to his. Her smile washed away. The flame in her eyes turned to ice. An ice that froze her in place. She drew a hand to her chest.

William's heart shriveled.

"William?" Annie managed to breathe out in a halting sob.

"I'm afraid so." Though he wanted to turn away, to spare her the horrendous sight, he kept his gaze steady upon her, waiting—waiting to see love sweep away the shock and horror in her eyes.

Instead she lowered her chin and turned her face away. Gripping the banister, she wobbled.

Risking her repulsion, William vaulted the steps between them and grabbed her by the waist before she fell. She stiffened at his touch. Permelia reached her other side and after exchanging a compassionate look with William, led her sister down the stairs and into the parlor.

William hesitated, his insides crumbling. Should he follow? Was he welcome? But Permelia's gentle smile beckoned him onward.

The servant woman he remembered as a slave brought tea and William chose a cushioned seat in the shadows. Annie sat on the sofa, staring at the cold hearth.

Permelia approached him. "Colonel, please join us." She gestured toward one of the chairs in the center of the room. "It's only the shock, I'm afraid."

"Please call me William." He heaved a sigh. "And I won't be staying."

Annie's eyes shot his way.

Permelia smiled. "Don't be silly, William. You've no doubt had an arduous journey and are welcome to stay with us as long as you wish." She made her way to the table and began pouring tea.

"Either way, I have only a week before I must report back for duty." William shifted in his seat. His gaze wandered to the door, silently chastising himself. He'd put his selfish desire to see Annie above any thought of how the sight of him would shock her. Now he'd upset her. Which was the last thing he'd wanted to do. He should leave.

Miss Permelia handed her sister a cup. "William must stay. Isn't that right, Annie?"

A visible sob shook his beloved Annie. Sipping the tea, she set it down with a delicate clank as his future, his heart, hung precariously on her response.

"Of course, William. We'll not hear another word about it." Annie's sweet voice brought his gaze back to her, where he was graced with one of her smiles. A smile that warmed him down to his toes—as it always used to do. Hope stirred. Then grew stagnant again as she added, "But surely you must return to your regiment?" It wasn't so much the question but the expectation in her tone that set William aback.

"After the terms of surrender were signed, my commanding officer granted me a month's leave." He coughed. "To settle my affairs."

Annie spread her skirts around her in a festoon of velvet braids and ruffles. "You must forgive me, William." She raised the back of her hand to her mouth, sorrow crumpling her features. "Seeing you. . .like this. . .it is such a shock."

Miss Permelia gave her sister an odd look before she settled into a chair between them. "William was injured in the war, Annie."

"Of course. I can see that," Annie snapped. Then the sharp lines of her face softened. "I'm so sorry, William. I hope you didn't suffer."

Not nearly as much as he was suffering now. "No, not overmuch."

Rising, Annie swooshed to the mantel, eyeing the gilded clock and bronze figurines sitting atop it. "We feared you had died." Yet there was no fear in her voice.

Permelia sipped her tea. "It is very good to see you, William."

"Yes, of course." Annie forced a smile, tried to look at him, then glanced back at the mantel.

Unease prickled over William, his thoughts traveling to his last visit to the Shaw estate—when he'd been welcomed with open arms, enjoyed the richest foods, the southern charm of Mrs. Shaw, and the hustle and bustle of a prosperous tobacco plantation. "Where are your mother and father? Your brother?" William sipped the bitter tea. He never did enjoy it without sugar.

"They are all gone." Miss Permelia stared at the teacup in her lap. "Except perhaps Samuel. We do not yet know his fate."

"I hate this detestable war! It's taken everything from me!" Annie fisted her hands beneath lacy cuffs.

Gone. William nearly dropped his cup. Instead, he set it down on the table beside him and rose. He longed to swallow Annie up in his arms, comfort her. "How? When? Why didn't you tell me in your letters?"

Annie's brow crumpled.

Permelia shifted in her seat. "Father died at Cross Keys. And Mother became ill and joined him last year."

"So it is just the two of you here?"

"And Elijah, Martha, and Ruth," Miss Permelia said.

Sorrow, coupled with alarm, assailed William. "How have you managed?"

Annie sank to the sofa in a sob, drawing a handkerchief to her eyes.

"Better than most." Miss Permelia moved to sit beside her sister. "We keep a garden and Elijah hunts. In addition, by God's grace, we hope to harvest our first crop of tobacco this year." Golden specks of hope and sincerity sparked in her eyes.

William wondered why he'd never noticed how beautiful they were before.

"We've had to sacrifice so much." Annie's voice broke, tearing at his heart.

A lump formed in his throat. "I'm so sorry. You never mentioned it." He could only surmise that in her selfless love, Annie had wanted to keep him from worrying while he was on the battlefield. Warmed by the thought, he gazed about the room, noting the rosewood center table, painted porcelain vases, gilded mirror and assorted oil paintings hanging on the wall, and the mahogany Grecian sofa upon which Annie sat. "But how were you able to keep so many of your nice things?"

Clutching her handkerchief, Annie straightened her back and glanced out the window. "We've made friends with some of the Union soldiers."

"Ah, then we are not all such bellicose toads?" William chuckled.

A smile flickered then faded on Annie's lips. "Why have you returned, William?" Her eyes swept to his. And finally remained.

And it gave him the impetus to answer her question.

"To marry you, Annie. If you'll still have me."

Chapter 3

Permelia set the candle atop her dressing bureau and knelt beside the trunk at the foot of her bed. Her heart felt as heavy and dark as the sultry night lurking outside her window—a night that barely entertained a whisper of a breeze to stir the curtains framing the leaded glass. Silver moonlight spilled upon the woven rug and toyed with the hem of her gown as if trying to improve her mood.

Wiping moisture from her eyes, she chastised herself. She should be happy for her sister. Happy that William had returned to claim her as his bride. Deep down, she *was* happy for Annie. Although at the moment, that joy seemed smothered by her own selfish agony. *Please forgive me, Lord.*

Oh, why hadn't Annie answered William's question? If he had asked Permelia to marry him, she would have leaped into his arms on the spot. Instead, Annie had promised to discuss his proposal tomorrow and promptly left the parlor. Perhaps she engaged in some sort of amorous dalliance, as she often liked to do with men—flirtatious behavior Permelia had never quite mastered.

She opened the trunk and drew her mother's shawl to her nose. The slight hint of jasmine still lingered on the cashmere. She breathed it in, wishing her mother were still in her chamber a few steps down the hallway. Though they'd never been close—not like her mother and Annie had been—Permelia missed her terribly. And if there was ever a time she needed a mother's advice, it was now. Now when her heart was a jumble of discordant thoughts and feelings. Most of which she'd never experienced before.

Setting the shawl aside, she pulled out the bundle of letters and held them against her chest.

Ah, William! He was here! She could hardly believe it.

The air stirred outside her window, fluttering leaves and entering her room to caress her face—as she had longed to do with William's. To caress away his pain, kiss away his scars. Lowering the bundle to her lap, she brushed her fingers over the crinkled vellum. Such sweet words they had shared, such intimacies, dreams, and hopes.

A tear slid down her cheek and plopped onto the paper. She quickly dabbed it with her sleeve, lest it destroy one precious word. But these letters were not meant for her. William thought he had been writing to Annie. When he penned each word, each loving phrase, it was Annie's face that filled his thoughts, his heart.

Not Permelia's.

"Oh, Lord, I never meant to deceive him. Please forgive me." She squeezed her eyes shut as more tears escaped. She had only meant to comfort him. To give him hope in the midst of the horrors of war. Words from someone who cared. But when William had mistook her signature, P. A. Shaw, for Annie, and his letter had been so filled with joy at hearing from her, Permelia hadn't the heart to tell him that Annie had given up writing to him.

That she had turned her affections to another.

Then the years passed and the letters continued, and Permelia found herself waiting for each missive with giddy expectation. For out from the penned words, emerged a hero. A man of honor, nobility, and courage. Yet with a kind, gentle heart and a wit that never failed to make her smile.

And she had fallen in love with him.

But now, he had come for Annie. As it should be. Permelia should be thankful that she had been able to offer William some solace during his darkest hours. Placing a gentle kiss on the bundle, she put them back in the chest, covered them with her mother's shawl, and closed the lid. At least she would always have his letters. No one could take away the precious words she'd shared with William.

A cloud swallowed up the moonlight, leaving her with only the flicker of a single candle to chase away the gloom.

God, help me to forget him. Help me to be happy for him and Annie. If not, she feared she would shrivel up and die.

∽

William stood beside the men under his command. Ten companies in all. Behind them, Union soldiers lined up like incoming waves before a storm. Early morning fog shrouded the field in a white veil, muffling the sounds of boots on grass, the cocking of rifles. The heavy breaths of jittery soldiers. The frenzied thud of their hearts.

The crack, crack, crack *of gunfire split the mist. A flock of birds fluttered into the sky and disappeared.*

"Fire!" William shouted. The soldiers raised their guns and ignited thunderous pandemonium.

Enemy bullets whined past William's ears. "Forward march!" The men parted the tall grass.

Yellow flashes sparked in the distant mist.

The air filled with smoke and screams and ear-pounding explosions. William grabbed the man to his right to usher him forward. He toppled to the dirt. A red pool bubbled from his chest. His eyes gaped toward heaven in vacant shock.

William crumbled beside him.

The boy was only eighteen. William had met his mother back in

Philadelphia and had promised her he'd look out for him. Brushing his fingers over the boy's eyes, he closed them forever.

A cannonball struck the ground nearby. The shock sent William flying. He landed in mud. Pain throbbed in his shoulder. A loud buzzing filled his ears. Accompanied by the thump, thump *of his heart. Shaking his head, he looked up just in time to see the tip of a Rebel saber headed for his chest.*

William snapped his eyes open. The blur of thick timbers crisscrossing the ceiling came into focus. The *cluck, cluck* of a chicken sounded. Where was he? He shot up and gazed over the gloomy room. Sunlight speared through small glass windows on either side of a door, which stood slightly ajar. A chicken perched in the entryway, staring at him. She clucked, bobbed her head up and down, then ruffled her back feathers and left.

He snorted. Even a chicken couldn't stand the sight of him.

Tossing his legs over the side of the cot, William raked both hands through his hair and drew in a deep breath, wondering when the nightmares would stop. He rubbed his sore neck and took in the one-room house that had once been the slave quarters. At least that's what Miss Permelia had told him when she and Elijah had escorted him there last night. Since it wouldn't be proper for him to stay in the main house, and the overseer's quarters had been burned to the ground last year, this was all they had to offer. Little did Miss Permelia know that compared to where he'd been sleeping the past four years, these quarters might as well be a room at the Fifth Avenue Hotel in New York.

He struggled to his feet, stretched out the aches still resident from his long ride, and made his way to the washbasin with one thought in mind. *Annie.* After making himself as presentable as possible, he intended to spend the day with her. Woo her and charm her like he used to do before this hellish war had separated them. He stopped to ensure the letters were still safe in the coat he'd slung over the back of a chair. He drew them out, flipped open his knapsack, and gently placed them inside. Better not to carry them around and risk losing them.

For to him, they were the essence of the woman he loved and the reason his sentiments for Annie had grown so deeply, despite his extended absence—despite her reaction to him last night.

Cringing at the memory, he made his way to the basin Elijah had filled with water. How could he blame her? Perhaps William should have written of his arrival. Perhaps he should have written about his scars. Deep down, he supposed he'd hoped they wouldn't matter; he'd hoped the woman he'd grown to love wouldn't care.

But what he hadn't considered was how much suffering Annie had faced in the past four years. Besides, when he'd posed his question of marriage last night, she had not turned him down. In fact, he thought he saw a spark of love in her eyes.

Halting before the worn chest of drawers, William gazed at his reflection in the mirror. Sunlight rippled over his puckered flesh, accentuating the purple divots and the pale, distended skin. He slammed his eyes shut. Would he ever get used to the sight? How could he expect someone as beautiful as Annie to love such a monster?

After washing and shaving, he donned a fresh uniform, minus his coat, and headed outside. The smell of freshly turned dirt, horseflesh, and wild oregano combined in an oddly pleasant scent as his glance took in the wide expanse of the plantation. Behind the main house stood the kitchen, dairy, and smokehouse. Off in the distance the barn rose stark before the encroaching forest. To its right stood the stables, once brimming with horses, but now eerily silent.

Laughter drew his gaze to a field to his left. He halted at the sight of a woman, hoe in hand, tending the soil beside Elijah.

Curiosity drew him toward her. Surely Miss Permelia hadn't meant that *she* worked in the fields. Absurd!

Yet, as he came closer, his suspicions were confirmed, for there she stood, dirt smudged on her arms and neck and perspiration beading on her brow. The hem of her cotton skirt was gathered and tucked within her belt, revealing a soiled petticoat and ankle boots covered in mud. But it was the healthy color of her cheeks and the way the sun flung golden ribbons through the brown hair dancing about her waist that drew William's attention.

Shielding her eyes, she gazed up at him and quickly lowered the folds of her gown. "William, good morning. Did you sleep well?" The red on her cheeks darkened.

Elijah leaned on his shovel. "I always slept well in that house. Lots o' good memories in there."

William flinched, wondering how a slave could have any good memories. "I did sleep well. Thank you." He stared at her aghast. "This is hardly suitable work for a young lady." His voice came out more pretentious than he intended.

"I beg your pardon, Colonel, but this particular lady does not wish to starve. Nor see her sister starve. I hardly think that either of those options would be more suitable than this breech of propriety."

The way she tossed her pert little nose in the air made him want to chuckle. Instead he cleared his throat. "Forgive me. I meant no insult."

"Quite all right." She set her hoe aside and stomped toward him, dirt clumping on her boots. "We've already planted the carrots, chard, green onions, and basil." She pointed to another large field next to what used to be the storehouse, if William's memory served, where tiny green sprouts dotted the fresh earth.

"And what are you planting here?"

"Tobacco." Lifting the brim of her straw bonnet, she gazed

over the field. "Our first attempt. Now that the war is over, we hope to be able to make some profit from it like Papa did."

William wondered how they would manage all the work it required to process tobacco but dared not ask. He had a feeling this resolute woman already had a plan.

She wiped her face, leaving a smudge of dirt. William found it adorable. "You must be hungry," she said.

He should be. He hadn't eaten since early yesterday. But his stomach had been nothing but a cyclone of nerves since he'd arrived. "In truth, no. I would, however, like to see Annie."

Elijah chuckled.

Miss Permelia gazed at the sun. "I fear you'll have a few hours' wait. She never rises before noon."

William jerked at the statement, concern flooding him. "Does she suffer from some malady?"

Permelia shook her head. "It's the war. It has taken a toll on her, I'm afraid."

William frowned. "A toll I only increased with my sudden appearance last night."

Permelia looked at him, neither avoiding the scarred side of his face, nor flinching at the sight of it. "I'm sorry for her reaction, Col—William. She's not been herself lately." She gestured toward the small brick house where ribbons of smoke spiraled from the chimney. "Help yourself to biscuits and coffee in the kitchen. Martha and Ruth will be happy to see you." Gathering her skirts she headed toward the main house. "Forgive me, but I haven't the time to entertain you properly. I must get cleaned up and head into town."

Wiping his arm over his forehead, Elijah returned to his work.

"Alone?" William shouted after her.

She faced him. "I need to bring the wild blueberries Elijah and I picked this morning to sell at market, and"—she hesitated—"attend to another matter."

"Unescorted?" William could not conceive of a woman traveling alone during such tremulous times.

"I have no choice, Colonel. Elijah is needed here." Her tone was clipped as she marched toward the house.

This time he couldn't help but chuckle. Turning, she gazed at him quizzically. "And just what is so amusing?"

William caught up to her. "You call me colonel when you become cross."

"I do?" She laughed. "But I'm not cross. It's just that many things have changed since your last visit." She continued onward.

He walked beside her. "If you'll permit me, I'd love to accompany you. Though I am not on duty, I should report my presence to Lieutenant Lee, the provost marshal." Besides, he found himself longing to spend more time with this fascinating woman, a woman who didn't shy away from dirt, hard labor, or working side by side with a freed slave.

"I'd be delighted." Her blue eyes flashed with an emotion he could not place before she turned away.

Five hours later, William strode down the Duke of Gloucester Street in Williamsburg, ignoring the sordid glares from both the citizens and returning Confederate soldiers. He could hardly blame them. He had reported to Lieutenant Lee and found him to be a pompous buffoon, who no doubt had entertained himself by reigning terror over the poor inhabitants.

Tipping his hat at a passing lady and her child, William continued onward, noting how she cringed when she saw his face and hurried to the other side of the street. How different from the way he'd been received by ladies before the war. He pictured himself, dressed in his velvet cape and top hat, strolling down The Boulevard in New York City, showered with the flirtatious smiles of ladies who all but swooned as they passed him by.

Yet he was the same man as before. Perhaps even a better man for all he'd endured.

His glance took in the buildings along the side of the road, and he realized Williamsburg had endured much as well. Yards once filled with flowers stood trampled and vacant, outbuildings had been burned, porches lay neglected and crumbling. Gaping holes glared at him from walls like angry eyes where windows and doors had once stood.

A group of Confederate soldiers, bandages around the arms and legs of their stained uniforms, loitered in front of Vest's store. The sharp scent of alcohol stung William's nose as he passed. Their gazes locked upon him like a dozen rifles, following him down the street and making him think that it hadn't been such a good idea to wear his uniform.

He quickened his pace to the Baptist Church, where Permelia had said to meet her. Church. He hadn't stepped inside a real church in years—only attended services when it was required of him in the Army. And even then, he had ceased to listen to the sermons. He still believed in God. But if he had to admit it, William supposed he was angry at a God who would allow the misery he'd witnessed on the battlefield. Men torn forever from their families. Young boys mutilated, their lives ripped from them before they'd even lived. And for what?

The United States would continue on as before. Yes, the slaves were freed—as evidenced by the many Negro freedmen walking the streets, receiving nearly as much scorn as William. But had the war really been about slavery? Or was it about men grasping for the same things that had caused all the conflicts throughout time: greed and power?

Shoving his cap farther on his head to shadow his scars as much as possible, he wiped the sweat from his neck. May, and already the unbearably hot Virginia summer was forcing its way onto citizens who had suffered enough. Looking forward to a reprieve from the sun, he entered the foyer of the church.

He halted as if he'd slammed into a brick wall.

What he had expected to see was a group of people kneeling in prayer or listening to the endless droll of some parson demanding recompense for the damages done by the North. Or perhaps a group of the faithful gathered to complain and whine about the occupation. Instead his eyes landed on a pile of amputated limbs stacked in the corner like discarded pieces of rotting wood. A horde of flies swarmed around them. William's stomach vaulted. He forced his eyes to cots that lined a room where pews must have once stood. The injured, maimed, and sickly writhed upon them like churning, restless waves at sea. Women in bloodstained aprons, carrying buckets and bandages, flitted between the patients, ministering to their needs. A stench he'd only smelled once before, on the battlefield of Chancellorsville, where the Union had lost over fourteen thousand men, assaulted him—the sour, putrid smell of death. Hand pressed to his belly, William stepped outside for air before he made a fool of himself.

"William." He turned around to see Permelia wiping her hands on her stained apron and looking at him with concern. "Are you unwell?"

Forcing a smile, William gathered his resolve. "No. Forgive me. I hadn't expected. . ."

"To see so many injured?" She brushed strands of hair from her face. Red stains marred her fingers.

"No, not here, in a church."

She glanced over her shoulder at the mayhem, genuine sorrow on her face. "We have been tending the wounded here ever since the war began." She sighed. "Despite the peace, the injured still pour in."

Moans shot from the open door, drawing William's gaze to a Union uniform draped over the bottom of a cot. He blinked. "Both sides?"

She gave him an incredulous look. "Of course. God loves Yankees, too, William." One corner of her mouth lifted.

He smiled, delighting in the sparkle in her eyes, present despite the misery surrounding her. After all she'd suffered and lost, after shouldering the burden of providing for her and her family, she still took time to help others. "How often do you assist here?"

"Twice a week, or as needed. The doctor sends for me if we receive a large number of wounded."

A woman called to her from within the church. Excusing herself, Permelia dashed off, promising to meet him outside as soon as possible.

Happy to oblige her, William wandered around the church grounds, stopping at the west side of the building where group graves marked the passing of many soldiers from this world.

"We ran out of space for them." Permelia's voice startled him, and he caught the mist in her eyes before she turned away.

He wanted to apologize, wanted to erase the pain from her face. But instead he offered his arm and led her away from the church.

Guilt assailed Permelia as she wandered down the street on the arm of her sister's fiancé. Not guilt in the act, for it was innocent enough, but guilt that she enjoyed William's company so much—his voice, his words, his touch. Thrilled that he had offered her his arm. Proud to be walking by his side, despite the belligerent gazes scouring them. Throughout the occupation, many of Williamsburg's citizens had grown to loathe the Yankees. With God's grace, Permelia saw them as mere humans on the other side of a nonsensical dispute that had been caused by man's foolish sinfulness.

Adjusting her bonnet, she peeked at William sauntering

beside her. The way the fringed epaulettes perched on his broad shoulders shimmered in the sun, the brass buttons lining his long blue coat, his leather belt and baldric, the red sash about his waist, the service sword at his side. And she had never seen a more handsome figure. Though she had tried to quell her reaction to his close proximity, she'd finally given in to the flutter in her belly and thump of her heart and decided she might as well enjoy this time with him. Soon he and Annie would be gone. To New York City, where they would marry, have a bevy of children, and live a happy life together.

On the wagon ride into town, he had hardly spoken, and Permelia sensed a deep sorrow within him. She longed to discuss the things they'd written of in their letters but dared not. Though she knew him intimately, he treated her as a mere acquaintance. But of course, to him, she was. It pained her nonetheless. So she'd spent the hour sneaking glimpses of him, admiring the assertive way he sat, directing the horses, the way his hair, the color of rich earth, fluttered against his collar. The stiff angle of his jaw and chin. And his deep-set eyes, so full of pain she longed to wrap her arms around him. Now, walking beside her in his crisp Union blues, he carried himself with an authority that set her at ease, a protectiveness that made her feel safe.

And she hadn't felt safe in a long time.

"It grieves me to see your fair town in this condition," he said as a horse and carriage rattled by, stirring up dust.

Permelia glanced over the spot where the hotel had once stood. "Every vacant house was torn down by the soldiers for wood. They stripped the ones left standing of anything valuable." She nodded to Mrs. Milligan, who was standing in her yard, eyeing them with curiosity. Permelia strolling on the arm of a Union officer would certainly give the elderly gossip something to talk about.

"I apologize for what my fellow soldiers have done, Permelia. It appears they have not behaved as gentlemen." Genuine sorrow tainted his voice. He laid his hand upon hers tucked within the crook of his elbow.

A thrill spun in her belly. "Some have been quite kind. But it seems war brings out the worst in men."

He gave her a look that said he understood that fact all too well. "Still I am both astonished and overjoyed that the Yankees, as you call them, left your home unharmed."

"They didn't at first. We quite feared for our lives." Permelia shivered as memories of those first few weeks of occupation marched across her thoughts. "But God took care of us. He has blessed us greatly."

William seemed surprised at her statement, but he only offered her a smile in reply.

Up ahead, a familiar face twisted a knot in Permelia's gut. *Jackson.* She wished Annie could see him now as he flirted with two young, attractive ladies. Upon spotting her, he started her way, his pointed gaze taking in William like a hawk would newfound prey. When his eyes focused on William's face, he flinched, halted before them, and offered a salute with languid enthusiasm.

"Good day, Jackson," Permelia said, wiggling her nose at the cedar oil he sprinkled in his hair.

"Miss Permelia." He removed his hat and dipped a bow.

"Sergeant Jackson Steele, may I present Colonel William Wolfe."

Jackson stood at attention, staring at William's coat. "Welcome, Colonel. I had not heard of additional officers arriving."

"At ease, Sergeant." William seemed unaffected by the man's inability to gaze upon his face. "I am not on duty at the moment. Though I do not find it surprising that you are not made aware of the movement of every officer." His tone had turned superior.

Jackson's eyes narrowed at the insult. Easing his stance, he slid his fingers over the oiled hair at his temples. "Regardless, it is good to see Miss Permelia on the arm of a gentleman. I've warned her more than once that she is fast becoming an old spinster."

Heat rose on Permelia's neck that had nothing to do with the hot sun beating down on them.

William cleared his throat.

"I fear you are mistaken," Permelia began. "William is but an acquaintance." How could she tell the man the truth? But it must come out sooner or later. Though she wasn't overly fond of Jackson, she didn't wish to hurt him either. "In fact," she continued, "you should know that he is Annie's fiancé from New York, come to claim her."

For the first time since she'd known Jackson, the supercilious facade slipped from his face. Yet, what replaced it terrified Permelia. Pure hatred. He slid a finger over his mustache and stretched his shoulders beneath his blue coat as if shrugging off the information. Once again the mask of imperious charm stiffened his features. He forced a smile, revealing a row of gleaming teeth that reminded Permelia of a horse neighing its displeasure.

"Well, that is quite impossible, Colonel," he said, "since Annie is already engaged to me."

Chapter 4

Y ou can't avoid him forever, Annie." Permelia spun around from her spot by the chamber window.

"Tighter, Ruth." Annie gripped the bedpost as the young Negro girl yanked on the lacings of her corset. Fear of displeasing her mistress was still resident in her wide eyes, though she'd been freed three years ago.

"I am quite aware of that, dear sister, which is why I intend to take a stroll with him today." Annie twisted her lips. "That is far too tight, stupid girl."

Ruth's hands shook.

Permelia approached, gave Ruth a sympathetic look and took over the lacing. "Ruth, would you please assist your mother in the kitchen." After the young girl left, Permelia finished the binding and helped Annie on with her petticoats. "Ruth is no longer our slave, Annie. You mustn't be so cruel to her."

"Oh, fiddle. I know. I'm sorry." Annie adjusted her crinoline. "I'm just so tired. And seeing William has been so. . .so difficult."

Permelia frowned. "I would think you'd be thrilled to finally see him." As Permelia was. Far too thrilled.

"Of course I am." Annie puckered her lips as Permelia assisted her with her final muslin petticoat before draping her skirt over the top.

"Then why have you been feigning illness these past two

days?" Permelia planted her hands at her hips and gave her sister a look of reprimand.

"Oh Permi." Annie dropped onto her bed, fluffing out her silver-blue skirts around her. "He's just so hard to look upon."

Permelia had no such difficulty. With a sigh she strolled back to the window, preferring to watch William working in the fields than to see her sister's pouting face. Shovel in hand and stripped to the waist, he helped Elijah dig irrigation ditches. The sun glistened off his powerful chest and arms, both rippling beneath the exertion. Her belly fluttered, and she hugged it in an effort to stifle the pleasant feelings, all the while growing accustomed to them. She had also grown accustomed to the absence of hunger pains since William had arrived. For he'd purchased a fresh pig and enough rice and grain to feed them for a month.

Annie's voice whined behind Permelia like an annoying gnat, but she couldn't tear her gaze from William. The son of a wealthy shipbuilder, a graduate of West Point, and an officer in the Union army, out working in the fields beside an ex-slave. Laughter rose on the wind as he and Elijah shared a joke. Permelia smiled. Perhaps the war had indeed changed him.

"I fear you are mistaken, Annie, about his appearance. He's not hard to look upon at all." The thoughts filling Permelia's mind slipped off her lips unawares. She nearly gasped at her sensuous tone—a tone that drew her sister to the window where she followed Permelia's gaze down to William. An unusual look contorted her features. Almost like jealousy. But that couldn't be. Annie would never be jealous of Permelia.

As if reading her thoughts, Annie flounced to the dressing glass and cocked her head, sending her golden curls bouncing as she admired her reflection. "You know what I mean, Permi. His face. It's hideous."

"You shouldn't say such things. It's him you love, not his face, Annie."

Her sister didn't answer. Instead she held a string of pearls around her neck. "Can you hook these?" The necklace Jackson Steele had given her, no doubt stolen from some other Virginia woman.

"You shouldn't wear those."

"Why not? They are beautiful."

"They are too fine a gift from a man who isn't your fiancé."

"What does that matter?"

If Annie didn't know, Permelia wouldn't tell her. Besides, when did her sister ever listen to her? Permelia latched the hook.

Annie swerved about, sending her skirts swaying back and forth like a church bell. "Stop being such a sanctimonious sprite, Permi. You always were so perfect. Never did anything wrong, anything dangerous. Don't you want to live a little, enjoy life?" A devilish gleam sparkled in her eyes.

Permelia squelched her rising frustration at the insignia she'd been branded with since childhood. Even the children in town had teased her when she wouldn't join them in their shenanigans. She hadn't wanted to disappoint her parents. She wanted to make everyone happy. To not hurt anyone's feelings. But she'd been a hopeless failure at that as well. "Of course I want to enjoy life. But you don't have to be evil to do so."

"But you can be a bit naughty now and then." One side of Annie's rosy lips lifted in a mischievous grin. "Come now, I'll wager you've never kissed a man."

Permelia swallowed and dropped her gaze to the wool rug.

"No, of course you haven't." Annie gave a ladylike snort and laid a hand on her heart, gazing upward. "Kissing a man is so heavenly."

Permelia gasped. "Don't tell me you've kissed Jackson?"

"Of course I have." Annie pinned silk flowers in her hair.

Permelia rubbed her arms and gazed back at William in the field. Her heart ached for him. While he had been fighting on the battlefield, his fiancée was in another man's arms.

"There's no harm in a simple kiss," Annie continued with a pout.

Permelia eased back the curtains as a breeze fluttered the lace at her neckline and helped cool her anger toward her sister. "Now that William is here, you should reserve your affections solely for him."

"I don't know if I can kiss him, Permi," Annie whined and crossed the room, plopping back onto her bed. "He's so. . ." She shuddered, and Permelia knelt before her, grasping her hands.

"Annie, of course you can. He's beautiful inside. I assure you, you will grow so accustomed to the scars, you'll hardly notice them." As Permelia had done these past few days. Forced to entertain William in Annie's absence, she had enjoyed every minute of their time together—despite his constant inquiries about Annie. Yet the pain in his voice had prompted Permelia to do all she could to encourage Annie to rekindle their relationship.

Though it tore Permelia up inside.

"He must leave in a few days, Annie. And you never gave him your answer."

Annie leaned on the bedpost. "Is it possible to love two men?"

"I have no idea." Rising, Permelia eased a lock of Annie's hair from her forehead. "But you can't be engaged to two men. You need to call it off with Jackson."

"Humph. I already tried." Annie folded her lips then cast Permelia a venomous look. "And I know you told him about William."

Permelia began to straighten the pillows on Annie's bed. "I had no choice." Perhaps she should have told her sister about the encounter in town. But wait. Permelia stared at Annie. "What do you mean you tried already? Tell me Jackson hasn't come to call."

Annie sashayed to her dressing table and dabbed perfume on her neck. "He came by last night, after you retired."

"Highly inappropriate."

"Don't be silly." Annie's voice was patronizing. "I assured him that I hadn't made up my mind yet." She paused, glancing at her reflection in the dressing glass again. "Jackson is so handsome, so charming, so romantic." She sighed. "But he has no money."

Pamela rubbed the ache rising behind her temples. Sometimes she felt as though she didn't know her sister at all. "You're promised to William. Please give him a chance." Though the thought broke her heart, Permelia wanted to see William happy above all else.

And from all indications, he truly loved Annie.

Annie adjusted her skirts. "I've never seen Jackson quite so enraged. Though I don't know why. I informed him about William years ago." She faced Permelia. "I simply can't know what's he's going to do. He all but declared he will not let me go without a fight. Isn't that romantic?"

At the look of excitement in her sister's eyes, Permelia spun back around. Jackson Steele was not a man to be trifled with. She recalled the way he had glared at William in town as if he were an enemy on the battlefield. A knot formed in Permelia's throat. Certainly the man wouldn't harm William. Would he?

A warm spring breeze wafted over William as he strolled along the stone path marking the outskirts of the Shaw plantation. The scent of dogwood and cedar filled the air as the honeyed voice of Annie filled his ears, bringing him a contentment he'd not felt since he arrived in Virginia. Not only had Annie finally recovered from her illness, but she agreed to spend some time alone with him. Just like they used to do when he'd come courting, walking this same path, arm in arm.

Although the scenery had changed.

Fields that used to be brimming with tobacco plants lay overgrown with weeds. Instead of the chatter of activity, whinny of horses, grate of ploughs, and laughter of children, only the buzz of insects and the chirp of birds accompanied the tap of their shoes over the thistle-infested flagstone.

Yet with Annie's delicate hand once again on his arm, his mind wandered back to former days, to a happier time when they had strolled down the bustling streets of New York, drawing the gazes of society matrons all abuzz at their famed courtship. William Wolfe, inheritor of Wolfe Shipbuilding and the most handsome eligible bachelor in town. Ah, yes, those were grand days!

"I'm most pleased you are feeling better, Annie."

Adjusting her parasol against the hot sun, she smiled but did not meet his gaze. "I am not sure what came over me." She hesitated. "It is truly good to see you, William."

See him? Since they'd left the house, she hadn't *seen* him at all. Not once had she looked his way. Though he couldn't attest to the same. In fact, he couldn't keep his eyes off her. The way the sunlight glittered off her skin and hair in a shower of brilliant diamonds, her lips the shade of the wild geraniums doting the landscape, moist with dew. He swallowed the desire to kiss them. Though he had taken such liberties in New York, he felt no such offer extended to him here. At least not yet. And not before he discovered who this Jackson fellow was and why he was under the mistaken notion that he was engaged to Annie. But he'd wait to pursue that topic. William did not wish to spoil the first happy moment he and Annie had shared since his arrival.

"This war has done no disservice to your beauty, dear. You are the picture of loveliness as always."

Voices drew his gaze to Miss Permelia helping Elijah load the wagon with vegetables to exchange in town for much-needed supplies. Absent from the younger sister were the sparkling jewels, the bead-laced coiffure, the bell skirt that fairly floated over the ground. Instead, with loose hair flowing down her back, Permelia wore a simple cotton gown fringed in nothing but dirt.

"Why, how kind of you to say, William." Annie giggled, drawing his gaze back to her.

He kissed her forehead, inhaling her fragrance of lilac. A fragrance that brought back memories of the last time he saw her on Bow Bridge in Central Park four years ago. He could picture them so clearly standing on the snowy bridge: the way her distraught sighs had emerged in sweet puffs upon the icy winter air, her glistening eyes so full of love, her father's carriage in the distance waiting to take her back to Virginia, and William commanded to report to his captain that afternoon and be sent off to fight.

"I cannot stand to be apart from you," she had said, falling into his embrace. *"I hate this war already. Why can't we be married now?"*

William had reluctantly nudged her back. Taking her shoulders, he'd studied her face, trying to memorize each line and curve, the graceful shape of her nose, her thick lashes now wet with tears. *"Because your father will not permit us to marry until this war is over."* Reaching into his pocket, he'd pulled out the coin and handed it to her.

"What is this?"

"My pledge to you, darling."

She examined the engraving. "It says 'Love never fails. W.W. Central Park.'" A tear slipped down her cheek.

He wiped it away. "This coin is my pledge to marry you on this very spot as soon as the war is over."

"Oh William." She stood on her tiptoes and smothered him with kisses.

Even now, four years later, William warmed at the memories. Especially with her once again by his side. "Where is that coin I gave you?"

Pushing away from him, she fingered the top of a tall weed. "I have it somewhere. I don't remember." She started walking again.

William's jaw tightened. *Don't remember?* Did his pledge to marry her mean so little?

A group of wood swallows flitted between the limbs of a mighty oak to William's left, serenading them in a celebratory chorus. Or was it a warning?

The silence stiffened between them, and William sought the words to ask her once again if she would accompany him to New York. If she still wished to marry him.

Perhaps sensing the oncoming question, she began chattering about all the difficulties she had endured during the war.

A squirrel halted on the path ahead of them and stared at them curiously before scurrying away.

Taking her hand, he slid it in the crook of his elbow once again. "I cannot imagine what you suffered, darling. I wish I had been here to help, to comfort you, when you heard of your father's death."

"And we were left defenseless." She sobbed, though no tears filled her eyes. "All our slaves ran off. Can you believe it?" She flashed a glance at him but quickly averted her eyes. He remembered that expression of hers so well, like a spoiled little girl who didn't get her way. It used to charm him. But now, he found it oddly annoying.

He halted. "All men have a right to live free, Annie."

Huffing, she snapped her parasol shut. "Of course I know that." She leaned her head on his shoulder. "But it was so frightening, William. Just Permi and me. And then the soldiers ransacked our house, I feared for our. . ." She bit her lip. "Well, you know. . . . I feared they would. . ."

Gripping her shoulders, William turned her to face him. "Did they?"

She lowered her chin. "No. But Permi shot one of them."

"Shot?" He glanced at Permelia hefting a small crate onto the back of a wagon.

"Yes, it was horrifying."

Horrifying for Permelia, no doubt. He glanced at the pearls around Annie's neck and her elaborate gown. "Yet you seem to have kept most of your nice things."

"Only because of Ja—well, a lady needs such fripperies, William." She gave him a coy smile, her gaze avoiding the scarred side of his face. "How else am I to charm my fiancé when he arrives?"

Which fiancé? William wondered. "Because of Mr. Jackson Steele, you meant to say."

Her lips slanted, and she continued forward.

William wiped the sweat from the back of his neck. "I met him in town. The man swears you are engaged to him."

Halting beneath the shade of a hickory tree, she turned her back to him. "You do not understand. I had to ensure our survival."

Agony caught in her voice, lowering William's defenses. He was behaving like a jealous ogre. He touched her shoulders. She didn't recoil. Turning her around, he took her in his arms. "Forgive me, Annie. I didn't mean to distress you."

She looked up at him then out onto the fields, her eyes blue jewels in a creamy pond. "While Permi grows her meager crops, it is I who's been forced into frightening alliances with the enemy."

"Of course, darling. I'm behaving the cad." Though William could not entirely understand why she had to go as far as espousing herself to Jackson, he *did* understand the desperate measures one had to take during wartime to survive.

She laid her head on his chest and sniffled. "The sacrifices I've made. And here you accuse me of. . .of. . ."

"I am truly sorry." He caressed her back, wondering why his body did not react to the press of her curves—a sensation he had longed to feel during the endless years of war. But it was her letters that had kept him going. Her sweet letters—filled with words that had caused him to fall even more deeply in love with her.

Chapter 5

Flirtatious laughter spilled from the front parlor. Halting at the door, Permelia took a moment to brace her heart before entering the room, tea service in hand. She knew what her eyes would see. What they had seen all day. Her sister clinging to William, chattering and fluttering her fan about like a lovesick bird—like she always did when eligible men were present.

Any eligible man.

Earlier Permelia had been forced to witness the amorous playact as the couple strolled about the plantation grounds. Now, in early evening, the heartrending performance continued incessantly in the house.

Silently begging God's forgiveness for her jealousy and for the strength to endure the night, Permelia set the tray down and gazed at the couple sitting side by side on the sofa. She supposed the sight would settle better with her if William looked at all pleased. But a perpetual glimmer of suspicion and unease had sparked in his eyes ever since they'd entered the house.

Completely unnoticed by Annie, of course, who continued to regale him with gossip from town.

"You don't need to do that, Permi. That's why we have Martha and Ruth." Annie waved her fan in Permelia's direction.

"Martha and Ruth are otherwise occupied preparing our

supper." Permelia forced a smile and handed William his tea. "For which we have you to thank, William. I must say, we haven't had such abundance in years."

Taking his glass, William's eyes locked with hers. Something flickered within them she could not place. But whatever it was, it sent her heart thumping. Turning, she strolled to the open window. Shadows drizzled over the trees like molasses, transforming their bright greens into a dull gray. A breeze cooled the perspiration on her neck. Absently slipping her hand into her pocket, she fingered the coin, the feel of it helping to assuage her sorrow. She'd meant to give it back to Annie but had forgotten. Or had she? She couldn't imagine being without it. Besides the letters, it was her only link to William. A link that had shamelessly fed her fantasy all these years that he'd pledged his love to her instead of Annie.

Which was ludicrous, of course.

She sipped her tea. A burst of mint followed the cool liquid down her throat.

"So, dear William, tell me how your family fares?" Annie asked. "Were you able to visit them after the war?"

"Indeed. I paid them a visit before traveling here. They are all well."

"And your family's shipbuilding business. Did it suffer much during the hostilities?"

Permelia spun around and lowered herself into a chair.

William glanced toward her, sending a thrill through her once again. "Quite the opposite, in fact," he said. "War increases the need for sturdy, well-built ships. My father informed me production has nearly doubled." He'd abandoned his uniform for civilian clothes: black trousers stuffed within knee-high boots, a gray waistcoat over a simple white shirt, a black neck cloth neatly tied about his throat. Yet even without the epaulettes and stripes, his commanding presence permeated the room.

"I am so pleased to hear it." Annie flashed one of her beguiling smiles and sipped her tea. "You'll no doubt be taking over the business in a few years as your father promised?"

"That is my plan." Again, he looked at Permelia. She averted her eyes. Why was he torturing her so?

His answer seemed to please Annie as she squirmed in delight, sending her curls bouncing over the nape of her neck. Candlelight shimmered over her cream-colored gown and reflected a luminous glow from the pearls at her neck and ears and the beads adorning her hair. Even her turquoise eyes glittered like the sea under a noon sun.

Permelia glanced down at her plain, soiled gown, suddenly wishing she could fade into the velvet fabric of her chair. After working in the fields, traveling to town and back, and spending an hour helping Martha in the kitchen, she had forgotten to change for supper.

Running a hand through his hair, William leaned back on the sofa and gazed at Annie as she continued prattling. How could Permelia blame him for being so enchanted with Annie's beauty?

Or was he?

Setting down her tea, Permelia studied the odd expression on his face, which harbored more confusion than admiration. Annie would have noticed it, too, if she took the time to look at him. But even sitting on his unscarred side, she barely glanced his way.

Permelia, on the other hand, found it increasingly difficult to tear her gaze from him. In fact, she hardly noticed his rippled flesh anymore.

Annie pouted. "How nice to hear that not everything was destroyed by this horrid war. Why, we have struggled for so long, I cannot imagine living without worrying every day how we are to survive."

William laid a hand over hers. "When we are married, you need never concern yourself with such things again." He turned to Permelia. "And of course I will institute a good overseer for the plantation. You will be well cared for here."

"You are too kind." Emotion burned in Permelia's throat, and she gazed down at her hands folded in her lap. She was truly happy for Annie and William. Their marriage would be good for everyone. They would be happy, and Permelia would not have to worry about money ever again. Then why were her insides flopping like a fish caught in a jumbled net of jealousy? Just being with them, watching them together, drained the life from her soul. She had always prided herself on her kindness, charity, and her obedience to God. What was wrong with her?

Standing, she intended to excuse herself to see about supper when the front door slammed open. Boot steps pounded over the marble foyer, and all eyes turned to see Sergeant Jackson Steele appear in the doorway.

William rose slowly. Something on the man's face had him reaching for the sword at his hip. Which was absent, of course.

Jackson's sword, however, was not. In fact, the polished metal winked at William in the final rays of the setting sun angling through the window.

Permelia gasped.

Annie froze. Her eyes took on a skittish look. "Whatever are you doing here, Jackson?"

The man sauntered into the parlor as if he'd been there a thousand times before. "I came to set things straight." Dressed in a freshly pressed dark uniform with light blue stripes, he held his cap in one hand while the other hovered precariously over the hilt of his sword. Sharp gray eyes scanned the room with impunity from within a finely sculptured face.

Annie struggled to stand. "Jackson, may I introduce William Wo—"

"We've met, love." Jackson sneered.

Love. The hair on the back of William's neck stood at attention.

Pressing down her skirts, Annie sashayed toward the intruder. "This is hardly the time, Jackson." She clutched his arm and attempted to tug him out the door.

"Let him speak," William said. It was fine time he discovered the truth. Annie certainly wasn't being forthright. And Permelia, sweet Permelia, never said a disparaging word about anyone.

Disgust at William's scarred face reflected in Jackson's eyes. "Annie and I are engaged, Colonel." He took Annie's hand and threaded it through his outstretched arm. "And I insist you leave at once. It isn't proper for you to be lodging with two unattached women."

Pulling away from Jackson. Annie's face paled. She lifted a hand to her forehead while Permelia rushed to her side.

"You would be well advised to curb your tone when speaking to a superior, Sergeant," William said as both confusion and fury rampaged through him.

"You pull rank on me in so personal a matter?" He gave a tight grin. "Very well, I will alter my tone, but that does not alter the truth that Annie is still engaged to me."

William glanced at his fiancée, hoping she'd tell the man the truth, but she seemed to be having trouble breathing. "The lady tells a different story, Sergeant. As I understand it, she offered you her kind regard in exchange for protection from vandalism. That is all."

Jackson snorted. "Kind regard. Is that what she's calling it?" A salacious gleam sparked in his eyes as they swept over Annie.

William took a step toward him. Sword or not, he would

put this mongrel in his place if he dared say another word to impugn Annie's reputation.

"Please go, Jackson," she breathed out as Permelia led her to a chair.

"Not until you tell him the truth, love."

"There is no need for an altercation," Permelia pleaded. "I'm sure we can work this out."

"Indeed we can." Jackson said, gesturing toward William. "If this man leaves." He raised his brows toward Annie. "Love, do tell the Colonel."

Annie stared at William, her wide eyes brimming with tears. Her lips trembled. Her gaze bounced between William and Jackson. She opened her mouth then slammed it shut. Finally, clutching her skirts, she darted from the room. The pitter-patter of her shoes and whimper of her tears echoed down the stairs.

Jackson glared at William. "If you aren't gone by tomorrow, I assure you, sir, you will regret my acquaintance."

"I fear it is too late for that, Sergeant." William returned his glare.

"We shall see." Shoving his hat atop his head, Jackson spun around and stormed from the room. A second later the front door slammed with an ominous thud.

William glanced at the stairs where Annie had fled. Should he follow her? Comfort her? Demand the truth? But no, that wouldn't be proper.

Permelia sank into the chair her sister had vacated. "Please forgive her, William. I warned her not to entertain that man's affections. But. . . Well, she's endured so much pain."

"No more than you, and you haven't aligned yourself with a blackguard."

She gave a bitter chuckle. "I'm afraid that option was not open to me. I lack both the charm and beauty of my sister."

She pressed her hands over her skirts as if trying to smooth the wrinkles and remove the stains.

William found the action adorable. He wanted to tell her that she was wrong on both counts. He wanted to tell her that he'd been unable to keep his eyes from her ever since she'd walked into the room. Now, gazing at her sun-pinked cheeks and the way the loose strands of her cinnamon-colored hair wisped across her neck, his heart took an odd leap.

"Besides, God has protected us," she said, "not Jackson."

As if drawn by an invisible rope, William took a step toward her. "Such resilient faith."

She graced him with a smile. "Isn't it trials that strengthen our faith? I'm sure you found much solace in God's presence during the war."

William swallowed. "Quite the opposite." He rubbed his mutilated cheek, numb to the touch. "I could not reconcile a loving God with the horrors I witnessed."

Gripping the chair, she stood, her forehead wrinkling. "Do not say such things, William. You cannot blame God for man's failings."

William stared at her, studying her humble stance, her graceful neck and delicate jaw. Before he could stop himself, he reached for her hand and laced his fingers through hers. "You make me want to believe that."

Her eyes flitted between his like skittish doves afraid to land. Fear and a yearning that surprised him flashed across them. She tried to say something, but the air between them had vanished, replaced by her scent of wildflowers and sunshine. He drew in a deep breath and caressed her hand, his body thrilling at the feel of her skin. "Why do I feel as though I know you so well, Permelia?" He sighed. "While Annie seems like a stranger to me."

"Please don't say such things." She tugged her hand from

his, making him regret his honesty. "Annie doesn't mean to be cruel. She is confused, hurting." She looked away.

"Why do you always make excuses for her behavior?" Reaching up, he touched her chin and brought her gaze back to his. A curl fell across her cheek. He eased it behind her ear, running his thumb over her skin—soft like the petal of a rose.

A tremble ran through her. She closed her eyes.

And William's restraint abandoned him. He lowered his lips to hers. Moist and soft. Just as he had imagined them. But what he had not imagined was how welcoming they would be. The room dissolved around him. Nothing mattered but Permelia and the press of her lips on his, her sweet scent, her taste. Then she pulled away, but ever so slightly. Their breath mingled in the air between them. What was he doing? He tried to shake off her spell, but it wrapped around his heart, refusing to let go.

She raised her gaze to his, candlelight reflecting both confusion and desire.

He ran the back of his hand over her cheek, longing to draw out the precious moment. Pressing his lips on hers once again, he pulled her close.

When a footfall padded outside the parlor.

Followed by a gasp.

Permelia pushed away from him. Remorse screamed from her eyes before she darted from the room.

∞

Tossing off her quilt, Permelia swung her legs over the bed and lit a candle. She'd spent the past several hours listening to the wind whistling past her window, the distant hoot of an owl, and the creak of the house settling. Or was someone else up and moving about? She gave up trying to tell. Regardless, sleep eluded her. Along with her sanity and possibly her salvation.

She had kissed William! She'd allowed him to touch the bare skin of her hands, her cheek. Her lips.

Shame lowered her gaze to the sheen of moonlight covering the wooden floor. There was no excuse for her behavior. She knew that. Had begged God for His forgiveness. Had prayed it had all been a dream. But the tingle that still coursed through her body told her otherwise.

When William had grabbed her hand, her heart had all but stopped. She should have pulled away then. Should have resisted him. Then when he had caressed her cheek, her breath escaped. And she couldn't move.

But when his lips had met hers, Permelia's world exploded in a plethora of sensations: the scratch of his stubble on her chin, his masculine scent filling her nose, his warm breath caressing her cheek. She felt as though she were another woman in another world. A world where William loved her, not Annie.

Thank God a noise from the foyer had stopped them or who knows how far into debauchery she would have sunk.

Sliding from her bed, Permelia hugged herself and started toward the window. But why had William kissed her? She could make no sense of it. No doubt it was simply an emotional response, a need for comfort in the face of Jackson's threats and Annie's rejection.

Hinges creaked behind her. A loud crash sent her heart into her throat. She spun around to see the door bouncing off the wall and Annie charging into the room like an angry apparition. Setting her candle down, she approached Permelia, her eyes molten steel.

And Permelia knew she had seen William kiss her. She tried to back away, but Annie raised a hand and struck her across the cheek. "How dare you?"

Pain radiated across Permelia's face and down her neck. Laying a hand on her stinging skin, she lowered her gaze. "I'm sorry. I. . .he. . .I don't know how it happened." A sob caught in her throat. "Oh Annie, I'm so sorry. It was nothing." But she lied even now. William's kiss had meant everything. Even so, she was nothing but a shameless hussy—a woman who had kissed another woman's fiancé.

"You're sorry! That's all you have to say for yourself?" Annie's voice boiled. "I've been pacing my room all night trying to figure out how my loving sister could justify kissing my fiancé."

Permelia had no answer. No excuse. Gathering her resolve, she finally looked at her sister, absorbing the scorn, the hatred searing in her eyes. Permelia deserved it all. The vision of her sister blurred beneath a torrent of tears.

The fury on Annie's face faded, replaced by a haunted look. "Wasn't it enough that you stole Father's heart from me? That he always loved you more than me?"

"That isn't true." Permelia took a step toward her, her mind reeling.

Annie spun around, sending her silk night robe twirling in the moonlight. She lowered her head and sobbed. "Yes it is. And you know it. Perfect little Permelia." She waved a hand over her shoulder. "Papa's eyes always lit up when you came in the room."

Permelia's heart sank. She'd never realized. Everyone adored Annie. All the young boys at school. All her friends. Mother. "I'm so sorry, Annie, I didn't—"

Annie's eyes flashed. "William doesn't love you." Her gaze traveled over Permelia with disdain. "How could he love someone like you?" Then with a lift of her chin, she floated from the room on a puff of white silk.

The slam of the chamber door thundered through Permelia's heart. Her legs gave way. Sinking to the floor, she dropped her head into her hands and sobbed. How could she have missed Annie's pain all these years? The rejection she had felt from

their father? While Permelia had relished in her father's ado-
ration, Annie's heart had been breaking. Selfish, insensitive
girl. Permelia pounded the carpet with her fists, watching her
tears fall and sink into the stiff fibers. Finally, hours later, she
collapsed in a fit of exhaustion.

The sweet trill of birds drifted on the first glow of dawn.
Permelia woke with a start. Struggling to stand, she brushed
the tear-caked hair from her face and gazed out the window.
Across the fields, darkness retreated from the advancing light.

And she remembered that God's mercy was new every
morning.

"Thank You, Lord. Thank You for Your mercy and
forgiveness."

Now she must do her best to gain Annie's. And to be a
better sister. A better follower of Christ.

But one thing was for sure. For the remainder of William's
time at the plantation, Permelia must do everything in her
power to avoid him.

Chapter 6

Rubbing his eyes, William entered the dining room, lured by the smell of coffee and biscuits and the hope that he'd have a chance to speak with Permelia about their kiss. A kiss that had kept him up most of the night. A kiss that still lingered like a sweet whisper on his lips. A kiss he should never have stolen. A touch of her skin he should never have enjoyed. All behaviors so unlike him. Behaviors that were no doubt caused by the weariness of war, coupled with the pain of Annie's inability to look at his face.

He sighed. Regardless of his attraction to Permelia, he had vowed to marry Annie. And a Wolfe never went back on his word.

Approaching the buffet table, William poured a cup of coffee when a sound brought his gaze to the door. Pressing down the sides of her skirt, Annie flounced into the room. Her bright eyes glanced over him but did not remain.

"William, I hoped to find you here."

He froze, stunned by her presence so early in the morning.

"Well, don't just stand there, William." She tilted her head, a coy smile on her lips. "Tell me how beautiful I look." She sashayed toward him. "Like you used to do."

William sipped his coffee, admiring the way the sunlight caressed her golden hair. "You know how beautiful you are, Annie. You need no affirmation from me." He stepped aside as she poured herself a cup of tea, a pleased look on her face. Had she always been this vain?

He cleared his throat. "What I'd like to know is the truth, Annie."

"About what?" She plucked a biscuit from a tray, grabbed her tea, and moved to the table.

"You know about what." His gaze followed her, though he found no allure in the bow-like pout on her lips or the sway of her silk bustle. "I refer to Jackson Steele. You left before answering the sergeant's question."

She waited for him to pull out her chair. "Why William, I've already told you why I befriended the man."

After seating her, William retrieved his coffee from the buffet and sat opposite her. "Somehow he seems to have gotten the wrong impression."

"Indeed. He's become quite obstinate." She bit her biscuit.

"Perhaps because you refuse to tell him the truth. Or perhaps it's me to whom you're lying?" He raised his brows.

"How can you suggest such a thing?" Sky-blue eyes locked upon his then shifted to the right side of his face. Gulping, Annie looked away.

Oddly, her aversion no longer pained him. He thought of the familiar way Jackson had gazed at her. The way he had called her "love" still rankled William but not in the way it should.

"I find Sergeant Steele's intimate tone with you most inappropriate."

"What are you implying?" Her eyes misted. Four years ago, those glistening tears would have brought him to his knees before her, begging her forgiveness.

Instead they pricked his suspicion. "Nothing. I demand honesty. And that you choose one of us."

"Why, William, I have chosen." Yet the wobble in her voice did not convince him. She set down her biscuit and dabbed a napkin over her lips. "Let's go for a picnic today, shall we? Perhaps if we spent time together. . .like old times." She gave a sad smile and gazed out the window before facing him again.

William finished his coffee, setting the cup a bit too hard on the table. Perhaps she was right. Perhaps he had expected too much from someone as delicate as Annie—expected her to accept his disfigurement as if everything were the same. He chastised himself for his impatience. Beneath all the fluff and southern charm, lurked a woman of substance, of character, and of faith—the woman he had fallen in love with through her letters. Perhaps it would just take time for that part of her to surface.

And for the first time since he arrived, Annie seemed willing to try.

Permelia entered the room. Tossing his napkin on the table, William stood, an unavoidable smile spreading across his lips.

She flinched as if shocked to find them there. A breeze toyed with the hem of her lacy petticoat. She'd arranged her hair in one long braid that hung down the front of her gown. Her eyes latched upon his then quickly sped away as a pink hue crept up her neck onto her face.

"Oh Permi." Annie rose, pressed down her skirts, and glided to William's side. Flinging her arms about his neck, she kissed him on the cheek. His good cheek, of course. "William and I are going to take the carriage out for a picnic today. Aren't we, William?"

William blinked, confused at the sudden display of affection. "Just for a short while." He conceded. "However, Miss Permelia, I fully intend to help you and Elijah with the chores." He *wanted* to help with the chores.

Permelia gazed out the window. "Do not concern yourself, William. You and Annie need time to become reacquainted." Yet, she wouldn't look at her sister. That coupled with the palpable tension in the room since her arrival made William wonder if the noise he'd heard in the foyer last night had been Annie.

"Besides, Elijah and I are going into town." Permelia turned to leave.

The room threatened to grow cold in her absence. "To help at the hospital?" William asked.

She halted but did not turn around. "I teach Negro children to read and write at the church once a week." Then she disappeared, the clip of her boots fading down the hallway.

Annie released his arm and sighed. "Have you ever heard such a thing? A few years ago, a person could be hanged for teaching slaves. Why ever do Negros need to read and write anyway?"

Dragging the stool to his bedside, William set the lantern atop it and sat on his straw-stuffed mattress. A night breeze strolled through his window, bringing with it a reprieve from the day's heat and the scent of wild violet and hay. Despite the pleasant evening, William had been unable to fall sleep. He untied the bundle of letters in his hand and opened the first one. Holding it up to the light, he scanned the elegant pen and sweet words of his precious Annie:

> *Dearest William,*
>
> *Your last letter brought me great joy as well as deep sorrow. Joy to know that you survived your last battle and sorrow to hear of the death of your friend, Major Mankins. I know how much his good company meant to you, and I grieve alongside you for the loss. May God fill you with His comfort as you continue to fight this senseless war. Know that you are not alone in your suffering. I cry*

along with you and long for the day when I can cry in your
arms. Tears of joy instead of pain.

You asked how we fared here under the occupation.
I suppose now that word has reached you of the fate of
Williamsburg I can mention our predicament. For I did
not wish to burden you with our meager problems when
you have so much responsibility weighing upon your
shoulders. But let me allay your fears, dear William. The
Shaw plantation stands, and we are all well. God's wings
of protection cover us, and in Him we abide.

Please know you are not alone. God and my love are
with you always.

Oh brave, wise William. You are ever in my heart and
prayers. . . . Annie

Releasing a heavy sigh, William gently folded the letter and set it on top of the others on his bed. Confusion stormed through him, muddling his thoughts and twisting his heart. Nothing made sense anymore.

He'd spent the day with Annie. First they'd taken a carriage ride through the country, followed by a lovely picnic beside a creek, and finally ending with afternoon tea in her father's library.

And he could find no trace of the kindhearted, humble, godly woman in these letters in the primped, vainglorious Annie.

Though her attitude toward him had vastly improved.

Though she seemed more accepting of his appearance.

Had she always been this way? Or had the war changed her? Perhaps the war had changed him. He dropped his head into his hands and scrubbed his face.

Even worse, all the while Annie chittered and chattered about this and that, William's thoughts had been on Permelia. Though Elijah accompanied her into town, he wondered how she fared, what she was doing, who she spoke to.

Whether she thought of him.

And teaching Negro children to read and write. Her kindness astounded him. In all his prior visits to the Shaw plantation, why had he not noticed her? Had he been so dazzled by Annie's beauty that he'd been blinded to the golden heart within her sister?

But he had no choice now. He was espoused to Annie. And to break off the engagement would bring irreparable shame to her, not to mention to his family. The Wolfe honor was as solid as the ships they built.

And just as unsinkable.

Picking up the letters, he pressed them against his chest. He must set aside his foolish admiration of Permelia and trust that eventually the real Annie would shine forth. Hopefully before he had to leave in two days to report to his commanding officer. He would love to have his engagement settled by then so he could enlist his mother to begin arrangements for the ceremony in New York while he served his remaining months in the Army.

Mind cluttered with these thoughts, William lay back on his bed, arms beneath his head when the faint whinny of a horse and stomp of hooves wandered over his ears. Odd. He'd helped Elijah secure the two remaining horses in the stables for the night. Unease slithered over him. Shrugging it off to exhaustion, he sat up, tied a cord around the letters, and packed them away in his knapsack. He strode to the window. Wind stirred the leaves of an elm tree, causing them to shiver in an eerie cacophony. Well past midnight, the main house loomed dark and large in the distance.

Light flickered in an upstairs room.

William scratched his chin. Who else would be up at this hour?

Shaking his head, he started back to his bed when a woman's scream pierced the night.

∽

An odd sensation crept through Permelia's slumberous mind, stirring her consciousness. A sensation of danger, of warning. But she didn't want to wake up. It had taken her far too long to fall asleep after her long day of trying to avoid William and Annie. A scuffing sound prickled her spine. Her stomach complained. Begging off with an excuse of a headache, she'd forsaken her supper, not able to tolerate watching Annie unleash the full flood of her charm and flirtation on William. Knowing it was merely an act to prove to Permelia where William's true affections lie.

Permelia sighed, her mind now fully awake. She opened her eyes. Movement focused her gaze to the right. The dark silhouette of a man stood by her bed. A clawlike hand reached for her throat.

Permelia screamed.

Skin, thick and scabrous and smelling of tobacco and sweat, slammed over her mouth. She tasted blood and fear. Pain throbbed in her chin, her gums. Her cries for help clumped in her throat. The glint of moonlight on steel revealed a knife in his other hand, floating over her bed like the scythe of the grim reaper.

"Well, if it ain't the prim and proper Miss Shaw." His voice spiked with angry sarcasm. "I'm goin' to take away my hand. If you so much as utter a peep, I'll slit your throat. Understood?"

Lifting a harried prayer to the Lord, Permelia nodded. Blood thundered in her ears. Was this to be her end? A violent death?

He removed his grip on her mouth, waving the knife before her. His face blurred in the darkness, but she felt his gaze scouring over her. "Yankee lover!" He spat to the side. "Where is that stinkin' Yankee hiding? Tell me now, or I'll finish you off in your bed."

A thud sounded on the floorboards behind the man, followed by a commanding voice. "Looking for me?"

Chapter 7

Relief flooded Permelia at the sound of William's voice. But terror quickly returned. The intruder swung about, knife clutched in his hand. Moonlight coated William in milky light. He stood by the door, arms crossed over his chest as if he were attending a country ball, not confronting an armed assailant.

Permelia struggled to sit.

The man took a step toward William, a sordid chuckle emerging from his lips.

William spread his arms out. "If it's me you're looking for, here I am. Leave the lady be."

He carried no weapons. Fear for William's safety choked Permelia's self-preservation, sending her leaping from the bed in search of anything with which to strike the man.

He must have heard her, for he swerved about and grabbed her by the waist.

"Let me go!" She struggled, trying to pound him with her fists, but he tightened a meaty arm around her chest and arms, pinning her to him.

He pressed the knife to her throat. Pain pinched her skin. Something warm trickled down her neck.

William's confident stance transformed into one of fury. "What do you want?"

"We want you, Colonel."

"We?"

"Me and the soldiers of the Confederate 17th Infantry Regiment." His hot breath wafted over Permelia's neck. "At least those who are left."

"And what do you want with me?"

"Because we was there. At the Second Manassas. We lost forty-eight men that day. Good men."

A flicker of emotion sparked in William's eyes.

"Ah yes." The soldier snickered. "We know you were there, too, commanding your Yanks to slaughter us."

William's jaw hardened. "We were all forced to do our duty that day, sir. The war is over." He gestured with his hand. "Lower the knife."

"It will never be over, Colonel." Spite dripped from the man's lips. "You will leave with me now. We have a lynching party ready for you. An' I'll bring the lady along so you'll behave."

Permelia's breath came quick and hard. The knife pierced deeper into her skin.

"No need, sir." William took a step forward. "Leave her here. I'll come with you."

"No, William!" Her words garbled beneath the press of the blade.

William swallowed. "Very well. Just don't harm her." His tone was conciliatory but a fire ignited in his eyes. They narrowed. Stretching his jaw, he headed for the door.

The intruder followed him. "Easy now, Colonel. One false move and I'll gut her."

Permelia's legs grew numb.

Something flashed in her vision. *Slam. Thud.* The assailant groaned. Yelping, he fell away from her. Pain burned across her throat. She gasped and raised a hand to the cut. William shook his hand from the strike. Stumbling, the man attempted to regain his composure, but William was already on him. He jerked him up by the collar and slugged him across the face. The knife flew from the man's hand, clanking to the floor.

The assailant's face twisted into a maniacal mixture of fear and fury. He rose to his impressive stature, even towering over William. Terrified, Permelia dropped to the floor and groped for the knife.

Yet William's expression remained confident. "Leave now, sir, while you are still able."

The man wiped blood from his jaw. "I came for you, and I'm not leaving without you."

William released an exasperated sigh. The man charged him. Permelia gasped. She shrank into the corner. In movements quicker than her eyes could follow, William blocked three of the man's strikes then leveled one of his own into his belly. The man bent over clutching his middle. He barreled toward William again. William grabbed his head and slammed him into the far wall. The snap of wood cracked the air. The assailant toppled to the ground. William seized him by the shirt and jerked him to his feet. The man held up his arms to block the next strike.

Clutching him with one hand, William dragged him out the door. Permelia found the knife and followed him. She halted at the top of the stairs, her legs nearly folding beneath her. She heard the man's boots thumping down each tread, saw the front door open in a flood of moonlight, and watched as William tossed him onto the porch.

Elijah appeared beside her, lantern in hand. "What's happening, miss?"

"An intruder. Go help William." She pointed below, sending Elijah racing down the stairs. Not that William needed any help, however. Clutching the banister, she followed him.

"Who put you up to this?" William demanded, gripping the man by the collar. "Who told you I was here?"

The man cowered. His chest heaved. Blood spilled from his swollen lip.

Elijah set the lantern on the railing and stepped beside William.

"Who sent you?" William asked again. Permelia had never heard his voice so full of rage.

"Steele." The man seethed.

Permelia's breath escaped her. She leaned on the doorframe.

"Jackson Steele?" William asked. "Isn't he also a Yank?"

"Not one who slaughtered my friends."

Yanking him down the porch stairs, William shoved him to the ground. "You tell Sergeant Steele that if he has an argument with me, he's welcome to come and issue a proper challenge. Soldier to soldier."

The man struggled to his feet and wiped a hand over his mouth.

William's face became flint. "If I ever see you here again, you'll be the one hanging from a tree."

Turning, the man slinked away, muttering "Yankee lover" under his breath.

Elijah rubbed the back of his neck. "Sorry I didn't hear nothin' till a few minutes ago. I was dead asleep."

"It's quite all right, Elijah." William's gaze followed the intruder. "No harm done."

Elijah started down the stairs. "I'll make sure he leaves."

Permelia stepped onto the porch. Her knuckles hurt, and she released her tight grip on the knife.

William's shoulders lowered as he shook off the stiff cloak of a warrior.

A breeze fluttered his hair, his shirt, and toyed with the hem of her nightdress. She hugged herself, gazing at him. She'd never seen anything like it before. The way he had dispatched the man with such skill and confidence. He'd protected her.

Saved her life. Her heart didn't know whether to embrace the thrill of his chivalry or shrink from the terror of her ordeal. She chose the former. Especially when he turned around and rushed to take her in his arms.

Halting, he grabbed the handle of the knife. "I'll take that." The kindness reappeared in his voice.

Happily relinquishing it, Permelia's legs wobbled, and William took her waist and drew her near. She collapsed in his arms. Muscles, strong and hard, surrounded her, encasing her in a safe fortress.

"You are safe now, sweet Permelia. Sweet, sweet Permelia."

She drew in a deep breath of his scent and leaned her cheek on his chest. "You saved me. I thought. . .I thought I was. . .I thought that man. . ."

"Shh, dearest. All is well."

And surrounded by William's arms, feeling the rapid beat of his heart against her cheek, she believed all was well indeed.

Until a startled cry jerked her away from him, and she turned to see Annie, lantern in hand, crystalline hair tumbling like a silken waterfall over her robe, standing in the foyer.

Her jealous glare bore into Permelia.

Throwing a hand to her forehead, she closed her eyes and started to swoon.

Abandoning Permelia, William dashed toward Annie just in time to grab the lantern and capture her in his arms before she toppled to the marble floor.

William settled a sniffling Annie onto the sofa in the parlor then struck a match and lit the oil lamp sitting on the table. A golden glow flickered over the room, sparkling the tears sliding down her cheeks. Holding a hand out to him, she beckoned him to sit beside her. "It is all so horrible, William. An intruder in our house? Utterly terrifying. Do tell me what happened."

With her pink nose, golden hair cascading over her silk robe, her full lips, she truly was a beauty. He remembered how she could captivate him with one glance of those blue eyes, one lift of those moist lips.

But he felt nothing as she gazed at him now, her eyes settling on the left side of his face. Instead he glanced toward the door where Permelia had announced she'd go make some tea. He longed for her return, longed to know how she fared after her harrowing ordeal.

"Oh William, I need you." Annie's sob drew his attention. Taking her trembling hand in his, he sat beside her.

"Just an angry, bitter soldier returning from the battlefield, I'm afraid." He wouldn't tell her about Jackson. It would only upset her further and serve no purpose. William would have to deal with the man on his own.

Footsteps sounded, and he knew Permelia had entered. He knew because the innocent sheen hardened over Annie's eyes as they shot toward the door.

"Here we are. Perhaps this will settle our nerves." Permelia set down the tray and began pouring tea into a trio of china cups. Her hand quivered, spilling some of the hot liquid, and William longed to grab it, caress it. Kiss it. She raised her gaze to his. Pain and confusion stretched a cord between them, locking their eyes in place.

Annie cleared her throat, snapping William from his trance. She accepted the cup from Permelia. "Thank you, Permi. No need to stay up. I'm sure you're exhausted."

Permelia touched the thin red line etched across her throat. She'd tossed a gown over her nightdress, but the lace peeked out from her neckline and hem. William remembered the way she'd clutched the knife and followed him downstairs. So brave.

"Yes, I am rather tired." She smiled.

Concern punched William's heart, and he leaned forward on his knees. "Would you like me to attend to that?" He gestured toward her wound. "I acquired some medical experience during the war."

"No." Permelia looked down. "I can take care of it, thank you."

Annie moaned. "Are we safe here, William?" She clutched his arm and drew him back toward her. "Will the intruder return?"

He patted her hand. "Never fear, I will guard the house while you and Permelia sleep."

"Sleep! I could never after such a horrifying event. Oh, do stay with me, William." She puckered her lips as a child would when begging a father for a treat.

William turned to face Permelia. To tell her she must stay with them as well.

But she was gone.

Hiking her skirts into her belt, Permelia knelt beside the row of cabbage and began pulling weeds from around the tender plants. Why did weeds always grow among the good sprouts, sucking the life from them? Her precious cabbage wouldn't stand a chance at surviving if she didn't come out here daily to pluck the offenders. She was reminded of the parable Jesus told of the wheat and the tares. The wheat represented God's beloved children, and the tares were those who didn't know Him—those destined to be pulled and tossed into the fire. As she was doing now. Yanking one particularly thorny interloper, she threw it atop a growing pile in her bucket then wiped her sleeve across her forehead. The afternoon sun lashed her with hot rays as the air weighed upon her, heavy with moisture.

But the work had to be done or they would not have enough

food come winter. That was, unless William and Annie married. Another reason why Permelia should stay away from him. Then why did the prospect make her so sad? She inched down the row of plants and plucked another weed. Better to keep busy. Better to keep her mind off of William. Off of Annie. And off of the threats made against him last night. Perhaps it was for the best that he was leaving soon. She'd never survive if any harm came to him.

Her thoughts sped to his chivalrous rescue last night. And the way she'd felt so safe and loved in his arms. Her heart swelled. But she quickly squelched it. She must not think of such things.

She hadn't seen William or Annie all day. They were no doubt entertaining themselves in the parlor or strolling about the grounds. Reigniting their love. Planning their wedding.

Yanking another weed, Permelia tossed it in her pail and stood, pressing a hand on her back. A man emerged from the tree line at the edge of the plantation. A light-skinned man. Her heart jolted. She grabbed the rifle lying atop the dirt, cocked it, and leveled it at the intruder. Fear set every nerve on edge as the seconds brought him more clearly into view. His confident gait. The wide spread of his shoulders. Dark hair spilling from beneath his hat.

William.

She lowered the rifle.

He hefted his gun onto his shoulder. Two rabbits swung from the barrel. With a wide grin, he halted before her. "Permelia." Her name emerged from his lips as if it were precious to him.

She brushed dirt from her skirts. "I thought you were with Annie."

His eyes wouldn't leave her. "I left before dawn to hunt."

"So I see. How kind of you."

He stepped toward her. His fingers brushed the bandage at

her throat. "How are you?"

Shaking off the daze caused by his touch, she retreated. "It is nothing. Thanks to you."

"When I saw that knife at your throat"—he gulped and drew a breath—"I was so frightened."

She looked away.

He leaned toward her. "I couldn't bear the thought of losing you." His breath caressed her cheek. He smelled like cedar and hay.

Permelia's heart sped. Was it possible this man returned her affection? She searched his face: his dark, imposing eyes; strong jaw; straight nose; and the rippled flesh on his right cheek. She longed to kiss away the scars. "You shouldn't say such things." Confusion tumbled her thoughts until she couldn't separate reason from desire. And that's what frightened her the most.

"I know. Forgive me." Resignation weighted his voice as he squinted toward the house. "I'm leaving tomorrow."

Permelia's heart sank.

"Before I leave, I will insist Annie tell me whether she still wishes to marry me."

"She'd be a fool not to." The words had escaped her lips before Permelia could stop them.

"No, I'm afraid I've been the fool." He cupped her cheek, and she leaned into his rough hand.

If only for a moment. Just one moment. So, he did feel something for her. Her heart took up a rapid pace again. But no. She stepped back. Whatever was between them, they must end it now. She was about to tell him just that when the *thu-ump, thu-ump* of a galloping horse drew their gazes to the front of the main house. A rider dressed in Union blues hastened down the tree-lined path and jerked his horse to a halt before the front porch. Sliding from the saddle, Jackson Steele grabbed his sword from his pouch, spotted them in the field, and shouted. "I've answered your call, Wolfe! A duel to the death!"

Chapter 8

Permelia gaped at Jackson, not trusting her ears with the words she'd just heard. *A duel?* William's jaw knotted. He faced her with determination. "Where is Elijah?"

Permelia swallowed. "In town."

"Gather Martha and Ruth and get inside the house."

"But what are you going to do?"

Gripping his rifle, he marched toward the slave quarters, the rabbits swaying from the gun's barrel with each step. "Ensure Annie is still inside and then bolt the doors and windows."

"Surely you aren't thinking of—"

He swung about. The stern look on his face clipped the words from her lips. "Take your gun, and do not leave the house. No matter what." His brows drew into a stern line. "That's an order."

For the first time Permelia imagined what the men under William's command must have felt when they stared into those commanding eyes, ignited with intent and purpose.

But she wasn't under his command.

She spun around and stormed toward Jackson, leveling her gun upon the knave. "Leave my property at once, sir, or I will fire upon you."

Jackson planted his sword in the dirt and leaned on the hilt. "Hiding behind a woman, eh, Wolfe?"

The heavy gun shook in her grip. Her hands grew moist.

Perspiration slid down her back. But she wouldn't relent. She couldn't let this man hurt William. Or ruin their lives as he seemed intent on doing.

She heard the crunch of gravel behind her. William appeared at her side. Placing a hand on the barrel of her gun, he gently lowered it, admiration in his gaze. "I must settle this once and for all, don't you see, Permelia?" His voice, gentle at first, hardened with conviction. "The man will simply come back at another time. Most likely after I've left and you're here all alone." He brushed a thumb over her jaw.

"And I couldn't stand for that." He flattened his lips. "Now do as I say." Then turning, he stomped away.

Permelia gave Jackson a venomous look. He chuckled. Clutching her rifle, she headed toward the kitchen house. Fear curdled in her belly. She could barely gather her thoughts. *Oh, Lord, please protect William. Please let no one die today.*

Within minutes, Permelia hurried a wide-eyed Martha and jittery Ruth in through the back entrance of the main house. After checking on Annie, who was sulking in the library, Permelia bolted all the doors then dashed to the front window of the parlor. She leaned the rifle against the wall and rubbed her aching hand.

Sunlight glared off Jackson's saber as he swung it before him with ease. Attired in his dress uniform, complete with blue striped coat lined with brass buttons, it was obvious he had complete confidence in his skills and intended to use the entire heinous performance as a means to impress Annie.

"I wish Elijah were here," Martha said as she took her daughter's hand and stood to the left of the window.

Annie swept into the room. "What is all the fuss about?" She pushed back the curtains and cocked her head.

"Jackson has called William out to a duel." Permelia bit her lip as an idea sprang into her mind. "Perhaps you could stop them, Annie?"

"Why would I do that?" Annie peered out the window. Her eyes lit up. "They are dueling over me." She released a satisfied sigh. "How romantic, don't you think?"

Martha clucked her tongue but gave no other indication of the disgust written on her face.

Permelia cringed. "How can you say such a thing? One of them could get hurt, possibly killed."

"Oh, fiddle. Boys will be boys." Annie plucked out her fan and fluttered it around her face. "It's hot in here. Open the window. I want to hear what's going on."

"William said not to." Permelia gripped her sister's arm. "Please, Annie. You must stop this."

Annie looked at her as if she'd lost her mind before tugging from her grasp.

The sight of William drew Permelia's gaze back out the window. He stormed into view, his service sword in hand. He stopped to speak to Jackson, hopefully to try and talk some sense into him. *Please, Lord, let him succeed.*

"I'm going onto the porch. I can't see anything from here," Annie announced, exiting the room before Permelia could protest.

The front door opened and angry voices rode upon a burst of heated wind. Grabbing the rifle, Permelia instructed Martha to stay put then followed Annie.

"Next time, don't send one of your lackeys to do your dirty work for you." William tossed his hat onto the dirt and flung his sword out before him.

Jackson smiled and opened his arms wide. "Your wish is my command, Colonel."

"You could have injured one of the ladies," William added.

"A Confederate would not injure his own."

"Tell that to Permelia. Your man held a knife to her throat."

Jackson's gaze shot to Permelia and then over to Annie, still batting her fan about her face.

"Jackson, whatever are you doing?" Annie feigned disapproval. "You stop misbehaving at once." Her flippant tone brought a smile to Jackson's lips.

Bile lurched into Permelia's throat.

"You look stunning, love." Jackson dipped a bow. "I fear I must inform this man of our engagement in the only language he understands."

William faced Annie, anger rumbling across his features. "If the lady would break off our engagement and tell me to leave, we could avoid this foolishness."

Annie seemed to falter beneath both men's gazes. She leaned against the post.

Permelia whispered prayers that her sister would finally speak the truth. "Tell them, Annie, for goodness' sake, before someone gets hurt."

Annie slapped her fan shut and flattened her lips, glancing up at the sky as if it contained the answer. "I don't rightly know what to say."

Permelia closed her eyes, trying to corral her anger. This was all just a game to her sister. "Choose one of them, dear sister, or your choice will be made for you," she seethed.

Annie tilted her head. "Then let it be made. And may the best man win."

William ran a hand through his hair and snorted his disgust. He turned to Jackson. "Regardless, you attempted to have me murdered in my bed. And now you dare challenge me. I cannot allow such an affront to pass."

Jackson leaned on his sword. "To the death then? Or until one of us forfeits." He snickered.

Annie gasped. Her wide eyes shot to Permelia as if she only now understood the deadly implications.

But it was too late. With a swoosh of his blade, Jackson

sauntered to William, leveling it at his chest.

William slapped the offending sword away with an ominous *ching* and eyed his opponent. Jackson circled him then swept down on William's right. Blade met blade with a resounding *clang* that filled the air and sent a shiver through Permelia.

William flung his sword back and forth with speed and agility, countering each of Jackson's blows. Jackson halted. Sweat shone on his handsome brow. William charged forward. Their blades rang together as he forced Jackson back over the dirt.

Permelia pressed a hand over her rattling chest.

Jackson's face reddened. "You're more skilled than I thought, Colonel."

"And you're not nearly as skilled as I thought."

Hatred fumed from Jackson's eyes. "We shall see." He spun about and dipped to William's left, striking him on the leg. A red stripe appeared across his trousers.

Both Permelia and Annie gasped at the same time. Permelia glanced at her sister, wondering if she truly cared for William, but Annie's eyes were riveted on Jackson.

"Ah ha!" Jackson boasted, strolling in a circle of victory as he caught his breath.

William, however, seemed barely out of breath. Neither did he seem concerned. Instead he lunged toward Jackson, this time lifting his blade high. Caught off guard, Jackson turned and met the attack with equal force, their blades locking. William grunted as he forced the man backward then shoved him against the bark of a tree.

The arrogant grin slipped from Jackson's face, replaced by fear.

"Don't hurt him, William," Annie whined.

William shoved his blade toward Jackson's shoulder. The man slipped away. The point stuck in the tree.

William tried to pull it free.

Jackson grinned, slowly approaching him like a cougar on wounded prey.

Abandoning the blade, William plucked a knife from his boot and faced Jackson.

"Perhaps you'll forfeit the fight, Colonel, and leave Virginia immediately?" Jackson sneered. "Rather that than suffer a humiliating death in front of the ladies."

William wiped the sweat from his brow. "Not until you promise the same."

Jackson slashed toward William.

William leaped out the way. No fear, no emotion at all, registered on his face. Just the confident expression of a warrior.

"I grow tired of this dance, Colonel." Jackson's face hardened and he stormed toward William in a vicious onslaught. He thrust the tip of his blade toward William's chest.

Permelia screamed.

Tucking in his arm, William dipped and rolled across the dirt, landing on his feet. He thrust his boot in the air, knocking Jackson's blade from his hand and sending him sprawling to the ground. Before the man could recover, William picked up the sword and leveled the tip against Jackson's pristine blue coat. The man's eyes erupted into volcanoes of hatred. "Go ahead, Colonel. Kill me." He gulped for air, thrusting out a defiant chin.

"No!" A woman's scream filled the air as Annie dashed down the stairs and knelt before Jackson, shielding him with her billowing skirts.

Stunned, William backed up and lowered his sword. So Annie did love Jackson, after all. Sudden pain throbbed in William's thigh. His legs gave out and he sank to the ground.

In an instant, an angel appeared beside him, embracing him, her tears dampening his cheeks. Like an elixir they stirred his soul back to life. Permelia. Plucking her handkerchief from within her pocket she pressed it on his wound. Terror, relief, and something else he couldn't place burned in her gaze. "I was so worried, William."

He reached up and wiped the tears from her cheeks. Over her shoulder, Jackson rose to his full height. Annie clutched his arm. Jealous fury faded from his features, replaced by a conciliatory respect. He dipped his head slightly. "You have won fairly, Colonel. And because I still have my life, I will honor my vow to never call on Annie again." He kissed her cheek, his face somber and determined. Then nudging her aside, he mounted his horse and rode away.

Lifting a hand to her mouth, Annie fled into the house, hysterical sobs trailing in her wake.

Permelia helped William to his feet. Grabbing his sword, he sheathed it and drew her close, kissing her forehead.

"I've never seen such bravery, William." Permelia leaned against his shirt. "Forgive Annie. When she calms down, she'll see things differently, I'm sure."

"I'm not of the same mind." William huffed. Why did this sweet woman always try to spare his feelings and defend her sister? Releasing Permelia, he wiped the hair from her face. He should tell her what his heart was bursting to say. That he loved her. That he wanted to marry her, not Annie. He opened his mouth to do so when a glare blinded his eyes, drawing his gaze to something on the ground. Leaning over, he picked up a coin. His coin. Shock sped through him.

He flipped it over. The coin he'd given Annie as a pledge of their love and marriage. He gazed at Permelia, confused.

Her eyes shifted from the coin to him. Her face paled.

"Where did this come from?" he asked.

She glanced down.

Placing a finger under her chin, he lifted her gaze to his. "I know you won't lie to me."

"It must have fallen from my pocket."

He stepped back, more shocked than angry. Annie had already made her sentiments quite clear. But what of Permelia? Yes, she had kissed him, and he thought he'd seen affection in her eyes more than once. But perhaps that was simply his desperate yearning for it to be true. Now he longed to hear the words from her mouth. "Why was it in your pocket?"

But instead of answering him, her lip quivered and her eyes filled with tears. Then clutching her skirts, she dashed into the house.

Permelia slammed the door of her chamber and fell into a heap on the floor. Dropping her head into her hands, she sobbed. Sobbed to release the terror that had gripped her as she'd watched Jackson and William duel. Sobbed to release the shame of her feelings for him. Sobbed because she couldn't tell him the real reason she kept the coin in her pocket. If he discovered that Annie had tossed it from the window, that she thought so little of it, William would be wounded far deeper than the cut on his thigh. Oh, why hadn't she given the coin back to Annie? Why had she been so selfish? *Thank You, Lord, for protecting him. But please send him and Annie to New York to marry. I do not think I can stand this torture anymore.*

Opening her trunk, she pulled out the letters and held them to her nose. They smelled of gunpowder and William. Wailing filtered down the hall from Annie's chamber, pricking Permelia's guilt. She should go to her. Comfort her. But she knew her sister's tears were for Jackson. Confusion tore through Permelia as desire and duty fought their own duel within her.

She covered her ears but could not muffle her sister's sobs. Finally Permelia left the room, went downstairs and out the back door. A walk about the grounds would do her good, clear her mind, give her a chance to hear from God.

William approached Permelia's chamber door. It stood slightly ajar, yet no sounds came from within. He knew he shouldn't be sneaking about a lady's bedchambers, but his tormented thoughts would allow him no peace until he found out the truth of where Permelia's sentiments lay. More importantly, why had she run away when he found the coin? He must know, and he must know tonight. For tomorrow he had to leave, report back to his commanding officer, serve out his remaining months in the Army.

He eased the door aside. "Permelia." No answer. He inched inside, gave a quick scan of the room, and upon finding it empty, moved to the foot of a four-poster bed, decorated with a simple quilt. A dressing table and mirror stood against the far wall beside an armoire. On the other side of the room, a writing desk, littered with pens, paper, and a Bible sat beneath the window.

Pain lanced through his thigh, and he pressed a hand over the wound. At least the bleeding had stopped. A burst of wind blew through the window, stirring something on the floor. Paper crinkled, and William knelt to find a bundle of letters tied with a thread beside an open trunk. Gathering them, he started to place them back in the chest when their familiarity struck him.

His heart stopped. Sliding the first one out from the cord, he unfolded it and scanned the words.

His letters. His letters to Annie.

The *tap tap* of steps and a tiny gasp drew William's gaze to the door, where Permelia stood, her hair tousled by the wind and smelling of wildflowers and horses. He held the letters up to her, unable to speak, unable to find the words. Unsure if he found them, that they'd be very kind. He could think of only one reason she would have them. Anger replaced confusion in his gut. Anger that this woman, this precious woman he thought he loved, had betrayed him!

Chapter 9

Permelia entered her chamber. A tremble threatened to buckle her legs. "I can explain."

William held up the bundle of letters, one of them open in his hand. "Why do you have the letters I wrote to Annie?"

Permelia tried to speak, but the words knotted in her throat. He would hate her if he knew. And she couldn't bear that.

He glanced at the letters then back at her, shock and pain drawing lines on his forehead. "You."

Making her way to the bedpost, Permelia clung to it, afraid her legs would crumple beneath her.

"You wrote the letters I received," he repeated.

She couldn't meet his gaze. Couldn't bear the agony in his voice, let alone the pain she would see in his eyes. "Not all."

"How many?" The agony turned to anger. He marched toward her and thrust the letters in her face. "How many?"

She flinched. "I started writing you after the occupation." She finally raised her gaze to his. "I didn't mean to deceive you, William. You mistook my P. A. Shaw for Annie."

Fire burned in his eyes. "So my mistake gave you license to pretend to be your sister?"

A tear slid down her cheek. She batted it away. "I hoped only to spare your feelings."

"Spared from wha—" William jerked as if someone struck

him. "Of course. Annie stopped writing to me." He took up a pace, his boots thundering over the wooden floor. "When Jackson Steele came into town, no doubt."

Though longing to ease his pain, Permelia clung to the bedpost and said nothing. All her attempts to spare him, to comfort him, had only caused him more grief in the end.

"You lied to me." He halted. The rage on his face stabbed her heart. "You should have told me the truth."

"I couldn't." She managed past the sorrow bunching in her throat. "You were out on the battlefield, enduring horrors beyond imagination. How could I tell you that your fiancée fell in love with another man?"

He snorted and ran a hand through his hair. "Sweet, sweet Permelia." He spat the words as if they were a curse. His eyes latched upon the letters. His face reddened. "I shared such intimacies with you."

"And I, you." Things she had never shared with anyone.

He shook his head. "And the coin?" He plucked it from his waistcoat pocket and held it up. Sunlight angled through the window and sought it out, setting it aglow. "Did Annie toss this aside as easily as she did our love?"

Permelia wiped another tear with the back of her hand and sank onto the bed.

"Why did you have it?" he demanded.

What did it matter now if she told him the truth? He was lost to her anyway. "I carried it because it made me feel close to you."

He flinched, his eyes narrowing.

"Because I love you." She looked up at him, his visage blurred through her tears.

Her words seemed to loosen the tightness in his face. But then his eyes narrowed again. "Love doesn't deceive." Tossing the letters into the trunk, he stormed from her chamber.

William pulled his stool to the rickety dresser and sat, releasing a heavy sigh. Light from a single candle flickered over the blank sheet of paper, daring him to write. But words escaped him. At least the right words. He propped his elbows on the dresser and dropped his head into his hands. A breeze from the slave quarters' window wafted around him, bringing the scent of primrose as katydids chirped a nighttime chorus.

He must leave first thing in the morning. And he had no idea what to do about Annie. Or Permelia. Or if he should do anything at all. Even if he resigned his commission, it would be months before he could return to Virginia. He raked both hands through his hair. Why didn't Annie simply break off their engagement? She'd made her feelings quite clear. And though he'd attempted to speak with her all day, she'd refused to see him.

His thoughts drifted to Permelia. She said she loved him. At the time he was too angry to let the words sink into his heart. But now, a thrill sped through him at the knowledge. Pushing back the stool, he made his way to his knapsack and took out the letters. He gently thumbed through them, remembering all the sweet words, the comforts, the fears, the laughs they contained. He had fallen in love with the woman in these letters. At least now he could make sense of the disparity between that woman and Annie. Permelia, sweet Permelia. Even the reason for her deception had been selfless and loving. It had taken him most of the day to break through his pride and fully understand that. He drew the letters to his chest.

He did love her. More than anything. He longed to go to her, tell her he understood her reasons for deceiving him. But it wouldn't be right to declare his love while he was still engaged to Annie. And now he had no time left to sort out the mess between them all.

Oh, God, what am I to do? He uttered his first prayer in years, spurred on by Permelia's unyielding faith—the way she spoke so lovingly, so reverently of her Father in heaven despite the tragedies that had struck her.

A breeze from the window stirred the dust at his feet. A cloud moved. Moonlight flooded him. He fell to his knees. "Forgive me, God, for abandoning You when I needed You the most. For being angry at You."

"I have always been with you, son."

William scanned the room for the source of the words. But no one was there. No one but him and God. "I've been such a fool." But he wouldn't be a fool anymore. From now on, he would talk to God often, praise Him daily. "I need Your help, God. Please tell me what to do."

"Love never fails."

The words swirled around him, stirring his faith and guiding his thoughts.

Finally he stood, straightening his shoulders. He knew exactly what to do. "Thank You, God." Then setting the letters down, he slipped onto the stool once again.

And began to write.

A glow shifted over Permelia's eyelids, growing brighter and brighter. A chorus of birds filled her ears. She popped her eyes open. Jerking upright, she glanced toward the window. The early blush of dawn had long since passed, giving rise to a bright midmorning sun. Rubbing her eyes, she leaped from the bed, slid into her slippers, tossed her robe about her, and dashed out the door. She'd stayed up far too late last night, pacing her chamber, crying and praying, until she'd finally given everything over to God and accepted His will—whatever that turned out to be. Even if it meant life without William. Afterward, a peace had settled on her, and she had fallen fast asleep.

But she had wanted to at least say good-bye to William. To tell him how sorry she was one last time. Hurrying down the stairs, she flung open the front door and made her way to the slave quarters. Darting inside the open door, she scanned the room. It was empty. All William's things were gone. Her heart as heavy as a brick, she dashed to the stables where she discovered what she had already guessed. His horse was nowhere to be seen.

William was gone.

Tears spilled down her cheeks as she dragged herself back into the main house and sat upon the sofa in the parlor. Numb. Dazed. Her mind reeled with sorrow. He hadn't even said good-bye. But after what she'd done, what did she expect?

Something winked at her from the table, drawing her gaze. The coin, sitting atop a folded piece of paper. She grabbed it, fingering the gold as a smile played on her lips. At least she still had the coin. Laying it aside, she picked up the letter. The words *Annie and Permelia* were written on the outside. Her chest tightened.

Shuffling noises brought her gaze to the door. Annie entered, her eyes puffy and red and her hair askew. She gave Permelia a seething look then dropped into a chair. "I suppose you're happy now."

Permelia gripped the letter, longing to open it, desperate to know what it said. "Why would I be happy?"

"Now that Jackson is gone forever."

"I'm not happy, Annie. I didn't want them to fight at all." She touched Annie's arm. "I'm truly sorry you are so upset."

Annie sighed and played with a ring on her finger.

"You should know that William left," Permelia said.

Annie's brow wrinkled. "Without saying good-bye?"

"You wouldn't even see him yesterday."

"I was upset." She pouted. "Now what am I to do? You've gone and chased off both my good prospects!"

Permelia would be angry if the accusation weren't so absurd. "What is that?" Annie pointed at the letter.

"It's from William, addressed to both of us."

Scooting to the edge of her seat, Annie snatched it from Permelia, scanned it for a moment, then began to read out loud:

Dearest Annie and Permelia,

Forgive me for not saying good-bye, but under the circumstances, I thought it best to leave without causing further heartache. I plan to serve the remainder of my time in the Army and then resign my commission at the end of the year. I have but one final request of you both. Search your hearts and decide what each of you truly wants. Honor forbids me to choose between you, so I have left the outcome in the hands of God. Should one of you decide you love this disfigured warrior enough to marry me, then meet me on Bow Bridge in Central Park on January 1st of next year at noon. I will be waiting.

William.

Permelia's hands trembled. She clasped them together in her lap as Annie gaped at her. "Do you think he is serious?"

"It would seem so." Permelia couldn't help but cling to the hope that, should Annie decide not to meet him, William would be hers. Surely this proved that he loved her. Otherwise, why would he have included her in the ultimatum? He loved her! Her breath caught in her throat.

"So, he would accept you as his wife?" Annie's face scrunched.

"Is it so hard to believe?"

Standing, Annie sauntered about the room, her silk night

rail streaming behind her.

Permelia stood. "If you break the engagement, Annie, I'm sure William will not hold Jackson to his vow."

"Of course I know that." Annie waved a hand in the air.

"Why can't you simply choose? Don't you see the mess you've created?"

Annie spun to face her. "How can I choose between great wealth and great attraction?"

"You mean beauty. If William wasn't scarred, you'd have no trouble deciding."

"Oh, fiddle. You just want William's money for yourself."

Permelia shook her head, her heart plummeting at her sister's accusation. How could she tell Annie that she loved William? How could her sister understand something so deep and abiding? Yet why, oh why, was Permelia's future, her very life, in the hands of her selfish sister?

Love never fails.

The words settled on her heart, chasing away her fears. God's love for Permelia never failed. And no matter what He had planned for her, it would be for her good and His glory. Even if it meant that Annie married William. No, Permelia's future was not in her sister's hands, but safely tucked within God's.

She faced her sister. "What are you going to do, Annie?"

Flipping up the collar of his wool cloak, William blew into his hands as he ascended the bridge, retracing the footprints he'd left in the snow only moments ago. His nervous breath puffed around his face. He'd been waiting for this day for seven months. Could hardly believe it had arrived. And now that it had, he wondered at the sanity of the ultimatum he'd left Permelia and Annie. He crested the bridge, swiped off the snow on the railing, and watched it tumble into the icy river below.

Tumble down like his dreams would if this day did not turn out as he hoped. He pulled his pocket watch from his waistcoat and glanced at the time. Nearly noon. Soon the months of waiting would end, and he would know who would become his wife. Or if he would have a wife at all. He glanced in both directions. A group of children built a snowman in the field beyond the river, their playful laughter bubbling through the crisp air. Sunlight glinted off freshly fallen snow and sparkled off icicles hanging from bare tree limbs. A lady and gentleman approached from the left. William tipped his hat. At the sight of his face, the woman's smile fell from her lips. She turned away.

He turned toward the river again. Would the pain of people's revulsion ever fade?

The sound of bells, clack of carriages, and stomp of horses' hooves drifted on muted conversations coming from New York City. A distant clock chimed the time. Each resounding clang tightened William's nerves. Finally the twelfth one sounded. He shoved off from the railing and began his trek down the other side of the bridge.

Then he saw her.

A woman coming toward him on the shaded path. Billowing lavender skirts peeked out from her long wool mantle. Her hands disappeared inside a furry muff while a wide-brimmed bonnet hid the color of her hair.

Oh, Lord, let it be brown.

Let it be Permelia, sweet Permelia. Though he had resigned himself to God's will, it had been Permelia who had filled his thoughts, his dreams, these long months. It had been Permelia he longed for. Loved with all his heart.

A heart that now thrashed in his chest with each step she took.

He tried to go to her, but his feet were frozen in place. His heavy breath puffed about his face, clouding his vision.

She moved into the sunlight. And stopped. Straining, William made out the details of her face.

∽

Permelia stepped into the sunshine. The trembling that had begun when she'd first spotted William increased in fervor. Accompanied by a racing heart. She could hardly believe her eyes. There he was! On the bridge just like he'd said he would be. And as handsome as ever in his black velvet-trimmed cape and high silk hat. But, why wasn't he moving? Why wasn't he coming to her?

She stopped, her heart constricting. Perhaps he had hoped to see Annie instead. Perhaps he was overcome with disappointment. She glanced over her shoulder, wondering if she should leave, but when she faced him again, recognition flashed across his eyes and a wide smile spread upon his lips. He hastened forward, arms wide.

Grabbing her skirts, Permelia darted toward him and fell into his embrace. Thick arms circled her in a cocoon of strength and warmth. She drew a deep breath of his scent. William. At last. She could hardly believe it. Easing her away, he cupped her face in his hands and swept his gaze over her as if memorizing every detail. "I'm so happy it's you, Permelia." He wiped her tears with his thumb. "I hoped, I prayed it would be you."

Permelia's laughter broke in between sobs. "You did?"

"Of course. I love you, Permelia. I love you." Leaning over, he pressed his lips to hers. At first gentle and soft, like the flutter of a butterfly, his warm breath caressed her cheek. Heat sped through her, swirling in her belly. Her legs quivered. Then he deepened the kiss. Like a man desperate for more of her.

Permelia's world spun. He tasted of spice and William, and she wished the moment would never end.

He withdrew.

"I love you, too, William," she said. "I always have."

He tenderly brushed a curl from her cheek. "But tell me, what of Annie?"

Permelia bit her lip. How would he take the news? Did he still care for her?

His brows drew together. "She is ill?"

"Not as far as we know. You see, my brother arrived home and—"

"That is wonderful news." He lifted one of her hands and kissed it.

"Not for Annie, I'm afraid," Permelia said. "He forbade her to marry Jackson. Said the man was a hooligan."

William snorted. "A good judge of character, this brother of yours."

"Indeed." Permelia smiled.

"What of Elijah, Martha, and Ruth?"

"Samuel hired them, along with many other workers. Thanks be to God, the plantation is doing quite well." Permelia couldn't keep her eyes off William, afraid he would vanish like the mist rising off the frozen river. Her thoughts shifted to Annie, and she frowned. "However, I'm afraid Annie ran away with Jackson anyway."

William flinched. "Eloped?"

Permelia nodded, happy when she saw no pain, no sorrow, in his eyes.

"She always was a bit pernicious." He chuckled.

Permelia looked down. "I fear for her well-being. In truth, I miss her."

He brushed a thumb over her cheek. "Then we shall pray for their happiness."

Reaching inside her muff, Permelia pulled out the coin and held it out to him. "I believe this is yours, sir?"

He smiled then closed her hand over it. "I know it was intended for Annie, but it would honor me if you would keep it. As my pledge to love you forever."

Emotion burned in her throat. But before she could find her voice to respond, he lowered himself on one knee. Brown eyes, brimming with joy and expectation, stared up at her. "Will you marry me, Permelia?"

She caressed his scarred cheek, hardly daring to believe his words. "Yes. Oh yes, indeed."

Mist covered his eyes as he rose and lifted her in his arms, spinning her around and around. Their laughter mingled in the air above them as Permelia gazed into the sky and thanked God for William, for his love, and for proving to her that, indeed. . .

Love never fails.

DREAM A LITTLE DREAM
PART 4

by Ronie Kendig

Chapter 11

The flutter of a butterfly, the fluid grace of a hummingbird, had nothing on the movements of Jamie Russo.

Sean couldn't help the thoughts as he stood tucked into the corner at the rear of the auditorium as Jamie proved her mettle. His heart soared, watching her chase her dreams. He'd thought she'd given up when he got the medallion in the mail. It'd taken him a week to muster the courage and determination to talk to her, to not soak in pity. But when he went to the studio to make amends, her best friend sent him here. Did this mean she'd found a way to pay her tuition? He'd give anything to see her get this.

She'd once said that he was a hypocrite for not even having a dream, but fixing motorcycles had aroused in him a deep sense of satisfaction. Warmth spread through him when he realized they were both hunting down their dreams. If only. . .if only she hadn't shoved him away.

William Wolfe had experienced rejection. For him, war and burn injuries tore from his hands what he thought he wanted—the love of a woman. The wrong woman. Sean could relate. His deployments, his injury sent his fiancée into the arms of another. At the time, Sean had let that wound fester, infect his soul. He'd heard it said that God never wastes a hurt. True enough, Sean stood watching something he wanted even more than marrying a shallow socialite.

A woman's voice rang through the auditorium, dismissing them but not before informing them that those accepted would receive an e-mail notice within a week. As soon as the white-haired matriarch left, the dancers rushed out the back with an electric hum.

Sean hurried after them, anxious to catch a glimpse of Jamie's face. She'd make it. He had no doubt. She was a fighter and an amazing dancer. His phone belted out "American Hero" as he stepped onto the main floor, and he answered it. "Sean Wolfe."

"Mr. Wolfe. I hear you got the Harley working. Have you reconsidered my offer?"

Sean sighed as he stared down the narrow corridor where the dancers huddled. "I'm sorry, Mr. Riordan. The bike's not for sale."

"I'll increase my offer."

Sean chuckled. "Sorry. I'm not willing to give it up."

"Thirty-five thousand is my last offer."

Almost choking, Sean fisted a hand over his mouth. "That's obscene. It's not even worth that."

"It is to me. And listen—this isn't the only bike I'd like you to fix. Partner with me. I'll track down the good ones, you fix them, and we'll split the profit."

He had to be kidding. The deal was ludicrously slanted in Sean's favor. Getting to restore bikes *and* make money? "I'd be willing to work together, but this Harley's not for sale."

Hoots and hollers mingled with groans and sobs, cutting off the conversation. Sean said good-bye and looked for Jamie amid the group. His breath backed into his throat.

Jamie turned sobbing, hands pressed to her face.

No. It wasn't possible—she *had* to make it.

A tall guy—no wait, that was her dance studio instructor. The same one who'd told Sean to get lost weeks back—pulled her into his arms.

Everything in Sean closed up. That embrace looked. . . intimate.

The guy rubbed her back. A girl hugged Jamie, smiled, then strode toward Sean.

Sean fisted a hand as he edged into the girl's path. "So. . .she didn't make it? What's wrong?"

"Officially, nobody's made it—yet. Those who are accepted get e-mailed, but Madame Faultier told Martin she was handpicking Jamie."

Just then, Jamie stepped out of Martin's hold. Her gaze collided with Sean's. She drew herself straight and came toward him, the guy on her heels.

"Why are you here?" Jamie asked, her voice cracking.

"To see you live your dream."

A tear rolled down her cheek, and it took everything in Sean not to wipe it away. "Well"—she sniffled—"I did. And now it's dead."

"But—"

"I can't afford it. I told you."

"Then why are you here, auditioning?"

Martin eased in. "Hey, now—"

"Stay out of this." Sean hated the growl in his voice, but he wasn't going to back down either. He hesitated, taking in her wet eyes, trembling chin, and knotted brow. She'd made it. And she was upset. Which meant she *didn't* have the funds, though he'd hoped a way would present itself for her.

"Don't you see?" More tears. "Now I have to humiliate myself—again—and tell them I can't go. I should never have come for the callbacks. But I just. . ."

"Jamie—"

"This." Anger vaulted over her grief. "*This* is why I didn't turn in my application."

Sean stepped closer, but at the same time, so did the guy behind her. Their eyes locked, and Sean sent him the hardest look he could muster. He dared this guy to challenge him. When Martin's shoulders lowered, Sean refocused on Jamie.

"Listen," he said, as he cupped her face. "You belong here, Jamie. You do. I could see it while you were dancing."

"But I don't have—"

"Let God handle that, okay?" He lifted her chin so she looked into his eyes. "Trust me on this. It'll get paid. I don't know how, but it will. Don't throw away your dream." He inched closer. "This time, it's about you."

She caught his wrists and tugged them free. "I want to believe that. It'd be. . .wonderful." Jamie sniffled again. "But I have to be realistic. I know I have what it takes, but now I need to get a job and figure out what to do with the rest of my life."

"Jamie—"

"It's okay, Sean." She nodded. "I'll be okay. But I have to go."

Panic streaked through him like a branding iron. "You're just walking away?" His pulse ratcheted. "Just like that." *From this? From me?*

"I have to, Sean. I can't live hoping and"—her lips quirked—"dreaming my life away."

Each molecule of air felt like a ten-pound weight. "Who's the one who told me I was too chicken to dream?"

More hesitation. Then she straightened. "Good-bye, Sean."

"Good-bye?"

A tremor ran through her chin. She turned and faded into the shadows with the entourage of dancers.

Chapter 12

Eight months later. . .

Light glittered and snow fluttered from the machines placed along the sides of the stage as Jamie took the stage for a final bow after the performance of her first recital with The Juilliard. Deafening and enthusiastic, the applause rang through the theater.

For you, Dad and Mom. . . I did it!

Roses sailed through the air, landing with soft thumps at her feet as she smiled at Uncle Alan, who sat on the front row with Gail. Beside them, an empty chair.

Jamie hauled in a breath. *Sean?*

She swallowed the painful thought. No, he wouldn't come. She'd walked away from him that day in the theater, so terrified her dreams would end when Madame Faultier discovered she could not pay the tuition.

Lifting a rose from the stage, she blew a kiss as the others did the same. Backstage, she found herself wondering for the millionth time where the money had come from for the tuition. She'd never forget arguing with the admin offices, but they'd insisted her account had been paid in full.

Dressed, she hurried out to the lobby to find her uncle and his wife. Both embraced her warmly.

"I am so proud of you, James," Uncle Alan said, planting a solid kiss on her temple as he hugged her. "Your father and mother would've been so proud of you, to see you living your dream." He guided her through the doors into the crisp December air.

Dream. If it hadn't been for Sean sending in her application. . . The weight sat heavy and prominent in her mind. She wanted to make things right, but he'd never talk to her. Not after the way she'd treated him and these months of silence.

"You were amazing!" Gail passed an enormous bouquet of parchment roses.

The deep rattle of a motorcycle drowned her thanks. A Harley—*No!* Not just a Harley. The one Sean had been restoring—she remembered the stenciled flames on the tank. But that wasn't possible.

"Excuse me." Jamie found herself speaking to the driver. "Where did you get this bike?"

"Like it, do you?" With an appraising look, he grinned. "Kind of crazy, driving it on New Year's Eve when there's supposed to be a storm, but it's a pride thing, I guess you could say."

"Why are you driving Sean's bike?" she demanded, her heart thrumming.

The man's eyes narrowed. "You know Sean Wolfe?"

Anger spiraled through her. "Why do you have his bike?"

"Sorry, it's mine. He sold it to me. We're partners." He offered his hand. "Marc Riordan."

"*Sold* it?" She couldn't help but gape. "But he—it was his father's!"

"I know. And he took me to the bank for it, too. Dragged thirty-five grand out of me. But she's a beauty—it was worth it. I'd better get inside before my date abandons me." He nodded then strolled into a nearby restaurant.

Sean had sold the bike? But he loved that thing. Said it was like having his dad back.

"Jamie?"

She turned toward her uncle's voice. "I...I don't understand."

Snow fluttered around them, spiraling as the cold wind kicked up.

"What don't you understand, Jamie-girl?"

Had her mind disengaged? "Why would he sell it? It was so important to him."

Uncle Alan's face filled with a sad smile. "I think something else was more important."

"What?" She swallowed, the cold drying her mouth almost instantly. "What could be more important than living his dreams?"

"You living yours." Gail's gentle words held no reproach. "He wanted that for you, even if you weren't for him."

Jamie hauled in a sudden breath at what they were saying. "No." He'd sold his bike to pay for The Juilliard? He sold *his* bike, *his* dream, for *hers*? It couldn't be. Her vision blurred, and she clamped a hand over her mouth to stifle a sob. She shook her head, and an unbelievable inadequacy engulfed her. "No." *I don't deserve it.* Not after being so angry with him she'd said good-bye and walked out on him. She gulped the anguish. "He told you. . .?"

"He didn't tell us that, exactly. But it wasn't hard to figure out when he started having to walk everywhere, and you suddenly had your account paid." Uncle Alan looked absolutely miserable. "That boy—when he gets an idea in his head, there's no digging it out."

Gail touched Jamie's elbow. "He was here tonight."

A tear slipped free. Jamie opened her mouth to say something, blanking at the thought of Sean watching her dance. Watching her do something he'd paid for.

"He went for a walk." Gail looked down the road.

Jamie followed her gaze. Draped in a blanket of white, with ethereal glowing lanterns dotting the darkened entrance, Central Park beckoned.

Elbows pressed to the snow-laden cast-iron rail, Sean threaded his fingers into a fist and squeezed. It was painful to watch her. Watch and know that she would never be his. Know that the one thing he'd wanted in life—her—wouldn't happen. Despite being a first-year student, she was taking the dance world by storm. No doubt existed that she held a promising future. She'd dance around the globe. She'd live her dream.

He pivoted around and dropped back against the rail. Arms folded, he let out a breath that puffed in his face. Cold nipped at his nose and ears, at the scar marring his neck. She deserved someone better, stronger, not broken. She'd get that now. She had a chance.

Sean stuffed his cold-stiffened hands in his pockets—and stilled. He drew out the coin. A new ache wove through him. This piece had made it through hundreds of years, through numerous relationships. . .and now failed.

He'd found the right girl.

But she didn't want me.

Head lowered, Sean closed his eyes. He pinched the bridge of his nose as he returned the coin to his pocket. What was the point of reading the letters? Of learning about his ancestors? Sure, he got a good history lesson. Maybe he didn't think of himself as a loser anymore. But in a way, he'd thought of the coin as a magic talisman. Not intentionally, of course, but just reading those stories, seeing how his aunt found her first true love. . .

Why can't it happen for me?

"I want her, God." He turned back to the frozen lake, the fat flakes coming down in drifts. "It's selfish, and probably unrealistic, but I want her. Next to You, she's all I want in life."

Love perseveres.

Hadn't he done that? Letting her walk away, paying for he school, helping her fulfill her dreams?

The sound of clopping drew his gaze around. Only darkness and the silent sentry lamppost stretched before him. The sound grew louder. . .closer.

A form raced under the halo of light and snow. She stopped, cupped a hand over her mouth, then darted toward him.

His heart kick-started. "Jamie."

She flew into his arms, thudding against his chest as her arms coiled around his neck. He snapped his arms around her waist and drew her firmly against him. She trembled.

"Why didn't you tell me?" she mumbled against his neck.

He held the back of her head, amazed at the miracle of this moment. "Tell you what?"

She eased away to look at him. "You sold your bike." Tears twinkled in her eyes. "For me?"

His chest tightened. "I'd do that and much more."

Tears streamed down her face as she relaxed against him. "Really?" she squeaked.

"I. . ." Sean's focus dropped to her mouth. He angled in, uncertain and hesitating, then captured her mouth with his. He'd never imagined a woman like her could accept a guy like him. But holding her, kissing her, savoring this moment, a thrill sped through him.

He broke off and brushed the hair from her face, his mind racing. Only one thought hit him, kept hitting him.

Oh man. Could he say it? Why was it hard to breathe? "You told me I was pathetic once because I didn't dare to dream. I thought the bike was my dream, but I've realized in the last six months, *you're* my dream. I love you, Jamie."

"I love you, too, Sean." She kissed him.

"Would you. . . ?" He drew the coin from his pocket and held it out.

With more tears, she nodded.

Sean slipped the pendant over her head, his hand tracing the line of her jaw. "Dare to dream a little dream with me."

Ronie Kendig grew up an Army brat, married a veteran, and they now have four children and a golden retriever. She has a BS in psychology, speaks to various groups, volunteers with the American Christian Fiction Writers (ACFW), and mentors new writers.

Dineen Miller readily admits one of life's greatest lessons is that there's purpose in our trials. Her years as a youth counselor, Stephen Minister, women's ministry leader, and small group leader fuel her desire to ignite the souls of others through words of truth. Married for more than twenty-four years, she shares her life with a great guy and her two grown daughters.

Kim Vogel Sawyer, a lifelong Kansas resident, is a wife, mother, grandmother, singer of songs, and lover of cats and chocolate. From the time she was a very little girl, she knew she wanted to be a writer, and seeing her words in print is the culmination of a lifelong dream. Kim relishes her time with family and friends, and stays active in her church by leading women's fellowship and participating in music ministry.

MaryLu Tyndall, a Christy Award Finalist and bestselling author, is known for her adventurous historical romances filled with deep spiritual themes. She holds a degree in math and worked as a software engineer for fifteen years before testing the waters as a writer. MaryLu currently writes full-time and makes her home on the California coast with her husband, six kids, and four cats.